Readers love the All for Love series
by NICKI BENNETT AND ARIEL TACHNA

Checkmate

"Strong characters, and intriguing plot premise, and enough historical
flare to satisfy most lovers of period fiction, all combine to give this
book some very strong bones."

—Joyfully Jay

"…a very engaging read, with dynamic characters, that evolved
through the book. I'm definitely looking forward to reading more in
this series world."

—Two Chicks Obsessed

All for One

"The story is well written with an interesting, complex plot and unique,
new characters as well as five others from the first book in the series."

—Rainbow Book Reviews

By NICKI BENNETT

Always a Bridesmaid
The Cattle Baron's Bogus Boyfriend
Evan's Heaven
Flight
Home for Christmas
New Traditions

With Ariel Tachna
Under the Skin

ALL FOR LOVE
Checkmate
All for One
Stronghold

HOT CARGO STORIES
Hot Cargo
Something About Harry

THE EXPLORING LIMITS SERIES
Exploring Limits
Stretching Limits
Refining Limits
Breaking Limits
Transcending Limits
No Limits

Published by DREAMSPINNER PRESS
www.dreamspinnerpress.com

Published by DREAMSPINNER PRESS
www.dreamspinnerpress.com

STRONGHOLD

Nicki Bennett
and
Ariel Tachna

Published by

DREAMSPINNER PRESS

5032 Capital Circle SW, Suite 2, PMB# 279, Tallahassee, FL 32305-7886 USA
www.dreamspinnerpress.com

Stronghold
© 2016 Nicki Bennett and Ariel Tachna.

Cover Art
© 2016 Reese Dante.
http://www.reesedante.com
Cover content is for illustrative purposes only and any person depicted on the cover is a model.
Interior Illustration © 2016 Anne Cain annecain.art@gmail.com

ISBN: 978-1-63477-466-6
Digital ISBN: 978-1-63477-467-3
Library of Congress Control Number: 2016910634
Published November 2016
v. 1.0

Printed in the United States of America
∞
This paper meets the requirements of
ANSI/NISO Z39.48-1992 (Permanence of Paper).

To Mary, who never stopped believing we would finish this one day.

ONE

"I SHOULD leave in the morning," Gerrard Hawkins said with a deep sigh. "I don't want to, but if I must go, the sooner I leave, the sooner I will be able to return."

The room was cool despite the unseasonably warm April weather, but the thick walls of Ambassador Blackwood's *hôtel particulier*, where he and Raúl had been guests for over six months, kept the heat out, and Gerrard was glad of the warmth from the fire at his back.

"I won't be gone more than a month. Two at the most."

The shiver that curled up the nerves of Raúl's spine had nothing to do with the coolness of the room. His eyelids flickered shut, the vision lasting only a moment, though that was enough to chill him even further. Drawing a breath, he opened his hazel eyes to fix on Gerrard, replacing the illusion with the reality of Gerrard's presence for as long as it was still his to claim.

"Of course you must go," Raúl said. "The claims of family are not to be ignored. And you have been absent from them far longer than they ever expected."

Gerrard rolled his eyes. "Were it not for my nephew's death and my brother James's illness, my father would be happy never to see me again. He made his opinion quite clear before I left England with Christian. I am far happier with you than I ever was in his house. I will do my duty by them and return to your side, where I belong." Rising from his seat, he drew Raúl into his arms, bending to kiss the slender column of his neck. Raúl's willowy figure had deceived Gerrard when they first met, but no longer. He knew the steely strength belied by the lithe form and fully intended to take advantage of it before the night was over.

Letting Gerrard pull him into an embrace, Raúl raised a hand to brush through the crisp, dark hair, longer than it had been when they first met six years before, though still far shorter than his own. He indulged in the warmth of Gerrard's lips against his throat until the need to taste in return became too strong to resist. Closing his fingers around the silken strands, he urged Gerrard's dark head down, claiming his full lips in a demanding kiss.

Gerrard gave in eagerly to Raúl's demand, parting his lips so Raúl could ravish his mouth. The thought of being separated for the first time in almost six years tore at his heart. Pulling away, he caught Raúl's face between his hands. "Give me something to remember you by," he pleaded. "Some token to carry with me while we're apart."

The love, tinged with anticipated sorrow, lighting Gerrard's deep brown eyes so filled Raúl's thoughts that the words did not at first register. When they did, he smiled, tugging gently with the hand still woven in Gerrard's hair. "A token?" he repeated. "A scarf, perhaps, to cover your hair like a Rom's? You might set a new fashion in England."

Gerrard laughed. "I think perhaps my father might object to that." He fingered the gold loop that pierced Raúl's ear. "Then again, I suspect he would object to anything associated with you and my new life, but many a Rom has a scarf. I was hoping for something more intimate."

"More intimate? You already carry my heart with you," Raúl answered, the words full of meaning for all they were spoken with a lilt of humor. "I fear any more intimate portions of my anatomy must await your return. But what think you of this?" He swept the dark hair behind Gerrard's ear, tracing his fingers over the whorled shell to linger at the lobe. "A ring to mark you as Rom." *As mine*, his heart whispered as he rubbed his thumb over the pendant flesh. "Your hair is long enough that it may escape your father's notice."

"I care not if he notices," Gerrard said, voice rough with desire. He leaned into Raúl's touch, his body tingling with the thought of his gypsy leaving a permanent record of their relationship. "Mark me as yours, love."

Never proof against that tone in Gerrard's voice, Raúl claimed his lips again before drawing away with reluctance. "Sit there by the fire while I gather what I need."

His gaze returned often to the strong, graceful form as he located a slender needle, a bottle of astringent liquid, and a square of soft cloth from the healer's supplies he always carried with him. Returning to the fireside, he bent before the hearth, holding the needle in the flame until the tip glowed red. Turning back to Gerrard, he straddled his legs, not surprised to feel the swell of Gerrard's erection press against his thigh as he lowered himself to sit. That arousal might not survive what he was about to do, but then he would have the pleasure of wakening it again.

"So you think to hold me down as you have your wicked way with me?" Gerrard said with a laugh, bringing his arms to rest around Raúl's waist. "You know I am yours to do with as you please."

"At the moment, it pleases me to feel you beneath me like this." Raúl pressed a kiss to each fan of dark lashes before nipping at Gerrard's lower lip. "Doubtless later I will expect you to return the favor." He let Gerrard pull him into a deeper kiss but drew back before the glide of his large, knowing hands could become too distracting.

After wetting the cloth with the astringent, he cleaned the skin of Gerrard's ear and then pinched the lobe between his thumb and forefinger. Drawing the skin taut, he thrust the needle through in one swift motion, catching the droplet of blood that welled from it with the damp cloth.

The jolt of pain was not unexpected, given the hot, sharp instrument Raúl had in his hands, but Gerrard winced nonetheless. "And what makes you think I have any desire to move from where I am right now?" he teased when he caught his breath again.

"Because," Raúl replied, his gentle touch drawing away the unavoidable pain, "having pierced you thus, I would fain feel you piercing me in turn." Reaching up, he removed the thin golden ring from his ear and fastened it in Gerrard's, then pressed a kiss to the spot where it entered the skin. "Make me feel you as long as I may after you have gone."

"A wish I shall gladly grant," Gerrard replied, his body quickening at the thought, "but that hardly requires me to move. I need not be above you to give you what you desire." He reached up and fingered the hoop that had only recently graced Raúl's ear. The thought that he wore not only a ring because Raúl had given it to him, but that he wore Raúl's ring, moved him deeply. "However, we are both much overdressed for such endeavors."

"That is easily remedied." Raúl made short work of the ties that secured Gerrard's doublet, before lifting it and the shirt over his head with care not to catch the newly inserted hoop. He lowered his head to the broad chest, inhaling the scent of Gerrard's skin as he sought out with lips and fingers all the most sensitive spots he had discovered in six years of loving the man beneath him.

Gerrard leaned back on his hands, offering his body for Raúl's delectation. He arched into the masterful touches, his blood racing as it had every time Raúl touched him, from the first time he laid hands on Gerrard to tend the wound he'd sustained saving Christian from the *conde* de la Rocha's blade. The faint scar on his upper arm seemed a small price to pay for the incredible richness that now filled his life. "I don't want to go," he gasped as Raúl's fingers found his nipples. "I cannot fathom how I will survive without you."

"We will survive because we must." Raúl followed the trail of dark hair from Gerrard's chest down the quivering muscles of his abdomen, dipping below the waist of his breeches, imprinting the rasp of the crisp curls onto his fingertips. The touch was not enough, and he leaned in to retrace the path with lips and tongue as he spread the placket of Gerrard's breeches. He curled his fist around the hot, thick shaft he would soon feel inside him, forcing away the flash of vision that haunted him. "Because I would not face a future without you at my side."

"'Tis not a future you need fear." Gerrard moaned, lifting his hips into Raúl's touch. "No power on earth could keep me from your side. I will go home and acquit myself of my duty, and I will return to you as swiftly as may be." He reached for Raúl, only to have him slip through his fingers. "Come here where I can touch you as well."

After stripping himself of the garments that thwarted his sudden need to feel Gerrard's body against his, skin to skin, Raúl once again straddled his lap. He coasted a thumb over the slick fluid wetting Gerrard's cockhead and raised it to his lips before aligning himself over the heavy shaft. If he would need endure weeks, if not months, of Gerrard's absence, he needed the memory of being filled by him, claimed by him as he had given himself to no other.

"No," Gerrard ordered, catching Raúl's hips. "You'll not deny me the pleasure of driving you out of your mind. I'll give you as long and hard a ride as you please, but only after I'm sure it won't hurt you. I know you can't heal yourself the way you heal others." Keeping one hand heavy on Raúl's hip to ensure his compliance, he fumbled for the oil they kept near to hand, spilled some over his fingers, and slid one into Raúl's entrance.

Uncharacteristic need consuming him, Raúl sank down on the thick digit, too impatient to wait for Gerrard to ease the way. In truth he wanted to feel the burn, wanted to carry the aches and marks of being well and truly loved. "More," he demanded, clenching around the invasive appendage. "Let me feel you stretching me, filling me. Loving me."

Gerrard nodded, freeing his finger and working the oil over his thick shaft. He thought he understood the need in Raúl's voice for the welcome pain of their joining. Usually he resisted, wanting to be able to make love again quickly, but that would not be an option tomorrow. Or for some time hence. "Take me in at your own pace if you will not let me prepare you. I would not hurt you unintentionally."

Raúl did not usually find pleasure in pain, nor was he a greedy lover, preferring to take the time to cherish his partner. But tonight he felt all too acutely how little time they had left together. Mating one of his hands to Gerrard's larger one, he intertwined their fingers while he guided Gerrard's shaft with his other hand. As soon as the crown nudged his portal, he pushed down, taking the full length in one thrust.

Gerrard groaned in delight at the sudden heat and pressure on his cock. He resisted the urge to thrust upward, rocking against Raúl as if he could burrow even deeper into the silken passage. Experience had taught him exactly how deep he could go, exactly how much Raúl could take, but he was tempted to disregard that and push for more, driven by the awareness of time passing and the need to leave as indelible a mark as Raúl had left on him. He settled his hands around Raúl's hips, holding him in place as he thrust upward, winning a hoarse cry from his lips.

Raúl clutched Gerrard's shoulders, finding a rhythm to their movements that drove the steely shaft deeper with each clap of their flesh. He clenched his muscles each time Gerrard drew back, massaging the thick rod with each inward stroke. Gerrard shifted him with ease, positioning him with the unconscious skill of one who knew Raúl's body as well as he knew it himself, so that each stroke rubbed over the sensitive seat of his pleasure. Raúl gasped Gerrard's name and bent forward to join their lips, plundering Gerrard's mouth with the same urgency.

Suddenly needing more range of movement than his seated position allowed, Gerrard rolled Raúl backward onto the thick rug and mound of pillows that covered the stone floor. *Once a gypsy, always a gypsy*, he'd teased when Raúl scattered the exotic accoutrements from his rooms in Madrid around the guest chamber in Christian's new home, but he was grateful for it now, the cushions providing a nest for them. The moment he had Raúl settled, he began to move again, pounding into his body as fast and as hard as his considerable strength would allow.

Raúl might have protested losing the freedom of motion had not the weight of Gerrard's body covering his more than made up for the loss. Curling his legs around Gerrard's thighs, he used the leverage to urge him on even more. Despite his larger size, Gerrard seldom dominated their lovemaking, letting Raúl set the pace, but tonight Raúl could bear no such restraint. He dug his fingers into the broad muscles of Gerrard's back, pulling him closer, meeting each thrust and demanding more. "All of you. Give me everything."

What little control Gerrard had left evaporated, and he gripped Raúl's thighs hard enough to bruise as he hiked them higher and onto his shoulders, nearly bending Raúl in half as he pummeled his upturned ass. Heedless of the awkward position, he leaned forward until he could mate his lips with Raúl's, joining them in as many ways as possible.

Speech, breath, thought became impossible as Gerrard finally claimed Raúl in the manner his senses demanded, taking and giving with each fierce stroke. Raúl answered his kiss, claiming Gerrard's mouth as he yielded his body, his mind, his soul to Gerrard's keeping. An especially powerful thrust set his eyes rolling shut, but he forced them to open, burning the sight of Gerrard's face, dark hair clinging damply as he bit at Raúl's lips, into the memory that would have to suffice him until Gerrard's return.

Gerrard moaned into Raúl's mouth, delving deep one last time before rearing up on his elbows so he could stare down into the hazel eyes, so unusual for his countrymen, as he chased their release frantically. Balancing on his knees and one arm, he slipped the other hand between them to find Raúl's erection, stroking it rapidly. He didn't know how much longer he'd be able to wait, and he intended to take Raúl with him. "Come for me, lover."

As much as he had needed Gerrard to take him, Raúl wanted to draw out these moments when they were joined in the ultimate intimacy, but he had no defense against those words spoken in Gerrard's lust-roughened voice. Heat flared through his veins, a ruddy haze darkening his vision; every muscle in his body seized and then shook with the force of his climax. Even as his senses swam to the point he felt near to losing consciousness, his body sought more, driving his cock through the sticky grip of Gerrard's fist while arching up into the pummeling.

Gerrard had known from their first night together that Raúl was as generous a lover as he was a healer, but tonight felt different in ways he couldn't begin to describe, the connection between them so real he could almost imagine the links of the chain being forged by their lovemaking, the bond so strong that neither distance nor time could touch it. "I love you," he gasped, losing his battle with control and filling the narrow sheath with the proof of his devotion.

Still breathless from his own climax, Raúl drank in the sight of Gerrard's face transformed by repletion—dark lashes fluttering over widened eyes, white teeth biting into his lower lip. He reached up to run his thumb over the abused flesh, and Gerrard nipped at the pad before drawing it into his mouth. A tremor shook through Raúl, and he tightened around Gerrard's softening shaft, winning a groan. "Te amo," Raúl murmured, nudging at Gerrard's elbow to encourage him to ease his weight back down. He needed the feel of Gerrard's body atop his for as long as he could have it.

Gerrard settled against Raúl's slighter form, the familiarity of years assuring him he wouldn't crush Raúl beneath him despite his greater size. As his pulse slowed, he turned his head and kissed the earlobe where the ring currently gracing his ear had once resided. "Do you suppose I'll remember how to speak English?" he asked idly as his thoughts turned to his family and the trip he was about to undertake. "I don't think I've used it since Christian and Teo left Spain."

"After a few days, you're more likely to forget you once spoke Spanish." Raúl tucked a strand of sweat-damp hair behind Gerrard's ear, not allowing himself to think of what else Gerrard might forget once he returned to his homeland. He had no doubt of Gerrard's love, nor was he a simpering miss to protest a duty he could not in honor expect Gerrard to refuse.

Gerrard shook his head. "Never," he swore, "for while English may be the language of my birth, Spanish is the language of my heart." He kissed Raúl tenderly. "It will only be for a month or two, *querido*. You'll hardly realize I'm gone before I'm at your side again." He knew the words to be a lie before he ever uttered them, for he knew how each minute apart would tear at him, but he hoped they would provide some consolation, or a smile at the least.

"You've turned into a poet." Raúl returned the kiss, their lips parting only to return again and again. "I would never have suspected it of the man I met storming Teo's lodgings to rescue his countryman." He smiled at the memory, and at how little he'd expected his physical attraction to Gerrard to grow into a love that had changed his life. "I have never needed anyone at my side," he admitted. "Until you."

The memory of their first meeting still had the ability to make Gerrard flush, but he'd more than learned his lesson and Raúl's worth in the intervening years. "You know—tell me you know there is nowhere I would rather be than by your side," he said urgently. "You have but to say the word and I will cast off this duty the way my family cast me off before we met."

While Raúl might cavil for any lesser reason, he would never protest the claims of family, the more so as he had no such claims of his own, beyond his self-assumed responsibilities to his fellow Rom. "I know," he assured Gerrard, emphasizing the words with another slow kiss. "But in sending for you, your father has taken the first step to mend the break between you. I could not hold you back when he needs you." Even if the separation would prove how much Raúl needed Gerrard as well.

"You are more generous than I would be were our situations reversed," Gerrard admitted. "I will hear him out, but there is no place for me in England anymore. I have no interest in the estate or in the title. My life is with you now. Nothing he says or offers will change that." He yawned widely. "Hold me one more night before I leave."

"You would need to fight me to let you go." Raúl shifted to let Gerrard settle more closely against him, resting his head against Gerrard's broad shoulder. "Sleep now. I mean to have my fill of you again before morning light."

Gerrard smiled against Raúl's black hair. "You will hear no argument from me."

TWO

RAÚL ENDURED three days after Gerrard's departure before the silence of the rooms they had shared grew too oppressive for him to bear. As ambassador of England to the French court, Christian had followed the king and queen to the Château de Fontainebleau, and since the only servant he and Teodoro kept was a kitchen maid who was too much in awe of Raúl to do more than serve him his meals and disappear back into the sanctum of her scullery, Raúl had the Paris town house to himself. Christian had sent word that the royal court would be returning to the Louvre within the week, the missive arriving the same day as the letter that had summoned Gerrard back to England. Raúl had meant to remain until Christian and Teodoro returned, not wanting to abuse his friends' hospitality by disappearing before their arrival, but two sleepless nights in the bed he and Gerrard had enjoyed for almost half a year had sapped him of his spirit. He had his clothing packed in a knapsack and was sitting down at the escritoire to write a letter of explanation to Christian and Teodoro when a clatter of noise in the entrance hall announced their homecoming.

"Raúl? Gerrard?" Christian's voice echoed through the suddenly bustling halls. "We're home."

The joy in those simple words was clear in Christian's voice. Home had always been a mutable concept to Raúl, as it was for most Rom, but in the years since he and Gerrard had been together, his home had been with his lover. He had not realized how much that foundation had come to mean to him until he felt its lack. That could not be allowed to mar his friends' return, though. "Welcome home!" he called, descending the curved staircase from the suite of rooms he and Gerrard had shared to the entrance hall.

"Have you finally left Gerrard so exhausted he cannot leave your bed?" Teodoro teased when Raúl came close enough to embrace him. "'Tis not good manners to leave your lover too exhausted to walk."

Teodoro Ciéza de Vivar, in addition to being Christian's bodyguard and lover, was Raúl's closest friend, but his jesting remark was another cut to Raúl's aching heart. "As if you do not plan to barricade yourself and Cristian in your bedchamber for the rest of the day and night?" he answered in kind, masking his grief. "Gerrard sends his regrets that he could not remain to welcome you home. He received an urgent summons from his father and is even now on his way back to England."

"I am sorry," Teodoro said, his face betraying his remorse. "I meant to tease you, not to be cruel."

"A message from his father?" Christian repeated. "They have not spoken since Gerrard came to Spain with me seven years ago. What could have happened to make his father break his silence now?"

"An outbreak of illness," Raúl answered, with a silent prayer for Gerrard's safety, though he knew there had not yet been time for him to reach the harbor at Boulogne. "There have been several deaths among his family, and his father wished him to return home at once."

"Then of course he would wish to go," Teodoro agreed.

"It must be serious indeed for his father to write to him after all this time," Christian mused aloud. "Gerrard always said his father was too rigid to ever unbend, especially after his mother died—not that Gerrard is any less stubborn."

In the years they had spent together, Raúl had found diverse means to make his lover tractable, but he suspected none were methods of which Gerrard's father would approve. "Doubtless they are much alike."

"What caused their falling-out?" Teodoro asked.

"Why are you still standing in the foyer?" Javier Montega, Christian's secretary, asked, coming into the house behind them. "Go in one of the salons so you will not block the way for the servants." As if they were recalcitrant children, he shooed them toward the intimate salon they used most often when they did not have guests.

Christian chuckled as the door to the salon closed behind him. "One day, the members of my household will remember I'm an ambassador and heir to the Ranleigh estate."

"But Javier so enjoys playing mother hen to us all." Esteban Ciéza de Vivar, Teodoro's son and Christian's junior secretary, had followed them into the salon and stretched his long legs out before him as he sat on one of the couches. "Why did you not go with Gerrard to England, Raúl?" he asked.

"You know I go to Saintes-Maries-de-la-Mer every year at the end of May for the feast of Sainte Sara," Raúl chided. "Gerrard could not hope to go to England and return in time for us to travel south. He will join me there when he can." Raúl did not add their concern about upsetting Gerrard's father even worse with news of their relationship. From all Gerrard had told Raúl, the old man would have a fit of apoplexy at the very thought.

From the look on Teodoro's face, he at least was not convinced by Raúl's facile answer. Taking a seat on another divan, Teodoro pulled Christian down next to him and closed an arm around his shoulders. "What caused Gerrard and his father to fall out?" he asked again, his dark eyes fixed on Raúl.

When Raúl remained silent, Christian answered in his stead. "He wanted to marry a young woman from the village near his father's estate," Christian explained. "He was a second son, never much in his father's favor, and so he had little expectation of wealth to support an aristocratic wife and family. The girl he met was amenable, even knowing Gerrard would never inherit the title. Gerrard's father, Sir Harald, categorically refused to have his son marry the daughter of a farmer and threatened to cut him off completely if he went through with the ceremony. Gerrard chose to leave instead."

"And earn his livelihood hiring out his sword," Raúl added with a smile, since it was Gerrard's putative role as Christian's protector while his father, the Duke of Ranleigh, was negotiating a treaty between England and Spain that had led to their first meeting. His expression sobering, he continued, "Perhaps this will be the occasion of a rapprochement between them. Sir Harald will surely see that his son has matured into a man any father would be proud of."

"He has you to thank for much of that," Christian said. "He was still very much the hothead when we first met you. Living with the Rom has tempered that."

Dwelling on the years he had lived with Gerrard would come close to undoing him, and Christian had just given Raúl the opening he needed to announce his departure. "As Gerrard does not anticipate returning for several months, I thought to join a group of Rom making the pilgrimage to la Camargue. There is always a family willing to welcome a healer into their caravan."

"You know you're welcome to stay here," Christian said. "With or without Gerrard, you are as much a part of this family as Teo or me."

Christian's words echoed in Raúl's ears and a sudden, momentary flash of vision blinded him to his surroundings. He could not say where he was, only that it was cold and dark and he was alone. "Without Gerrard." *Without Gerrard.* Had he not been leaning against the doorjamb, Raúl would have staggered. Drawing a deep breath, he blinked, but the moment of prescience had vanished as abruptly as it came, leaving him with only an uneasy dread of he knew not what.

"Raúl?" Teodoro said. "Are you well?"

"Perhaps Gerrard has exhausted me," he answered lightly, unwilling to speak of the vision even to Teodoro, as if giving it voice could somehow make it real. "'Tis as well I had a day or two to regain my strength before I start on my way."

"Gerrard can be exhausting, no doubt," Christian quipped, "but you've never had trouble keeping up with him before now. I have some correspondence I need to see to. Esteban, I believe I will need your help with it." He caught Teodoro's gaze and looked meaningfully in Raúl's direction as he left the room.

"His correspondence must be of grave import indeed if it can distract him from marking your return home." Raúl pushed off from the doorway, hoping to forestall Teodoro from more questions by proving he had recovered from the moment's weakness. "I know how difficult it is for the two of you to be circumspect while dancing attendance on His Majesty."

He might have saved his breath.

"What are you not telling us?" Teodoro completely ignored Raúl's comment. "And do not tell me it is nothing. We have known each other too long. You have never let me keep secrets from you. Don't expect to keep them from me now."

Raúl crossed to the tall windows overlooking the street, avoiding Teodoro's too-perceptive gaze. "Why must it be any more than the prospect of several months without my lover?"

"Because you are more troubled than that," Teodoro replied. "Either there is more to Gerrard's departure than you have told us or you have had one of your visions. Since neither bodes well for your peace of mind, I would have the truth so I know how much to worry about you."

Raúl turned to find Teodoro standing behind him, his dark eyes narrowed with concern. The two of them had always guarded each other's backs, from the earliest days they served together in the Spanish war in Flanders. This was not the kind of trouble that could be faced down at the length of a sword, but even so, there was no one he would rather have at his side than Teodoro Ciéza de Vivar. Except, of course, for Gerrard Hawkins.

"'Twas but a premonition. It had naught to do with Gerrard," Raúl answered. That was true enough, though it was Gerrard's very absence that gave the foresight its power. "He will, we hope, mend the breach with his father and then return to meet me at Saintes-Maries-de-la-Mer."

Dza devlesa, Raúl murmured to himself. *May God go with him.*

"Do you want us to come with you?" Teodoro asked. "Or perhaps not 'us' since I doubt Cristian could be absent from court that long, but I could come with you. If I spoke to our friends among the musketeers, I could probably even manage not to worry about him while we were gone."

"I appreciate the offer," Raúl said sincerely, clapping Teodoro on the shoulder, "but one of us missing our lover is enough. There is no reason for you and Cristian to share my misery. I will be fine once I am on my way." He stepped away from the windows toward the door. "Everything here reminds me of him. When I am on the road with other Rom, the time will pass more quickly." Or so he could hope.

"If you say so, amigo," Teodoro replied, "but you must promise to send for me if you need me. Cristian would understand."

"What do you expect to happen?" Raúl answered with a wry smile. "I am but going on pilgrimage to the seashore, not storming an enemy's stronghold to rescue a king!"

"I do not expect anything to happen," Teodoro said, "but trouble seems to find us at the oddest times. Twice, now, we have found ourselves embroiled in plots against a king. It seems prudent to be on our guard."

"When have you known me not to be on my guard?" Raúl shook his head, as much at himself as at Teodoro. He should have learned by now that there was little he could do to influence his presentiments. What would come to pass would come to pass in its time, and it did him no good to fret about it beforehand. "Come, I have kept you from Cristian long enough. Ask your groom to saddle my horse and let me be off."

Teodoro looked like he wanted to argue, but he finally relented, clasping Raúl's shoulder tightly. "Do not let too much time pass without news from you," he ordered. "I expect to hear you are reunited with your *inglés* before long."

"May God will it to be so," Raúl answered, returning the embrace. "I would ask you to give my love to your Cristian, but you doubtless have more and to spare of your own to offer him, so please give him my thanks once again for the hospitality of his home." By the time he had retrieved his bags from the bedchamber, Christian's groom had his horse, Martiya, waiting in the entry yard. Once he secured his belongings to the saddle, Raúl mounted and waved his farewell to Teodoro, turning the spirited black stallion toward the Porte d'Italie and the road south.

Memories crowded his thoughts as he traveled, thoughts of a harried ride through the Spanish countryside, Teodoro and Christian at his side and Gerrard hanging stubbornly to the back of a horse too small for his large frame, determined to keep the pace no matter the consequences. They had teased him when they stopped at an inn for lunch, Teodoro and Christian stealing a few minutes alone, but Raúl's respect had grown apace as the day wore on into night and Gerrard had kept up without complaint.

That had all coalesced when the *conde* de la Rocha attacked Christian rather than let him speak before the Spanish king. Neither he nor Teodoro had been close enough to intervene, but Gerrard had lunged for Christian, knocking him aside and taking a slice on his shoulder that would surely have ended Christian's life had it fallen true.

Gerrard had insisted the cut was too slight to need tending, but Raúl persevered, intent by that point on getting his hands on the big Englishman. He cleaned and bandaged the wound, and then expended a little of the healing energy he could sometimes bring to bear to the benefit of his patients. No sooner had his palms settled over the smooth, warm flesh than a vision seared itself across his mind, the two of them tangled in an intimate embrace. If most of his presentiments were a flicker of shadow cast in candlelight, this was a lightning bolt, electric in its intensity. He managed to mask his shock from Gerrard, certain the prospect was only a projection of his own desire. After all, only the night before they had ridden to King Philip's rescue, Gerrard had spent the evening in the arms of Aldonza de la Cerda, one of Madrid's most desirable procuresses.

"This should heal well," Raúl said softly as the muscle flexed beneath his fingertips. Powerful men had ever been his weakness, and Gerrard was a powerful man indeed. He kept his voice steady through force of will alone, but it was not enough, not with the way Gerrard looked at him as he insisted again that his wound was not serious.

He smothered a sigh at the subtle rebuff and prepared the herbs he would use for the poultice. Gerrard's muscles twitched beneath his hands as he cleaned the cut and spread his paste over the injury.

"What's that?" Gerrard asked sharply.

"Merely a poultice, made with comfrey to speed healing," Raúl answered, well used to the distrust the *gaje* had for his herbs and potions. "Are you always so—agitated—over a cut that isn't serious?"

"I don't like being fussed over," Gerrard retorted. "And don't tell me I'm the first person to chafe at your medicines. I don't see Ciéza de Vivar submitting easily to your attentions."

"Teodoro never submits easily to anything," Raúl agreed, unrolling the bandage around Gerrard's broad chest with careful fingers. "Witness how long he fought against his feelings for Cristian."

"Did he fight his feelings for you as hard?"

Raúl was surprised by the words—it almost sounded as if the *inglés* was feeling the pinch of jealousy. "Friendship is the one thing Teodoro has never fought," he replied, leaning closer to tie off the bandage.

"What magic is this?" Gerrard muttered, pulling away and turning to face Raúl, arms crossed protectively across his chest. "What have you done to me that I react to you like a jealous lover? I've never sought the company of men the way Christian has!"

"I have never needed a spell to attract a lover," Raúl answered, his smile hiding the sudden pounding of his heart. Perhaps Gerrard was as affected as Raúl by the sudden tension in the room. "Are you surprised that strength is drawn to strength?" Gerrard's bewildered expression tempted him to step into those strong arms and show him what he had been missing, but the first move had to be Gerrard's.

"But why now?" Gerrard demanded.

"That is a question even the wisest man cannot answer," Raúl responded, feeling the tremor of Gerrard's muscle where his hand still rested on the bigger man's chest. He took a step closer, ready to back away if he felt Gerrard withdraw, but the *inglés* stood his ground. "Does it matter?"

"I don't know," Gerrard replied honestly, closing his hand over the one against his skin. "I've never felt this way before. I only know I don't want it to stop."

"Only if you ask to stop." Raúl lifted his other hand to Gerrard's broad chest and raised his head to brush their lips together softly.

Slowly, as if he had to convince himself this was really happening, Gerrard moved his hands to Raúl's shoulders and then into his thick black hair, tilting his head to better mate their mouths one to another.

A jostling as his horse moved to avoid a cart passing them on the road recalled Raúl's attention to his surroundings. "Your master is a fool, Martiya," he murmured, stroking the dark stallion's mane. Gerrard had asked him once why he hadn't gelded the beast to make him more biddable.

"How would you like to be gelded?" he'd retorted, tracing his fingers over Gerrard's equally impressive cock. Gerrard had shuddered, seemingly equal parts arousal and revulsion, making Raúl laugh. "I don't need to geld my horse to control it."

The recollections were having their own effect on Raúl's shaft, and he pushed them resolutely from his mind. There was nothing pleasant about riding with an erection. He would save the rest of his memories for when he was alone and could indulge in reliving those early days with Gerrard in more comfort.

THREE

GERRARD RODE hard for Boulogne, not sure how long it had taken his father's letter to find him, but even so, it took six days to reach the coast. Six long days of missing his lover, worrying about his brother, dreading meeting his father again after seven years of absence.

He drew up in front of a tavern in Boulogne, tossing his reins to the stableboy who ran out to meet him. "Take good care of him," Gerrard ordered. "He's worked hard this last week."

"Oui, monsieur," the stableboy said, taking Nubarrón's reins and leading him to the stable. Gerrard shouldered his saddlebag and strode into the inn. His garments were no longer those of an aristocrat, but he had not forgotten all the lessons on carriage and comportment his father had drilled into his sons. He drew himself up to his full height as he passed beneath the lintel. He did not call for the innkeeper, preferring to let the man's attention come to him of its own accord. He would garner far more respect that way than demanding it, a trick he had learned from Christian. His father had certainly never learned it.

Sir Harald preferred to toss his status around at every possible occasion, as if by reminding people of who he was he could improve his standing in society. Gerrard had seen Christian use his title to gain entrance to certain circles on occasion, but the rarity of it made it effective. His friend and former employer would never draw that kind of attention to himself in an inn like this one.

"Can I help you, monsieur?" the innkeeper asked, catching sight of Gerrard and bustling over to him. "A bite to eat, perhaps a bottle of wine?"

"Both," Gerrard said, "and a room for the night if you have one."

"Of course," the innkeeper said. "Find a seat and I'll bring dinner. My missus roasted a ham today."

Gerrard took a seat against the far wall so he had the entire taproom in his line of sight. He had no reason to think anyone was following him or that anyone would care what he was doing, but he had earned his living by the sword for too many years to let those habits die now.

As he stretched his legs under the table to work out the tightness from days in the saddle, he glanced around at the other occupants of the taproom, another habit learned through long experience. Most appeared to be travelers like himself, merchants heading to the coast to meet cargo ships or returning with their goods to Paris, while a few he took to be local townsfolk in for a drink and some news. Seeing none that warranted his concern, he relaxed slightly when the innkeeper brought him a plate of ham with roasted potatoes and a bottle of dry Vouvray wine.

The meal was hearty and filling, though Gerrard ate it with little of the appreciation the innkeeper's wife's efforts deserved. His attention was not on his food but on the journey ahead of him. Unless weather held them back, it shouldn't take more than half a day for even the slowest ship to get him back to England, and another five days' ride after that to the family lands in Essex. He'd have to make arrangements for Nubarrón to make the crossing with him, he decided. It might cost him nearly as much as buying a new horse when he reached England, but as heavily as he rode, there was no guarantee he could readily find a mount up to his weight in Dover. Besides, he'd grown attached to Nubarrón. Not many weeks after the headlong ride to the *conde* de la Rocha's estate that had led to his wounding and discovering his feelings for Raúl, his lover had taken him to a gypsy camp where, he had assured Gerrard, they would be able to find a horse that could match him. Nubarrón might not be the speediest horse, but he'd carried Gerrard through many a long, hard ride, and Gerrard would not leave him behind now. Not when he would be the only link Gerrard had left to Spain, to France, and to Raúl.

Finished with his meal, he thanked the innkeeper and asked to see his room. The man led him upstairs to a garret room. "I hope this will meet your satisfaction, monsieur. It's the only bedchamber we had left when you arrived."

The ceiling was low on the sides of the room, but the bed was generously sized for a tavern such as this one, and Gerrard was only planning on staying one night. "It will do fine."

The innkeeper left him alone, and Gerrard locked the door behind him. After stripping down, he climbed in bed and struggled to find a comfortable position. These last six nights had been the first in over five years he had slept alone. He found it surprisingly difficult to settle. Far more difficult than he had found it to sleep next to Raúl those first few nights when he couldn't quite believe what he was doing.

When the Duke of Ranleigh had hired him to serve as his son Christian's protector, Gerrard had been shocked to discover that Viscount Aldwych preferred lovers of his own sex. As he had come to know and admire the young nobleman, he had been able to put aside his shock, but he had still not understood the attraction. Gerrard liked women, and most of them seemed to be pleased with him. He had never imagined any circumstance in which he might find himself aroused by another male.

And then he met Raúl.

Raúl had defied Gerrard's expectations from the moment he laid eyes on the gypsy when he burst into Ciéza de Vivar's apartments expecting to rescue his kidnapped charge. Christian refused to leave, and Raúl made a fool of Gerrard in seconds, forcing him to reconsider his opinion of the man and his appraisal of the situation. It only got worse from there. Raúl seemed omniscient and omnipotent over the next few days, making arrangements and providing what they needed in the nick of time even when he had no warning. Esteban, Teodoro's son, claimed Raúl could do anything. Gerrard wasn't sure that was an exaggeration. In a matter of days, Raúl had gotten Teodoro on the mend from a brutal beating by the Inquisition, placed his men in de la Rocha's castle, and even arranged a horse for Gerrard to join them on their frantic ride through the country before anyone told him Gerrard might be coming. It should have come as no surprise that Raúl would insist on seeing to his wounded shoulder. It came as a great surprise when the touch of those magic hands on his bare skin had a far different reaction than either of them expected.

Gerrard had tensed, shocked to feel his cock hardening at the gentle brush of Raúl's fingertips over the slash the *conde*'s sword had scored on his shoulder. There was nothing blatantly erotic about the touch, and he tried to dismiss the reaction as his body's way of countering the discomfort. Never mind that he had never had that reaction any of the other times he'd been wounded. He clenched his teeth as Raúl cleaned the cut, remarking as he did that it would heal well, but when the gypsy rubbed a thick unguent into the muscle of his shoulder, his bollocks tightened, and he pulled back, stammering some awkward excuse.

Smiling at the memory, Gerrard wrapped a hand around his shaft, stroking it slowly. He'd accused Raúl of bespelling him with his potions, and Raúl had laughed. "I've never needed a spell to lure a partner to my bed," he'd protested.

Gerrard believed it now, but at the time he had still been uncertain even as he had given in to the enticement of Raúl's hand on his bare chest. That first kiss had been so tentative, so light he had barely felt it on his lips. It had rocked him to the depths of his soul. He had pulled away in surprise, only to dive in for a second kiss, the need to feel more nearly overwhelming.

Even now, nothing aroused him as quickly as Raúl's mouth against his. He would have to do without that tonight if he intended to find release, but he could close his eyes and remember what it felt like to kiss Raúl, that first tender, hesitant kiss followed by more passionate ones and then finally by the loving ones that had bound him to Raúl for life.

His palm caught the fluid that seeped from his cock at the memory of those first kisses, spreading it down the shaft as he stroked himself. Raúl's body should have felt wrong against his, with none of the soft, rounded curves Gerrard had sought out in his previous lovers, but they had fit together naturally, the hard planes of Raúl's chest rubbing against Gerrard's in all the right places. "Why now?" he'd asked when he'd raised his head long enough to catch the breath Raúl's kisses had stolen. *Why you?* he'd wondered but hadn't asked aloud.

"Are you surprised that strength is drawn to strength?" Raúl had answered.

He had been then, though he had stopped questioning it in the time they'd been together. He had been desired for his strength, both as a lover and as a hired sword, before Raúl first seduced him, but he had never sought strength in return. Not in a lover, leastways. He had always sought his opposite where his lovers were concerned, their softness yielding to his strength. He had learned the allure of strength yielding to strength that night with Raúl. In the days and years since then, Gerrard had learned both to give and to take, but that night, Raúl had ceded complete control to him, easing Gerrard's fears of losing his masculinity by allowing himself to be taken like a woman.

As many times as he had sunk into Raúl's depths, as many times as he had felt Raúl's cock spearing into him, that first night remained indelibly etched in his memory, the way his body had reacted to even the slightest touch with more fervor than any previous lover had ever evoked. Raúl's hand resting on his chest had alone been enough to pebble his nipples and raise gooseflesh over his chest and arms. Raúl's kiss had been enough to make his entire body ache for more. And when that hand and those lips began to wander, Gerrard had been lost beyond redemption.

There had been no thought of submission, for Raúl's hands and lips had stolen his ability to think. Only sensation was left, and no lover had ever aroused his senses as Raúl had. No woman he had ever lain with had the boldness to explore his body as completely as Raúl did, nor did any woman seem to know all the places where he was most responsive and exactly how to exploit them to bring him to the precipice and hold him there on the brink. Raúl might have taken him then, for he would have granted anything in that moment to achieve his relief, but with the awareness that even now Gerrard accepted without fully understanding, Raúl had not pressed his advantage as any other man might have. Instead, he had dipped into another of his pots of potions to open himself, a sight Gerrard had found almost as arousing as if Raúl's hands had still been on him, and then Raúl had straddled his hips, guiding Gerrard's cock to nudge his portal.

Gerrard's hand tightened around his cock at the memory of that slow, slick slide into Raúl's body, the channel squeezing around him so closely he could feel the beat of Raúl's pulse against his skin. His stroke stuttered and he closed his eyes, reliving the moment when he had first joined with Raúl in body and in spirit.

Neither of them had the patience to last long with adrenaline coursing through them from the wild ride and facing death before the king of Spain, yet it had not been a frantic coupling to mirror those Gerrard had engaged in postbattle at times to work off the bloodlust riding him hard. Even then, in the midst of surging passion, he had felt the undercurrent of true attachment, something beyond the sating of their lust. It had not shown in the way he thrust up into Raúl's body or the way Raúl had slammed down onto his cock, but rather in the way their lips continued to meet and cling, the way Raúl twined their hands, holding on for far more than dear life. When they had finally found release, Raúl had not pulled away in embarrassment or completion, but instead had curled against Gerrard's side, resting his head in the hollow of Gerrard's shoulder, their fingers still entwined. Gerrard had known then that this was different. Even with Rebecca, the woman he would have married had his father not forbidden it, he had never lain like that, as if they had not a care in the world and nothing would ever separate them.

When he had awakened the next morning, it was to find Raúl watching him, his eyes warm but with a shadow of wariness. A week before, he might have justified the night as battle lust, and he would certainly have taken his leave as quickly as he could pull his clothes back on. The shadow in Raúl's eyes told him the gypsy was prepared for Gerrard to do just that. But Gerrard was not the same man he had been when he first accompanied Christian to Spain, and he was certainly not the same man who had dismissed Raúl as no threat at the door to Teodoro's apartments. He had always been a quick study of what gave his partners pleasure, a skill that had served him in good stead with the women he'd bedded. Determined to repay the pleasure he had received the previous evening, he turned that skill to learning Raúl's body as Raúl had learned his, savoring each sigh and groan he won while exploring the smooth chest, the muscled arms, the sculpted abdomen, and lean legs of his new lover.

He had discovered that loving a man was not so different than loving a woman. Raúl gasped and moaned and writhed beneath him with all the passion Gerrard could have asked for, his body as responsive as a finely trained horse, arching into Gerrard's kisses and caresses with far more abandon—far more real abandon—than any lover Gerrard had ever known. By the time he reached the hurdle of stroking his new lover's cock, his delight in Raúl's sensitivity had outweighed his hesitations, and he had taken it in his hand, much as he stroked himself now, exploring the silk-over-steel column with tender dedication and growing wonder. He had become so engrossed in what he was doing that he had missed the signs of impending climax, Raúl's seed spilling over his hand much to his surprise and delight.

He fought not to climax now at the memory of Raúl's face lost in passion, because the memory of preparing and mounting him moments later was even more powerful, but he missed Raúl too much. With a low groan, he closed his eyes and pictured Raúl's beloved face as he gave in to his own need.

Pumping his fist over his engorged shaft, Gerrard conjured the image of Raúl's face when he'd entered him, his position between Raúl's widespread legs granting him the freedom to put to use all he'd learned about the other man's susceptibilities. With a low groan he spilled over his knuckles to the memory of Raúl grasping him by the hair and pulling him down into a passionate kiss. Even as he had spent himself that morning, he knew something more than lust lay between them. The days and nights and years that followed had taught him so much more about the man he had come to love and bound them together with ties that even this separation would not be able to sever.

"Sleep well, my love," Gerrard murmured, touching a finger to the earring Raúl had given him as tenderly as he would caress Raúl himself, before rolling the bedding around him and falling into sleep.

GERRARD AWOKE the next morning with no memory of his dreams, but they must have been of Raúl if the fresh spend coating his belly was any indication. With a sigh and a fleeting thought that he should have ignored his father's summons and stayed at Raúl's side, he rose from the bed and washed quickly in the ewer the innkeeper had provided. He longed for a proper bath, preferably with Raúl sharing the tub with him, but he would wait until he reached his father's keep for that. A quick wipe of his face, groin, and underarms would suffice for now.

Gathering his few belongings into his saddlebags, he descended into the main room of the tavern to the smell of fresh baked bread.

"Good morning, monsieur," the innkeeper said. "Would you break your fast before you leave us? My wife baked this morning."

"You tempt me," Gerrard replied, "but I must arrange passage to England this morn, and I dare not miss the tide."

The innkeeper crossed himself quickly. "God keep you safe in that devil-infested country."

Gerrard laughed, quite sure his father and brother would say the same of France. "I pray he will as well." He paid the bill and collected Nubarrón from the stable, then led him down to the wharf to negotiate passage for them both across the English Channel toward home.

He watched the activity at the harbor for a few moments, examining the boats before approaching the one that seemed to him the most seaworthy. It was a short crossing over the channel, but wind and wave had brought down many a ship, and he had no mind to join them. He might have driven a harder bargain with the captain for his passage, but in truth, as much as he hated leaving France, he was anxious to be gone. The sooner he left and mended things with his father, the sooner he would be able to return.

Having seen Nubarrón secured in the hold, Gerrard returned to the deck to monitor their progress. He was no sailor to help with the lines, but he could not stand being confined in a cabin or the hold, even for so short a crossing as Boulogne to Dover. Once they landed, it would be another few days' ride before he reached his father's land. Nubarrón would appreciate the exercise after being confined.

By the time they reached the cliffs of Dover, Gerrard had grown restless, pacing the bow of the boat until the captain lowered the gangplank and gave him permission to bring Nubarrón up from the hold.

The terrain might have been unfamiliar to Nubarrón, but Gerrard knew it well, and once they left the port city behind them, he gave the horse his head, letting the pace and the wind blow away the stiffness of the crossing. Over the days as he rode toward his family's estate, he was surprised at the swell of emotion he felt at passing familiar landmarks. He did not regret his decision to leave England, but it seemed the ties to the land of his childhood were not so easily broken.

Slowing Nubarrón's gait, Gerrard tried to foresee his father's reaction to his return. One might expect him to be pleased with his son's obedience, but Sir Harald would consider such filial obedience his due, never mind that it was Gerrard's rejection of his father's demands that had led to their falling-out. Try as he could, Gerrard could not see a way in which this meeting would end well. His father would doubtless expect him to remain in England and reform his way of life—meaning to conform to Sir Harald's wishes. That Gerrard meant to return to France as soon as he might would not sit well with the baronet. That his son was supporting himself by hiring his sword—to gypsies, no less!—would be even worse. His friendship with Viscount Aldwych, ambassador to the court of France and heir to the Duke of Ranleigh, would redeem some of these sins in his father's eyes, for he would see in it a means to enhance his own family's social status. Gerrard couldn't help but smile at the thought of the old man's reaction should he ever actually meet Christian.

Christian might draw the mantle of authority around him when doing so would protect his family or advance a cause he championed, but he had no patience for those who put on airs. He would take Sir Harald apart if the man tried to use their loose connection to improve his standing at court.

Gerrard hoped the passage of time and the death of his nephew would soften his father's attitude and make Gerrard's return a cause for happiness amidst the grief. If nothing else, perhaps his son, Randall, would be a point in his favor rather than a mark against him. Surely any heir, even one born out of wedlock, was better than none. But even that would not be enough to make Sir Harald accept Gerrard's relationship with Raúl. Some things were simply not within the realm of possibility.

FOUR

AFTER FOUR days on the road in which Raúl had passed few other travelers, leaving him far too much time to brood about missing Gerrard, he rode toward Auxerre with lightening spirits. The villages where he had stopped for the night had been little more than a collection of cottages and small shops to support the local farmers, but in a town of some size, he hoped to find others following his same route. He would far prefer the company of others to his own morose thoughts.

Circling the area, he searched the fields for signs of a Rom caravan, finally finding a circle of colorful wagons east of town. He hailed the caravan before approaching, not wanting to frighten the children.

A tall, swarthy man stepped from the protective circle in response to his call.

"Greetings," Raúl said. "I'm traveling to Saintes-Maries-de-la-Mer and looking for company. I'm something of a healer and would be glad to offer my services in exchange for riding with you."

"A healer?" the man replied anxiously. "The Holy Mother herself must have sent you. My daughter has been feverish for two nights now. We have been dosing her with yarrow tea, though it is helping but little, and the apothecary in town is none too happy to treat with us."

"I will see to her gladly." He dismounted and stepped forward, trusting Martiya to stay where he left him. "Raúl, at your service."

"Nikolae, at yours," the man said, grasping Raúl's outstretched hand.

"Let us see what I can do for your daughter," Raúl proposed. "If she has been sick for two days already, we should not delay any longer."

Nikolae led Raúl into the circle of *vardos* and up to the entrance of the largest wagon. Raúl paused to greet the old woman who sat on the steps up into their home. She smiled at him, crooked teeth flashing as she sketched the sign of the cross in blessing.

Raúl followed Nikolae inside and knelt on the floor next to the bed of a young girl, perhaps three or four years old. He touched her forehead gently, feeling the signs of a low fever. She roused and coughed wetly. "What's your name, love?"

"Nadya," the little girl replied in a pitiful voice. "The *gaje* call me Nadège."

"Then it's a good thing I'm not *gaje*. Where does it hurt, Nadya?" he asked.

"Chest," she said, her voice rough. "Ears."

Raúl lowered his head to her chest, listening for the rattle that would signify pneumonia, but he did not hear anything untoward. "I have something in my saddlebag that should help."

"Thank the Blessed Mother," Nikolae's wife said. "We have heard rumor of the plague and feared to lose her."

"She is not so sick as that," Raúl assured them. "A little mint oil to help clear her chest and head, some willow bark tea to lower her fever, and then plenty of rich broth to keep up her strength, and she should be well in a matter of days."

Leaving Nikolae's wife stroking the child's hair and murmuring softly to her, Raúl tethered Martiya to the back of the wagon and retrieved his pack of herbs from the saddlebag. When he returned to Nadya's side, he warmed a palmful of oil infused with mint and juniper before gently anointing her cheeks, throat, and chest with the fragrant balm. She managed a weak smile when he rubbed his fingers over the skin beneath her nose.

"Breathe in now, love," Raúl said, resting his palm over her heart and murmuring softly in a language most would no longer recognize. Nadya's chest rose and fell more easily, and Raúl closed his eyes to regroup his strength before pulling the blanket over her and turning to her relieved parents.

"Brew her a tea with this willow bark, and alternate it with broth as often as she will drink," he instructed. "Wash her down with cool water if her fever rises again, and then rub her with more of the oil. I will check on her again in the morning."

"Will you sup with us, monsieur?" Nikolae's wife asked.

"If you will call me Raúl, I would be honored to share your table," Raúl replied.

"And I am Mirela," she said. "Are you heading south?"

"I am," Raúl said, "on the way to Saintes-Maries-de-la-Mer."

"It is unusual to find a lone Rom," Mirela observed as she rose from her daughter's bedside. "I hope nothing has befallen your *familia*."

The words brought a pang to Raúl's heart. "My lover was called home. We were visiting friends in Paris who are not Rom and had intended to travel south together." He hesitated, unsure how his hosts would react if he admitted his lover was male. His own *familia* knew his inclination and had come to value Gerrard's place at his side, but not all Rom were as accepting.

"You are welcome to travel with us," Nikolae offered. "We had no destination in mind other than seeking warmer climes, but if our daughter recovers, I would gladly offer thanks at Saintes-Maries-de-la-Mer."

Over a dinner of stewed rabbit served up by Mirela, Nikolae asked Raúl to share some of his story if he were willing. "I judge by your accent, and since our paths have never crossed before, that Burgundy is not your home."

"My people live in Spain," Raúl answered, "though I have traveled much in recent years." As Teodoro had followed Christian in his rising diplomatic responsibilities through postings in Belgium, Austria, and Venice, the two had always invited Raúl and Gerrard to visit them. Christian's position as ambassador to France, and his involvement in uncovering the plot to discredit the head of the musketeers as a means of weakening protection to the French royal family, had kept them in France longer than Raúl expected. He had hoped to return with Gerrard to Spain following their pilgrimage, but Gerrard's summons had put those plans to naught. And Raúl had still not been able to shake the premonition that something—he had no idea what—was ahead that would keep him from Gerrard. Shaking his head to banish the vague disquiet, he returned his attention to his hosts. "Perhaps after the festival I will return there."

"You are far from home indeed," Mirela said. "It must be an interesting story to have brought you so far."

"Sometimes," Raúl said with a laugh, "although much of the time was simply spent with good friends."

IN A few days it was clear that Nadya was out of danger, the greatest challenge being to keep the lively child in bed until she had fully recovered her strength. When even telling her tales could no longer keep her interest, Raúl bethought himself of something he carried in his saddlebag.

"I have something for you, Nadya," he told her, offering her a small but intricately carved wooden figure. "His name is Boldo, and he needs someone to care for him."

The little girl smiled at the horse and held it to her breast, stroking the flowing mane. "Papa will not let me near the big horses," she said softly. "Now I have a horse of my very own."

"Until you are a little bigger, Boldo is a better size for you than the big horses," Raúl agreed. "Gerrard will be happy to know he's found such a good home."

Gerrard had been worried about how he would fit in with the caravan when he decided to stay in Spain with Raúl, but it had not taken long before he won everyone over with his charm and his gentleness. Raúl had seen Gerrard fight and knew how ruthless he could be when it came to defending himself and those he cared about, but with the Rom children, he was the gentle giant, content to sit on the ground with them and carve toys for them to play with, animals and dervishes and little wooden flutes. In the next town they visited, one of the local women asked about buying some of them, and Gerrard's place in the caravan was assured, as if his place as Raúl's lover had not already guaranteed his acceptance. In the intervening years, Gerrard had carved hundreds of such trinkets.

It had not been enough for Gerrard to be accepted, though. He had insisted on integrating as fully as possible, much to Raúl's delight and amusement. He sat with the children, learning Romani at their side.

"It's not necessary," Raúl had protested, though the sight of Gerrard dwarfing the caravan's children warmed his heart. "Most of us speak Spanish and some French as well, enough to converse with you."

"But it marks me out as different." Raúl refrained from pointing out the obvious fact that Gerrard's size alone marked him apart from the slighter Roms. "If I am to live with you, I want to fit in as one of you."

Raúl had not known how to argue with that, and Gerrard had learned, slowly and sometimes with amusing results, but he had learned, determined to fit in with his new home. He had been equally determined to contribute materially, with his carving and with his sword.

"Where did you learn to carve?" Raúl asked. He had experience with how gentle Gerrard's touch could be, but it was still surprising to see such large hands create such intricate detail.

"My nursemaid's husband worked as our family's master groom," Gerrard answered, putting the final details on a sheepdog carrying a puppy in its mouth. "I was fascinated by horses and spent every minute I could escape from my tutor in the stables haunting his footsteps. He put me to work doing what chores I could, but until I was old enough and large enough to be of real help, setting me in a corner carving kept me out from underfoot."

Raúl could imagine it so easily, the inquisitive boy wanting to help but unable to do anything useful. "You were not the typical aristocrat's son, were you?"

Gerrard chuckled. "No, I was not. I would not be here if I were. I spent far more time with the servants than I did with anyone my father approved of. We finally fought one time too many, and I chose to leave rather than do something I would regret. My temper has always been my downfall."

"'Tis nothing wrong with passion so long as it is guided to the proper channels," Raúl answered, running a palm over the muscle of Gerrard's arm.

"And what channels would those be?" Gerrard teased, his smile turning seductive.

"You're well familiar with at least one of those channels, I'd warrant," Raúl answered in kind. While he may have preferred the dominant role as a lover more often than not before this, he had found it no hardship to let Gerrard take the lead in exploring his new role as a lover of men—though he fully intended to be the only man in Gerrard's life, now and in the future.

"Then perhaps it is time to explore a different channel," Gerrard said slowly.

Raúl's blood, already heated by the husky tone Gerrard's voice took on when he turned amorous, pulsed through his veins at the suggestion, pooling in his groin and stirring his cock to full hardness. He had not pressed in this, understanding that Gerrard would come to readiness in his own time, but the thought of completing their union in his lover's body roused him to a state that demanded immediate release. Tamping down his impatience, he took the carving and knife from Gerrard's hands and set them aside. "Perhaps so, but in that case we should take this to a more private venue."

They retired to Raúl's wagon, the one he used when he traveled with the caravan of his family and friends—his *familia*. The temptation to hurry, to grab and take, was strong, but he understood the magnitude of this step for Gerrard, so he moved slowly as they undressed, taking his time to kiss and caress with the same slow tenderness as the first time they made love. Not that they had been rough since then, but familiarity had granted a certain ease and allowed for the occasional frantically eager coupling instead. That would not do for this time, though. Gerrard deserved to have his first time be as special as he was.

Despite his efforts, Raúl could feel the tenseness in Gerrard's muscles as he kissed his way up the inside of the strong thighs. Rising to his knees, he settled a palm on Gerrard's shoulder. "Roll over, love."

Gerrard tensed even more at the request, but Raúl soothed him with long, slow strokes of his hands up and down his back, kissing his way down Gerrard's spine to the curve of his buttocks. The gasp that escaped suggested Gerrard had guessed Raúl's destination, but he did not give his lover a chance to protest before burying his head between the firm cheeks and licking the length of Gerrard's crease.

The long, low groan and the shudder that ran the length of Gerrard's spine told Raúl that while he might have startled him, the attention was not unwelcome. Raúl settled in to ravish Gerrard in earnest, circling the spasming ring of muscle with teasing licks and slow, wet swipes of his tongue until it clenched at every touch. Raúl sucked gently at the pucker before pushing the tip of his tongue inside the hot, tight channel.

Gerrard howled—there was no other word for the sound that issued from his throat when Raúl's tongue breached him. Raúl ran a hand down his arm, and Gerrard clutched his fingers, squeezing them convulsively in a wordless plea for more.

Raúl gave it gladly, licking and thrusting and sucking on the tight ring of muscle until Gerrard was bucking back against him, curses streaming from his lips as he begged and pleaded and demanded. Sliding a slick finger inside was easy after that, and Raúl rubbed over the bundle of nerves until Gerrard warned that he was close.

It might have been easier on Gerrard to take him from behind, but Raúl needed the intimacy of seeing his face as he made love to him for the first time. After sliding his fingers free and bestowing a final lick down the now-sensitized crease, he touched Gerrard's shoulder. "Onto your back again, love."

Any uncertainty Raúl might have harbored about Gerrard's readiness was put to rest when he rolled over, spreading his legs wide, knees bent, soles planted on the mattress. Gerrard's cock, swollen and red and leaking, bobbed against his stomach, and Raúl couldn't resist leaning down to swipe his tongue over the dampened crown. Gerrard groaned and wove his fingers into Raúl's hair, pulling his head away. "Now," he panted, his voice heavy with desire. "I want to feel you inside me when I come."

Raúl was unable able to resist the plea, moving up between Gerrard's thighs until their groins met. He rocked against the cradle of Gerrard's hips, their cocks sliding wetly against one another until Gerrard grabbed Raúl's hips. "Enough. Do it now."

Even with Gerrard's demand adding to his own body's urges, Raúl was determined to take his time. Grasping his heated shaft with a squeeze to slow his own racing pulse, he nudged the crown against Gerrard's opening. The damp muscle accepted him readily, and he paused when just the head slipped inside, leaning forward to capture Gerrard's lips in a slow, sweet kiss. Gerrard pushed his tongue into Raúl's mouth in the same manner he doubtless wanted Raúl to plunge into him, but Raúl held his hips still, letting his kiss communicate his feelings. He had not yet told Gerrard that he loved him, a part of him still fearing to frighten Gerrard away, but he could show him without words.

Gerrard writhed beneath him, rocking up against Raúl until their bodies joined completely without Raúl ever having thrust into him. "I never imagined it could feel like this," Gerrard whispered, peppering Raúl's face with tender kisses. "I love you."

Even though it seemed he had worried for nothing, Raúl still hesitated to say the words in return. Instead he clasped Gerrard's hips and rocked in slow, gentle strokes until a hiss of startled breath told him he'd found the heart of Gerrard's pleasure. Trailing kisses down the corded muscles of Gerrard's throat as he arched beneath him, Raúl rubbed over the sensitive spot again and again. Gerrard's shaft dragged against his belly as they rocked together, but Raúl resisted the temptation to curl his palm around its generous length. Instead he teased his thumbs over Gerrard's chest, finding the nipples hidden in the dusting of dark hair. Gerrard wrapped a hand around Raúl's buttocks, pulling him closer, increasing the friction where his cock throbbed between them.

Raúl rested his full weight on Gerrard's body, uniting them as completely as he knew how, wrapping Gerrard's legs around his own waist, leaning down so their chests met, his smooth skin rasping against the hair on Gerrard's torso, their lips touching, parting, only to touch again.

When Gerrard's breathing grew short and erratic, he clenched around Raúl, the ripple of muscle nearly enough to steal Raúl's control. "Never felt... like this with... anyone else," he rasped, his voice hot against Raúl's ear.

Turning his head, Raúl claimed Gerrard's mouth, working a hand down the broad chest and between them. Gerrard's cock was slick in his palm, thrusting into his grasp with the same urgent tempo as Gerrard's tongue plundered his mouth. Groaning into the kiss, Gerrard tensed against him as his climax seized him, the sudden clench of his muscles pulling Raúl over the edge as well. Pleasure blazing through him, he raised his hands to cradle Gerrard's face and comb the sweat-damp hair from his brow. "Kamaù tut," Raúl murmured, his gaze meeting Gerrard's love-softened eyes. "I love you."

Gerrard echoed the words in his funny English accent, but to Raúl they were perfect, and Gerrard was diligent in his practice, saying them over and over until they sounded natural on his lips.

Not hearing them for the past few days was harder than Raúl could ever have imagined. He prayed fervently for the day to come quickly when he and Gerrard would be reunited and he could hear them once more in person rather than in the silent echo of his memories.

Nikolae's voice calling for the men to harness the horses so they could head out wrenched Raúl from his memories. Martiya would not be expected to pull his weight, but Raúl had no intention of shirking his share of the responsibilities. The trek to Saintes-Maries-de-la-Mer would take over a month with the caravan, and he wanted to arrive in time for the feast day.

FIVE

GERRARD REINED in his horse as he neared the edge of the Hawkins estate. As much as concern for his family had driven him, he was not quite ready to face his father. If he had learned anything from Raúl—and the list of things he had learned could fill a book—it was that information was his most valuable resource. Unless things had changed beyond all recognition, the best place in the village or on the estate to get information would be his former nursemaid, Agatha, and her husband, Colman.

Settling Nubarrón in the paddock beside their house, he brushed the dust off his clothes as well as he could and knocked on the door, hoping he still remembered how to speak English.

It seemed an eternity before he heard stirring inside, a familiar voice calling to wait a moment, and then the door opened and his old nursemaid stood in the entry. For an instant she seemed shocked into silence, and then she caught him in her arms, her head barely brushing his chin. "Gerrard Jules Hawkins! Lord love you, just look at you!" She drew away fleetingly, her gaze raking him up and down, before she pulled him into another embrace and then tugged him inside, closing the door behind him. "Just look at you! Seven years gone with nary a word while you traipsed over who knows what heathen lands! At least you seemed to have been eating well, wherever you've been," she tutted, lifting a corner of her apron to wipe her eyes. "I do believe you're even bigger than you were when you left. Or maybe I've just gotten used to people wasting away…." She sighed, shaking her head. "What am I thinking of, leaving you standing here in the doorway? Come into the kitchen and I'll put the kettle on for some tea."

Gerrard followed Agatha inside, feeling at once ten feet tall and ten years old again. It was good to know some things never changed. "Is Colman up at the stables?" Gerrard asked, looking around and seeing no sign of Agatha's husband. "I have so much to tell you that I don't even know where to start."

Agatha sighed again while filling a heavy kettle from a pitcher on the sideboard and then setting it on the hearth to warm. "Colman's been gone these three years past," she answered, cupping Gerrard's cheek. "He would have been so happy to see you home again. 'Always was the best of the Hawkinses,' that's what he always said of you."

"I have you and him to thank for that," Gerrard said, taking her hand. "I'm sorry. I should have tried to get word to you and gather the news from home more often, but I knew my father would not pass any messages along, and I did not know how James felt about my abrupt departure. I would have come home then if I had known."

"You couldn't have known, sweeting. I only wish you had better tidings to come home to now."

Gerrard nodded slowly, digesting what she said and what she had not said. "It's that bad?" he asked, leading her to the table and urging her to sit. He had learned self-sufficiency living with the gypsies. He could prepare Agatha a cup of tea to warm her old bones instead of expecting her to wait on him.

Agatha's gaze followed him as he reached into the cupboard for the tea, still in the same spot she'd kept it when she'd listened to his hurts and triumphs when he was a boy. "Come, sit beside me," she said, patting the chair next to her. When Gerrard settled, she took his hands between hers, and he thought how small and fragile they seemed compared to his. "They're all gone," she said gently. "Your father, your brother and his lady, and little Jamie. The plague took them all. Miss Philippa lasted the longest, but when Sir James went, she like to lost her will to live." She squeezed Gerrard's hands, her eyes filling with tears. "I'm so sorry."

Gerrard fought back his own hot tears at the thought of his gentle sister-in-law giving up on life. He could barely make sense of the news. All chance of reconciling with his father, gone. All chance of seeing his son one day recognized as part of the family, lost. And what of his life on the Continent? Raúl waited for his return in France. "I... I don't know what to do."

"Oh, child." His nurse gathered Gerrard to her as if he were still that young boy, rocking him in her arms as he let the sense of loss sweep through him. When his tears stopped, Agatha smoothed his hair and stood to make the tea. She set the two stoneware mugs on the table before them. "I might even have a bit of that honey raisin cake you like so much," she teased and cut him a hearty slice from a cloth-wrapped loaf before settling back beside him. "Troubles always seem worse on an empty stomach. Drink your tea, and then we'll see what's to be done."

Gerrard took a deep breath, wishing Raúl were there. His lover would know what to do. Raúl always knew what to do. That wasn't to be, though, so he sipped his tea and ate a slice of Agatha's special cake and let the feeling of being home again wash over him. He might have lived in the manor house until his falling-out with his father drove him to leave the country, but this kitchen in this little cottage had been home.

"What about the servants in the house?" Gerrard asked after a few sips of tea. "Is Reeves overseeing the estate in my father's stead?" If his father's man of business had the estate well in hand, perhaps Gerrard could settle matters quickly and return to Raúl without much delay.

"Your father dismissed Mr. Reeves, shortly after you left, it was." Agatha cut another slice of cake for Gerrard and sipped her own tea. "Word among the servants was that he refused to agree to one of Sir Harald's demands." Agatha didn't elaborate, but Gerrard had his suspicions. As angry as his father was at Gerrard's actions before his departure, he wouldn't put it past the old man to have tried to cut him out of the succession, and from what Gerrard remembered of Reeves, the man would never have agreed to such an act. Not that it would have been a concern then, with both James and his son in line to inherit before the family's black sheep. "Sir Harald never replaced him—said he'd see to his own concerns after that," Agatha continued.

Well, fuck. "Has anyone been caring for the estate since my father's death?" Gerrard asked, the enormity of the task facing him beginning to sink in. He briefly considered walking away from it all. The estate would simply cease to exist with no one to care for it. The servants would find other jobs and the villagers would go on as they always had without having to pay tithes to his family. In time another aristocrat might take the title or be granted it by the king, but it would be none of Gerrard's concern. He could return to Raúl free of entanglements. Then he looked into Agatha's lined face. She would not find another job at her age, and with no one to oversee the estate, she would not receive her pension either. And Randall would be left with even less than he had now if Gerrard relinquished his claim on the estate. "Or will I find complete chaos in the manor house?"

"Not *complete* chaos," Agatha said, patting Gerrard's hand. "And nothing you cannot soon set to rights. There was no one to collect the quarter settlements, though so many of the farmers suffered losses to the sickness that few would have been able to pay in any case. Some of the crofts have no one left to work them and will need to be assigned new tenants if they aren't to fall fallow. Those of us left at the manor have fared well enough living off the home garden, but there will be crops to bring in and the cellar to fill if we aren't to go hungry this winter."

"Then I suppose I should get started," he said with a sigh. "First, though, I must post a letter. I only pray the general direction I can give it will be enough for it to find its intended recipient. Would you have paper and a quill I could use?"

"Of course, lambkin." Agatha's thin lips curved into a smile as she rose to gather the requested items. "Some pretty young miss back in France waiting for word of your safe arrival, perhaps?"

"A dear friend," Gerrard said, reaching automatically for the earring Raúl had given him when they parted. "I had promised to meet him in southern France within the month, but since it will take me weeks to travel there, I will not make it as planned, and I would not have him worry for naught. He knew my family was ill. He will understand the delay." He took the paper from Agatha and wrote a short note to Raúl. He would have preferred to pour his heart out, but he dared not put such sentiments on paper where they could be used against either Raúl or himself. After finishing the letter, he sealed it and slid it in his pocket. "I suppose I should go up to the house now. Is there anyone there I will recognize or who will remember me?"

"Most of the servants are new since your time," Agatha answered, her gaze lingering on Gerrard for a moment before she picked up the empty cups and took them to the sink. "Sir Harald was never an easy master after your mother, the Lord bless her soul, was no longer here to soften him, but he grew even sterner once you left the manor. Not all had the patience to deal with his cantankerous ways. Many of those who stayed were no longer young enough to go looking for a new position, and so more susceptible to the sickness." She shook her head. "I sometimes questioned why God saw fit to spare me, especially with Colman gone, but I see now it was so I would be here for you when you returned."

"We will need to hire new servants, then," Gerrard declared. "The manor must be scrubbed from top to bottom and all the linens replaced if it's to be safe for use again. There are many things I haven't yet learned from Raúl, but the importance of cleanliness is one lesson he pounded into my head. Even if I don't stay for long, the manor should be habitable. I want to bring Randall here if nothing else. I have to return to the Continent for a time, title or not. Will you care for him in my absence?"

"Will not the boy's mother be here to care for him?" The nurse's face tightened into a frown. Agatha had never been overly fond of Rebecca when Gerrard had been courting her, though the older woman had never spoken disparagingly of his lover once he had announced his intention to wed, even when he had confessed that Rebecca was carrying his child.

"I cannot marry her," Gerrard explained. "My heart is given elsewhere, but Randall is still my son, and I would have him recognized as my heir since he is the only one I'm likely to have. I do not want to bring Rebecca here because I have no desire to give her false hope. I would have married her seven years ago if my father had allowed, but my life is different now."

For all her age, Agatha's gaze was still sharp as she considered Gerrard again before speaking. "It is never easy for a mother to give up a child she loves," she said finally. "Nor for the child to be supplanted when you are ready to provide a legitimate heir."

"Randall is the only heir I will ever have," Gerrard insisted. Raúl provided him many things—a check on his temper, a home for his heart, and a passion Gerrard had not imagined possible—but his lover would never give him another child. "I will speak with a solicitor and make sure everything is in order for Randall to inherit the title."

"No doubt that will make it easier for Rebecca," Agatha answered in the voice Gerrard had learned as a child to recognize for the warning it was. "You'll not stop her from seeing her son, no matter if you mean to recognize him or not."

"She will always be his mother, even if she will never be my wife," Gerrard assured her. He could all but see Agatha biting her tongue to stop from asking about his mystery lover, but since he had no desire to shock her on his first day home, he did not provide any other details. "Are you well enough to ride down to the village with me so I can see what condition everything is in? Nubarrón can carry us both."

"I may be old, but I was Colman's wife for nigh on fifty years," Agatha answered with a smile that made her look far younger. "It's been long since I've been on the back of a horse, but I warrant I haven't forgotten how to ride."

On impulse, Gerrard leaned over and kissed her lined cheek. "And I'll warrant I haven't forgotten how to ride double. It's good to be home. I've missed you."

THEY WALKED outside, and he helped her onto Nubarrón's back. The gelding snorted when he climbed atop his back as well, but he calmed the animal with firm hands and gentle words. Guiding his mount down the lanes of his childhood, he bypassed the manor in favor of the village where he had often played as a child.

As he entered the lane through the center of the village, he heard a shout of welcome from the blacksmith lounging outside his smithy. "Sir Gerrard! 'Tis good to see you home!" Blinking back his shock at the realization that since his father's death he was, in fact, Sir Gerrard, he slowed his horse to a stop. The smith—Warren, Gerrard thought his name was, still as large as ever, though far grayer than Gerrard remembered him—held Nubarrón's reins in one massive hand and clapped Gerrard on the back with the other with enough force to rock him forward against Agatha. His booming voice garnered the attention of others, and soon Gerrard found himself surrounded by a throng of villagers exclaiming, "Welcome home, Sir Gerrard!" and "Thank heavens you've come home, sir," and "We'll soon see things put to rights now that you're here, Sir Gerrard!"

Handing Agatha down into the smith's arms—ignoring her protests that she needed no help but not her blushes as the smith lowered her gently to the ground—Gerrard dismounted. Nubarrón nickered and tossed his head as the villagers closed around them, offering respectful curtseys and bows, the bolder ones touching his sleeve as if to confirm he was really there. Gerrard was surprised how many of the villagers he remembered by name and saddened by how many of those he remembered were missing, victims of the plague or simply the years he had been gone.

It would have been easy to remain aloof, to brush aside the welcome as either his due or somehow beneath him as his father had always done, but Gerrard had spent the past years learning another kind of leadership. "Warren, I need you to gather everyone at the chapel, if you would. I've been gone and I don't know everyone or what the needs of the village are anymore. We need a plan, and I can't come up with one on my own. I'll need everyone's help if we're to set Hawkins Hall back to rights."

The villagers seemed shocked, but Agatha's smile was proud as the blacksmith sent several of the younger men in the crowd scurrying to send word to any who hadn't already gathered. After securing Nubarrón's reins to a post outside the smithy, Gerrard took Agatha's arm and followed Warren to the chapel, where the new graves in the churchyard proved his earlier surmise correct.

It took time for everyone to gather, the younger villagers helping the remaining older ones into the church. Gerrard seated Agatha in the front pew and then wandered among the townspeople—*his* people—finding the elders he remembered, the ones whose wisdom he would need now to fill his father's shoes. One or two at a time, he led them to join Agatha in the front of the church. When Warren shut the door, indicating everyone had arrived, Gerrard walked back to the altar and turned to look into the expectant faces. "I need your help," he began without preamble. "I have been gone for seven years, and I don't know what decisions my father made, for good or for ill. I don't know what has changed and what has remained the same. I don't know what the village needs, but if I have learned one thing in my travels, it is where to find the answers to those questions, and that is with all of you."

There was silence as the villagers absorbed his words, doubtless pondering whether to believe them. But many of the elders remembered Gerrard from his youth and seemed to accept that he had not grown into his father's son. "Many of us have rents due," a wrinkled woman Gerrard recognized as the wife of the village baker said. He did not see her husband beside her, leading him to assume she had been widowed. "And few have had money or heart to shop since the sickness came."

"My son and his family survived, but he was ill and is still too weak to work his holding," another man added.

"Both my son and son-in-law are gone, and their widows and children have no one but us to care for them," a second elderly woman said.

"We no longer have a grocer or an apothecary," another said.

"First, no one will be evicted because of the rents," Gerrard declared. "We have lost enough people to the plague. We will not lose more because of money. Does everyone have a decent place to live, or are there houses in disrepair?"

"Most of the houses are fine, but a few had damage during the winter, and the plague hit before Sir Harald could begin repairs," Warren replied.

"Are there empty houses where those whose homes are damaged could live until we can complete repairs?" Gerrard asked.

"Far too many," another man replied sadly. "But who would want to live in them? The plague may still linger in them."

"They simply need to be cleaned," Gerrard said. Raúl had demonstrated to him over and again the value of sunlight, fresh air, and cleanliness in fighting off disease. Surely the plague could be no different. "Those who are strong enough can scrub them top to bottom, and then leave them open to the air for a few days to sweep out all the stale air."

A murmur ran through the room, but obedience to the aristocracy was too inbred for them to ignore a direct order. Gerrard wasn't entirely sure how he felt about that, but if he could use it to protect and shelter his people, it would be worth it. "Once that is done, I will ride to London to see if I can find a new grocer and apothecary for us, and while I am there, I will be naming my son, Randall, as my heir. I know my father would not let me wed his mother, but I would claim him before God and men, starting here today."

Looking around, Gerrard noted for the first time that neither of Rebecca's parents were among the gathered villagers, nor was Rebecca herself, or Randall. He glanced in alarm at Agatha, who smiled at him in reassurance.

"Jacob is working the farm, and Rebecca does not like to leave him alone. He recovered when her mother did not, but he is still not as strong as he was, and Rebecca worries about him," Agatha explained. "We can ride past their holding on the way back to the manor house, if you would like to stop and see them."

Gerrard considered he should probably warn Rebecca before he thrust their son into the spotlight. It was too late where the village was concerned, but they should talk before he went to London. "Our first order of business must be safe lodging for everyone. Gather all the soap and rags you have, and we will start with the empty houses. If we scrub them today and leave them open to air out tomorrow, people can move in the day after. Once that is done, we will see what else needs doing."

As the villagers filed out of the chapel to follow Gerrard's instructions, he took a moment to say a swift prayer for Raúl's safety. At least if he was busy, he would not have time to miss him.

SIX

THE CARAVAN rolled through the marshy plain approaching Saintes-Maries-de-la-Mer, though the land was too flat for Raúl to catch any glimpse of the coast yet. They'd been traveling more than a month since he'd left Paris, stopping in a number of small towns along the way so that Nikolae and Mirela could sell their wares and buy provisions, and several other wagons had joined theirs for the journey. More than once it had occurred to Raúl that he could have traveled far faster riding alone than at the slow pace the carts could move, but he reminded himself that he would simply have exchanged the long days waiting for the caravan to reach the coast for long days waiting alone for the festival to begin. At least traveling with the caravan, he had the company of the other Rom to distract him. Nadya, in particular, had occupied much of his time, asking him questions about his homeland and the countries he had visited in his journeys. Once the others who joined them on their pilgrimage learned he was a healer, he'd dealt with a number of minor illnesses and injuries, and he'd scavenged the countryside they passed through for fresh roots, barks, and herbs to replenish his supplies.

No matter how he filled his days, though, the nights belonged to Gerrard. On most nights when the weather was clear, Raúl slept in a blanket under the stars, leaving Nikolae and Mirela what privacy he could (especially once he found that Nikolae was prone to snoring). He'd begun by trying to imagine where Gerrard might be in his own journey, but for all that he was traveling to another country, Gerrard would have reached his family estates long before Raúl would reach the southern coast. Raúl wondered how Gerrard's father had reacted to his son's return. As much as he hoped for Gerrard's sake that the two could reconcile their differences, he couldn't escape the niggle of worry that Sir Harald might convince Gerrard to remain in England. Gerrard had promised to return, and Raúl had no reason to doubt him, but neither could he forget the flash of foresight that had shown him alone.

In the light of day, it was easier to ignore such forebodings. Raúl told himself that Gerrard might well have completed his business with his father by now, that he might already be crossing the channel back to France or even on the road behind them. Even so, he could not help wishing they could move just a little faster to reach Saintes-Maries-de-la-Mer. Each day closer to the festival was a day closer to being reunited with Gerrard.

"Monsieur Raúl," Nadya called, running up to him. "We've almost arrived."

"So we have," Raúl agreed. "Is this your first trip for the festival?"

"I went to the festival when I was one years old, Mama says, but I don't 'member much. This time I 'member better."

"I'm sure you will," Raúl said, lifting the child into his arms as he strode along at Martiya's side. "You're a big girl now."

"Can I ride Martiya?" Nadya asked.

Raúl chuckled. He should have known the child had ulterior motives in coming to talk to him. "I suppose it will be all right," he said, setting her on the saddle before swinging up behind her. "Hold tight to his mane so you don't fall."

She tangled her little fingers in the dark strands of Martiya's mane as Raúl tightened the reins to keep the stallion in check. The horse shook his head but did not fight Raúl's control.

Several more minutes passed before Nadya leaned back against Raúl. "Mama says you are sad. Why are you sad, monsieur Raúl?"

Raúl raised a hand to smooth the little girl's hair. He hadn't been aware his mood was so obvious; he would have to keep a tighter rein on his own emotions. There was no need to make the people around him deal with his humors. "A friend of mine had to go away, and I miss him," he said, putting the situation in terms the child could understand.

"He'll come back soon," Nadya said with the assurance only a child could possess. "Papa always does when Mama misses him."

"I'm sure you're right," Raúl agreed. Martiya tossed his head as if adding his own assertion to the statement. At the same time, a shout arose from the lead wagon.

"I can see the church!" Nikolae called out eagerly. The tall triple bell towers of the fortified church were visible for miles inland. Scattered cries of excitement echoed through the caravan as the word spread. Martiya danced beneath the reins, and Raúl might have given him his head had Nadya not been sitting before him. "Let's ride up ahead with your parents," he suggested instead. "You can be the first to enter the village. That will bring you extra blessings."

Nadya bounced excitedly in Raúl's arms, her enthusiasm enough to set Martiya sidestepping again. Raúl frowned. He would have to pass Nadya off to her parents and let the stallion have a run, or the horse would not be fit for stabling tonight. It suited him better anyway to enter the village alone. If Gerrard had been with him, it would have been different, like it had been in previous years when they rode into the village together at the head of Raúl's caravan, but Gerrard was still in England or somewhere on the road behind him.

Nikolae and Mirela took Nadya back from him despite her protests, but Raúl would let them deal with their daughter. He had his own concerns. Turning Martiya away from the caravan, he spurred the horse across the marsh, taking him away from the caravan and the friendly faces, but nothing could take him away from his memories.

The wind whipped a strand of his long hair loose from the kerchief that covered it as Martiya galloped, and Raúl could not help but remember the wild ride from Madrid to the *conde* de la Rocha's estate, when his eyes had first opened to Gerrard's worth. "May the wind bring you back to me soon, *querido*," Raúl murmured as Martiya's hooves rang over the cobbled road entering Saintes-Maries-de-la-Mer.

The actual pilgrimage procession would not take place until May 24, but Raúl rode up to the church anyway, leaving Martiya tethered at the entrance as he went inside and lit a candle to Saint Christopher for Gerrard's safety.

That done, he set out to find lodgings for himself, since he would not be leaving Saintes-Maries-de-la-Mer until Gerrard met him there some weeks hence.

A WEEK later Raúl had come no closer to resolving his restlessness, even though he had found a group of his own friends from Spain in one of the many encampments around the town. He needed Gerrard, but while he could leave in a matter of days after the festival ended, the risk of missing Gerrard on the road was too great for him to leave for England.

"Now there's a welcome sight! Well met, Raúl."

The sound of his name drew Raúl from his pensiveness, and he looked up to find Esteban striding across the courtyard with all the brashness that marked him as Teodoro's son. Time would temper that

with control, but Raúl saw much of his friend in the young man who
joined him now.

"*Hola*, whelp!" Raúl responded, breaking into a smile. "Does the
court travel to Saintes-Maries-de-la-Mer?" He had seen no sign of the
kind of chaos that would surely accompany a royal visit, and indeed
the village had no accommodations worthy of King Louis and Queen
Anne, let alone enough to house the train of courtiers, ladies-in-waiting,
and hangers-on that would invariably accompany them. "Or have you
slipped your father's leash so that I should forget having met you?"

"Neither," Esteban replied with a courtly bow. "The court has
come to Tarascon, to the royal chateau there, and as a servant of the
ambassador, I have come with them. Cristian and Teo have taken rooms
in Arles, preferring not to be dependent on the king for their residence,
and Teo sent me to find you and invite you to join us there anytime you
weary of your little village."

"I will join you and them gladly," Raúl said. "I have seen enough
kings that I would as soon avoid the royal court myself. Attention from the
throne rarely bodes well for Roms." He was not surprised that Christian
and Teodoro chose to keep some distance from the king as well—gossip
still held that Louis was more interested in his male courtiers than his
queen, and Raúl had himself witnessed more than one lingering glance
from the throne directed at the English ambassador. He knew his friend's
temper well enough that Teodoro would have little tolerance for such
scrutiny of Christian, no matter how regal the beholder.

"You should be able to avoid royal attention, but do not think
to avoid the musketeers. I swear, those four spend more time in our
courtyard than they do guarding the king," Esteban muttered.

"I take it you have yet to best any of them," Raúl teased. "If
you would spend as much time working on your swordplay as you
do wooing the chambermaids at court, you would perhaps reach that
worthy goal."

"I will have you know I have no interest in chambermaids," Esteban
said haughtily. "I have gained the affections of one of Queen Anne's
ladies-in-waiting."

"Indeed! Then I am even more honored that you have been able
to tear yourself away long enough to search me out." Though his tone
was light, he remembered being Esteban's age. In fact, if Gerrard were
present.... He put a stop to that thought before it could continue and

smiled. "Let me saddle Martiya and let the friends I've been staying with know I will be away."

"Teo threatened sufficiently dire consequence if I returned without news of you that I thought it prudent to do as he said," Esteban admitted, following Raúl through the streets to the encampment, where he shouted his destination to Fonso and Emilio in case Gerrard should arrive while he lingered in Arles.

Saddling Martiya took only moments more, and then they were racing north to Arles and the comfort of friends who would understand his pensiveness and distraction.

"Look who I've found," Esteban called a couple of hours later when they clattered into the courtyard of the inn where Christian and Teodoro had taken up temporary residence.

True to Esteban's prediction, they found Christian lounging on a bundle of hay outside the stables as Teodoro and another man in the livery of the royal musketeers—Léandre, Raúl recognized by the straw-colored hair—sparred in the open space between the stables and the inn. Aristide, the oldest of the foursome of musketeers they'd met while visiting Christian in Paris, leaned against a banister in the shade of the inn's eaves. Teodoro and Léandre both had stripped off their outer coats in deference to the sun's warmth, and the back of Léandre's linen shirt was damp with sweat.

Aristide bowed in Raúl's direction, but Christian jumped up and wrapped him into a hug, calling to Teo to stop playing about and welcome their friend. With a seemingly effortless move, Teodoro knocked the sword from Léandre's grip and sheathed his own with a hiss of fine Toledo steel before striding across the dusty yard to clasp Raúl's shoulder.

"I expected to find you sparring with Aristide," Raúl observed to Teodoro as Léandre recovered his sword and the two musketeers crossed the courtyard to greet him. From what Raúl had observed, the older musketeer was the only one with the skill to offer Teodoro a true challenge.

"Aristide decided I could teach his companions more than he could," Teodoro explained. "You are here alone. I take it you have no word from Gerrard?"

"It has barely been a month," Raúl said. "The time for him to travel home, see his father, and then reach the south of France is prohibitive."

Teodoro nodded, dark eyes searching Raúl's lighter ones thoroughly. "Aristide! Pick up your sword and come give Raúl a challenge. You've learned all my tricks. 'Tis time you learned his as well."

The leonine musketeer unfastened his black surcoat, draping it carefully over the rail before rolling up his sleeves and stepping into the courtyard. He unsheathed his blade without flourish and raised it in a silent salute before standing at ready, waiting for Raúl to make the first move.

Raúl tossed his leather jerkin to Esteban, who had returned from leading their horses into the stable, and adjusted the scabbard on his hip, taking a moment to study his opponent. Aristide was nearly as tall as Gerrard if not quite as sturdy; his height would give him the advantage of reach, but Raúl had found his smaller size often led adversaries to underestimate him. Forcing back the memory of his first meeting with Gerrard, Raúl drew his blade and met Aristide's with a clang of steel.

Raúl had sparred, and indeed fought, enough unfamiliar foes in his lifetime to be capable of adapting to different styles of attack, so Aristide's first move did not catch him unawares. He could see Teodoro's tuition in the way Aristide watched his left side, although the musketeer did not have a *daga izquierda* that Raúl could see.

By the time Raúl found an opening in Aristide's defenses and disarmed him, they had both worked up a sweat, and Raúl had lost all track of how much time had passed.

"Well played," Raúl said with a bow to Aristide. "I foresee spending much time honing my skills against yours. Rarely has anyone other than Teo pressed me the way you did today."

"Your friend has taught me much, and I look forward to learning from you as well," Aristide answered, saluting again before sheathing his blade. "I hope you were taking note," he added to Léandre with a grin.

"Enough to show Perrin a new trick or two when he gets off duty," Léandre retorted, wincing as he pulled his surcoat over his head. "Though Teodoro here has left me feeling as gangling as a new recruit. I'm not sure I'll have the strength left to tussle with Perrin, lounging as he is in the royal presence."

"You always have strength enough to tussle with Perrin," Benoît retorted, coming out of the stable in time to hear Léandre's final comment. "Even when you haven't the strength for anything else." He crossed the courtyard to Raúl. "Good to see you again, Raúl. I hope you've fared well since last we met."

Raúl smiled to see how casually Benoît moved to Aristide after clasping his hand and how naturally he settled into the arm the musketeer draped around his shoulder. "Well enough, though you seem to have fared better, my friend."

"They despair of making a musketeer of me," Benoît replied with a fond smile for Aristide, "but they are content enough to make use of my skills in the forge. It is a reason to stay in Paris."

"'Tis not only your skills at the forge that are valued," Léandre interjected, while Aristide bent closer to murmur something into Benoît's ear that made him flush and swat at his lover. The interaction warmed Raúl's heart, even as it made him ache for the closeness he missed.

"They still despair of making a musketeer of me," Benoît insisted, "unless you can work magic here as you did when you saved Aristide's life. It would seem I am hopeless with a sword."

"Swordplay is not the only skill of value, even among the musketeers," Raúl countered. "Do not discount your contributions to your friends, to say nothing of what you give to Aristide."

"He is the sun in my heavens," Aristide agreed, tightening the embrace briefly. Here among friends the musketeers allowed themselves a freedom they would not express at court, even in Paris where such relationships were, if not accepted, at least pointedly ignored.

"He is a besotted fool," Benoît retorted, though his words bore no heat and the expression on his face assured Raúl he was far more charmed than offended by the tender words and loving kiss.

Christian moved to Raúl's side before he could decide how to reply to that. "Come walk with me," he said. "Leave the children to their swords and keep me company for a time."

Raúl looked to Teodoro as Christian linked their arms and turned away from the inn, but Teodoro merely inclined his head and called that he was going inside to wash up. Raúl knew Teodoro would not have been as complacent with anyone else, but if there was one person he would trust to watch over Christian as he would himself, it was Raúl.

"Do not think Gerrard has forgotten you," Christian said when they had walked out of earshot of the others. "We don't know what situation he has found at home. If his brother did not recover from the illness that took his nephew, he is the heir to the title now, and if his father succumbed as well, he now holds the title. Yes, it is a minor one, but not something to be brushed aside lightly. He will have people who depend on his decisions, and they will not understand his desire to return to you. He will do it because he loves you, as if you needed me to tell you that, but however difficult his relationship with his father, Gerrard grew up in an aristocratic family. He understands his responsibilities to his people and the estate."

"He is likely on his way back even now," Raúl answered. "He could be riding into Saintes-Maries-de-la-Mer as we speak." Only his quickened pulse revealed how fervently he wished it were so.

"Your words in God's ear," Christian said, "but if he is not, if he does not arrive tomorrow or next week or next month, it does not mean he has changed his mind about you. He *will* come as he promised because he belongs with you as I belong with Teo."

"I believe that is so," Raúl agreed. He smiled ruefully at Christian, trusting the *inglés* with an admission he could not even concede to Teodoro. "That does not make it any easier to wait."

"No, I'm quite sure it does not," Christian allowed. "For as long as the court is in the south, you are welcome here if we can provide some distraction to the passage of time."

"Your friendship is more than distraction," Raúl said, turning back toward the entrance to the inn. "So long as it does not interfere with your responsibilities, I will welcome your company."

"If nothing else, you can keep Teo from killing someone while I am at court," Christian said with a laugh.

"We have not had much luck in that regard in the past," Raúl said with an answering laugh, "but I will do my best."

"We live in hope."

SEVEN

GERRARD SAT at his father's desk—it still didn't feel like his own—
staring at the ledgers in front of him and trying to make sense of the
entries. The days in the month since his arrival at Hawkins Hall had
passed far more quickly than he could have expected, filled with repairs
to the village and the business of the estate. The nights had passed with
agonizing slowness as he ached from the empty spot beside him. He
missed Raúl terribly, and no amount of dreaming or remembering could
lessen that pain. Not even the few moments he had been able to eke out
to spend with Randall could distract him completely.

"Excuse me, Sir Gerrard." Herndon, Sir Harald's retired butler,
whom Gerrard had convinced to return to Hawkins Hall until someone
could be trained to take his place, appeared in the doorway as if by magic,
a feat Gerrard had always envied and never understood. "Sir Thomas
Beecham wishes to know if you are receiving."

Thomas Beecham had been James's friend more than Gerrard's,
but Gerrard had fond memories of following the two older boys on their
adventures before they outgrew childhood games. Thomas would have
a different view of the events in the neighborhood than the villagers did
and could perhaps help Gerrard find his feet more quickly so he could
return to the Continent and Raúl.

"Offer him brandy—" Herndon's disapproving look made Gerrard
feel five years old again. "Fine, offer him tea and tell him I will be down
momentarily. I should find my doublet, I suppose."

"It is here, sir—you left it over the back of your chair at breakfast
this morning." Herndon's face wore the same chastening frown as when
he'd caught a much younger Gerrard stuffing his pockets full of apples
to feed to the horses at the stables. "I would also suggest neatening your
hair before you greet Sir Thomas. It looks as though you'd not combed it
upon rising from your bed this morning."

Gerrard had in fact arranged his hair as part of his morning ablutions,
Agatha being as much of a stickler about the appearance proper to Sir
Gerrard Hawkins of Hawkins Hall as ever Herndon could be, and even

less reticent about expressing herself. He must have been running his hands through it again. Smoothing the recalcitrant strands down with his palms, he resisted the urge to confirm his appearance reflected in the panes of glass in the study window. He was not some dandy trying to impress society with his airs. After tugging down the hem of his loose shirt, he pulled on the doublet Herndon handed him and followed the older man down to the drawing room.

Gerrard resisted the urge to lift a hand to the earring Raúl had given him. Agatha already eyed it with far too much curiosity. Gerrard did not want the rest of his small staff doing the same.

"Beecham," Gerrard said, extending his hand as he walked into the drawing room where the other man waited. "Good to see you again. How is your family?"

"Well enough, thank you," Sir Thomas answered, shaking Gerrard's hand warmly. "I was fortunate enough to retire to London before the illness grew widespread. We tried to convince your father to do the same, but you know how stubborn Sir Harald could be…."

"No one knows that better than I," Gerrard agreed. "I wish James at least had listened." If he had, Gerrard could still have been in France with Raúl. "As it is, I find myself distinctly ill-equipped to deal with my new position. My father dismissed his man of business some years ago, and I have yet to find one I trust to run the estate while I am away."

"You do not plan to remain in residence, then?" Beecham asked. "I have seen the improvements you made in the village. Indeed, they are the talk of the countryside. Your father was a worthy man, but careful with his coin. He was not one to sink money into anything that was not falling down about his ears."

"I left behind a life on the Continent to come home, knowing only that my nephew had died," Gerrard explained. "I didn't learn of my father's and brother's deaths until I arrived. Even if eventually I do decide to live here most of the time, I must return and settle my business there, because I did not leave intending to stay away for more than a month or two. It has already been over a month. I know I have responsibilities here, but I have them there as well."

"I must say, I remembered you most as the little brother who followed James about and always spoiled our fun by sticking his nose in our business," Beecham said with a grin. "I came calling half to satisfy my curiosity about what kind of man you'd grown into. From what I've seen of how you're pulling things into shape here, you've matured well. The county needs Hawkins Hall well-run and caring for its own, and you're seeing to both." Beecham paused for a moment, considering. "I may be able to help you with your most pressing need. I have a cousin who is looking for a position. He grew up on an estate in Suffolk very like Hawkins Hall and came to London for his education. He's a younger son and has been keeping his father's books since the old man's health started to fail, but since Sir Andrew's death, he and his older brother have butted heads. It would be as well to put some distance between them, and Kellan would serve your interests well, I'm sure."

"He is in London now?" Gerrard asked. "I will almost certainly have to travel to London again in the next week or two, and it would save me a trip if we could meet at the same time."

"Yes, he has taken lodgings there." Beecham smiled. "Let me give you his direction, and I will write to let him know to expect you. It would be good to have him closer, and I give you my bond he'll serve you well. He has a good head on his shoulders and always dealt well with the tenants on his father's lands."

"That is good to hear," Gerrard said. "I would not wish to leave my tenants in unscrupulous hands, even for the months it would take me to travel abroad and return, and if it turns out that I cannot return quickly or stay here long, it will be even more important." He could see the question in Beecham's eyes. "I have been attached to the retinue of Ambassador Blackwood." If that was not exactly the truth in the present, he had been living under Christian's roof for the previous six months, and he had been in Christian's employ still when he met Raúl and embarked on the most fulfilling adventure of his life. "I should return and take my leave officially, if nothing else."

"Speak with Kellan and see what you think," Beecham said. "If you find him acceptable, he can divide his time between London and Hawkins Hall, or move here fully if you prefer. Not that I think he'll need it, but I'd be happy to keep an eye on the lad until your return if that would help ease your concerns."

"If you recommend him so highly, I'm sure he will be fine, but I will meet with him, and should he suit, I will suggest he consult you on any matters outside of the routine," Gerrard agreed. "Did you lose many tenants to the plague? I was horrified at how many cottages I found empty upon my return."

"Aye, on mine as well, and those who are left worn from working the land of those who are gone. 'Twill be hard to bring in the harvest without more men. Come fall, perhaps we can pool our resources if need be. We are close enough neighbors to help one another."

Gerrard spared a thought for Raúl and his gypsies. If they were there, harvesting both his fields and Beecham's would be easy, but Gerrard did not know if Raúl would be willing to come to England, much less if the others would consider it. "I think that is a fine idea. Neither of us would benefit from the other failing, and we have much to gain by reaping more than our tenants can use. With the plague having struck so hard in the shires, I imagine there will be quite the demand in town."

The conversation turned then to London, and Beecham related news to Gerrard of several mutual acquaintances and how they had fared in the years since Gerrard had seen them last. After a quarter of an hour, the older man rose to take his leave, first writing the name and direction of the relation he'd suggested. "Come visit us at the Beeches some time, Hawkins. My wife will be happy to meet you, and my mother will be glad of a single gentleman in the neighborhood to even out the numbers when we entertain."

"I would be honored to meet your wife, but while I will happily round out the table at dinner, I fear your mother is doomed to disappointment if she seeks to find me a wife," Gerrard replied with, he hoped, an amused chuckle. "I have named Randall as my heir, although I will wait until I return from the Continent to move him into the Hall. I have no intention of marrying."

Beecham smiled in return. "Do not tell her that. 'Twill make her all the more determined to see you wed. Unless perhaps you have some tragic tale of the lady you loved and lost on the Continent?"

"Nothing so tragic," Gerrard assured him, "although perhaps I will not tell her that."

"I will leave it to you what tale you spin for her," Beecham said, "but do not wait too long to come tell it, or she will have words with both of us. I should be off. It is my day to make the rounds of the neighborhood. The things I do for peace in my home."

"And you wonder why I choose to remain single," Gerrard said, showing Beecham to the door. "I will call before I leave for London."

Beecham took his leave, and Gerrard returned to his rooms to change into breeches suited for riding. He would saddle Nubarrón and ride into the village to see if anyone needed anything from London since he was going. He had hired a new grocer and apothecary with promises to stock their businesses as necessary, but neither of them had brought him a list yet.

Half an hour later, he rode into the village square, unable to stop a smile at the progress he found in every quarter. Roofs had been repaired or replaced. Walls were shored up where the storm had damaged them. Fresh flowers bloomed in planters and beds around the occupied cottages.

He left Nubarrón with Warren, asking the blacksmith to check the horse's shoes before he rode into London later in the week, and walked to the town green. The children called to him as they ran by. He pulled a carving from his pocket to give to the youngest girl, Amanda, who trailed behind. She gave him an angelic smile and ran off after the others again.

"You always had a soft spot for the little ones," Agatha said, coming out of the bakery in time to see Amanda pocket her toy. "I figured you would have a brood of your own by now."

"I have Randall," Gerrard said for what seemed like the thousandth time since he returned home. "I do not need other children of my own. I have a village full to keep me entertained." And that many more among the gypsies he had come to think of as his family as he traveled with Raúl. "The villagers still try to hide things from me. Does the baker have everything he needs to run his business?"

"The bakery seemed well stocked," Agatha assured him, "but you should check with the others. The apothecary used many of his herbs and tinctures trying to help those stricken by the plague before it took him as well, and we used many more cleaning the Hall and the cottages."

"What do you think of the new apothecary?" Gerrard asked, offering her his arm as they walked toward the shop in question.

"He seems knowledgeable enough," Agatha allowed, "and willing to listen to sense when he hears it."

"That is good," Gerrard said. "I will speak with him. Perhaps if I ask for an inventory, I can determine what is missing."

"You do seem to have learned a good deal of herb lore while you were away," Agatha observed, her sharp gaze raking over his riding garb and the earring that adorned his lobe. "I might ask what company you kept while you were gone."

"The very best," Gerrard assured her.

"I can believe that is true," his nurse agreed, "for you left here still a boy for all the years you carried. You have come back a man. I don't scruple to tell you that there were some who feared you might prove a wastrel or worse on your return, caring for naught but what value you could strip from the estate. Few expected you to put the energy and coin you have into restoring what had fallen into ruin. Whatever company you kept in the time you were gone, I could not have wished for a better influence upon you."

Gerrard wondered if she would still say that if she met Raúl. He had no doubt she would approve of Christian since he fit everything she believed an aristocrat should be, but he didn't know what she would make of Teodoro and the musketeers. "Ambassador Blackwood would be glad to hear it," he said instead. "I will leave you here unless you wish to speak to the apothecary as well."

"Nay, we have all we need at the Hall for the nonce." She stretched on her toes to give Gerrard a buss on the cheek. "You should visit Rebecca again while you are here. Jacob has little energy left to spend with Randall after working the farm all day, and the boy needs a father."

"And I will be one to him," Gerrard promised. "Let me finish with my business and then I will see to my family. That way I can spend as much time with him as Rebecca will allow."

"You may find Rebecca has something to occupy her time as well," Agatha said, patting Gerrard's cheek and walking away before he could ask what she meant by the cryptic remark. Noticing that her path took her toward the stables, Gerrard wondered if she planned to share her purchases from the bakery with a certain blacksmith. If nothing else, he had something to tease her with should she begin to question too closely into his own romantic relations, or lack of them.

Shaking his head, Gerrard walked into the apothecary, pleased to see the man he had engaged tidying the shelves. "You have made good progress in here, Mr. Turner," Gerrard said. "Much of the mess is cleared away. Have you prepared a list of what needs to be ordered?"

"Not yet, Sir Gerrard," Turner said. "I've been trying to take an inventory as I straightened up, but as you warned me, there was much work to be done."

"Let's start with the inventory, then," Gerrard suggested. "I can see what you have and decide what to purchase when I ride to London later in the week."

The apothecary looked skeptical, but Gerrard had not been Raúl's lover and helper for more than five years without learning some of the gypsy's secrets. He went through the list, murmuring barely loud enough for Turner to hear him. Looking up finally, he said, "We will need lavender for sure, comfrey, feverfew, foxglove, poppy, and sage, as well as willow bark and yarrow if I can find them."

"You surprise me, Sir Gerrard," Turner said. "I don't think I've encountered such awareness outside of my colleagues."

"I have spent much of my time away with one of your colleagues," Gerrard explained. "I learned a thing or two at his elbow."

"So I see. If you could indeed bring back everything you just listed, I would be most grateful and much better able to see to the needs of the village."

"I will bring back all of it I can find," Gerrard agreed. "And perhaps we can use some of the vacant garden lots to grow anything I can't find. It will be a few months before we can grow enough to support the apothecary completely, but I would rather depend on a local supply than on whatever we might or might not find in London."

"Very wise," Turner replied. "I'm sure some of the locals can be persuaded to help us tend the gardens."

"I think they could be persuaded to do most anything that would help them avoid another plague," Gerrard replied sadly. "Having enough medicine that treating the sick would be an option will be as logical to them as it is to us. Now, is there anything else you need? Mortar and pestle, bottles or brews of any kind?"

"Nothing," Turner assured him, "and yes, I would tell you if I needed anything. Some lords are so suspicious of anything outside their ken that working for them is dangerous at times, but I see it will not be that way here."

"As long as you do not play us false, you will be safe here," Gerrard said. "Now, I have other stops to make before the afternoon is out, so I will bid you good day."

"Good day to you as well, Sir Gerrard."

Gerrard left the apothecary and checked in with the other merchants in town, finding all in order, to his relief. The sooner the village was back on its feet and functioning normally, the sooner he could leave to find Raúl again. Reclaiming Nubarrón, he headed in the direction of Rebecca's family's farm. He found Rebecca alone in the farmhouse.

"Hello, Rebecca."

"Hello, Gerrard," she said. "I suppose I should call you Sir Gerrard like everyone else."

"That seems a little awkward given our past," Gerrard replied. "It is hard enough hearing it from everyone else. Hearing it from you, it feels mocking."

"I did not mean to offend."

"You haven't. I came to see Randall and to tell you both I am leaving for London again in a few days. The solicitor should have finished drawing up the papers naming Randall my heir, but I hope you will keep him here for a little while longer. I must return to France, and I would rather have him here with you than alone in the Hall while I am gone."

"He needs his father," Rebecca insisted. "He does not understand your absences or the fact that his parents are not married."

"He is my son," Gerrard said. "I have claimed him in the village and by law. Whatever else happens, nothing can change that. As for his parents being married, I explained that when I came before. No matter what we might have felt before he was born, we do not know each other anymore, much less love each other."

"No, we do not," Rebecca agreed. "How soon do you expect to move him to the Hall?"

"You sound almost eager to have him gone."

"Not eager to have him gone," Rebecca said, "but eager to have this resolved. The baker at the Beeches has made an offer for my hand, and I cannot leave while Randall is unsettled."

"If my trip to London goes as I hope it will, I should be able to leave for France within a week or two. Then it is a matter of finding my companions and deciding what we will do next," Gerrard replied. "I could be back in as little as six weeks or it could be as much as three months, depending on the travel conditions and whether I can find a ship to take me to Bordeaux or if I must cross France on horseback."

"I don't understand why it is so important that you go back," Rebecca said. "What is on that cursed Continent that draws you?"

Gerrard wondered whether Rebecca still resented having to remain behind the first time he'd left England. "I couldn't take you with me,"

Gerrard reminded her. "I did not know how I would earn my own living, much less support a family."

"But you said you would come back for me," Rebecca retorted.

"I took employment with Viscount Aldwych as his bodyguard," Gerrard replied, bristling at the criticism. "By the time my service to him ended, too much time had already passed."

"So what did you do after that? Your letters grew less frequent the longer you were gone, and it was hard for me to reply when I never knew where you might be. Though I must admit you always managed to send funds for Randall's care," Rebecca allowed.

"I offered my sword to a band of traveling merchants," Gerrard replied honestly, though the truth was far more complex than that, "and have been with them ever since." He did not mention that he had remained in close contact with the ambassador, still less that he and Raúl had been Christian's frequent guests over the intervening years. He suspected that would do little to ease Rebecca's ill humor. "While I hope they will return to Hawkins Hall with me, even if they do not, I must apprise them of my change in situation. They depend on me."

"And we do not?"

"I intend to hire a man of business, hopefully a cousin of Sir Thomas Beecham's, who will manage the estate while I am gone, but I can hardly ask him to manage a boy of seven as well."

"Agatha could watch him, and should he not have a tutor?"

"He will have one when I return," Gerrard snapped. He took a deep breath, drawing on Raúl's lessons of calm and control. "Listen to us, Rebecca. We cannot even discuss the welfare of our son, the one thing we should be able to agree on, without snapping at each other. We would have made each other miserable if we had found a way to be together. Whatever we thought we felt all those years ago, we were not in love. You are, however, the mother of my heir, and I know you have his best interests at heart. Can we agree to work together to see to his future?"

"I have been the only one seeing to his future since he was born," Rebecca answered, but her voice had lost a bit of its sharp edge. "I am glad you mean to do what is right by him, Gerrard, but simply naming him your heir and disappearing again is not enough. He needs to know his father, and unless you mean to be a real father to him, you would be better to leave him with me and Ben to raise. He is a good man, and will prove a good father, I'm sure."

"I am not 'disappearing again,' as you put it," Gerrard insisted. "My father left behind a tangle that is beyond my head for numbers, so I must find a man of business who can handle the affairs of the estate whether I am resident or not, so the trip to London is a necessity, and I owe my friends in France an explanation. I *will* return and I *will* be a father to Randall—a real father, the kind I never had either—but I must do these two things first. I need you to help him understand that."

"So long as you keep your word to him better than you did to me." Rebecca stared up at Gerrard, her hands planted on her hips. "I may understand you, Gerrard Hawkins, but he cannot."

Gerrard swallowed another sharp retort. He had defended himself with all the excuses he had. Rebecca would accept them or not. Far more important was Randall's reaction. "Where is he? I would like to see him."

"In the fields with Father," Rebecca said. "He is the nearest thing to a father Randall knows."

"If my friends will return with me, he will have more fathers than he will know what to do with," Gerrard said, thinking of Raúl and the gypsies and the care he had seen all the men show to the caravan's children. "And even if they don't, I hope I have learned enough from them to know how to be a father to him upon my return."

"They are in the barley field to the west of the house." Rebecca's expression softened. "If you like, you can stay to dinner with us. It may not be the fancy fare you're used to, but I can put a fair meal on the table, and it will give you more time to spend with your son."

Gerrard laughed. "What fancy fare do you think I found in a merchant caravan wandering around Europe? I would be honored to join you for dinner. Perhaps I can even give your father a hand with the work that remains for the day. As you said, he is no longer a young man." He bowed slightly and took his leave, walking quickly toward the field Rebecca had indicated. He found his son all but dancing around his grandfather with excitement. "Randall," he called, "give your grandfather a moment's peace and come give me a hug."

"Papa!" Randall shouted, running toward him. The boy was tall but slender, as if the rest of his body had yet to catch up with his inches. His blue eyes favored his mother, but the brown hair curling around his head marked him as Gerrard's son. "Did you ride Nubarrón today? Can you take me riding on him, please?" Reaching Gerrard, he hugged him tightly, laughing when Gerrard lifted him up and spun him around.

"Let me answer one question before you ask a dozen more," Gerrard scolded, his deeper laughter mingling with his son's. Rebecca might be justifiably bitter where Gerrard was concerned, but it had not carried over to Randall. "Yes, I rode Nubarrón, and yes, I will take you riding on him, but first we must help your grandfather finish in the fields so your mother will not scold us all at dinner."

"Welcome, Sir Gerrard." Jacob Chapman approached more slowly and bowed his head in greeting. "It wouldn't be right for you to work the fields with me, but I've about finished for the day in any case. Between us, Randall and I managed to clear out the worst of the weeds, from this field, at least."

"I've been working with my hands for the past six years," Gerrard said with a chuckle, "but if you're sure you're done, I'll take Randall for a short ride and give you a brief respite from his company."

"I expect I'll be missing his company before much longer," Jacob replied quietly, picking up his tools before starting back to the house. Randall tugged at Gerrard's hand, dragging him after his grandfather with unrestrained eagerness.

"You will be as welcome in the Hall as Randall will be," Gerrard said. "I won't forget your care of him simply because I now share that responsibility. Now, Randall, shall we go for a ride?"

"Yes, yes!" Randall chanted, pulling his father around the side of the house to where Nubarrón stood placidly chewing a mouthful of grass. Randall paused, hesitant to approach too near the big horse until Gerrard nudged him forward.

"He likes children," Gerrard said reassuringly. "As long as you don't run up to him and startle him, he'll be as gentle as a lamb." A vision of Martiya snapping at the children running by brought a smile to his face. Nubarrón didn't have the stallion's fire. "If Raúl comes to visit, though, you must not go near his horse alone. Promise me you will be careful around Martiya if they come to live here."

"Who is Raúl?" Randall asked as Gerrard helped lift him up into the saddle. "Will you be staying here now? Mother says I shouldn't get my hopes up, but I wish you would stay so I can see you and Nubarrón more often."

Gerrard decided he should be pleased to rank above his horse rather than after him in Randall's esteem. "Raúl is a very dear friend of mine," Gerrard said. "He is in France right now, visiting a special church. I was supposed to meet him there, along with the rest of his caravan, because I live with them. I didn't know about Sir Harald and Sir James being ill. Now that they're gone, I have to live here at least some of the time, but first I have to tell Raúl everything that has happened. I'm hoping he and his caravan will come back and live here with us, but I don't know yet what they will say."

"I go to church with Mother and Grandfather," Randall announced. "We say prayers for Grandmother, now that she is in heaven, and for you wherever you are. Except now you're here!" He grinned, squirming happily while Gerrard mounted behind him. "Is Raúl a gypsy?" he asked, not pausing long enough for Gerrard to answer. "I saw a caravan once. They came to the village, but Mother wouldn't let me go to see them. She says gypsies take children away from their families."

"Yes, Raúl is a gypsy," Gerrard said, picking out the most important part of what Randall had asked. His temper flared at hearing the same prejudice against the gypsies from his son's mouth that he had encountered all over Europe, but he bit it back. Yelling at Randall for repeating what he was told would serve no purpose. If Raúl agreed to come to England with him, Gerrard would have a few words with Rebecca about her preconceived notions. "You don't have to worry about gypsies stealing you away. They take in children who have nowhere else to go, but they would never take a child who has a family to take care of them." He pulled his hair back so the hoop in his ear was clearly visible. "See what Raúl gave me?"

"Does that mean you're a gypsy too? Did it hurt? Can I have one?"

"It means I live with the gypsies," Gerrard agreed, "and it hurt a little, but not too much. As for whether you can have one, we'll wait until you're a little older before we make that decision. You might decide you don't like the gypsies after you meet them." He couldn't actually imagine that coming to pass, given Randall's sense of adventure and the gypsies' sense of family, but one delaying tactic was as good as another at this point. "But don't tell your mother just yet. She'll fuss at me again for telling you tall tales, even if every word is the truth."

"I wish you could live here with me," Randall said. "You'd let me visit the caravan, and I could ride Nubarrón whenever I wanted."

The plaintive words tugged at Gerrard's heart, but he did not tell Randall of his plans to move the boy to the Hall. He hoped Raúl would agree to come back to England with him, but if he refused, Gerrard was not sure duty would win the battle of wills that would follow. If he returned only rarely, it would be hard enough on Randall without broken promises between them. "We shall see if I can persuade Raúl and his friends to return to Hawkins Hall with me. How does that sound?"

"Will you have to go away to ask him? Could you just write to him and tell him to come here?" Randall asked.

"I have written to him already," Gerrard said, "but it is like my letters to you and your mother. Sometimes letters get lost, and I promised Raúl I would meet him in Saintes-Maries-de-la-Mer. I try not to break my promises so I shall go and fetch him, but I promise *you* I will come back. It may take some time, but I will return."

"I wish I could go with you and have adventures like you do." Randall sighed heavily. "Mother and Grandfather never let me do anything fun. They are always afraid I will get hurt or sick. But I am not a baby anymore. I am almost eight years old."

"I know you are," Gerrard said with a hug for his son. "I have counted every year that passed. I cannot take you with me this time, but when I get back, we will have adventures aplenty."

"Then I hope you and your friend come back soon." Randall grasped Nubarrón's reins more firmly and smiled over his shoulder at Gerrard. "Now can we make Nubarrón gallop?"

EIGHT

A FEW days before the festival, Raúl thanked Teodoro and Christian for their hospitality and rode back to Saintes-Maries-de-la-Mer. The grand procession would not take place until the twenty-fourth, but the smaller celebrations would already have begun, and he had his own personal devotions to see to. He had left word with his friends to send Gerrard on to Arles if he were to arrive while Raúl was gone, but a part of him still hoped to find him at the encampment when he returned.

The marshland of the Camargue stretched out before him as he headed south, all wide-open spaces with flamingos along the waterways. He had always loved the long-legged birds with their somewhat awkward gait and brilliantly colored plumage. As a child he had chased through the waters, trying to catch them. The memory of it brought a smile to his face, a much-needed burst of happy memories in the midst of the loneliness that plagued him despite Teodoro's best efforts. The festival had always been a place of happy memories for him, from his earliest childhood to the first time he discovered his gift of healing, all the way through bringing Gerrard with him the first May after they met. It would be strange not to have Gerrard with him this year, but he would not fail in his devotion to Sainte Sara.

Dotted along the firmer ground as the marsh gave way to the town were clusters of wagons, many of the vardos decorated with colorful banners and garlands of flowers. A few bonfires were already lit in anticipation of the coming nightfall. Rom from several caravans waved and called out to Raúl as he rode past, inviting him to join them. He returned the greetings and stopped to speak with some of those he knew from earlier festivals, but the church beckoned him, and before he joined any of the festivities he needed to pay his respects to Sainte Sara. He paused only to purchase a nosegay from a wagon surrounded by colorful and fragrant blooms before continuing on to the church.

When he reached the sturdy stone building, he dismounted and tethered Martiya to a nearby tree before entering the sanctuary. It took a few moments for his eyes to adjust from the dusk outside to the shadowy interior of the church, its darkness broken by the oil lamps hanging from the ceiling and the rows of votive candles surrounding the altar and the niches dedicated to the saints who gave the church and the town their name.

He had turned toward the crypt at the left of the altar when a soft voice behind him called his name.

"Welcome back, Raúl," Father Bernard said with a smile. Raúl smiled automatically in return. Father Bernard had been a young man, just out of the seminary, when Raúl was a child. He had ever been Raúl's friend and the closest thing to a confessor he had allowed himself. "I wondered when you would arrive. Has the year treated you well?"

"It has had its blessings as well as darker days," he answered, the emptiness of Gerrard's absence weighing heavily on his heart. "I find myself wearied," he admitted, "and hope Sainte Sara may renew me."

"Then let us take your offering to her," Father Bernard suggested. He walked with Raúl down into the crypt where the statue of Sainte Sara made its home except during the festival. The base of the statue was surrounded by flowers and the stubs of white wax candles, some still guttering, others completely burned out. Raúl placed his flowers with the others and knelt before the simple plaster statue, peering up at the benevolent, dark-skinned saint. She had none of the inherent opulence of the statues of the Saintes Maries in their boat in the church above, but already the pilgrims had adorned her with cloaks and a crown.

"She smiles down on you as she has always done," Father Bernard commented softly. "Whatever troubles you carry, her intercessions will lighten that yoke."

Nothing but Gerrard's return would do that completely, Raúl knew, but he closed his eyes, letting the strain of the last weeks ebb away in the cool peacefulness of the crypt. Wordlessly he opened his soul, offering up his memories of the year past and adding a prayer for the saint to watch over Gerrard as she had ever succored him.

He had been little more than a child the first time he felt the brush of grace across his soul, but the intervening years had done nothing to inure him to the humbling effect of kneeling before his patroness and feeling that grace once again. Raúl had never claimed to understand the power that had filled him the day he rushed to the side of a man who collapsed under the strain of carrying Sainte Sara's statue toward the sea. Like so many others, he had intended to help the other porters keep the statue from falling, but before he could reach for the litter, he felt a compulsion to check on the fallen man instead. He laid hands on the man's arm and felt the tingling he now associated with healing energy. At the time, it had scared him almost to the point of pulling away.

Something told him to stay where he was, despite the odd sensation, until the man's racing pulse slowed beneath his palms. His head swum and he felt near to passing out himself when old Jinoquio, his caravan's healer, finally made his way through the press of bodies to kneel beside him. He spread a hand over the man's chest and then looked at Raúl in wonder. "Sainte Sara has smiled on you," he murmured softly enough that only Raúl could hear him. "You have her gift."

"Gift?" he repeated numbly, feeling as weak as if he'd run all the way to the festival rather than riding in his parents' vardo.

"The gift of healing," Phuro Jinoquio said, "though I expect at the moment you're not feeling it much of a blessing. You're Tomasis and Alamina's son, aren't you? Healthy enough that I haven't needed to tend to you since your birth. I'll have a word with your parents. There is much you need to learn to foster and safeguard your calling."

He spent the next four years at Phuro Jinoquio's side, learning all he could about herb lore and more, before war had come and he'd been conscripted into the army. Given that his service had brought Teodoro to his side, he couldn't complain too much about that. When he returned from the war, Jinoquio had grown too feeble to continue as the caravan's healer, and Raúl had stepped tearfully into his place, seeing to his family as Jinoquio had always done. Years later, his calling had brought Gerrard to him as well, and he would never stop being thankful for that blessing, for in Gerrard he had found strength when he was weak, comfort when he was weary, and a love to last this lifetime and beyond.

Peace suffused him as he knelt in the crypt, and for a few quiet moments, he could rest.

Gradually his weariness eased, and though the core of loneliness remained, he found it easier to bear. Gerrard could even now be on his way to Saintes-Marie-de-la-Mer. Opening his eyes, Raúl gazed up at the saint's humble plaster image. "May I always be worthy of your blessings," he murmured before rising to his feet. With a final bow to the richly bedecked statue, he turned and made his way from the crypt to the main nave of the church.

"Will you sup with me?" Father Bernard asked. "Gerrard is welcome to join us as well, of course, even if he does not come to pray with you."

Father Bernard doubtless expected Raúl to smile at the quip as he had always done, but Raúl could not summon a smile for him today, not with Gerrard so far away. "I will join you gladly, but Gerrard is not with me this year. Family obligations called him away."

"Ah, that accounts for your melancholy countenance when you arrived." Father Bernard patted Raúl's arm. "Well, if Sainte Sara has restored your spirits, I will see what I can do to restore you in body. My housekeeper always prepares more than I can eat myself." Raúl doubted that was true—since the church for the most part ministered to a wandering congregation of Rom and the local fishermen, it was far from a wealthy parish—but he followed Father Bernard to the vicarage feeling lighter in spirit than when he had arrived.

The small terrace behind the priest's home was surrounded with flowering bushes growing up over the stone walls, giving the garden a wild and magical feel. Raúl had always loved it there, ever since the first time Father Bernard had showed it to him. Then he'd been afraid of the priest's reaction to the "miracle child," as people had called him before he learned to hide his abilities under a cloak of herb lore and discretion. Father Bernard, though, had never treated him as anything other than another boy in need of spiritual direction. Father Bernard gestured for Raúl to take a seat at the heavy wooden table in the shade of a large wisteria.

"Where have your travels taken you since last we met?"

"Paris, for the most part, when we were not with our caravan in Spain." The "we" threatened to reopen the wound of Gerrard's absence, but he refused to let it darken his time with Father Bernard. "We were guests of Gerrard's countryman, Viscount Aldwych."

"Heathens, the lot of them," Father Bernard said, his smile removing any sting from his words. "I despair of my good Catholic boys taking up with godless Englishmen. At least in Paris, I can hope you found time to tend to your soul."

"Most churches, even in Paris, are not so tolerant of Rom as you are, my friend," Raúl answered with a shake of his head. Though not as vicious as the Inquisition they had faced down in Spain, most French churches were just as suspicious of the itinerant Romani. "They would look on my calling as witchery, if not worse." To say nothing of his sharing his life and his bed with another man, but while Raúl knew the priest was aware of his relationship with Gerrard, he would not force him to acknowledge it here on church grounds.

Father Bernard shook his head. "I will never understand my brethren who forget that our Savior ate with sinners, prostitutes, and tax collectors. If he chose to do that, who are we to judge the merit of any man? You—and Gerrard—will always be welcome here. If I could wish for more, that is out of my hands."

"If more priests were as enlightened as you, I might perform my devotions more regularly," Raúl replied. "As it is, I find it best to avoid bringing myself to their attention." He supposed by the standards of most clerics he was a poor Catholic, but he had never felt comfortable in the soaring marble-and-gilt sanctuaries that seemed monuments to men's power and glory rather than to the God they purported to worship. He did his best to use his gifts for the benefit of those around him and trusted that would count for something when it came time for him to face his judgment. Raúl shook his head at his unusually somber thoughts. For the most part, he lived for each day and let the future see to itself. Perhaps the uncertainty of his future with Gerrard made him more introspective than his wont. "Tell me about the preparations for the festival," he said to turn his mind to less weighty topics.

"All is as it has always been. The caravans gather in the plains around the city. More gypsies come into town each day, bringing offerings to Sainte Sara. Music and dancing fill the streets at all hours of the day and night, and the city bells toll for joy. Will you help carry the statues in the procession this year?"

Raúl shook his head. "I thank you for the honor, but I already have Sainte Sara's benefaction. Give others the chance to win her graces."

"You were ever one to seek the shadows rather than the accolades of others. I see nothing has changed."

THE MORNING of May 24 dawned clear and cool, though Raúl expected the sun would warm things up as the day went on. He broke his fast quickly and headed into town for Mass and the procession to the sea. All around him other Rom were doing the same, everyone dressed in their best, most colorful attire. Many people carried musical instruments—

guitars, violins, mandolins, tambours, pan flutes, and more—and as they walked into town, one of the men struck up a tune. Others quickly picked it up, to the delight of the children who gamboled at everyone's heels. Raúl caught one girl just as she stumbled and set her back on her feet. She smiled at him before running off to rejoin her friends.

They gathered on the parvis outside the church, the noise and color a stark contrast to the solid stone of the church walls, more fortress in appearance than anything else. It brought a smile to Raúl's face. His people had so few places to call their own, and some might argue that even here, they were not at home, but he had never felt that way. Here, in the town square of this little village of less than a thousand people, Raúl belonged in a way he didn't anywhere other than in Gerrard's arms.

The worshippers filled the dark church to overflowing. Most of them, like Raúl, who stood against a cool stone wall near the back of the sanctuary, could barely hear the priest's voice, but they followed the rituals of the Mass by rote, and Father Bernard made sure that everyone who wished received the Eucharist, even those who had not been able to fit into the church itself and milled on the plaza outside. When the rite was finished, a select group carefully raised the statue of Sainte Sara from the crypt, where Father Bernard sprinkled them with holy water in blessing before they brought it outside into the sunlight.

A troupe of riders on white Camargue horses led the procession, carrying lances topped with colorful banners that snapped in the breeze off the sea. Sainte Sara's statue, her dark face almost obscured by layers of silk and velvet robes, necklaces, and garlands of flowers, swayed on a wooden platform borne on the shoulders of a dozen men. Others carried tapestry banners and ornately carved crucifixes, also bedecked with flowers. The cavalcade threaded through the narrow streets toward the shore, the music and laughter and cries of "Vive Sainte Sara" offsetting the press of bodies crowded together. A young woman caught Raúl by the hand and swung him around, smiling as she offered him a flower from the mass of blooms she cradled in her other arm. He accepted it with a bow and an answering smile before she turned away to share her joy with another stranger.

They reached the shoreline, but the procession did not slow, the entire mass of people and animals continuing into the surf until it came up to their waists. Some years the water had been a welcome relief from the heat. Other years it had been barely tolerable with the chill, but this time it was a cool caress against Raúl's thighs without being so cold he shivered from it. The hymns and songs continued, and all around him his people celebrated. He looked up at the statue of Sainte Sara and smiled. The day was as close to perfect as it could be without Gerrard in the water next to him.

"Sainte Sara, set us on the right path, give us your beautiful luck, and give us health. And if someone thinks bad of us, change his heart so that he thinks good of us. Amen." Raúl spoke the traditional words softly, adding his private prayer that Gerrard would return to him soon.

NINE

"TEO! CRISTIAN!"

The sound of Esteban's frantic voice rose from the courtyard below the windows in the salon where Teodoro, Christian, and Raúl had chosen to retreat from the afternoon heat. As the king seemed in no hurry to return the court to Paris, Christian had removed from the inn to a villa that allowed them more space. "We're upstairs," Christian called, leaning out the window to summon his secretary.

Moments later, Esteban burst into the room. "Have you seen— Raúl! You're here. Thank God. The queen is taken ill, and Marie-Agnès fears she will lose the child she carries. Will you come to Tarascon and help her?"

Esteban's concern was palpable, but Raúl hesitated to respond. He'd agreed to stay at the ambassador's villa after the festival ended and the caravans he'd stayed with during the fete began returning north again. While visiting with Teodoro and Christian could not keep him from missing Gerrard, at least they had never stayed together at this residence. It was easier here than in the caravans, where each time he turned around he was assailed with memories of his lover carving gifts for the children or loving him sweetly inside one of the colorful vardos.

The villa Christian had rented in Arles was near enough to the castle Louis maintained in the south that he and Teodoro could ride there when court business required, but Raúl had never accompanied them. As far as he was concerned, the farther he stayed from royal attentions, the better. "I am sure the king's physicians are capable of caring for her," he answered.

"They want to bleed her," Esteban said, his lips twisting in disgust. "Please, Raúl. I spent my childhood watching you help those around you recover from wounds and illnesses I know should have been far more serious than they were. Will you help?"

"I doubt they would let me in to see her," Raúl temporized, though the healer in him recoiled from the crude and debilitating "treatment."

He had no idea what ailed the queen, but bleeding "to let out the ill humors" would do little but weaken her when she needed strength to fight off her illness.

"Marie-Agnès said she would let you in," Esteban said. "I told her about you, and she said you could come in through the servants' entrance. No one would ever see you."

Even though Esteban was a man grown, his expression was that of the young boy who had grown up believing there was nothing Raúl could not do. Despite his misgivings, Raúl could not deny that expectation if there were anything he might do to help. "If they will allow me in to see her, I will do what I can," he agreed.

"Thank you," Esteban said, embracing Raúl impulsively. "I knew you would help."

"Esteban, have our horses saddled," Christian requested, exchanging a glance with Teodoro, who inclined his head in silent agreement. "We will ride with you to Tarascon."

Before Raúl could protest that he did not need an escort, Teodoro crossed the room to his side. "This is Cristian's world," he said softly, his pride in his lover evident in his eyes. "He will not interfere if he is not needed, but it is always well to have a friend at court."

"Then we should ride," Raúl said, acceding to his friends' wisdom.

They rode north to Tarascon. When they reached the royal chateau, Christian and Teodoro left them, Christian's status as ambassador too great to allow him to pass unnoticed. Raúl followed Esteban to a side door, where a young woman with tear-stained eyes met them. "Thank you, monsieur, for coming," she said, taking Raúl's hand. "The fever grows worse, and the royal physicians despair of helping her."

"How long has she been ill?" Raúl asked in a soft voice as they followed the lady-in-waiting through thick-carpeted corridors. Esteban took the young woman's hand and murmured something into her ear that brought a small smile to her face.

"Nearly a week, monsieur," she answered. "Nothing the physicians have tried has done any good. Esteban told me he was sure you could help her. I pray he is right."

So did Raúl, though he didn't think it would help the maid's confidence any to say so. At the end of the corridor, she rapped on a heavy wooden door before pushing it open and gesturing them into the room.

The bedchamber was dark and stale, the curtains pulled tightly over the windows and around the bed. "Esteban, open the windows," Raúl ordered. "We need light and fresh air. Mademoiselle, will you tell your mistress I am here? I would not wish to startle her."

"I told her you were coming," Marie-Agnès said. "She said she would be glad of someone from her native land. I will tell her you're here."

The lady-in-waiting parted the curtains on the bed and spoke with the person inside. Permission given, she opened the curtains more widely. Raúl bowed deeply. "Will you tell me what ails Your Majesty?"

The pale, slender woman on the bed bore small resemblance to the charming and luminous description he had heard from Christian. A flush reddened her sunken cheeks, and a sheen of sweat dampened her forehead and her light nightdress. "Chills and fever," the queen answered in a mild voice roughened by a bout of coughing. "I feel as if I cannot draw a full breath. Most of all, I fear for the health of my child."

Any hesitance Raúl might have felt at treating a member of the royal court was forgotten as his healing instincts rose to the fore. "If I may?" he asked, his hand hovering over the queen's wrist. At her nod, he clasped his fingers loosely over the pallid skin, his lips tightening at the thready, weakened pulse. He did not need to lean forward to hear the rasp in the queen's breathing.

Meeting Esteban's worried gaze, he summoned a smile he hoped would pass as reassuring. "A pitcher of cool water, a basin, and a cloth?" he asked. The lady-in-waiting scurried off to gather the items he requested. Opening the pouch at his belt, he drew out a handful of healing herbs and a small jar of salve and set them on the table at the queen's bedside.

Marie-Agnès returned a moment later with everything Raúl had asked for. He poured a little of the water into the basin, dipped the cloth in the water, and draped it across the queen's forehead. Then he poured a goblet of water and measured a dose of powdered willow bark into it. "This will taste bitter," he warned her, "but it will help your fever, and that is the greatest danger to your child right now."

Helping the queen to sit forward, Raúl supported her with an arm behind her shoulders and held the goblet to her lips with the other. As she sipped slowly, he closed his eyes and murmured a voiceless invocation, all his healing energies focused on the two patients in his care.

Anne trembled against him as she sipped the potion, but when she leaned back against the pillows again, Raúl was pleased to see that her color had improved. "It will take a few days, but if we can keep your fever down, you should be on the mend before long."

He handed the salve and the packet of willow bark to Marie-Agnès. "Rub her chest with the salve to help with her breathing," he instructed, "and make a tea of the willow bark and have her drink it on rising, at noon, and at bedtime. Leave the windows open to let fresh air into the room, and wash her down with cool water should the fever rise again." He breathed deeply, gathering the strength he had left. "Do not try to rise too soon, Your Majesty," he advised the queen. "Once the fever has gone for a day and a night, you may sit up and perhaps take a turn around the room, but rest and eat to rebuild your strength before you try anything more."

"Thank you," Anne said, offering her hand to Raúl again. "I will not forget your kindness in coming to help me."

"I serve at Your Majesty's will," Raúl said, bowing over her knuckles. "Your lady-in-waiting knows how to find me should you need me again."

"Will she recover?" Esteban asked after Marie-Agnès had escorted them from the room.

"With rest, and if your amour can keep the court physicians from sapping her strength, both the queen and her son should be well."

"Her son?" Esteban's brows rose, for though he was only a page to the English ambassador, all the world knew how desperately Louis wished for an heir.

"Her child, I should say." Fortunately Esteban did not linger on Raúl's slip of the tongue, chattering instead about how worried Marie-Agnès had been and how grateful she would be once the queen was fully recovered.

Raúl smiled encouragingly, recognizing the first flush of young love. He sincerely hoped everything would work out for Esteban, the closest to a son he would ever have.

"HOW FARES the queen?" Christian asked when Raúl and Esteban rejoined him.

"Let us return to your villa," Raúl replied. "We can talk more easily there."

When they reached the villa, Raúl left Esteban to hand their horses off to the groom and followed Christian and Teodoro inside. He sank into a chair in the salon, where Teodoro poured him a glass of wine, knowing from long experience how much of his energy Raúl spent when healing.

"She has an inflammation of the lungs, but if her fever can be kept down, and if the damned court physicians do not sap her strength even further through bleeding her, she and the child may well recover."

"That is good to hear," Teodoro said. "After all the trouble we went to with the Queen Mother, it would be a shame to lose her to illness now."

"Anne is a charming woman, and the court would be a far sadder place for her loss, the more so for the child she carries. She has lost two through miscarriage before this, and Louis has high hopes she will bring this one to term." Christian crossed the room, his hand trailing over Teodoro's back as he passed. "I will leave you to rest in case your services are needed again."

Teodoro's gaze followed Christian until he left the room. When they were alone, he asked, "Have you heard from Gerrard?"

"No, though I little hoped to do so. If all has gone as planned, he should be on his way back to France by now." *And I would far rather see his face than any letter*, Raúl thought wearily. He had grown used to having Gerrard's strength and love to lean on when his own resources were spent, and Teodoro's well-meaning inquiry brought his absence to the fore.

"And if all has not gone as planned?" Teodoro asked.

Unbidden, the memory of the flash of vision he'd seen before Gerrard's departure assailed him—darkness, and alone, so alone. He shook his head, taking another sip of wine. "Then he will come when he may," Raúl said firmly, assuring himself as much as Teodoro. "You and Cristian will just have to suffer my presence until he does."

"You know you are welcome here for as long as you need or want to stay," Teodoro said. "I was more concerned about you than about the duration of your visit. It is hard to be separated from the one you love."

"I fear it may be something I will need to become accustomed to," Raúl answered. "If Gerrard and his father reach a rapprochement, he may wish to return to England more often. Or perhaps even make his home there once again." The thought chilled his soul, but he could not let his own selfish desire keep Gerrard estranged from his family.

"Would it be so terrible to go to England with him?" Teodoro asked seriously. "While it is not my favorite of the places I have visited at Cristian's side, I would rather be with him than in any earthly paradise."

"In what role?" Raúl hoped he'd managed to keep his growing disquiet from his voice, but Teodoro's raised eyebrow told him he hadn't succeeded. "In the eyes of the world, at least, you are Ambassador Blackwood's bodyguard. Even were someone to suspect your relationship is more than that, you have a legitimate reason to be together. There is no such role I could fill for Gerrard, and my very presence in his life would raise suspicions. From what I have heard from Cristian, England is not as fanatical as Spain in its persecution, but I would do nothing to place Gerrard in danger, even if that only meant ostracism within his society."

"You are a healer," Teodoro pointed out. "You could serve as the village apothecary, perhaps, and from what I understand from Cristian, Gerrard's family is not a highly placed one. Even were the worst to come to pass with his family's illness, he would never be a scion of society the way Cristian will someday be. You would not need the same excuse to be at his side as I have."

"That assumes his village would stand for a Rom to live in their midst, let alone trust him enough to come to him for healing." Raúl knew he was viewing the situation in the worst possible light, but the longer Gerrard was absent, the harder it was to convince himself that they could find the means to stay together. He had kept Gerrard in his world for the years they were together, but it was surely foolish to expect an English nobleman, no matter how minor his title, to turn his back on that lineage to roam as a wandering gypsy the rest of his life.

"You are borrowing trouble," Teodoro said with a shake of his head. "How often did you ask me why I was denying Cristian when I kept searching for reasons why our future could not be? You were right to chide me then. Take your own advice now."

"How can I argue against my own wisdom?" Raúl finished the wine and rose to his feet, feeling a bit steadier now. Sleep would be the quickest means to restore the rest of his strength, though Gerrard's return would be the best medicine of all. "Go find your Cristian and celebrate your happiness."

"That is advice I will follow with pleasure," Teodoro responded, pulling Raúl into a soldier's embrace. "One thing I have learned of your Gerrard is how steadfast his regard is once given. Do not give in to doubt. He will return to you. I am as sure of this as I am of the welcome I will find in my Cristian's arms."

Teodoro's certainty gave Raúl enough strength to smile at his friend. There could be no doubt of Teodoro's welcome in Christian's arms. Leaving the salon as well, he retired to bed to rest.

"RAÚL! YOU must come again. The queen has taken a turn for the worse," Esteban cried, bursting into the room. "Marie-Agnès said the court physicians took credit for her recovery and insisted on bleeding her again. Marie-Agnès fears she is miscarrying."

"*Béngalo dili*," Raúl spat. If there were one thing he could ban from this earth, it would be the practice of bleeding the sick. All too often the "cure" did more harm than the illness it was meant to treat. "Get Martiya saddled. I will ride as fast as I can and pray it is not too late."

"I told the groom to ready Martiya as soon as I returned," Esteban answered breathlessly.

"Then let me get my pouch, and we will ride at once."

Raúl kept up a string of curses the entire way north to Tarascon, the ride reminiscent of too many he had taken in the company of his friends. "Will we be allowed admittance?" Raúl asked Esteban as they neared the palace.

"Marie-Agnès said the queen told the king the truth, but only after the court physicians bled her again. The king is desperate for an heir. Desperate enough even to send for a gypsy."

If the queen had already been bled again, Raúl feared his own skill and strength might not be enough, but he kept that doubt to himself. Expecting to face resistance from the palace guards despite Esteban's assurances, his spirits rose slightly at seeing a familiar face above the black musketeer tabard.

"Aristide! Is the queen any better?" Esteban asked.

"Not that I have heard," Aristide answered grimly. "Raúl, well met. When Esteban told us you were staying with the *vicomte*, our hopes rose. If there is any hope to save the queen and her child, it lies in your hands."

"We shall see what state I find her in," Raúl replied. "I will do what I can, of course, but not even I can bring the dead back to life."

Aristide led them through the chateau to the doorway of the royal chambers. "M. de Tréville," Aristide said with a bow. "We have brought the man who saved my life when I was wounded last fall. Hopefully he will be able to help Her Majesty."

"We will pray you are right," M. de Tréville said, opening the door to allow Raúl to pass.

Once again the curtains were pulled closed, darkening the room. "Open the curtains," Raúl ordered. "I will need water and clean rags. Clean ones, mind you." He bowed to the queen. "Madame, will you let me examine you?"

The voice that answered him was so weak Raúl could scarcely hear it; the color that had returned after he had last treated the queen was gone. Silently repeating his curse, Raúl reached for the pouch at his waist when a bout of coughing racked the queen. Her face constricted in pain, and she cried out, a sudden rush of blood staining the sheets.

"Where are the rags?" Raúl snapped, pulling the sheets aside. "We must stop the bleeding if we have any hope of saving the babe. You must lie as still and quiet as you can, Madame. I know it hurts, but you must let me help you." The others in the room crowded closer, raising Raúl's hackles. "Clear the room. Whatever happens, your presence here will not help her. She does not need the whole court bearing witness to her distress."

"Out!" the king ordered in a voice that brooked no disobedience. "I, however, will stay."

"As you wish, Majesty," Raúl said, "but stay out of my way. 'Tis the life of your wife and child at stake."

Marie-Agnès returned with the rags. Raúl packed them as tightly as he could, trying to stop the bleeding. It slowed, but when he placed his hands on Anne's belly, he could feel no spark of life within her. Stifling a curse, he did what he could, hoping it would be enough to keep her alive.

Raúl was vaguely aware of Marie-Agnès wiping the queen down with cool water, of the voices around him as her coughing eased, his attention focused on the thread of life that still bound his patient to the world. When his sight darkened to a shadowed haze, he forced himself to pull away, praying it would be enough. He reached for his herbs with shaking hands and crumbled a mixture into the goblet resting at the bedside.

"Help her to drink it," he murmured, wishing in vain for Gerrard's strong arms to lean into. He staggered to a chair against the wall, his head falling forward, the breath rasping from his lungs. When his vision stopped swimming, he raised his head to meet the king's worried gaze.

"The queen should recover," he said wearily. "So long as you keep those leeches from bleeding her near to death again. The babe...." His voice faltered. As hard as it was to feel any life slip away, to lose a child before it had any chance was a pain that always bruised his heart.

"You treated her before without my knowledge, and she improved," the king said, his voice hard, "so I will not blame you for the loss of the child, but you need to leave now, before my grief overcomes my better judgment."

Raúl nodded, forcing himself to stand. "Do not let them bleed her again, Your Majesty, or you will be mourning your wife as well as your unborn child." He bowed as best as he could and left by the servants' entrance he had first used to gain admittance to the queen's chambers. The last thing he needed was to face the court at the moment.

To his relief, Aristide and Perrin stood inside the corridor. "We will show you out," Aristide said. "Are you well enough to ride?"

"Martiya will not let me come to harm." Raúl breathed deeply, gathering what strength he had left.

"Thank you," Perrin said softly, gripping his elbow. "I can't pretend to know what magic it is you do, but it was clear to see by the color in Her Majesty's cheeks and how much more easily she was breathing the last time you visited that you have helped her."

Raúl shook his head. "Fresh air, cool baths, and herbs to lower the fever and ease her breathing are no magic. And could you have kept the court physicians from draining her strength with her blood, she might yet have kept her child."

"You did all you could," Aristide assured him, pulling him in an embrace. For a moment Raúl closed his eyes and let himself imagine it was Gerrard who held him before he returned the clasp and stepped back. "Though all the court will mourn, no one blames you for what has come to pass. Go with our thanks, and know that the musketeers will never forget what you have done for our queen."

Raúl hoped Aristide was right and that blame would not fall on him, because while he knew Aristide was a man of his word, he did not know who would win a struggle between duty and honor if the king ordered him arrested or killed. "If you see the ambassador or his entourage, will you tell them I have returned to Arles to rest?"

"Of course," Perrin said. "We will find them as quickly as we can."

"Discreetly," Raúl insisted. "There is no need to draw attention to my departure. My arrival drew attention enough."

When he stepped into the courtyard, Esteban stood with Martiya's reins in his hand. "Do you need me to return with you?"

"Stay and comfort your Marie-Agnès." Raúl mounted, the stallion's restive manner stilling when he settled into the saddle. "I can find my way back to the ambassador's villa, and once there I plan nothing more than a good night's sleep." More than ever, he regretted that it could not be in Gerrard's arms.

TEN

AS GERRARD rode into London, he grimaced at the dust and noise and smells. He had grown used to the fresh air and quiet of the countryside around Hawkins Hall. After that and living with the gypsies, mostly avoiding large cities unless they were visiting Christian and Teodoro, the bustle of the English capital was nearly overwhelming. Muffling a curse, Gerrard rode toward the inn where he had stayed the last time he was in London. He had the direction of Beecham's cousin, Kellan, but he would need to freshen up from the journey and send word to the man to set up a meeting rather than drop in on him unannounced.

The innkeeper remembered him, at least, and arranged a room for him immediately, saving Gerrard the need to haggle for a bed. He ordered a bath brought so he could clean up and change for dinner. He would find someone to take his card to Kellan tonight, and tomorrow he would hopefully hire a new man of business and find a messenger to carry word to Raúl about the delay and the possible change of plans.

He missed his lover. He could not shake the feeling that Raúl was in trouble, and it was making him short-tempered, something he thought he had outgrown in the time he lived with Raúl. He only hoped being reunited with Raúl would cure him of that affliction again as he had once before.

The inn boasted a decent cellar, so Gerrard finished off a bottle of wine along with his dinner, hoping it would help him sleep amid the noise of the busy inn and the London streets. After his meal he wrote a short note to Beecham's cousin, introducing himself and requesting the opportunity to meet to discuss a business offer. Having arranged with the innkeeper to have a groom deliver it to the man's residence, Gerrard climbed the stairs to his room, where he pulled off his garments and settled in for the night.

Even after all the weeks of their separation, Gerrard found it hard to fall asleep without Raúl's body warm against his. He tried to imagine where Raúl would be at this moment. The festival had ended, he knew, resolving again to find a ship or merchant on the morrow who was heading to France and would be willing to carry a message to Saintes-Maries-de-la-Mer. He hoped Raúl had found a group of gypsies who had made the pilgrimage and were willing to wait with him until Gerrard could return. The thought of Raúl waiting alone, wondering why he hadn't arrived, filled Gerrard with guilt, but there was no way he could leave until he had someone trustworthy to care for Hawkins Hall and its dependents in his absence. Surely Raúl would understand once he could explain the circumstances to him.

He tossed in the bed, trying to remember the last time he had slept alone before leaving for England. He was not entirely sure, but he thought it was the night Raúl had locked him out of their rooms for being a jealous fool—and then sought him out in the middle of the night because he could no more sleep than Gerrard could. In retrospect it struck him as funny, but at the time he had been insane with the thought that Raúl might be done with him.

It had all started when they arrived in Brussels, the site of Christian's first diplomatic posting. They had written ahead to inform Christian of their intended arrival, and Christian had sent back a note assuring them of their welcome. They stabled their horses and walked inside, knowing Christian kept no servants. Walking into the salon, they found Christian and Teodoro half-undressed, clearly about to make love. Gerrard had intended simply to withdraw and knock, giving the two men time to dress, but Raúl had no such hesitations.

"Now there's a sight I never thought to see again," he teased, his gaze roaming over Teodoro's bare chest in a way that roiled Gerrard's temper.

"You say that every time you see it," Teodoro retorted dryly, accepting the shirt Christian handed him after reclaiming it from the floor where it had fallen. "At least I am not flat on my back in bed this time."

Gerrard's gaze flew to Christian, who to his surprise appeared to be holding back laughter.

Christian straightened his own clothes, clearly unconcerned by the exchange between the two men as he crossed the room and embraced Gerrard and Raúl warmly. "Ignore them," he told Gerrard. "They say things like that to shock us. Raúl would no more leave you than Teo would leave me."

Gerrard let Christian's words mollify him for the moment, but the spark of jealousy was slow to die, fanned all evening by Raúl and

Teodoro's teasing comments and obvious familiarity with each other. Whatever their relationship was, it had clearly been a deep and intimate one. By the time he and Raúl went upstairs to the rooms Christian offered them, Gerrard's temper was on full boil.

"What do you take me for?" Gerrard demanded as soon as the door closed behind Christian, leaving them alone for the first time since their arrival.

"Take you?" Raúl's eyes shimmered with humor and something deeper. "If that is your preference, it will be my pleasure to indulge you."

"After the way you acted with Ciéza tonight, I'm surprised you have a thought for anything but slipping away to meet him," Gerrard grumbled. "Does Christian know about you?"

Raúl smiled, refusing to give Gerrard the fight he wasn't sure why he wanted. "Cristian could not bring himself to ask either, but I will tell you as I told him. Teo and I once were lovers, though neither of us was foolish enough to fancy himself in love. Cristian is wise enough to see that he alone has ever touched Teo's heart."

That did not help at all. "It's not Ciéza's heart I'm interested in," Gerrard shouted. "You say you love me and then you act like... like that!"

"Like what?" Raúl asked, his voice still level but the laughter leaving his eyes. "This is not the first time you have made assumptions about me, though I believed you had learned better since then."

"Like you still want him," Gerrard said, his voice breaking at the thought of Raúl having taken Gerrard as his lover only because he could not have Teodoro. "I don't have much in this world, but I do still have my pride. Would you go back to him if he asked?"

"He would never ask," Raúl said, shaking his head. "Cristian knows that, though you clearly do not. But if you do not have enough trust in us to ask the question, perhaps you would prefer to make other arrangements for the night."

Gerrard recoiled from the suggestion, the ache in his chest so strong he wanted to scream. Instead he turned for the door. "Perhaps that would be best."

Finding an empty room was easy. Christian's villa in Brussels was large enough for a much larger entourage. Finding a comfortable position in the cold bed was far harder.

He had no idea how long he tossed in restless irritation, trying to fuel the waning embers of his anger. The image of Raúl entwined in Teodoro's arms refused to leave him, though as he calmed he realized Raúl was right. He had seen for himself what Teodoro had endured for Christian's sake and what Christian had risked for Teodoro. No one who saw them together in the rare moments when they dropped the discreet façade they wore before the rest of the world could doubt what they meant to each other. Christian had been able to put the time before Teodoro met him behind them. Unless Gerrard could do the same, he risked losing the greatest happiness to ever come into his life.

Sitting up, he had just decided to find Raúl and ask—beg, if he had to—for his forgiveness when a tap sounded at his door. Hoping it was Christian rather than Teodoro coming to talk some sense into him, he called out, "Come in."

To his surprise Raúl entered, his deceptively slim form silhouetted against the light from the window in the corridor before he closed the door behind him. "I ought to crack your thick skull for your stupidity, but I find I cannot sleep with this unresolved between us. What proof will satisfy you that there is no more between Teo and me than a long and enduring friendship?"

"You are here," Gerrard replied, his voice hoarse with emotion. He stretched out his hands in entreaty. "Forgive me. I have a temper, and nothing sparks it more quickly than feeling slighted, however illogically. I was coming to look for you because I could not sleep either. You have never given me any reason to doubt you, but even now, I do not always understand how you are here with me, and the thought of losing you—"

Raúl silenced his apology with a slow, deep kiss. "It is your strength that first drew me to you, and I find it hard to credit that you can question what I feel for you. Be assured, I value Teo's friendship deeply, for it was formed and hardened in the fiercest of crucibles. But he is no threat to you. I know only a little of your history before we met, but nothing that happened before that day matters. You, and no other, hold my heart."

Gerrard found it hard to credit that Raúl could forgive him so easily. He wrapped his arms around his lover, drawing him down into the bed, intending to make slow, sweet love to him to round off his apology.

To his surprise Raúl shifted onto his back, pulling Gerrard's heavier body on top of him. "Take me," he demanded, canting his hips so their arousals slid slickly against each other. "Give me all of your strength." He grasped Gerrard's buttocks, dragging him closer. "To everyone else, even Teo, I am the healer, the miracle worker. Only to you can I confess how much I rely upon your strength—how much I need you."

That silenced any doubts Gerrard had left. He knew the strong side of Raúl's personality, watched it every time Raúl took charge of a sickroom or the gypsy caravan. He had never paid any attention to how rarely Raúl showed his softer side, but his words drove home the reality that only Gerrard saw that side of him. If Teodoro had ever seen it, and Raúl's words seemed to suggest he had not, it had not happened since Gerrard met them. "My strength, my heart, my body, and my life," Gerrard promised, pressing down against Raúl. "I had thought to take my time and prove the depths of my regret in speaking rashly, but you press my control."

Raúl shimmied decadently beneath him, his tongue tracing fire up the column of Gerrard's throat. "Forget control," he murmured, wrapping his legs around Gerrard's thighs and arching upward. "Prove you need me as fiercely as I need you."

All hope of slow and gentle disappeared with those words. Gerrard cursed silently when he realized they had nothing in this borrowed bedroom to ease the way, and nothing even in the one they had intended to call their own. He pulled back roughly before diving between Raúl's thighs to lick wetly at the entrance he intended to breach. His patience would not last long with Raúl's provocation ringing in his ears, but he would not hurt him unnecessarily.

Raúl tangled long fingers in his hair, holding Gerrard's head in place as he pushed up to meet him. Raúl's groan when Gerrard pressed his tongue inside nearly broke his control, but he took his time in this at least, knowing his passion would take over once he replaced the wet muscle with his cock. Not until Raúl was cursing steadily in Rom and tugging almost hard enough to pull his hair from its roots did Gerrard allow himself to be urged upward. Raúl claimed his mouth as soon as he was within reach, tongues dueling in a battle Gerrard was happy to let him win.

His patience at an end, he pressed the head of his erection against Raúl's entrance, alert for any sign of distress, but Raúl only kissed him even more wildly, his feet planted on the bed to push up against Gerrard's ingress. Once he was fully seated, he shifted his weight to pin Raúl's hips to the bed until he could free one hand to do the job instead. Keeping Raúl still, he pulled back and thrust as hard as he could, giving Raúl his full strength just as he had asked.

Raúl met each thrust, letting his head fall back as he strained to join them even deeper. When Gerrard nearly slipped free when pulling back for his next stroke, Raúl twisted and rose to his knees, dragging Gerrard's head down to his shoulder for an awkward, biting kiss. "Harder," he urged, lifting his hips. "Make me feel you."

The sight of Raúl's upturned backside begging for his attention was more than Gerrard's nearly frayed control could stand. He grabbed Raúl's flanks, holding him steady and pounding into him with all his might. Raúl grunted with each stroke, but since he rocked back into every one, Gerrard did not worry he was hurting him. "Is this hard enough?" he taunted, though what he would do if Raúl said no, he had no idea.

"Never enough," Raúl panted, his chest heaving beneath Gerrard's, his muscles clenching around Gerrard's cock as if he were fighting to hold it inside.

It would never be enough as far as Gerrard was concerned either. He could spend his life making love with this man, and he would still bemoan the lack of time. Releasing one hand's grip from Raúl's side, he slid his hand between them, gripping Raúl's leaking cock, shuttling his hand up and down the slender length, trying to add another layer of sensation.

Raúl arched his back, his hips stuttering between Gerrard's rough grip and pounding cock. Sweat dripped from the hair clinging to Gerrard's brow, but he couldn't spare a hand to wipe it away. With a smothered cry, Raúl stiffened beneath him, every muscle frozen until his cock jerked in Gerrard's grasp, pulsing hot fluid over his fingers.

That was all it took to finish Gerrard, his own release stealing his breath and his strength so that he collapsed forward against Raúl, pushing them both onto the mattress. "I love you," he said, his lips moving against Raúl's sweaty neck. "I'll never doubt you again."

"I will be pleased to prove it to you again whenever you require, if this is the result," Raúl murmured, finding Gerrard's hand and intertwining their fingers, though he made no effort to move from beneath Gerrard's weight. "I assure you I feel thoroughly loved."

"As long as the proof is not preceded by another fight, I will indulge you whenever you wish," Gerrard said. They curled together that night, warming the sheets even without the benefit of a warming pan.

Gerrard was not so lucky tonight. The heat of summer kept his bed from being cold, but nothing could replace Raúl at his side. He turned over, trying to find a comfortable position alone in a strange bed, but the memories had raised a passion that demanded to be assuaged. He took himself in hand, tugging a few times until his cock spilled, but he felt none of the satisfaction he knew with Raúl. It was release, nothing more. With a sigh and a fervent prayer that they would be reunited soon, he closed his eyes and tried to sleep.

GERRARD ROSE early the next morning, dressing carefully and taking only the time to eat before going to his meeting with Kellan. While he was supposed to be the one conducting the interview, he still felt the need to make a good impression. He wanted Kellan to respect him, not merely view him as an employer.

He found Kellan's lodgings easily, simple rooms in a simple building, but well maintained from what Gerrard could see. He knocked on the door and waited to be admitted.

The man who answered the door looked far younger than Gerrard expected, though he could see the family resemblance to Sir Thomas. "Kellan Beecham?" he asked, wondering if he could trust the management of his estates to someone who barely seemed old enough to shave. Still, Sir Thomas said Kellan had handled affairs for his father before the older man's death. He would talk with the young man first before drawing any rash conclusions—another lesson Raúl had taught him. "I am Gerrard Hawkins. Your cousin, Sir Thomas Beecham, recommended I speak with you."

"Yes, he wrote to tell me you might be calling on me. Please, come in." Kellan stepped aside to let Gerrard enter. "I was just about to make myself a cup of tea. Will you join me?"

"Gladly," Gerrard said, walking inside. The inside of the lodgings was no fancier than the outside, but the rooms were meticulously kept, an encouraging sign. A man who favored order in his surroundings would surely favor them in his business as well. He waited patiently while Kellan prepared their tea. Once the young man took a seat across from him, Gerrard brought back up the subject of his call. "I don't know exactly what Sir Thomas told you, but I am in need of some… assistance with my estate."

Kellan nodded. "My father was in failing health for some time, and I managed things for him from the time I left university until his death last fall. Since my elder brother inherited the title, he… prefers to see to things himself." The younger man broke off awkwardly, and Gerrard remembered Sir Thomas saying that there was some friction between the two brothers. "I am not sure what reference he might give you, but I can provide the names of several of the tenants and shopkeepers on the estate who could vouch for me."

"Sir Thomas gave an excellent reference already, but I will accept the other names as well," Gerrard said. "I must travel abroad shortly and will need someone trustworthy to oversee the estate while I'm away. I hope not to be gone more than a few months, but traveling in France is unpredictable at the best of times." Traveling with a band of gypsies made it even more unpredictable, but Gerrard kept that thought to himself. He would spring Raúl and the others on his tenants when the need arose. "Would you be comfortable doing that? Not immediately, of course. We would need time to discuss where things stand and where they need to go before I leave, but in a matter of a month or six weeks, could you see taking on that responsibility?"

"I would do so gladly, if you would trust me to do so," Kellan answered with a wide smile. "I much prefer country life to London and would be available whenever you require me. In fact," he said, "if you plan to return to your estate once you finish your business here, I could accompany you if you wish. I could take over as much of the management as you like while you are still in England—a sort of probationary apprenticeship, if you will—and if you are satisfied with the results, we can discuss terms for a more permanent relationship."

Kellan's willingness to accept a trial period settled all of Gerrard's concerns but one, but given that he did not even know if Raúl would agree to return to England with him, Gerrard chose not to broach the matter, however obliquely. If Kellan had issue with it upon Gerrard's return, Gerrard would deal with it then, when he was in a position of again doing without a man of business if necessary. "I should probably explain about my son," he said instead. "I left England eight years ago because my father refused to let me marry the girl I thought I loved. I have named our son as my heir even though the girl and I have decided against marrying as she found someone else in my absence. I hope this won't pose a problem for you."

"Not in the least," Kellan assured him. "I find my brother's children far easier to deal with than my brother himself. How old is the boy, if I may ask?"

"Seven," Gerrard said. "He was born a few months after my departure for Spain. At the moment he lives with his mother and will remain there until I return, since it would be unfair to him and to the staff to foist him off on them in my absence, but once I return, he will move into the manor with me and begin to learn everything he will need to know as my successor."

"I have a nephew near that age myself," Kellan replied. "Was the estate much affected by the plague?" They spoke of the depredations the sickness had wrought in both the country and the capitol, the questions Kellan asked about the situation of the remaining tenants doing much to convince Gerrard that he would be able to handle the responsibilities of dealing with their needs.

"I have one other matter I must attend to this afternoon," Gerrard said, "but I had intended to return to Hawkins Hall in the morning, provided our meeting went well. Is that enough notice for you to accompany me, or do you need a few days to set your affairs in order before joining me there? We will see how the next few weeks go and discuss a more permanent appointment before I leave for France."

"There is nothing to hold me in London," Kellan replied. "Is your business anything I can assist you with?"

"Only if you know of a ship bound for France and a courier for hire willing to take a message to the southern coast," Gerrard said wistfully. "I have friends there who will be anxious for news, and I would not have them worry about me any longer."

"My acquaintance does not extend to ship captains, regrettably, but I would be happy to accompany you to the docks to make enquiries," Kellan offered. "With two of us asking, we may find what you seek more quickly than you would alone."

"If you are sure I won't be keeping you from anything, I would appreciate the help," Gerrard said. "Nor, despite my friends' best efforts, is negotiating a strength of mine."

"In that I may be able to assist you," Kellan said, finishing his tea. "If you are ready, I am at your service."

ELEVEN

"RAÚL?"

Struggling to remain in the dream where he rested against Gerrard's broad chest, Raúl dragged the quilt over his head and burrowed deeper into the pillows.

"Raúl? My apologies for waking you, amigo, but you have a visitor." Teodoro's deep tone finally broke through the somnolent haze, and Raúl sat up quickly. The slight shake of Teodoro's head, however, quickly disabused him of the hope that Gerrard had returned.

"Who is it?" he asked, scratching his head, which still felt heavy despite the night's rest. "I know of no one who would call upon me here."

"Some local count," Teodoro said as Raúl pulled on his trousers. "Cristian met him at a court event and mentioned we had taken a villa here." He handed Raúl a fresh shirt from the armoire, which Raúl pulled over his shoulders. After drawing his hair into a rough queue, he bound it back and gestured for Teodoro to precede him down the stairs to the salon where Christian entertained visitors.

"Ah, Raúl, there you are," Christian said when they came in. While he did not acknowledge Teodoro by name, Raúl saw the look that passed between them, the one only a blind man would miss. It amazed him how blind most people were. "This is Henri, *comte* du Saint-Rémy de Provence. He heard of your success in helping Her Majesty and hoped he might prevail on you to examine his son as well."

Though Raúl could hardly consider the loss of the unborn babe a success, he did not protest Christian's words, instead offering the *comte* a bow. To his surprise the noble extended his hand, which Raúl accepted after a brief hesitation. "Milord," he said, noting the dark circles beneath the man's eyes. "How may I be of service?"

"It's my son, sir," the *comte* explained. "He has a fever and chills, and now he's started to cough. It sounds just like the foul malady that nearly took Her Majesty, and when I heard the ambassador knew the man who saved our gracious queen, I prevailed on him to introduce us in the hope you would help my son as well."

"I will do what I may," Raúl answered, determined not to lose another child to the illness if there were any way he could prevent it. "Let me gather a few things, and then you may bring me to him."

"Thank you, sir," the *comte* said, his gratitude visible on his face. "You are welcome to stay in my home rather than riding back and forth if that would be easier for you. I have plenty of space."

Raúl hoped it would not come to that, but he bowed again to the *comte* and returned to his rooms, adding a set of linen and a spare shirt to the bag in which he gathered his herbs and healing supplies. After tying a scarf over his head, he descended to the hall where the count was trying not to pace. "Should Gerrard arrive while I am gone...," he began.

"We will tell him where you are," Christian assured him. "I doubt it would come as a surprise to him to find you out helping others."

Raúl summoned a smile, hoping it was more robust than it felt, and turned to the *comte*. "I am at your service. Shall we go?"

The *comte* led Raúl out to his carriage, a finely appointed one, Raúl noticed idly, and instructed his driver to return them to his village. When they pulled into the courtyard, Raúl looked at the windows on the upper floors, seeing them all closed tightly. "The first thing you must do," he said, "is open all the windows. Fresh air is your greatest defense against illness. The disease breeds in dank, foul places. It cannot breed where there is light and fresh air and cleanliness."

The *comte* looked dubious but to his credit did not argue. As soon as the doors of the villa were swept open before them, he gave orders for all the windows to be opened. A handful of servants scurried to do his bidding, while another led them up the arched marble staircase to a bedroom on the upper story. A young child of no more than five or six lay in an enormous bed, looking pale and lost behind the heavy hangings.

Raúl swept the velvet bed-curtains aside and nodded for the *comte* to open the window casement. "Bonjour, young friend," he said quietly, sitting on the edge of the mattress. "I am Raúl. Can you tell me your name?"

A fit of coughing was Raúl's first answer. Eventually, though, the boy brought it under control. "I am Louis," he said. "My father named me for the king."

"An honorable namesake," Raúl agreed, taking Louis's hand in his and feeling for his pulse. It was rapid but strong, a good sign. As long as the boy's strength held on, Raúl could probably treat him with herbs rather than having to expend his own strength. "I'm going to make something for you to drink. It won't taste very good, but it will help you feel better."

"He has vomited up most of what we have given him to eat," the *comte* interjected as Raúl crossed the room to pour a glass of water from the ewer that stood on the dressing table. Raúl opened his pouch and crumbled a handful of herbs into the liquid, adding something to settle the boy's stomach as well as ease his fever. He would have the child's caretakers boil the water and steep the herbs into a tea after this, but he wanted to get the first dose into him immediately.

"Now, drink all this up, Louis," Raúl instructed, helping the boy to sit forward and sip at the glass. Several more bouts of coughing interrupted them, but eventually the glass was emptied. "Well done!" Raúl praised, easing the child back onto the pillows and ruffling his damp hair. Folding away all of the heavy bedding except for a thin undersheet, he turned to the servant, perhaps the boy's nursemaid, who hovered behind the *comte*.

"Bring some cloths and cool water," Raúl said. "Bathe him down every few hours, and don't smother him beneath all these heavy blankets. Let his body breathe and he'll rid himself of the fever sooner."

"But he'll take a chill if you leave him uncovered that way," the servant protested. "My lord, are you sure you trust this… man to help Louis?"

"This *healer* saved Her Majesty the queen," the *comte* answered in a voice that sent the nursemaid off with a shake of her head. Raúl combed his hand through Louis's hair, soothing him as the herbs did their work, the next round of coughing already subdued.

"I apologize," the *comte* said. "Isabeau has been with us for a long time, and her devotion to the family is unswerving, but—"

"But I am an unknown and a threat to her charge," Raúl said. "I do understand how she feels, even if I would do nothing to harm the boy. Whatever you do, do not let her convince you to have him bled. It nearly killed the queen and cost her the life of her child."

"I won't," the *comte* replied. "Will you stay for luncheon? My wife and I would be honored to have you at our table."

And if that were not proof of how much the *comte* loved his son, Raúl thought, he needed no further evidence. "Let me be sure Louis is fed first," he answered. "Some rich beef broth would be best to build up his strength until he can hold down solid food again." He rose from the bedside and dug into his pouch, arranging his packets and sachets on the dressing table, taking note of the herbs he would soon need to make a trip to the market to replenish—or hunt for himself. "And if you would, have a pot for boiling water brought up from the kitchens." A small fire would not warm the boy too much, especially with the fresh breeze from the windows, and he could boil water for the teas he would have Louis drink every few hours.

"I will order it done right away," the *comte* said, "as well as make it clear to the servants that a request from you should be followed as if it came from me. I cannot lose my son."

Raúl nodded. "I will get him settled, and then this afternoon, I must make a trip to the market to see if I can purchase more herbs. I am running low on some things he will need."

The *comte* nodded and, after bending to place a kiss on his son's forehead, left the room. Raúl ran a hand down the drowsing boy's cheek, feeling the heat already beginning to dissipate from the flushed skin. He stretched as he stood and walked to the window, looking out over the ornate gardens toward the harbor. It was too far to see the water from here, but the crisp air carried the tang of the sea. *May it carry Gerrard to me soon*, he prayed silently before turning away, stifling a sigh. Gerrard would come when he could and no sooner; in the meantime he had a patient to claim his attention.

Glancing again at the stock of medicines depleted from treating both Queen Anne and young Louis, Raúl wished he had been able to ride Martiya to the *comte*'s. The market square would be a long walk from the *comte*'s villa, and without a mount he would be dependent on the *comte*'s coach to take him to town. Or to return him to Christian's.

Deciding there was nothing for it but to impose on the *comte*'s servants at least this once, Raúl descended to the courtyard and found the coachman who had brought him there. To his relief, the man did not seem at all disturbed by Raúl's request and drove him back to Christian's lodgings with a minimum of fuss.

"Back already?" Christian asked. "I didn't expect to see you for a few more hours at least."

"How fares the boy?" Teodoro added, either ignorant of or ignoring the shirttail that hung free of his pantaloons. Raúl hid his smile; he could hardly begrudge the two their moments together.

"Poorly enough for his father's fears to be justified, but strong enough yet to recover so long as he is not treated as barbarously as the queen," he answered. "I came to fetch Martiya before refreshing my supply of herbs. It will take several days' doses before young Louis will be wholly out of danger."

"Do you want us to come with you?" Christian offered. "You are in good favor at court at the moment, but I know not if that will carry over to the villagers as well."

"The *comte* is most accommodating," Raúl replied. "He has instructed his servants to follow my requests as if they came directly from him. I do not know what more you or Teo could do to assist that they cannot. Besides," he added dryly, "I would not want Teo to accuse me again of interrupting your more private moments."

"You have never interrupted us needlessly," Christian reminded them all. "While we cherish our private moments, we would rather be interrupted than ignorant of events conspiring against us."

Teodoro raised an eyebrow but did not dispute Christian's statement. "Go gather the rest of your things—I will see Martiya saddled for you." Leaning forward, he murmured something into Christian's ear, pressing a kiss to the side of his throat before heading toward the stables.

Raúl considered asking Christian what Teodoro had said but ultimately decided against it. Some things were best shared only between lovers, something he and Teodoro had chosen long ago not to be. "Thank you for your unfailing support," he said instead. "It is reassuring knowing I am not alone here."

"If Gerrard hasn't returned, there is a reason," Christian insisted. "Do you want me to see what I can find out? I have connections in England who could find out the situation of his family, perhaps to give you a better idea of when to expect him."

Raúl shook his head. While he was grateful for the offer, he would not have Gerrard feel Raúl needed Christian's influence to track him down as if he could not be trusted. "He will return when he may. And I suspect the *conde*'s son will keep me occupied until that time."

"He *will* return," Christian asserted again. "Now, you should gather your things, as Teo undoubtedly has Martiya waiting for you impatiently in the courtyard by now."

After clasping Christian's hand in thanks, Raúl climbed the stairs to the bedchamber that held his things. He selected a few more days' garments, his comb, razor, and other necessities he had not taken the time to gather at the *comte*'s initial summons. Pausing a moment, he added the last of the wooden animals Gerrard had carved for the Rom children in Raúl's *familia*. Perhaps he would give it to young Louis, but just having it with him brought Gerrard a bit closer.

He shoved his things into a pack, then returned downstairs, finding Teodoro back in the main entryway, his arm around Christian's waist. "You may want to take Martiya for a run before you go to the market," Teodoro warned, "else he may not take well to being forced to mince along the crowded streets."

"Unlike some of my patients, he will do what I ask of him," Raúl answered with a smile. "I will return as soon as I can."

"We will be here," Teodoro said philosophically. "Watch your back, *amigo mío*, since you will not allow me to watch it for you. Your Gerrard would have a few choice words to say if I let you come to harm."

Raúl held back the retort that he was well able to fend for himself. While he had done so before and would doubtless do so again, it was good to have friends who cared as Teodoro and Christian did. "And since when have you begun fearing what Gerrard may say?" he replied instead.

Teodoro shrugged. "He is wise enough to know what he has in you. There is hope for him yet."

Raúl choked back a snort of laughter at Teodoro's taciturn response. He should have known better than to hope to win a true compliment in Gerrard's regard from Teodoro's lips. It would have to be enough that Teodoro accepted Gerrard's presence at Raúl's side. "I will be in touch," he said simply, clasping Teodoro's shoulder before mounting his horse and riding for town again.

His thoughts raced as he gave Martiya his head, letting the stallion run out some of his energy. He had no doubt he could rein his mount in when they reached the market, but there was no reason to make that battle of wills more pointed than necessary. By the time Raúl reached the square, Martiya had wearied of racing and slowed to a gentle trot, making it easy to stop and study the wares of the different vendors.

More than a few of them scowled as he passed their stalls, standing in the doorway to block his view or pulling back their wares as if he would leap off his stallion's back to seize them. He had long since grown accustomed to the ignorance that equated Rom with thieves and swindlers, though it made it no easier to bear. Spotting an herb seller's stall, he dismounted from Martiya and whispered quietly to the stallion, leaving him standing outside as he entered.

"You aren't worried someone will decide your fine horse is fair game?" the man behind the stall asked as Raúl stepped inside. "Or that some child will run by and spook him, causing an accident?"

At least he hadn't accused him of stealing a stallion that was obviously too good for a gypsy, as Raúl had heard more than once. "He will stay there until I return, though anyone trying to steal him may be missing a few fingers if he tries," Raúl said. "I am looking for willow bark, feverfew, cinquefoil, foxglove, pennyroyal, primrose, and sage— as much as you have."

"I have rarely met a man with such faith in his mount," the vendor replied, beginning to gather the herbs Raúl had listed. "These are in high demand at the moment. They say the court has a new healer who is buying up all he can find."

Hiding a smile, Raúl refrained from admitting that he was the "new court healer." He doubted the herb seller would believe it any more than he believed Martiya would stand where Raúl left him. "A wise healer indeed," he remarked as he pinched a comfrey leaf between his finger and thumb. Not as fresh as he'd hoped, but without the time to roam the woods outside town to find what he could himself, it would have to do.

The herb seller wrapped the herbs Raúl selected after weighing them on the scale and named an exorbitant price. Raúl raised an eyebrow in disbelief.

"You think your court healer will journey all the way here to buy herbs from you?" he asked. "I will pay you half that amount, which is still more than they are worth, or you can lose any chance of selling them before their potency fades." The *comte* would not cavil at the cost, he knew, but he was not about to let the shopkeeper take advantage of him.

The herb seller's eyes narrowed. "It would seem there's more to you than meets the eye, and not merely the quality of your steed. I might have some more of the comfrey leaf, more recently picked, if you had the gold to purchase it."

Raúl settled in to haggle in earnest. The herbalist countered with suggestions about the efficacy of his remedies, some of which Raúl agreed with and others he refuted, finding the man more astute than many sellers he'd met who dealt in superstition as much as any real understanding of their wares. Finally agreeing on a price that was not out of reason for as much of the herbs he needed as the shopkeeper could provide, he handed over several coins and secured the packets in the pouch at his waist. Perhaps if Louis's condition improved in a day or so, he could ride to the woods and gather some fresh herbs for himself. "A pleasure doing business with you," he told the shopkeeper with a bow of his head.

The man returned the gesture. "The pleasure was mine. Remember me, should the court need more of your good care."

As surprised at the herbalist's acceptance as he was at his insight, Raúl bowed more deeply. "I see you are a wise man as well. If you have the chance to obtain more of these, I may have need of them within the week."

"I will see what I can obtain."

Nodding his thanks, Raúl left the shop and mounted Martiya, who had not moved from where Raúl had left him. "The world is full of surprises," he murmured to the stallion, turning him back to the *comte*'s villa.

The surprise that greeted him when he returned was not as welcome.

"Isabeau has fallen ill," the *comte*'s butler told Raúl as he led him up the stairs to the boy's room. "And Louis has been crying for her and working himself into a state." Raúl could understand the boy's need for familiar faces around him, and despite the nursemaid's disapproving attitude, he was sure she was a comforting presence to young Louis. He feared that given her age, she would be far less resilient than his young patient.

"Let me see Louis first, and then I will look in on her," Raúl offered, grateful he had stopped at the market but recognizing he would need to make time to hunt for more herbs himself until the herbalist laid in a fresh supply.

"Raúl," Louis whined when he entered his room. "I want to see Isabeau."

"I know you do," Raúl said, "but she is ill like you were and must needs rest as you do." He checked the boy's temperature and peered into his eyes. "Have you been coughing much while I was gone?"

"Only a little," Louis replied.

Raúl suspected it was more than a little, but the boy was in less distress than he had been. "Rest a little longer while I check on Isabeau, and then I will return and perhaps we can play chess."

"I don't want to be alone," Louis complained. "I'm tired of staying in bed. I want to go in the garden and play with the puppy Mama gave me."

The boy's returning energy was a good sign, but he needed to recover more of his strength before letting him out of bed would be a good idea. "Perhaps you would like to play with this until I return," Raúl suggested, delving into his pack and pulling out the horse Gerrard had carved. "A friend of mine made it."

Louis took the toy and galloped it across the quilt on his bed. "You'll come back soon?"

"As soon as I see what ails Isabeau," Raúl agreed. "You want her to get well so she can come play with you again, don't you?"

When Louis nodded, Raúl ruffled his hair before leaving to find the butler. The older man led him up a back staircase to the much smaller servants' quarters in the upper story.

"What—what is he doing here?" the nursemaid gasped between coughs, pulling the blankets up around her throat.

"Nothing, if you want me to leave," Raúl replied, "but if you will let me examine you, perhaps I can help you feel better."

Isabeau looked at him suspiciously. "With your foreign ways and wicked concoctions, you're like to kill me instead."

Suppressing a sigh, Raúl reminded himself that she was speaking out of ignorance. "I have helped young Louis, and if you will allow me, I will do my best to help you also." When her countenance did not clear, he played on what he hoped was her genuine affection for the boy. "He is asking for you. The sooner you are back on your feet, the sooner you can see to him again."

"Oh, very well," Isabeau said with a huff. "Do your worst."

Raúl had no intention of doing that, but he would do his best by her. As he suspected, she had the same symptoms of the illness that had affected Louis earlier, without the benefit of the boy's age and good health. He prepared the same brew for her to drink and a poultice for her chest. "Drink all of this," he urged. "It will help with the fever and cough."

Isabeau scowled but emptied the glass between bouts of coughing, but she vehemently refused to allow him to apply the poultice. He prepared the cloth and permitted her to place it beneath her nightshift. Given her age and the fever he could see flushing her skin, he would have liked to set someone to watch over her, but while the *comte* could be convinced to leave a housemaid with his son, he would be unlikely to spare another to tend to the nurse. Raúl would have to look in on her as often as he could.

"Rest for now," he told her. "I'm going to check on Louis again and see if anyone else has fallen ill. I will return to see how you are doing in an hour or two."

"I'm sure I'll be fine," Isabeau said primly. "You needn't worry more about me."

"I'll make that decision for myself," Raúl replied with a bow of his head. He glanced toward the window, locked tightly shut, but he didn't suggest she open it. Even if he opened it before he left, she would surely close it the moment he was gone, and she needed to stay in bed, not wander around the room.

After setting a glass of water on the small table beside her bed, Raúl returned to Louis's room, which was significantly cooler than the stuffy space under the roof. He was pleased to see that at least here his instructions regarding fresh air had been heeded, the curtains fluttering in the warm breeze. Louis was still happily prancing the wooden horse over the blankets and making whinnying noises.

The *comte* came in on Raúl's heels. "He seems much better."

"He's young and strong," Raúl replied. "With time and care, he will be fine. I saw to Isabeau as well. You need to check and see if any of the other servants have fallen ill. If so, I should care for them as quickly as possible as well. We do not want the illness to spread."

"Papa!" Louis exclaimed, looking up from his playing. "Come sit with me!"

The *comte* raised an eyebrow at the carved stallion his son proudly presented to him but praised its attributes with a fond smile. Raúl watched them for a few moments before leaving them to their time together. If Louis were his only patient, he would feel no qualms about returning to Christian's villa for the night, but he had promised to check on Isabeau in a few hours, and he had not yet determined whether he might need to treat any of the *comte*'s other servants. Climbing the stairs, he decided to see if there was an empty room in the servants' quarters.

TWELVE

GERRARD AND Kellan rode north to Hawkins Hall the next morning, the messenger Gerrard had hired with Kellan's help having been dispatched to France with all haste. They reached the Hall the next evening just before supper. Gerrard had enough time to introduce Kellan to Herndon and Agatha before they ate. They hadn't planned on guests, but Gerrard insisted he and Kellan could eat the same meal as the servants. After all the years of eating with Raúl and the gypsies, he was hardly one to stand on ceremony.

"You are not the typical English baronet," Kellan commented as they sat down to their meal of shepherd's pie. "I can't imagine my brother or my cousin accepting such a simple meal."

Gerrard shrugged. "When you have been hungry and not known where your next meal was coming from, you gain a bit of perspective on such things."

Kellan frowned. "I understood that you and your father had fallen out, but surely he did not leave you in such dire circumstances?"

"If there is one thing you must learn about Hawkinses, it is that our pride and our tempers often lead us into trouble," Gerrard admitted. "My father refused to let me marry Rebecca, so I left. I had no way to support her on the road, even if she hadn't been nearing her time. She was safer here, with her family, than she would have been with me in those days. I took the clothing I could carry in a saddlebag and the horse I had bought out of my allowance. Until I returned a few months ago, I took nothing from the estate or from my father, though I sent money for Randall whenever I could."

"That alone sets you apart from any other noble I have met," Kellan observed. "How then did you keep yourself until your return to England?"

"I saved the life of Viscount Aldwych," Gerrard explained. "His father, the Duke of Ranleigh, seemed to believe that deserved a favor in return and hired me to escort his son around the Continent. By the grace of God and the viscount's good will, I survived for two years, until the viscount found another protector. After that, I traveled with a band of merchants, offering my sword and whatever other skills could be of use."

"You are a resourceful man, Sir Gerrard. I suspect you will need such resourcefulness to deal with the conditions on your estate, if it was affected as severely as the tenants on my brother's land."

"Now you understand why I need someone here I can trust while I travel back to France," Gerrard said. "We have rebuilt the cottages that were damaged so that everyone who survived has a safe place to live, and we have brought in an apothecary and a grocer to replace the ones who did not survive, but we are severely lacking men to tend the fields and bring in the crops for winter."

"As are most of the estates I have had contact with," Kellan concurred. "The disease was so widespread, none have workers to spare."

Gerrard thought again of Raúl and the gypsies, all healthy and strong in France. If they could be persuaded to return with him, the harvest would be much easier, but first he had to be free to leave to rejoin them. The two months he had been gone seemed far longer than that. "If my trip is successful, we may have some respite. As I mentioned, I traveled with a band of wandering merchants. If they could be persuaded to return with me, as is my hope, we would have easily another twenty able-bodied men, plus women and children who could help with the harvest, but I doubt many will come if they must rely only on a written message. I would have far greater chance of persuading them in person."

"Then you must show me what needs to be done to allow you to leave," Kellan answered, mopping up the last of the gravy from his plate with a piece of bread. "Perhaps tonight you can show me your books, and in the morning I would like to visit the village with you. It will be easier to work with your tenants while you are gone if I have met them and they have seen us together before you leave."

"That sounds like an outstanding plan," Gerrard said. "If you have finished, we can take our port in the office instead of the drawing room and examine the books."

He caught Kellan's look of surprise and shrugged. "You must remember that my life has not been that of the typical baronet. I spent two years as the constant companion of Viscount Aldwych and then spent nearly six years with a band of gypsies. I have forgotten the meaning of class and choose to base my association on the character of the man, not his birthright."

Kellan's youthful face broke into a smile. "A band of gypsies! My cousin did not relate that part of your story. You will have to tell me more over our port."

Gerrard suspected Kellan would run out of interest before Gerrard ran out of stories, but it would be a relief to speak of them, even if he had to couch his adventures in general terms lest he reveal too much. "That's because Sir Thomas doesn't know that part of the story." He led Kellan upstairs to his office and poured them both a glass of port from the decanter on the sideboard. "I met Raúl and his band after Raúl's best friend tried to kill me and stole Christian—that is, Viscount Aldwych— out from under my nose."

The sip of port Kellan had taken turned into an inelegant sputter. "Since the viscount obviously survived to become ambassador to France, you must have won him back again," he said once he had recovered his aplomb.

"No, he decided his kidnapper was a better protector than I could ever be," Gerrard said. "Ciéza has been his bodyguard ever since, and since their acquaintance saved the life of King Philip of Spain and helped stop a plot to kill Louis XIII in France, I think few would disagree with me. For my part, it brought Raúl to me—to my attention, that is—and I have been grateful for that ever since."

"Gypsies for the most part are not well regarded here, though it seems your friend and his companions are not common gypsies." Kellen raised a hand before Gerrard could protest. "I did not say I share the opinion, but you should not be surprised to hear it, and not only from your tenants, should your friends indeed decide to travel to England."

"They are no better regarded anywhere else," Gerrard said with a sigh, "but I hope here, where I might expect to have some small influence on people's opinions, to give them a place to call home if they so desire. Their ways are different from the ways of those they offer their services to, but being different does not make them evil or laggard or any of the other vices of which they are often accused. Christian received credit for saving King Philip, but he could not have done it without the help of the gypsies. M. de Tréville, captain of the Royal Musketeers, received credit for foiling the plot to assassinate the king, but the musketeer who brought him the news would not have lived to tell the tale without Raúl's skills at healing. I don't expect to change the world, Kellan, but I would very much like to make one corner of it safe for my friends."

"Then I hope I shall have the chance to meet the men who have gained so much of your regard." Kellan drained his glass and set it to one side. "Now let us have a look at your books and see what I might take care of for you so you may return to them."

Kellan's acceptance bolstered Gerrard's confidence, and so he drew out the ledgers from his father's desk. "My father let his man of business go after my departure and did not retain another one. I fear we may never make sense of some of this, but that is less of a concern to me than making sure my decisions going forward are sound ones. I want my tenants housed and fed and the use of my land to support them and me as sensibly as possible. Everything else is secondary."

After poring over the documents for some time in silence, Kellan nodded. "The entries stop once your father fell sick, but before that he kept good records. I suppose that is not too surprising, given his reputation as a man fonder of keeping his coin than of spending it." He tapped the ledger thoughtfully. "Have you kept track of what you have spent since your return? Even without the most current quarter's receipts, there is sufficient here to see you through several poor harvests if need be, though I hope it will not come to that."

"From what I have seen as I have ridden around the estate, the harvest will not be poor if we can tend the crops and reap it in the fall," Gerrard said. "The fields are planted, and all appears to be in order. Obviously we must not count the gain until we have the crops in, but all the auspices are good."

"That is well," Kellan replied. "If you can provide me with the rents for the last quarter and the receipts for what you have outlaid in repairs, I will bring the ledgers up to date."

"I didn't collect the rents last quarter," Gerrard said. "I returned home to chaos, to people dead and families grieving, and everyone worried they would be turned out of the only homes they've ever known. I won't be that kind of landowner. They do the work, not me. If they can pay next quarter, we will collect then. If they have not yet recovered from the plague and the damage from the storms, then we will wait another quarter. I will not have my people turned out of their homes."

Kellan straightened in his chair, though his hazel eyes warmed as he held Gerrard's gaze. "I did not mean to imply any criticism of your decisions, Sir Gerrard. In truth, the reason my brother and I found ourselves so often at loggerheads after our father's death was due to his intent to wring every penny he could from the estate, at whatever cost to its tenants. I believe your methods, while costly in the short term, will pay far greater yields in times to come. I but need to ensure I have recorded an accurate total so I may keep the accounts going forward."

"I apologize for raising my voice," Gerrard said, flushing a little as he realized how easily he could have alienated the one person poised to let him return to Raúl's side. "My temper has been known to get the better of me on occasion. In my defense, at least this time I lost it defending my tenants rather than for less valid reasons. Most of the receipts are here in the desk." He drew out a sheaf of papers. "There may be a few in my chambers. I warned you I was in need of a man of business. I can barely remember to ask for a receipt, much less bring it here and record it in the ledgers."

"These will get me started." Kellan accepted the papers and flipped through them briefly, nodding to himself. "I will review them tonight and make note of any questions I may have. Bring me any others you may find, if you will. I shall draft a letter for you to your bank, naming me your man of business so that I may validate your funds and draw on them at need while you are gone. That will put your finances in order before you go, and I will keep all in order for you to review when you return. How else may I assist you?"

"For tonight, that will be more than enough," Gerrard said. "Tomorrow we will ride the estate, and I can show you what has been done and what must still be done. You will have to oversee the work while I'm gone. The villagers are eager to have everything set to rights, but that does not mean they always have the means to do so. I have done my best to address the needs they have brought to my attention, but other needs may well arise I have not taken into consideration. I do not want to lose people to the winter weather if it can be prevented with a little application of money and effort now. Shall we ride after breakfast in the morning?"

"I am at your convenience," Kellan replied.

"You may not want to say that until you hear your options for the night," Gerrard said with a self-deprecating smile. "I have spent my time and energy making sure the villagers all had roofs over their heads. The only rooms in the Hall that are habitable are mine and the servants' quarters. None of the guest rooms have been arranged since the plague. The other option is to return to Finchingfield, to the posting inn there, though I cannot swear the accommodations will be any better than the servants' rooms here, so small is the inn."

"A room in the servants' quarters will be fine for tonight," Kellan answered. "It is not so long since I shared a dormitory while at school. Perhaps tomorrow we can look for a likely cottage in the village to house me while you are on the continent."

"That is another problem," Gerrard explained. "The house intended for the estate manager is occupied. We had a family with no home and a home with no occupant. We will prepare a room here in the Hall for you, but as you said, it will have to be tomorrow. Thank you for your understanding. I know we are not the typical situation."

"As I well know I am not a typical estate manager, we should deal together admirably," Kellan replied. "Now, if you will spare me a candle and show me to the servants' quarters, I would like to dig deeper into the books before morning."

The following day dawned cool, not that anyone but Gerrard was up to see the dawn. He saw no reason to disturb the servants at that hour, when years on the Continent had taught him to see to himself. They would rise and breakfast would be ready in a couple of hours, but Gerrard enjoyed the quiet hours before then, time when he didn't have to be Sir Gerrard but could simply be himself.

Hiring Kellan brought him closer to being able to reclaim that life, or at least to being able to travel to France and reclaim Raúl. He hoped Raúl would be willing to return to England with him. Gerrard had not allowed himself to dwell on his home during the years of his absence, but he had missed it. He had missed Agatha's nagging and Herndon's unfailing support, even when it was masked by disapproval. He'd missed the cool mornings—nothing cool about summer in Spain ever—and snow in the winter. He'd missed the green hills and deep forests. And, he was discovering, he had missed the Hall itself, the sense of being connected to the past and a future that was greater than himself.

Now he just had to convince Raúl they could make a life together here.

With a sigh of frustration at the long separation, he turned and dressed for the day. The sooner he had Kellan established, the sooner he could find Raúl and resolve the tension inside him.

When he made his way into the kitchen to see when breakfast would be ready, he found Kellan already there, to his surprise, teasing the cook as if he had lived there all his life.

"Good morning, Sir Gerrard," Kellan greeted him with a smile while sneaking a piece of bacon from the platter Mrs. Cullen had just set on the table. "Did the scent of this wonderful food lure you here as it did me?"

"It lures me here every morning," Gerrard replied with a smile. "Mrs. Cullen spoils me with her cooking. Did you pass the night in reasonable comfort?"

"Perfectly well, though I suspect I will need to walk to the village to work off all the food I shall consume at breakfast." He smiled at the cook, who blushed like a maiden.

"You need some fattening up, sir. You're near as thin as Sir Gerrard has gotten. Don't know what kind of victuals he had to live on in those foreign parts, but now that he's home in England, he'll always have a decent meal on the table."

"And will always appreciate it," Gerrard said, leaning in to kiss the cook's rosy cheek before joining Kellan at the table. "We won't be back for lunch, I don't think, Mrs. Cullen. I need to show Mr. Beecham the estate, so I imagine we will lunch in the village or at the posting inn, which means we shall be famished for dinner since they won't be able to compete with your cooking."

"Never you mind, sir. I have a fine roast on hand to prepare for this evening, and a nice pudding to go with it, and peas fresh from the garden, and some of the currant cake you like so much for dessert."

"That sounds like a feast fit for a king," Gerrard said as he began to eat. After a few bites, he turned to Kellan. "I thought we'd start with the fields so you can see what's planted and where and then go on to the village so I can introduce you around. Is there aught else you need to see while we are out today?"

"Only to meet anyone I will need to deal with in your absence," Kellan answered. "It will be easier if they see me in your company to believe I have your confidence and your delegation until you return."

"We will visit the shopkeepers in the village," Gerrard agreed. "Many of them have been in the village all their lives, though not the grocer or apothecary." He finished his breakfast and took a few more sips of tea. "When you're ready."

"At your convenience, Sir Gerrard." Kellan rose as well, bowing his thanks to the cook. "Until this evening, Mrs. Cullen."

Gerrard led Kellan out to the stables. The grooms came running, apologizing for not having the horses ready, but Gerrard waved them aside. "Take care of Mr. Beecham's horse. I'll see to Nubarrón myself."

He saddled his mount and joined Kellan outside.

"I've brought your account books up to date," Kellan said once they had mounted and turned their horses toward the fields. "I will need to confirm the amounts with your banker to be sure we have not missed any expenditures that were unrecorded, but barring anything major gone missing, your finances are in good shape."

"That is reassuring," Gerrard said. "We have planted as many fields as we could manage, so as long as we can bring in the harvest, we should have supplies to hold us through the winter."

"I shall see about finding additional laborers during your absence," Kellen said.

Gerrard nodded and turned Nubarrón toward the farms. His tenants were already out in their fields, checking progress and fending off the weeds that would steal precious water from the wheat and oats and other crops. They spent the next two hours crisscrossing the estate until the midday sun and growing heat drove them toward the village. Gerrard silently cursed the trappings of his rank that kept him from stripping off his doublet, but he had learned his lessons at his father's side. The villagers needed to see him as the head of the estate. He had bucked those lessons at times since he had been home, but today would not be one of those days. "Perhaps a pint at the tavern to refresh ourselves before we make the rounds of the village?" he suggested.

"A cool mug of ale would not go amiss," Kellan agreed, pushing his hair back from his forehead. "I had forgotten what thirsty work it is to make the rounds of an estate of this size."

"Then we shall start our introductions with Warren, the blacksmith, where we can leave our horses, and then go on to the tavern and Cowden, the tavern keeper," Gerrard said, leading the way through the village to the forge where the clank of hammer on anvil greeted them. Nubarrón shook his head at the sound, but Gerrard ignored him, swinging down and leading the horse into the cool dimness of the stable.

"Warren!" he called when the sounds of smithing paused.

"Sir Gerrard!" Wiping his hands on his apron, the blacksmith walked into the stable. "'Tis good to see you again, sir." He glanced curiously at Kellan. "Mistress Agatha did not accompany you today?"

"Not today," Gerrard said, smiling at the thought of the burly blacksmith being sweet on his old nurse. "Warren, this is Mr. Beecham, my new man of business. We're making our rounds so everyone can meet him."

"I'm pleased to make your acquaintance," Kellan said, offering a hand that was dwarfed in the smith's larger one. "I have been meaning to have my horse reshod, but while living in London I have not found a smithy I trust."

"You leave him to me, Mr. Beecham, and I'll soon set him to rights," Warren assured them. "If you're planning to have your luncheon at the inn, I'll have him shod before you're ready to ride back to the Hall."

"We will be in the village for a couple of hours at least," Gerrard affirmed. "You won't find a better blacksmith in the area," he added for Kellan's benefit. "You should let him take care of him for you."

"Gladly," Kellan agreed. "After all, if he can handle that great animal you ride, my Decker will be no trouble for him at all."

Gerrard chuckled as they left the smithy. "No, the real test of his skill isn't Nubarrón. Big as he is, he has a placid disposition for the most part. The real test will be putting new shoes on Martiya. I have known Raúl for almost six years, and not once in that time could he find a blacksmith who could put new shoes on his stallion without Raúl holding his head the entire time. The inn is this way."

Kellan's keen eyes took in the buildings that lined the street as they crossed it to the small inn. A woman coming out of the bakery stared at them for a moment before dropping a curtsey to Gerrard. "I take it you are not in the habit of bringing visitors about," he said with a smile as they entered the taproom.

"When would I have had time?" Gerrard replied with a shake of his head. "Since I have been back, my sole focus has been setting things to rights after the plague." He only hoped the villagers could grow used to the sight of him with another man. If they couldn't, Kellan would have a much harder job than he'd anticipated when he'd agreed to come to Hawkins Hall. "If I know the tenants on my estate, you will not be a visitor for long. Then Agatha will fuss over you the way she does over me, and everyone else will presume on your long friendship, and you'll be just another part of the fabric of this place."

Before Kellan could answer, the innkeeper approached them, a smile beaming from his face when he recognized Gerrard. "Sir Gerrard, welcome, welcome! Please, come take a seat. What can I bring you and your friend, sir? A few pints of homebrew? The missus has some chickens fresh from the spit if you'd like something to eat, or there's some ham from last night and some cheese, or both if you'd like."

"What say you, Beecham?" Gerrard asked. "Have you burned off Mrs. Cullen's breakfast yet?"

"I wouldn't say no to a pint of homebrew to wash down some ham and cheese," Kellan replied with a grin. "My size notwithstanding, I have what my old nurse used to call 'a healthy appetite.'"

Gerrard chuckled. "That would be two of us."

They took a seat at one of the tables, and the innkeeper brought them two pints of ale. Gerrard lifted his glass in Kellan's direction. "To future collaborations."

Kellan raised his pint in kind. "And to my cousin Thomas, who has done me a good turn in bringing me to your notice. Perhaps I am speaking too soon, but I believe we shall deal excellently together."

As long as Kellan could accept Gerrard's association with Raúl, not just as friends, but as partners. "I believe you are right."

The innkeeper had just put their plates in front of them when Turner, the apothecary, came in. "Sir Gerrard, well met," Turner said, coming over to their table. "Thank you for the supplies. They arrived this morning. I believe I have the best-stocked apothecary outside of London."

"Good," Sir Gerrard said. "Turner, this is Mr. Beecham, my new man of business. If you should need something and I'm not available, please speak with him instead."

"Mr. Turner," Kellan said, rising to his feet and taking the man's hand. "I saw the effects of the plague on my brother's lands. If there is aught I can do to assist you in preserving the health of Sir Gerrard's tenants, you have but to ask."

"A pleasure, Mr. Beecham. At the moment Sir Gerrard has seen to my supplies, but if I run low, I will let one of you know. Sir Gerrard has been most clear about his intention for my apothecary to be well stocked."

"Have a seat, Turner. I'll pull you a pint as soon as I've seen to Sir Gerrard and Mr. Beecham," the tavern keeper called to the apothecary, bustling up to Gerrard's table. "Is all well, sir? Can I bring you each another ale?"

Gerrard cocked an eyebrow at Kellan, who shook his head. "No more for me if I am to stay on my horse. Is there anyone else we should visit here in the village? Or at the surrounding farms?"

"There is the grocer, the baker, and the tailor," Sir Gerrard said, "but we can meet them later as well. While I hope to be able to leave for France in a week or two, I was not planning on leaving tomorrow." He wished he could. He wanted nothing more than to drop everything and hie back to Raúl's side as fast as Nubarrón could carry him, but if the day had reminded him of anything, it was of how much depended on him and his responsible management of the estate. Spending today introducing Kellan around the village brought him one step closer to being able to follow his heart.

"And I will return on my own also, though it is good for the townsfolk to see you with me and know I have your confidence. It will induce their confidence in me as well, until such time as I can prove myself to them."

"I have no doubt that you will," Gerrard assured him. When they had finished their lunch and Turner his ale, Gerrard left a coin on the table to pay for their meal. As they exited the common room of the inn to return to the stables, a woman in a flounced dress, more elaborate than any other they had seen in the village, stepped up to them.

"Sir Gerrard," she said warmly, dropping a curtsey. "How happy I was to hear you had returned to us. And who is your companion?" she asked with an arch smile.

"Mr. Kellan Beecham, this is Mrs. Johnson, the wife of our local tailor," Gerrard said. "As you can see from her lovely frock, we are blessed with a most talented tailor. Mr. Beecham is my new man of business."

"My pleasure, madam," Kellan said with a bow. "I shall avail myself of your husband's services once I am established in the community. My wardrobe is sadly deficient in riding apparel, and I can see I must quickly remedy that lack."

"Our shop is just past the baker's at the end of the lane. My husband will be happy to provide whatever you need," Mrs. Johnson said. "A pleasure to meet you, Mr. Beecham. Sir Gerrard, you should visit us more often."

"I shall be a devotee of your husband's as soon as my business on the Continent is settled," Gerrard replied. "Now if you will excuse us, we must attend to the rest of our day."

Mrs. Johnson curtseyed again and bustled on down the lane. "The whole town will know your name by the end of the day," Gerrard said as they headed back toward the smithy. "Mrs. Johnson is the biggest gossip in the village."

"Then I shall make it my goal to charm her, though I suspect ordering several pair of breeches from her husband will serve as well," Kellan answered, a smile on his lips. "She is definitely a woman whose good opinion I will need to cultivate."

"Indeed," Gerrard said. "Just do not let her think you are in search of a wife, or she will introduce you to every eligible lass from here to London."

"I have no objection to meeting the local lasses," Kellan assured him. "Though I would prefer to establish myself before settling down with any one of them. I spent enough time with my nephew to know I would like children of my own someday, but I need to be able to provide for a family before that day."

"Then we should return to the Hall and ready a room for you," Gerrard said. "It won't quite be a home of your own, but it will be a start."

"I have no objection to remaining in the servants' quarters if you want to be off to France at once," Kellan said. "If you will let me know which room you would like to assign me, I can make the room habitable while you are away."

It was a tempting thought. He missed Raúl miserably, but his sense of responsibility demanded he see Kellan properly settled before he disappeared for an indefinite amount of time. "If we both work at it, we will have the room habitable within a matter of days."

"Let us start at once, then," Kellan replied. "I can see you are anxious about the business that takes you to France. And the sooner you are away, the sooner you can return."

"Thank you," Gerrard said as they retrieved their horses from the blacksmith.

The ride back to the Hall was considerably warmer than the ride out, the sun having reached its zenith, and Gerrard was grateful for the coolness of the Hall when they walked back inside. "Let us go upstairs. We'll find a room that will suit."

They climbed the stairs to the second floor, and Gerrard led the way down the hall to the room where he had spent his childhood. It was large enough to be comfortable and central enough to be accessible while still far enough away from the master bedroom for both of them to have their privacy.

"This will be a fine chamber with a bit of scrubbing." Kellan glanced around in appraisal. "There is plenty of space for a table and chair for me to work at, if we can find one in a storeroom somewhere, and the window offers a grand view of the tenant farms."

"We will find whatever you need," Gerrard said. "Between the attics and all the rooms currently standing empty, there is plenty to choose from. The schoolroom had chairs and tables if nothing else. The view is particularly grand in the summer when the sun sets directly behind those hills."

"Then it is decided," Kellan agreed. "We can open the casement overnight to air out the mustiness, and move the bedframe into the hall or another room in the morning. I will speak with Agatha to arrange for hot water and soap and cloths for cleaning. Perhaps we can look through the attics to see if there is furniture to suit while the light lasts, and after that it will be nearly time for dinner."

"The attics will be hot, as bright as the sun is today, so you may wish to remove your doublet. I promise not to be offended, if you will promise the same," Gerrard said with smile. "I have few enough doublets these days to want to ruin the ones I do have."

"Informality will never offend me," Kellan said, removing his own doublet and then hanging it upon the nearest bedpost. "In truth, I have been thinking of how cool it would feel to sit in my shirtsleeves in my chamber for a few minutes before dinner. It is a pleasure to feel a bit of breeze, even if we will soon swelter in the heat of the attic."

Gerrard laughed. "I have rarely worn a doublet except against the cold since I left England, so you can imagine how constrained I feel. Indeed, in the heat of the summer, even shirtsleeves were often optional. Gypsies are not the most formal of people. Let us finish sweltering, and then we can both relax in the cool breeze before we must satisfy Agatha and Herndon by putting on our doublets again."

Gerrard led Kellan upstairs to the attics he had spent many a childhood hour exploring. He and James had played at knights and pirates and all other manner of adventures among the covered furniture and chests and crates of outdated or outgrown clothes. "If memory serves, we put the tables and chairs from the schoolroom at the far end of the attic."

After rummaging through several holland-covered mounds, they uncovered a table and two chairs Kellan decided would suit. "And if I ever tire of dealing with the estate accounts, I can amuse myself trying to decide which of the letters scratched into the surface are yours," he told Gerrard with a grin. Wiping a runnel of sweat from his temple, he frowned at a streak of dust on his shirtsleeve. "I shall have to rinse out a shirt and hope it dries overnight, or I will have nothing clean to wear tomorrow."

"Take it off before it gets more soiled," Gerrard said, stripping his own shirt over his head. "You will still have to wash the sleeve, but that will dry faster than the entire shirt."

Kellan loosened his neckcloth and unfastened the buttons at his wrists before following suit. "I fear my build is no match for yours," he said regretfully, eying Gerrard's chest. "However you passed your time on the Continent, it was not poring over books as I have done."

"No, it was not," Gerrard agreed. He lifted several more covers, looking for a nicer armoire than the one currently in his old room. "Much of it was spent working alongside the gypsies or practicing swordplay with Raúl and his friends. I have learned more than a trick or two from his old compatriot. Ciéza was a soldier, a street brawler who will use any means necessary to win a fight. When you're fighting to defend the one you love, considerations like fair play seem of less importance."

Kellan shook his head. "I am sure that is true. How different your life is than what I have known! I imagine you must have quite a few stories to tell."

"Saving the life of the king of Spain?" Gerrard joked. "Or the king of France? Though that was hardly our everyday life."

"You will have to tell me more—that is, if you would," Kellan asked, lifting one of the chairs free of the jumble of other furniture.

"Though you may inspire me to follow you to France. Such excitement is not to be found within the pages of account books."

"The excitement was mine only peripherally," Gerrard admitted. "The story in Spain is truly Ambassador Blackwood's, and the story in France that of three of the king's musketeers, but I would be happy to regale you with my small part over dinner."

Kellan's muscles flexed as he pushed a couch aside to pull the table free as well, drawing Gerrard's attention. Raúl was similarly slender, but Kellan had none of Raúl's underlying steely strength. Gerrard could appreciate the man's appearance, but Kellan exerted none of the fascination that the sight of Raúl's bare chest had on Gerrard's senses.

"You travel in circles I can only imagine," Kellan remarked, pushing his damp hair back from his forehead. "The most exciting day of my life was when my father took me to court to be presented to the king. I did not even exchange words with him, and you speak so casually of saving the lives of royalty. I wonder whether you will not find life at Hawkins Hall deadly dull in comparison."

"Raúl will provide all the excitement I need," Gerrard said, the words slipping out before he could think better of them.

Kellan settled the second chair on the floor and paused. "You have spoken frequently of your friend Raúl," he said finally, his voice tentative. "It is he you go to find in France?"

"Yes," Gerrard said. He hadn't intended to say anything quite so bluntly, but if he was going to lose Kellan over this, better to do it now, before the man had blended into the fabric of the village. "It is my most fervent hope that he will return to Hawkins Hall with me."

"Then I hope so, too, for I look forward to meeting him." Kellan hesitated again. "Though if your village is any like my brother's, I fear you may find not all are well-disposed toward strangers, especially…" He seemed to be searching for a word before finally concluding "… gypsies."

Raúl being a gypsy would be the least of their problems, Gerrard feared, but he had already said more than he had intended. "I have spent six years watching him win people over. I choose to hope he will charm the villagers here as easily. If, of course, he agrees to return. He may choose not to leave France, or he may return to Spain." The thought filled him with dread, but he had to accept that Raúl might not be willing to upend his life because Gerrard's life had taken an unexpected turn.

The need to be off to France grew more urgent as his thoughts spiraled downward. "We should move this downstairs so we can dress for dinner."

Kellan picked up both their shirts and tucked them under his arm before maneuvering the two chairs seat to seat and lifting them. "Can you manage the table alone, or will we need to make a second trip?"

"I'll manage," Gerrard said, lifting the table and following Kellan down the stairs. He wasn't entirely sure Kellan understood the depth of his relationship with Raúl, but he hadn't run screaming at the suggestion that they were more than casual acquaintances.

As he carried the table down the stairs, he resolved to leave for France in a day or two, a week at the most.

THIRTEEN

TEODORO PACED the confines of Christian's drawing room, the click of his boot heels echoing on the marble floor. "It's been more than a week since your *comte* sent for Raúl, and beyond his returning the first day for more clothes, we have not seen or heard from him since. Something is amiss."

"He is hardly 'my' *comte*," Christian said mildly. "I met him at court, but that means little enough, as well you know. You also know Raúl would not likely leave once we heard there is sickness in the village."

"But not without sending word," Teodoro countered, his dark eyes narrowed in concern. "Knowing Raúl, he will have run low on his healing supplies by now, and even the herb sellers in Madrid could not always provide for his needs, let alone the market in a small village such as Saint-Rémy de Provence. He would have written to ask our assistance in finding more, if nothing else."

"What would you have me do?" Christian asked seriously, Teodoro's concern for their friend triggering his own alarm. "I can send a messenger to the *comte*, but I know not it if it will get through if the sickness has continued to spread. If Saint-Rémy is quarantined, it could be that no one is being allowed entrance or exit."

Before Teodoro could answer, the doors to the drawing room opened and Javier, Christian's secretary, entered. "Pardon, your Excellency, but a servant has arrived from the *comte* du Saint-Rémy de Provence with a letter for you." As Javier had been the recipient of Raúl's healing skills himself upon his rescue with Teodoro from the Inquisition, Christian was not surprised when he lingered as the liveried messenger handed him the missive. Doubtless he too hoped to hear news of their friend.

"Javier, would you please show the messenger to the kitchens for some refreshment while we see what the *comte* has to say?" Christian said, taking the letter and waiting for the servant to leave before breaking the seal.

Javier glanced from Christian to Teodoro, who gave a minute nod before Javier led the messenger from the room. "I am not the only one worried about Raúl," he said while Christian scanned the letter.

"I know that," Christian said, not looking up from his reading. "Javier will be back before I can finish this, I'm sure." He skimmed a little farther and stopped. "Perhaps you should fetch Esteban as well. This is more serious than I had thought."

"What has happened?" Teodoro demanded, crossing the room to Christian's side. "Is Raúl ill?"

Christian shook his head, but before he could speak, the doors opened again to both Javier and Esteban. "Is it news from Raúl?" Esteban asked, his worried gaze moving from Teodoro to Christian.

"Of Raúl," Christian amended. "It would seem the peasants in France have as much tolerance for gypsies as those in Spain. The *comte* writes that he has confined Raúl to his castle for Raúl's protection because the villagers have begun demanding a scapegoat for the worsening illness. While the *comte* knows Raúl has done nothing but help, he fears to allow Raúl to leave lest the townspeople seek revenge upon him despite his innocence."

"How can the villagers think Raúl had anything to do with bringing the illness?" Esteban protested. "He has done nothing but try to help them!"

"Fear and ignorance," Javier answered. "It was no different when I lived on the *conde* de la Roche's estate. When plague swept through the farmlands, people blamed the Jews, the gypsies—anyone and anything to try to find a reason for the sickness."

"Fortunately the *comte* seems to have the good sense not to believe their superstitions," Christian said, hoping to reassure the others and to keep Teodoro from rushing off rashly. "He says Raúl is welcome as his guest for as long as it takes for it to be safe to leave."

"Guest?" Teodoro snapped, scowling. "Raúl is his prisoner, no matter what polite words he uses to disguise it." He turned to Javier. "Have the groom saddle my horse. I will relieve the *comte* of the necessity for seeing to Raúl's 'safety.'"

"Teo," Christian said, rubbing his hand along Teodoro's arm. "We have the ball in honor of the queen's birthday tomorrow. We cannot be absent from court. Raúl will be safe for a few days longer, and once the birthday festivities have ended, we can ride together to Saint-Rémy and see what might be worked out."

"¡*Joder!*" Teodoro spat, his eyes sparking with anger. "The queen will survive her birthday without my presence. You may trust this *comte* with Raúl's life, but I do not. We are far more capable of seeing to his safety if such is needed."

Christian had not spent six years in Teodoro's near-constant presence without learning when not to push his fiery lover. "If you will not wait for me, then take Aristide with you. He may hide behind the tabard of a musketeer, but he is the *comte*'s equal in rank. His presence may indeed be more useful than mine."

Christian could see Teodoro's temper cool at his acquiescence. "If he is willing and his duties permit it, I would be glad for his company." Teodoro had spent enough time sparring with Aristide, Christian knew, that he would recognize his value as an ally should the *comte* prove reluctant to release Raúl to them. "But with or without him, I ride within the hour."

Christian grabbed Teodoro's shoulders, squeezing tightly. "Do not do anything rash," he ordered. "While I want to see Raúl safe as much as you do, I want you safe most of all. Do not come back to me with more rents in your skin. You have scars enough already."

"Most of them healed thanks to Raúl," Teodoro reminded him, raising Christian's chin with a knuckle to soften the comment with a kiss.

Christian only hoped Raúl would be around to heal any new ones.

TEODORO RODE into the courtyard of the building M. de Tréville, commander of the Royal Musketeers, occupied while the court resided in Tarascon. As he hoped, a contingent of musketeers filled the open area, practicing or taking their ease. While he did not see Aristide's distinctive leonine countenance among the group, he did spot two others he was well familiar with. "*Hola*—Léandre, Perrin!"

"Bonjour, Teodoro!" Léandre called, lowering his sword and moving toward Teodoro as he dismounted. "Come to teach Perrin here how to use his sword for more than batting at flies?"

"You had no complaints about how I wielded my sword last night," Perrin retorted softly enough for only Léandre and Teodoro to hear him. The sharp repartee between the two men was enough to tease a short laugh from Teodoro, but his mission was too serious for a battle of wits.

"Perhaps another day," Teodoro answered. "Do you know where I can find Aristide?"

"Practicing some swordplay of his own, no doubt," Perrin replied with a wink. "What new adventure is afoot?"

"No adventure, merely a ride to Saint-Rémy de Provence," Teodoro answered. "I hoped Aristide might accompany me."

"If we can pry him away, I'm sure he will," Perrin said. "Léandre and I will fetch him and meet you back at the ambassador's residence, half an hour hence? Or would you prefer to help us roust him from his bed?"

"Roust him or join him?" Teodoro asked, exchanging a glance with Léandre. "In either case it is a pleasure I must decline."

"Benoît would take his hammer to me if I tried," Perrin replied.

"And I'd plant my foot up your ass if you tried," Léandre threatened. "We none of us need to play those games anymore." He turned back to Teodoro, his attitude sobering. "All of us are off duty for the next few days. We'll ride with you on this not-an-adventure."

"In case it should become an adventure," Perrin added. "You never know when an extra sword might come in handy."

"We have proved that oft enough," Teodoro agreed.

THE POUNDING on the door was the only warning Aristide and Benoît had before the outer door to their rooms flew open. "Aristide, roust yourself from Benoît's embrace. Teodoro has brought us a new adventure."

Benoît groaned, rolling off Aristide and pulling the covers over them to preserve some degree of modesty, doubtless not willing to give Perrin and Léandre more fodder for their teasing. "I thought you locked the door," he murmured with a final kiss to Aristide's jaw.

"I had thought us past the need to do so." The sheet fell off Aristide's shoulder as he rose on an elbow to glower at the other two musketeers.

"Don't blame me—I knocked," Léandre countered, clouting Perrin on the shoulder. "Haven't I managed to teach you anything?"

"Monogamy," Perrin replied immediately. "Besides, it's not like we haven't seen Aristide naked before."

"You haven't seen me," Benoît retorted. "Wait in the other room. We will dress and join you in a moment."

Aristide pulled Benoît back into his arms without waiting to see if Léandre and Perrin obeyed. "I am sorry, but I'd best see what they are on about before they do anything rash. We will resume this later," he added, sealing the promise with a possessive kiss.

"Go," Benoît said, running his hands down Aristide's back to squeeze his ass before releasing him. They had enough experience with Léandre and Perrin's schemes, whether Teodoro was involved or not, to know not to tempt fate. "I will be here when you return."

The caress was enough to coax Aristide to remain in bed, Léandre and Perrin be damned, but Teodoro's involvement spurred him to action. The Spaniard was not one to ask for help lightly; if he needed them now, the situation, whatever it was, would be a serious one. After claiming a final kiss, he stood and pulled on his breeches before striding bare-chested into the main room of the small apartment he and Benoît shared.

Aristide did not expect Benoît to volunteer to accompany them. M. de Tréville had arranged for him to travel with the musketeers who accompanied the king, affirming he did not trust the state of his men's weapons to unknown blacksmiths, but Benoît claimed he really had the captain's romantic nature to thank for his presence there. He freely admitted he had no illusions about his ability to help in a fight, though Aristide did his best to convince Benoît not to belittle the services he did provide the company.

"So what is this new adventure that cannot wait for me to rise from bed to discuss?" Aristide asked, stretching his shoulders with a yawn.

"It's not our fault you're still in bed in the middle of the day," Perrin retorted. "Or did he lure you back with the offer of his sweet ass?"

Léandre clouted Perrin on the back of the head before Aristide could answer. "What Aristide does in bed is no longer your concern, *chipie*. Keep it up and I'll think you need a reminder of who your own sweet ass belongs to." He slid his hand down Perrin's strong back to squeeze the anatomy in question before he turned back to Aristide. "Teodoro has not told us why yet, but he asks our presence to accompany him to Saint-Rémy."

"You reminded me quite well last night," Perrin retorted. "Riding was not on my list of things to do today." Turning to Aristide he added,

"Teodoro claims it will not be an adventure, so I am sure we shall have a grand time."

"Your idea of a grand time is anything involving the prospect of a fight," Aristide countered. "Court gossip holds that the ambassador preferred to remain in Arles because of sickness spreading through the region around the village. Why would Teodoro need to travel there, unless…?" He paused, considering. "I have not seen Raúl around the court since their return." He and Benoît owed at least a part of their happiness to Raúl's influence; if he had been seeing to the sick and was in trouble now, which was the only reason he could think of for Teodoro to ride to the small town, Aristide would not hesitate to offer the support of his sword. "Let me finish dressing and saddle Orphée, and I am with you."

"Unless?" Perrin asked as Aristide returned to the other room. "I hate it when he doesn't finish his sentences."

"Unless something has happened to Raúl," Léandre answered. "He stayed with Aristide after the Queen Mother's men shot him while we brought word back to M. de Tréville in Paris, remember? He has reason to be grateful to the gypsy."

"Oh," Perrin said. "I hadn't thought of that."

Aristide and Benoît, both hastily dressed, rejoined their fellow musketeers a few moments later. "As late as we are setting out, it is doubtful I will return until tomorrow," Aristide told Benoît, caressing his cheek. "If we are gone beyond that, I will send word if I can."

"Be safe," Benoît said firmly. He followed Aristide into the other room. "Léandre, Perrin, I expect you to bring him back in one piece."

"We don't know there is any danger," Aristide said, settling his hat onto his head.

"You are walking out of my sight with those two and Teodoro," Benoît retorted. "I have no doubt danger will find you even if you don't go looking for it." Heedless of Perrin and Léandre standing there, he pulled Aristide into his arms for another kiss.

Aristide returned the kiss ardently, pulling back only when he and Benoît both had need to draw breath. "I will return as soon as I may, *mon cœur*."

CHRISTIAN STOOD at the door to his lodgings watching Teodoro pace as he waited for Aristide. He feared Teodoro would not wait much longer.

If it came to that, Christian would send Esteban with Teodoro now and send the musketeer after them when he arrived.

The outer gate opened and three horsemen rode in. Christian recognized the jaunty tilt of the plume on Léandre's hat.

"Teodoro, well met," Aristide said, swinging down from his horse. "Perrin and Léandre tell me we ride for Saint-Rémy, but they couldn't tell me why."

"Raúl has been treating the *comte* du Saint-Rémy de Provence's son, and knowing him, anyone else who has fallen ill in the village. As he has not been able to hold back the spread of the illness single-handedly, the townspeople have made him their scapegoat. You know enough of the attitude toward gypsies to imagine what that means. The *comte* has taken him prisoner, claiming it is for Raúl's protection, but I mean to bring him back before the *comte*'s resolution is put to the test."

"And he will not wait until I can accompany him," Christian added. "I know you have put those days behind you, but if I cannot be at Teo's side to remind him of how to approach an aristocrat, you are the best one to stand in my place. You will keep him from doing something rash, I hope."

"Rash?" Teodoro raised an eyebrow at his lover. "As long as the *comte* listens to reason and releases Raúl to us, we will have no issues."

"I have experience with how you persuade people to see reason," Christian reminded him. "Perhaps you should let Aristide do the talking."

"And if the *comte* is not inclined to be reasonable, he will have our swords at his back," Léandre added.

Christian looked at Aristide again. "Please don't let them do anything rash."

Aristide shrugged a shoulder, glancing over it at Léandre and Perrin. "I will do my best."

"I suppose that is the best I can ask." He wished he dared leave court with the men in front of him, but his position demanded his appearance at certain functions, and as much as he and Teodoro owed Raúl, he could not abandon his post for anything less than a threat of death.

"You worry too much." Teodoro drew Christian into an embrace, pushing back the waves of blond hair to press a kiss to the side of his neck. "Do not let the king forget himself and make advances toward you while I am gone."

Christian chuckled. "You have taught me to defend myself. My virtue will be safe until you return. *Te amo*," he added, dropping his voice so the others could not hear. He had no doubt they knew, but some things were private. He rested his hand on Teodoro's waist, feeling the *daga izquierda* on his belt. Teodoro might say he was going to persuade the *comte* to listen to reason, but he was armed for battle. As much as Christian hoped it would not come to that, the weapon's presence assured him. He had seen the men in the courtyard fight. It would take strong odds to defeat them.

"Try not to worry, *mi corazón*," Teodoro murmured, taking Christian's lips in a tender kiss. While Christian knew Teodoro had no real reason to fear for his safety, that made it no easier to think of the days and nights they would spend apart. "We will return with Raúl as quickly as we may." After claiming a final kiss, Teodoro strode to his horse and mounted quickly, curbing the steed's restive shuffling and moving in front of the musketeers.

Christian stood at the door watching until the four horsemen faded from his sight.

TEODORO REINED in his horse when the first glimpse of the castle of Saint-Rémy de Provence became visible through the trees. The white stone battlements topping the hill, around which the houses of the village were clustered, took on a reddish tinge in the light of the setting sun. While some might have taken that as an ill omen, Teodoro was not one to give credence to superstition. Still, he would feel far more comfortable when they had recovered Raúl from the *comte*'s dubious protection. Raúl would be the first to protest the need for protection at all, Teodoro thought wryly, but there were few he would trust more than the men at his side.

"So what are we doing now that we're here?" Perrin asked. "You're even more closemouthed than usual. I'm up for whatever it is, but I'd like to know what hornet's nest we're about to stir up. We are about to stir one up, aren't we?"

"As long as the *comte* allows Raúl to return with us, we shall merely have enjoyed a pleasant afternoon's ride in the countryside," Teodoro answered.

"What fun is that?" Perrin asked, his expression petulant. "We're stuck at court with nothing to pass the time, and then one bit of excitement comes along and you won't even let me enjoy it?"

"Have you forgotten M. de Tréville's reaction to the last bit of 'excitement' you and Léandre got up to?" Aristide asked, his voice stern, though the corners of his lips twitched.

"That was two months ago," Perrin said. "He's forgotten about that by now."

"I'd prefer not to bring it back to his attention," Léandre interjected. "Let's go talk to this *comte* and get this over with. All this riding has worked up my appetite."

"You can tell us the tale once Raúl is back with us." Teodoro nudged his horse forward, the musketeers following until they reached the outer wall encircling the village. A set of heavy wooden gates barred their way where the road met the walls.

Aristide glanced at Teodoro, frowning. "The village gates would usually stand open, unless they needed to keep attackers out."

"Or to keep someone inside," Teodoro answered, moving a hand to his sword hilt.

"Is there more to this than you've told us?" Léandre asked. "Not that I doubt your word, but this seems somewhat of an overreaction to the presence of one gypsy. Whether they desire to keep him in or out, he is still only one man."

"There is one way to learn the answer to that." Teodoro dismounted and strode to the gates, then pounded a fist against the weathered wood.

"Who is there?" a guard shouted from inside the gate. "Saint-Rémy is under quarantine. No one is allowed entrance unless you accept those strictures."

"Open in the name of the king's musketeers," Perrin shouted back. "Would you have us tell His Majesty you denied us passage?"

"Passage to where?" the guard retorted. "We are not a large city. Simply go around and be on your way."

"We have business with the *comte*," Teodoro answered, already growing frustrated. Dealing with words was Christian's skill; Teodoro preferred acting to talking, but even the four of them together could hardly knock down the gates and storm the castle.

"Then you'll have to stand your quarantine like everyone else," the guard insisted.

Before Teodoro could argue again, Aristide spoke up. "Would you consider taking him a message instead?"

The guard who poked his head over the wooden barrier looked hesitant, but he didn't refuse, so Aristide continued. "Tell him the brother of the *comte* de la Croix wishes to speak with him. Perhaps that will change his mind."

"I suppose there's no harm in passing on the message," the guard said, "but don't expect a different answer."

The moment the guard's head disappeared over the battlements, Perrin turned to Aristide. "You swore never to claim that title again."

Aristide shrugged. "I owe Raúl my life. I will do what it takes to aid him in return."

"And if the *comte* refuses to see us?" Léandre asked. "What then?"

"Then we wait until dark and find a low spot in the wall to climb inside," Perrin said. rubbing his hands together in anticipation.

"We can hardly wander the streets asking if anyone has seen a gypsy," Léandre objected.

"The *comte*'s letter said he had confined Raúl to the castle," Teodoro responded. "Though that could mean in the dungeons, like as not." Not that wherever the *comte* was keeping Raúl would stop Teodoro from finding him. Though the *comte*'s imprisonment would not be as harsh as the dungeons of the Inquisition, Teodoro would no more leave Raúl there than Raúl had left him to his fate. "If it comes to that, we will find a way to convince the *comte* to hand him over to us," he added, moving his hand to his sword hilt.

"Let us see what the *comte* replies first," Aristide said calmly.

Teodoro inclined his head, but his hand stayed on the woven grip of his sword.

AS THE lowering sunlight faded from the narrow window of the servants' chamber he had been given to sleep in, Raúl packed the dwindling amount of herbs he had remaining in the pouch he wore at his waist. He would need more soon if he was to continue treating the *comte*'s servants. He looked up when the door opened, wondering who had fallen ill now. His reserves of strength were running as low as his supply of herbs.

Instead Louis, the *comte*'s son, peeked his head inside. "You are still here!"

"What are you doing out of bed?" Raúl scolded, though the youngster looked much stronger than the last time Raúl had been allowed to see him. He ran a hand through Louis's tousled hair, relieved that he no longer felt feverish. "I'm sure your father would not want you wandering about."

"I won't tell him if you won't," Louis said with an impish grin. "I was lonely. No one has come to see me all day."

"Madame Isabeau is still ill herself," Raúl answered, though he was surprised the *comte* had not assigned another servant to watch over his son. Though judging by the number of housemaids and footmen he had treated, perhaps the *comte* felt he was protecting the boy by keeping him away from anyone else who might have the sickness.

"My father told me," Louis said, his voice small and sad. "So many people are sick. Are you helping them like you helped me?"

"I have tried," Raúl answered, hoping his frustration at not being able to do more did not color his voice. The *comte* had not allowed him to return to the market to obtain more herbs, not since the butcher who delivered meat to the castle complained about how many merchants had fallen ill since "that damned gypsy started skulking around the village." Many of the *comte*'s servants were no more willing than the boy's nursemaid to allow him to tend to them. "They are not all such good patients as you."

"That is silly," Louis declared. "You made me feel better. Why wouldn't they want you to help them the same way? I will have Father order them to stop their foolishness."

If it were only that simple, Raúl thought. Far from believing he could help them, many of the villagers apparently blamed him for causing the sickness, or at least bringing it to them. He had seen his fellow Rom blamed for matters they had no hand in often enough that he should have become inured to it, but whether the charges were made out of ignorance or spite, the repercussions often proved dire. The *comte* was sure the accusations would be forgotten once the worst of the illness had passed, but Raúl could not share his confidence. Had little Louis not responded to his healing, the *comte* himself might not be offering him the protection of his castle.

The door opened and the *comte* walked in. Louis's almost cocky demeanor changed immediately to one of contrition. "Don't scold Raúl,

Papa," the boy pleaded. "I snuck in to see him even though you told me not to leave my room."

"I wasn't looking for you, Louis," the *comte* said with an indulgent smile for his son, "though we will discuss how well you follow directions after I speak with Raúl. For now, though, you need to go back to bed and rest. You are not fully recovered. Raúl and I have business to discuss."

"*Oui*, Papa."

Raúl reached out to ruffle the boy's hair, winning a smile before Louis left to return to his rooms. "His strength is returning," he told the *comte*. "It will be a challenge to keep him in bed much longer."

"That may be, especially with Isabeau still recovering as well," the *comte* said, "but that is my problem, not yours, I'm afraid."

Though Raúl was not as confident the boy's nursemaid had sufficient strength to fight the illness as Louis had, given her age and unwillingness to submit to his treatments, he did not contradict his host. "I will need to go to the market for more herbs if I am to continue to treat her and the others," he stated instead, on the chance that seeing his son's improvement might soften the *comte*'s unwillingness to let him leave the castle.

"That is the business we need to discuss," the *comte* said. "The unrest in the village has grown too serious to ignore. The *prévôt* will be here in a few days. I will speak on your behalf, of course."

"*Prévôt*? Speak on my behalf in what regard?" Though he kept his voice level, Raúl's blood chilled at the *comte*'s words.

"The villagers have demanded you be put on trial for bringing the plague to the village," the *comte* said with a sigh. "I know it's not true. People were ill before you came, and some have recovered because you were here, but I must protect my family as well."

"Then let me leave," Raúl countered. He knew all too well the fear that drove panicked people to find a scapegoat for forces they felt powerless against. He held no hope that he would find any fair hearing, especially if the sickness continued to spread. "I will slip away without being seen."

"If I do that, it will be my head they demand when the *prévôt* arrives," the *comte* said. "We will have to trust in justice."

Raúl suspected that justice would look far differently to a man of the *comte*'s wealth and position than it did to a rootless Rom. Recognizing it would be useless to argue with the noble, however, Raúl simply nodded.

He wouldn't need the *comte*'s permission to find a way out of the chateau once night fell.

"We will need to change your lodgings until then, I'm afraid," the *comte* said. "I can't have you disappearing with the morning mist. You may bring whatever clothes or blanket you would like, but your sword must remain here. I hope you will be a gentleman and come with me willingly. I would rather not repay your kindness to my family by having my guards drag you to the dungeon like a common criminal."

For a moment Raúl considered fighting, but his sword was across the room—he hadn't been wearing it to tend to Louis or the servants—and before he could make a move for it, the door opened again to admit three of the *comte*'s men from the corridor outside. If his blade were still strapped to his waist he would have taken the odds, or even seized the *comte* and threatened his life unless they released him, though he knew he couldn't kill the man if they called his bluff. The *comte* might be a coward, but Raúl would not be the one to deprive Louis of his father. Shaking his head, he picked up his bag and a pillow and blanket from the bed. "It will be difficult to treat my patients from your dungeon," he said dryly as he stepped past the guards.

"You said yourself they are mostly recovered," the *comte* said, "and if they take a turn for the worse, I know where to find you." He led Raúl through the castle down to the cellar, where a room had been hewn out of rock. A thick wooden door with a metal bar across it marked it as a prison cell. He opened it and gestured for Raúl to go inside. "As hot as it is these days, the coolness should be a refreshing change."

"You are welcome to join me," Raúl offered, a shiver that had little to do with the cellar's temperature tightening his skin. He closed his eyes for a moment to gather his strength, but the sense of dizziness did not pass. He must be even weaker than he thought. The *comte* frowned and closed the door, the bar falling with a heavy thud that echoed against the bare stone walls. In the light that filtered through the door's small grated window, Raúl could see the guards who had followed the *comte* turn away.

"I will send a servant with breakfast in the morning," the *comte* said through the closed door before his footsteps faded from Raúl's hearing.

Raúl slumped against the wall, fighting another shiver as he glanced around the windowless room. A wooden cot was pushed against one wall; a small table holding a basin of water and concealing a chamber pot beneath was the only other furnishing. He had endured worse accommodation; he would endure this. Fortunately the *comte* had not bothered to have a guard search him or his belongings—besides the dagger concealed in his boot, he had several smaller blades among the medical supplies in his bag. He would simply have to watch for an opportune moment to use them. Perhaps when a servant brought the breakfast the *comte* promised.

Another wave of dizziness took him, and for an instant he was back in Gerrard's arms at Christian's villa, the night before Gerrard had left for England. He closed his eyes in an ache of longing. His heart leaden, he realized this was what he had seen in his flash of presentiment—the cold, the darkness, the emptiness without Gerrard. *Without Gerrard.* His lover should have returned from England by now, and in the dank cell it was easy to think of all the reasons that could have kept him away: highwaymen on the road, an accident at sea, the same illness that had claimed the villagers of Saint-Rémy. Or simply that on returning to his home and his family, Gerrard had changed his mind about committing to a wandering life with a homeless Rom.

Raúl shook his head, refuting the thought. He would not believe it—he did not believe it. Gerrard loved him; he was as sure of it as that the sun would rise on the morrow. Whatever the cause that had delayed him, he would return to France. The chill from the walls seeped into Raúl's bones, the silence whispering to him: *But will you be alive when he arrives?*

Fourteen

Gerrard unwrapped Randall's arms from around his neck. "I will be back before you know it." He pressed a kiss to the crown of his son's head and prayed he was not making a promise he could not keep. He clung desperately to the dream of having Raúl join him in what was becoming his new life. Now he had to convince Raúl that it could work, because no other alternative bore contemplation.

"Can't I go with you?" Randall asked with a woebegone expression. Gerrard wondered if he had sounded the same when he'd begged James to accompany him on some outing when he was a child. "There will be nothing to do but help Grandfather in the fields. I want to have adventures with you."

"Ah, *niño*," Gerrard sighed, the Spanish endearment slipping off his tongue with easy familiarity, "this won't be an adventure. This will just be a quick trip to find my friends and bring them home with me. When you're older, we'll go on a real adventure together. I'm sure Raúl and I can find something to satisfy even your wildest imaginings."

"Do you promise?" Randall insisted, looking up at Gerrard, his blue eyes filling with tears. "You won't leave and not come home again?"

"I promise." If Raúl could not be persuaded to come back to England with him, Gerrard would simply have to fetch Randall to live with them on the Continent. He wouldn't break a promise to his son.

"Come away, Randall," Rebecca said, taking the boy by his shoulders and leading him back toward their cottage. The look she threw over her shoulder at Gerrard before they entered told him he would do well to keep his promises to their son better than he had those to her. He didn't blame her for her protectiveness. He could not complain about the direction his life had taken when it had brought him to Raúl, but she didn't know that and wouldn't understand it even if she did.

He gave one last wave in Randall's direction when he turned back at the door before mounting Nubarrón and turning his head south toward the coast. Kellan had helped him secure passage on a ship sailing for Bordeaux. He had left everything else in Kellan's competent hands. He could sail for France with no concerns other than Raúl's reaction to his changed fortunes. So why was it so hard to leave?

He wished, not for the first time, that there were some way to know his messages had reached Raúl. Having come to learn the gypsies' dedication to family—whether by blood or adoption—he had no doubt Raúl would understand why he had needed to stay at Hawkins Hall to set things to rights. *If* he had received the messages. Gerrard's heart ached at the thought of what Raúl might be thinking if neither letter had reached him. Sending a silent pledge of his love, he could only trust Raúl's faith in him in the event both missives had gone astray.

The lodgings Gerrard found in Plymouth when he arrived there almost two weeks later were nowhere near as nice as most of the places he had managed to find in France or Spain, but Gerrard wasn't there for the quality of the bedding. He needed a place to lay his head for the night so he could sail with the tides in the morning. Though Dover was closer to Hawkins Hall, sailing from Plymouth would get him to Bordeaux, shortening the distance he'd have to ride across France.

He forced down a meal, though he couldn't have said later what he'd eaten. He considered taking a bottle of wine up to his room in the hopes it would help him sleep, but he didn't want to risk oversleeping in the morning and missing his ship. Nor would he care to risk the always unpredictable weather with a thick head—he was in general a fair sailor, but he had a long ride once he landed and didn't need to court seasickness. But that meant facing the empty bed, cold reminder of the many nights he and Raúl had spent in similar accommodations during their many travels, without even that comfort.

Only once had the inn been as run-down as this one. He had completely recovered from his wound by then and had decided to throw his lot in with Raúl and the gypsies. Christian and Teodoro had left Madrid for England, and Raúl had decided to rejoin his friends in the south. They intended to leave early enough to make the trip in one day, but instead a storm overtook them and forced them to find shelter. Unfortunately they were not the only travelers on the road that day, and even the basest of inns was full almost to capacity, giving them no choice but to share a room. Even had there been rooms available, they would have slept in only one, but that saved them the necessity of spending coin on two rooms to maintain appearances. The sheets smelled of mildew and the windows did not latch tightly enough to keep out the wind, but Gerrard gave no care to those things as they readied themselves for bed.

Always before that night, Raúl had been the instigator of their intimate moments, but Gerrard had spent the day trailing behind Raúl and Martiya, his gaze fixed on the vision of Raúl's ass in the saddle, and he had no patience for Raúl's usual careful approach.

Raúl's clothing clung to his body, thanks to the rain that had soaked them both, but Gerrard had no care for his own discomfort as he pinned his lover—he was finally beginning to think of Raúl in those terms—to the door of the dusty room. He pulled off the kerchief Raúl wore and tangled his fingers in the dark hair while he captured Raúl's lips in a fiercely possessive kiss. Whatever Raúl might have said about his uncharacteristic dominance was muffled since Gerrard had no intention of releasing his mouth anytime soon. Instead he moved his hands from the silkiness of Raúl's hair to the damp fabric that covered his chest, blindly finding the nipples beneath already pebbled, whether from the cold or from arousal. Whatever the cause, he dragged the pads of his thumbs over them, swallowing Raúl's groan and repeating the rough caress. He could continue this way, winning more of the wanton sounds, were his need to see and touch more of Raúl not more urgent.

He expected Raúl to challenge him for control, if only because up until that night, Raúl had led their interactions, no matter what position they ended up in, but Raúl melted into his touch, leaving Gerrard completely in charge. It made him wonder if he'd deprived Raúl, however unintentionally, of something he needed. He resolved that night to do everything he could to keep Raúl from ever doubting his interest. It had been too soon then to speak of love, but desire had been there from the first.

An especially deep groan as he flicked his thumbnails over the nubs of flesh finally won Gerrard's attention from the seduction of Raúl's mouth. Keeping one hand on Raúl's shoulder to prevent him from moving—not that he'd yet shown any intention to do so—he slid to his knees, admiring the shadow of dusky areolae visible through the wet fabric. Still teasing one nubbin with his thumbnail, he took the other between his lips, repeating the motion with his tongue.

"Gerrard," Raúl gasped, and the sound of his name in that broken voice rocked Gerrard to his core. *He* had done this to his usually composed lover. A kiss, a caress, the brush of his tongue, and he had reduced Raúl to this state already. What could he do, what sounds could he wring from Raúl, if he dared more? Possibilities raced through his mind. He might never have taken another man as a lover, but he had experience to spare with women—and his own preferences—to guide him. He reached blindly for the laces on Raúl's shirt to loosen them even as he sucked a little harder through the cloth. He would remove it in a moment, but first he would see just how far he could push.

Raúl's fingers combed through his hair, the contact sending tingles of arousal on a circuitous path from his head to his groin for all that it wasn't a touch he'd considered erotic before that day. Feeling bold, he closed his teeth over the bud of flesh, worrying it gently. Raúl's grip tightened, any discomfort Gerrard might have felt lost in recognition of the pleasure Raúl must be feeling. He nipped a bit harder before moving to repeat his attentions to its mate, sliding his free hand between the panels of Raúl's shirt to soothe the abused flesh with gentle fingers.

Raúl's skin was cool to the touch, legacy of the storm and his damp shirt, but it warmed quickly as Raúl arched against his fingers. He had come to expect it since that night, but then it had been a revelation to him, how sensitive Raúl's entire body was. He caught the taut peak between his thumb and forefinger to roll it between them, and Raúl jumped as if burned. Gerrard might have pulled back to check on him if Raúl hadn't pulled his head even more tightly against his chest. Gerrard shuddered with a need to match Raúl's own, the barrier of the shirt suddenly more than he could stand. He slipped his hand from its berth and pulled the hem free of Raúl's waistband. Catching on, Raúl lifted his arms to help free himself of the garment. The moment the cloth rose above the level of his nipples, Gerrard left Raúl to fend for himself and fell on his chest like a man half-starved.

Given the feast spread before him, Gerrard found his attention drawn from Raúl's soon-swollen nipples to the planes of his chest. The muscles beneath the olive skin might be less marked than his own, but experience had proven their strength, and Gerrard traced them beneath quivering flesh with tongue and lips, marking the spots that won the greatest reaction for future exploration. For now he was intent to leave no patch untouched by his mouth. The scent of sweat and horse and arousal grew as he moved down Raúl's abdomen, and he grasped Raúl's hips when Raúl arched into the moist kisses, holding him still against the door while he dipped his tongue into the well of Raúl's navel. Raúl tugged at his hair, and Gerrard circled the declivity with little catlike licks, his path any farther blocked by the waist of Raúl's breeches.

"You don't have to," Raúl began as Gerrard worked open his laces. Gerrard appreciated the offer, but he hadn't gotten enough of Raúl and had no intention of stopping yet. He had watched Raúl come undone beneath him, but always in encounters Raúl had guided until the very end. Not tonight. Tonight he would decide what and when and how. He jerked the fabric down, baring Raúl's full cock, and nuzzled into the thatch of hair at its base. The aroma of desire was strongest here, so close to its source, and he reveled in it.

Answering would mean losing contact with Raúl's skin, so Gerrard let his actions speak for him. Starting at the base, he used lips and tongue to map Raúl's shaft, the scent and heat only whetting his appetite for more. He could feel Raúl's pulse quickening in the vein beneath the skin as he moved upward slowly, reining in his own arousal to savor this treat as it deserved. When he reached the head, he darted his tongue to catch the pearl of moisture at its tip, spreading the saltiness over his lips before closing them around the loose flesh and drawing it back to bare the silky crown.

Raúl muffled a shout with his fist. Gerrard wanted to draw his hand away so he could drink in every sound, but the inn offered no real privacy. A closed door and four walls, but all so thin anyone walking by could hear them, and Gerrard found he was as possessive of Raúl's desirous cries as he was of everything else related to his new lover. Raúl was his, and he refused to share even the slightest part of his passion. He savored the newness of bestowing such pleasure on Raúl—the salty, slightly bitter taste, the weight against his tongue, the way his lips stretched to accommodate his girth.

Gerrard let his hands follow the planes of Raúl's abdomen and come to rest on his hips, holding him in place. With his palms flat against the winged bones, he could feel Raúl trembling, and he tilted his head back, taking him deeper into his throat as he sought to capture Raúl's gaze. Raúl's head was thrown back, leaning against the rough door panel, and Gerrard suddenly needed to see his eyes, to know that the possessiveness, the connection he felt was shared. He reluctantly slid back, letting his prize slip free from his lips long enough to murmur Raúl's name.

Raúl looked down at the sound of his name and stroked Gerrard's cheek with such tenderness that all Gerrard's doubts flew out of his mind. He turned his head to press a kiss to Raúl's palm. "Querido," Raúl murmured, and the Spanish endearment was still new enough to bring a thrill to Gerrard's heart. He'd wanted a sense of connection, and Raúl provided it in abundance. Thus assured, he returned his attention to bringing Raúl as much pleasure as he could manage.

The silken skin covering Raúl's shaft fascinated him, and after laving it from root to tip he closed his lips around it, letting them glide over it gently. A sound that was almost a whimper escaped Raúl's throat, making Gerrard smile. He swirled his tongue over the head and then lower as he took Raúl deeper, slowly at first, moving up and down until he found the pace that made Raúl quiver beneath his hands. He let his own eyes fall closed, all his focus on the hard flesh filling his mouth and the smooth flesh against his palms and the wanton sounds urging him on.

He'd never imagined being the one to provide such attention, but now that he tried it, he couldn't imagine going back. He knew all too well the pleasure Raúl was feeling, and the thought of being the one—the only one—to make Raúl feel this way left him hard and aching.

Lord willing, he'd spend the rest of his life finding ways to make Raúl happy. He just had to get back to him. He pushed the stray thought aside and focused on the memory of times spent together rather than on time spent apart. He was on his way to France, and they'd be together soon. Another two weeks, three at the most.

It would be so easy to sink back into the memory and find release in it, but he had grown tired of the feel of his own hand. He could wait until they were reunited. After all these months apart, Raúl would be as hungry for their lovemaking as he was, and it would be so much better than anything he could do to himself, even with his memories goading him on.

Closing his eyes, Gerrard called back the vision of Raúl's face contorted in ecstasy. "Soon, my love," he whispered, then burrowed deeper against the pillow and let sleep take him.

FIFTEEN

GERRARD PUSHED Nubarrón as hard as he dared, knowing he still had leagues to cover before he reached Saintes-Maries-de-la-Mer. Only the knowledge that running Nubarrón into the ground would ultimately delay his arrival kept him in check, though, for he could not shake the feeling that Raúl needed him. He rose at dawn each day and rode until it grew too dark to continue, finding inns when he could and sleeping under the stars when he couldn't.

He had dismounted in a field six days outside of Bordeaux when he heard a young voice. "Excuse me, monsieur. Are you going to sleep in our haystack?"

"I was going to," Gerrard replied, looking around for the owner of the voice. "If that meets Your Lordship's approval."

The child giggled and stepped out where Gerrard could see him better. "I'm not a lord. I'm Andreas."

The boy looked no more than eight or nine, dressed in the coarse homespun that would have identified him as a farmer's child even had he not claimed the haystack. Gerrard sketched a bow. "I am Gerrard, and my companion is Nubarrón. I promise he will not eat more than a mouthful or two of your hay, if you can spare it." To his relief, Andreas showed no signs of the gaunt body and vacant eyes that haunted him from the small village he'd ridden through that had been stricken by the plague earlier in the year. "Though perhaps I should ask your parents' permission as well?"

"They won't care," Andreas said, "except to tell you to sleep in the barn rather than the haystack. Have you had supper? It will be time to eat soon."

"I have not," Gerrard said. He'd intended to eat the crust of bread left from lunch until he could find somewhere to eat tomorrow.

"Then you must come home with me," Andreas said. He started through the fields toward a small collection of buildings. Gerrard followed, reminded terribly of Randall. He had spent so little of his son's life in the same village that he hadn't expected to miss him, and yet he did. Not with the same clawing ache that he missed Raúl, but he missed him all the same.

When Andreas introduced Gerrard to his parents, a hearty-looking farmer and his wife, they insisted he join them at their supper. It reminded him of the families in his village, many of whom had lost so much as a result of the illness that had taken so many lives, who were still willing to share the little they had with those who had even less. He hoped Kellan was moving ahead with the improvements they'd discussed before he left.

The cassoulet they placed on the table was simple fare, but Gerrard had spent enough years traveling with Raúl's gypsies not to care. "You have a fine son," he told them as they ate. "He reminds me of my own boy."

"Your son is not traveling with you?" the farmer's wife asked.

"No, he remains in my village in England. I am in haste, and he would slow me down. When he is older, perhaps I will bring him with me on another trip."

That would thrill Randall, he knew, imagining the boy joining them in Raúl's peripatetic travels. There would be other children for him to play with, and the *daya* would mother him like their own sons and daughters. Though Randall would be Sir Randall of Hawkins Hall one day, and Gerrard could imagine his father's horror at the idea of his grandson being raised in a gypsy caravan.

Then again, his father would be horrified at many things that were now staples in Gerrard's life, not the least of which would be the gold hoop in his earlobe, symbol of everything he and Raúl shared.

"If you travel in haste, you should rest so you can rise and travel on early in the morning," the farmer said. "I haven't a bed to offer you, but we can make a pallet of straw. 'Twill be more comfortable than an open field."

"I will take it willingly," Gerrard said, "but first I must see my horse settled."

"Andreas will help you," the farmer said. "He knows where everything is in the barn."

After thanking Andreas's mother for the meal, Gerrard retrieved Nubarrón from where he had been grazing placidly on the grass in front of the farmer's cottage and led him to the barn.

"He can stay here with our plow horse," Andreas offered, opening the large stall where a dappled gray draft horse munched contentedly from a trough of oats. "We had two, but Turgeon was old and passed earlier in the spring."

"It's fortunate Nubarrón has such a placid disposition," Gerrard answered as he led his mount into the stable. The two horses stared at each other for a moment before Nubarrón dipped his head to the trough, lipping up a mouthful of oats. "I can't imagine Martiya—" His voice caught for a moment at the memory of Raúl racing the spirited stallion across the Spanish countryside while he and Nubarrón plodded doggedly behind. "—my... friend's... stallion agreeing to share a stall so readily."

Andreas nodded sagely, as only a child his age could do. "Stallions are difficult. Marchand is much easier to work with. Where are you going when you leave here?"

"East," Gerrard said. "To Saintes-Maries-de-la-Mer. I have friends who await me there. Then I must return to England, for my son would be most unhappy with me if I did not."

"It must be exciting to ride wherever you wish," Andreas said wistfully, reminding Gerrard even more of Randall. "I have never traveled anywhere except to my grandparents' farm across the river."

"At times," Gerrard agreed, thinking of the places he had visited with Raúl, "but it can be wearying as well. Sometimes I wish for nothing more than to be at home with those I love." For most of the last six years and more, "home" had been wherever Raúl's travels or Christian and Teodoro's postings had taken him, but over the past weeks he had come to realize the claims Hawkins Hall and its tenants had on his responsibilities—and on his heart.

When he rode away after his falling-out with his father, with James and his nephew both hale, he had never expected to come into the title, but now that he had, he could not cast it aside as easily as he would once have thought.

"You must miss your wife," Andreas said.

Gerrard considered how to answer the question. He could hardly expect Andreas to understand or accept his relationship with Raúl, but he didn't want to lie either. "I'm not married," he said finally.

"I'm sorry. Did your wife die like Turgeon? Papa says that happens to people too."

Thinking of his brother and sister-in-law and nephew, not to mention his father and all the villagers taken by illness, made Gerrard glad Andreas had not yet known such loss. "My son, Randall, lives with his mother," he said, not adding *at least for the moment.* He could hardly explain the tangle his life had become to this innocent farm boy. "I am going to meet a dear friend of mine, and I hope we will return together to spend more time with my son."

Andreas didn't seem to know what to make of that, much to Gerrard's relief. Gerrard gave Nubarrón one last pat on the flank and headed back inside. Andreas's parents had prepared a pallet near the hearth in the kitchen, close enough to warm him during the night without having to worry about stray sparks. "Thank you," he said as he spread his blanket across the straw. "Your hospitality is all the more welcome for being unlooked for. I will be on my way at first light."

"After you have broken your fast," Andreas's mother insisted. "We rise early. You will have time to eat before you ride on."

When the family turned in for the night, Gerrard took several coins from his saddlebag and hid them beneath the straw pallet, where they wouldn't be found until after he left the next morning. He judged the family's pride would lead them to refuse any offer of payment for their hospitality he might make directly. After snuffing the remaining candle, he shifted on the makeshift bed, his muscles weary from the constant riding, but his mind refused to settle. He estimated about another week's travel before he reached Saintes-Maries-de-la-Mer, no matter how much he wished it could be faster. For the past several days he had felt a growing sense of urgency, greater than his missing Raúl alone could account for. It felt as if Raúl needed him. While he had come to share Esteban's belief that there was almost nothing Raúl could not do, he could not shake the foreboding. "I'm coming, *mi corazón,*" he vowed softly, willing his mind to rest so he would be ready to ride with the sun.

HALFWAY THROUGH the sixth day after leaving Andreas and his family behind, Gerrard hit the edges of the Camargue. Relief surged through him as he slowed Nubarrón to navigate the marshland paths with care. His sense of foreboding had only grown in the intervening days, leading him to ride even after sunset with the moon approaching full overhead.

He would stop for a few hours to allow Nubarrón to rest before rising and pushing on. Sleep eluded him regardless of whether he lay on the ground or sat astride Nubarrón. He saw no reason to linger when the horse was ready to move on. He only prayed he had arrived in time to forestall whatever had caused the worry that would not leave him.

As he reached the outskirts of the town, Gerrard saw most of the caravans had already departed in the weeks following the festival. He'd worried a bit about how he would find Raúl among the throngs of gypsies he'd seen when he'd accompanied Raúl on previous pilgrimages, but they had never stayed long after the festival themselves. Spotting an encampment ahead, he dismounted and led Nubarrón to the fire where several men sat around whatever they were roasting for dinner.

"*Sastímos*, uncle," he greeted the oldest man politely, hoping the Romani he'd picked up in Raúl's caravan would get him through a conversation with a group of strangers.

"*Sastímos*, young man," the man replied with a ready smile. "You're late if you've come for the festival, friend."

"Not for the festival but to find some who attended it," Gerrard explained. "I was supposed to meet him here. I am later than I'd hoped to be, but I believe he would have waited. Are there other caravans that still linger?"

"There are a few wagons still on the other side of town, near the vicarage. You might try there to see if they are the ones you seek," the man suggested.

"*Nais tuke*, uncle," Gerrard thanked him before remounting. The flare of uneasiness returned, but he tamped it down as he rode on. He could hardly expect to find Raúl in the first group of gypsies he met. As he passed the heavy stone church and spotted another cluster of *vardos*, his spirits lifted. He recognized the colorful wagons as some of those that traveled with Raúl's caravan.

"*Sastímos*, Emilio," he shouted before he even halted Nubarrón and slid from his back. "Is Raúl with you?"

"Gerrard, well met," Emilio answered. "We have been expecting you for weeks. Raúl was moping so much we sent him to Arles to stay with the ambassador. I don't know if it cheered him up, but at least it freed us of his sour disposition. Are you back to stay, then?"

"No, the situation at my family's estate was worse even than I feared. I must speak with Raúl first, but I may have a proposition for you all, depending on what he thinks of my idea. I will head to Arles to fetch him as soon as I have given Nubarrón a rest, and then we will return, hopefully in a few days, and explain more," Gerrard said. "Would you have oats I could give Nubarrón?"

"Of course," Emilio answered, rising to retrieve some from inside the wagon. When he had Nubarrón munching contentedly, Gerrard sat and accepted a mug of beer from another gypsy.

"He was well when he left for Arles?" he asked, the foreboding refusing to be shaken even though he knew no harm could come to Raúl with Christian and Teodoro. "Have you had any word from him since then? Did he say when he meant to return?"

"No word, but we didn't expect any. He left direction for us to send you on to him in Arles when you arrived. As much as he is one of us, he is at home with Ciéza in a way he is with few others but you. Don't worry. He can take care of himself. Don't you know… there's nothing he can't do."

Once, the reference to Raúl and Teodoro's closeness would have driven Gerrard mad with jealousy, but now it gave him some measure of comfort instead. Teodoro would no more let anything happen to Raúl than he would to Christian. If Raúl was with them, he was as safe as he could be. "You're right, of course. It will be good to see them again as well."

He finished his beer with the company as they told him about the festival but, with thanks, declined their offer to share their supper. Though he wouldn't reach Arles before nightfall, he could not sit idle when Raúl was so close. Shaking his head at their good-natured teasing, he remounted Nubarrón, who seemed equally refreshed after finishing his oats.

"*Latcho drom*, Gerrard," Emilio called, wishing him a good journey. "Don't wear Raúl out too much before you return to us."

The teasing no longer had the ability to embarrass him as it once had. He would never be the fixture among the gypsies that Raúl was, but at least those of Raúl's caravan had accepted Gerrard as Raúl's partner. They had few secrets among them, their peripatetic lives keeping them all in close company too much for anything to stay hidden long. "Then perhaps we should linger in Arles for a time so he is fit to ride when we return."

"Or so you are," Joachim called out as Gerrard wheeled Nubarrón back toward the road. He wanted to be sure he was past the treacherous marshlands surrounding the town before the sun set.

In fact it was well past dark before he left the wetlands behind. Fortunately the moon rose early, giving him some light, but he rode slowly, not wanting to risk Nubarrón twisting a leg or worse if the ground suddenly went out beneath them. Pure stubbornness kept him going until they left the marshes behind them, but it would be the middle of the night before he reached Arles, and since the gypsies did not know Christian's exact direction, he could hardly go knocking at doors at random hoping to find his residence. Biting back a curse, he stopped Nubarrón beneath a tree and prepared to spend one more night—the last, he fervently hoped—without Raúl.

Sixteen

"Messieurs, the *comte* will speak with the *comte* de la Croix. The rest of you must remain here," the guard declared when he returned some minutes later.

Aristide stepped forward with a nod. "I will return as quickly as I can, hopefully with good news and our friend in tow."

"You aren't going in there alone," Perrin protested. "What if something happens?"

"I'm a captain of the Royal Musketeers and the brother of the *comte* de la Croix. Our good host is not going to try anything that would run the risk of bringing the king's or my brother's wrath down on him. I will return shortly."

Perrin looked unconvinced, but Léandre silenced any further protest with a hand to his arm. Teodoro inclined his head, no doubt used to the measured pace of diplomatic negotiations even if his narrowed eyes hinted that he found it no easier to bear than Perrin did. With a nod in return and a silent glance at Perrin that warned him to stay out of trouble, Aristide turned to follow the guard.

The man unbolted the heavy wooden gates, opening one only enough to allow Aristide to pass through, as though he feared the other three would try to force their way in. *At least one of them would like to try*, Aristide thought as the guard led him through the large courtyard, empty save for a servant carrying a pile of linen to be washed. He wondered whether it was always this quiet, or whether the quarantine was indeed keeping the village's inhabitants sequestered.

Once they crossed the bridge over the moat and passed through the portcullis into the castle proper, the guard led Aristide up a staircase to a waiting room hung with somewhat faded tapestries. "The *comte* will join you shortly," the man said before leaving to return to his post.

Aristide brushed at the dust on his doublet, wondering if he should have donned his black uniform tabard instead. He had not anticipated needing to use his rank to gain audience with the *comte*, and now that he had, he wished he looked the part more. 'Twas too late to do anything about it, though, so he drew himself to his full height and pulled the air of authority he had learned as a captain around him, the better to impress the *comte* when he arrived.

"*Monsieur le comte* du Saint-Rémy de Provence," a servant announced.

Aristide turned to face his interlocutor. "Monsieur," he said with a slight nod of his head. A musketeer bowed only to the king and queen.

"*Monsieur le comte*, to what do I owe the pleasure of your visit?" the *comte* asked.

"My brother is the *comte*, not I," Aristide corrected. "As for my visit, a friend of mine dwells under your roof. I have come to escort him back to Tarascon." If the *comte* thought the request had the force of a royal summons, so much the better.

The *comte* studied Aristide for a moment before seeming to come to a conclusion Aristide was not sure he cared for. "Your younger brother, yes?" he asked, though the question was surely rhetorical. "I have heard some of your story. You claim unusual companions, monsieur."

"There is no shame in claiming friendship with one to whom I owe my life," Aristide replied, deliberately ignoring the question about his brother. The less said of his past, the better. "I would speak with Raúl." He invested his tone with the same steel that had sent lesser men running.

The *comte* shook his head. "I too owe the gypsy a debt," he said, his voice low with regret. "He saved my son's life, and I do not believe there is any evil in him." He met Aristide's gaze levelly. "The villagers, unfortunately, do not share my view. When the sickness continued to spread, they blamed him, whether since he was the only newcomer in the village or simply because he is a gypsy. I keep him here for his own protection."

"All the more reason to remove him from here entirely." Aristide recognized the *comte*'s type all too well. He reminded him of his father, caring more for the opinion of others than of doing what was right. Perhaps the possibility of royal disapproval might sway him. "My friends and I will gladly escort him back to Tarascon, where he will be safely out of reach of your villagers. He saved the life of the queen. You would not want to be the one to explain to Her Majesty how he came to harm."

"The townspeople know he is here." The *comte* shook his head again. "There have been nearly a dozen deaths since he arrived. Had I not kept him here for his own safety, they may well have stoned him in the street. I cannot simply let you leave with him—they would be calling for my head if I did. I expect the *prévôt* to arrive within the week to judge the circumstances."

Aristide considered his options for a reply. He already knew Teodoro would never wait that long, even if they could be assured of a favorable outcome of such a trial. As it was, the ruling would almost certainly go against Raúl, and Aristide could no more stand for that than Teodoro would. "Will you let me speak with him? I would assure our friends of his well-being until such time as they can be reunited."

"I go far in breaking the quarantine to speak with you," the *comte* answered. "Your rank, even though you choose not to claim it, can excuse that much, but I dare not allow more liberties than that. Your friend is well," he asserted, meeting Aristide's gaze and holding it. "He is confined, 'tis true, but the cell is as comfortable as I can make it. He receives hot meals, and the one guard is there for his protection only, so that none can come upon him unawares."

Aristide pondered the *comte*'s words. The man had all but told him where Raúl was being kept and that he was but lightly guarded. Perhaps, coward though he was, the *comte* would prefer his troublesome guest gone before he was judged and surely, as a foreigner and a gypsy, found guilty. "Thank you for your time. If you speak with Raúl, tell him Aristide sends his regards. Give him at least the comfort of knowing his friends have not forgotten him. I will return to speak for him at his trial." He gave another sharp nod and strode out of the room, not waiting for the *comte*'s reply. If he had to stay a moment longer in the company of the spineless worm, he would lose his temper and end up in a cell next to Raúl's, and despite his earlier assertions, neither his brother nor his king would ride to his rescue if he did.

"I don't like this," Perrin growled. "Waiting like a pack of dogs while hoping the *comte* will drop us a crumb."

"Then let us use the time to our advantage," Teodoro countered, nudging his horse into motion. "I find it useful to know the battlefield before beginning a skirmish."

"We don't know that it will come to that," Léandre said even as he followed Teodoro and Perrin around the outskirts of the wall. "Aristide can be damn persuasive when he puts his mind to it, and equally threatening if necessary."

The village, like so many others in rural France, was crammed inside heavy walls, with the castle set in the tallest section of the wall. Scaling that would be nearly impossible without ladders and more soldiers than they had at their disposal. They would have to rely on their wits and on the element of surprise if they intended to fight their way into the castle.

"I would prefer to avoid combat if we can," Teodoro agreed as he scanned the fortification for any potential weakness. "I like not the odds in a direct attack." He reined in his horse and pointed toward a small door in the wall ahead of them. It appeared unguarded, at least from the outside. "Would that lead into the keep?"

Léandre examined the position of the door. "Likely not. Probably just into the village, an entrance or exit for those without carts or wagons to require a large road, but once we are inside the village, there will be ways into the castle. They have locked down the town for their quarantine. They are trying to keep people in as much as they are to keep us out. If we knew where Raúl was, we could probably get to him before they knew we were there."

The three men continued their circuit of the village, finding a few spots where the wall dipped lower with the terrain but nothing else as promising as a means of ingress. "Let us hope Aristide has proved as persuasive as you believe him to be," Teodoro said as the gates came back into view.

They did not have to wait many minutes more before Aristide returned. "Alone," Perrin muttered. "We'll have a fight yet."

"What news?" Teodoro asked once Aristide had remounted Orphée and they rode slowly away from the fortifications.

"Not here," Aristide said. "Let them see us leaving. When we reach the tree line, we will stop and talk."

Teodoro nodded, and they rode on in silence until they were hidden within the forest out of sight of the guards. "The *comte* will not release him," Aristide said. "He fears a mob if he does. He has called for the *prévôt*, who will be here within the week. Raúl is in the dungeon with only one guard on him."

"You saw him?" Perrin asked.

"No, the *comte* told me. Though he did not say it in so many words, I think he would let Raúl go if he didn't fear the consequences of such a choice. If he hinders us, it will only be for show."

"We found a door on the outer wall that could get us inside," Perrin interjected. "No guards outside, and surely any within would be no match for the four of us."

"We should wait until dark, at least," Léandre added. "Let them think we've gone and they'll likely be unprepared. 'Tis not like they are at war, after all."

"They only think they are not," Teodoro said. "We are fortunate none of you are wearing your tabards. With luck we will be in and out with Raúl without incident, but should it come to fighting, 'twould be best if you were not known as musketeers."

"'Tis a pity we cannot get into the village to buy some scarves and such." Perrin grinned. "We could disguise ourselves as gypsies come to free one of our own."

"The *comte* already knows who I am," Aristide said, "both as a musketeer and by my title. I'm not sure we can escape notice if he chooses to denounce us."

"Do you think he will?" Léandre asked. "Surely he didn't give you all the information he did only to lure you into a trap."

"I don't believe he will, but we should be prepared to explain ourselves to M. de Tréville, just in case."

"We've gotten good at that," Perrin countered. "So what are we going to do to pass the time until it's dark enough to storm the castle?" He eyed Léandre, who bit back a laugh.

"See if we can find somewhere on the road to buy some wine," Léandre answered. "I think I remember seeing an inn not too far back toward Arles."

They found the inn a few leagues back, as Léandre had said. The innkeeper recognized the quality of their horses and swords even without the distinctive uniform of the musketeers and rushed to offer them the best his establishment had to offer.

"A room where we can dine in private, if you will, my good sir," Léandre said. "We would enjoy our repast away from prying eyes."

"Of course," the innkeeper replied, leading them through the taproom to a private chamber in the rear of the inn. "I will see to it that you aren't disturbed."

"Send in a bottle of your best wine," Perrin instructed over his shoulder as Léandre preceded him into the room. Before either of the others could follow, he closed the door behind them.

Teodoro reached for the door handle, but Aristide stopped him with a hand on his arm. "You'd do best to leave them to themselves for a time."

"Like that, is it?" Teodoro raised an eyebrow. "Well, I cannot begrudge them. Were our partners here with us, we might well wish for the same. Let us see what we can find to refresh ourselves in the common room, my friend."

Aristide followed Teodoro back into the taproom and took a table with his back to the wall. Teodoro settled in next to him, and they waited for the barmaid to come by. "I only hope they remember that we are not in Paris where they are known and ignored. I have no desire to be run out of here because of their noise."

"They are rash and full of bluster, but they are not stupid. They will be careful," Teodoro said.

Aristide looked doubtful, but they could do nothing about it from where they were sitting. If worst came to worst, they would deal with it then.

Either the two were discreet or the walls of the inn were thick, because no untoward sounds made their way to the common room. Aristide and Teodoro supped and shared a bottle of wine, but when the church bells tolled midnight without Perrin and Léandre joining them, Aristide rose from the table with a sigh. "I suppose we shall have to pound on the door to roust them, or they're like to forget our purpose and stay in there all night."

Teodoro stood as well, but before they could leave the common room, their companions appeared from down the hallway, smiling broadly.

"That's worked up an appetite! What's for dinner?" Perrin asked.

"You've had your refreshment for the night," Aristide answered. "It's time we ride."

Perrin looked like he was going to argue, but the dark look Teodoro shot his way dissuaded him. Raúl's safety was at stake. It was time for the musketeers to repay their debt to him.

They paid the innkeeper, collected their horses, and returned to Saint-Rémy. They found the village much as they had left it, with no visible guard on the small gate. They left the horses tethered inside the tree line where they would not be visible to any passersby and wrapped their cloaks around themselves to further obscure them in the darkness. The moon shone full overhead, making secrecy more difficult, but they made it to the secondary door unchallenged.

Not surprisingly, the door was locked. When no guard questioned their actions, Aristide pointed to the lintel above the door. "I think we can get over it, or one of us can, to open the door from the inside."

"Give me a leg up," Perrin said to Léandre, who grinned but linked his hands together. When Perrin stepped into the cupped palms, Léandre boosted him up. Perrin caught hold of the top of the entryway and swung over, opening the door to the other three a moment later.

"Sloppy," Teodoro murmured as they passed through. He closed the door behind them, leaving it unbarred in the event they needed to make a quick escape.

"They aren't expecting to be invaded." Aristide stood beside him against the wall, and they both scanned for guards, though judging from what the *comte* had told Aristide, Teodoro did not expect to encounter any patrols. "Which is as well for us."

"Now that we're in, how do we find Raúl?" Perrin asked.

"Without alerting the entire town that we're here," Léandre added with a nudge to Perrin to keep his voice down.

"If this castle is like de la Croix, there may be a way into the cellars," Aristide said. "One I can guarantee will not be guarded."

"Why do I have a feeling we won't like this way in?" Perrin muttered as they followed Aristide toward the castle.

"Because it wouldn't be unguarded if it were pleasant," Léandre replied. "We will do what must be done."

Keeping to the shadows of the wall, they circled the castle until Aristide spotted what he'd been searching for—an opening near the castle's foundation stones, only a few feet high, covered by a metal grating. "There," he whispered.

"I knew I wasn't going to like this," Perrin grumbled. "Are we sure there isn't another way in? We can take out a few guards if we need to."

"And alert the rest of the castle to our presence." Léandre frowned. "I'm not looking forward to this any more than you are, but if it gets us in undetected...."

While the two younger musketeers bickered, Teodoro approached the culvert and, with the aid of his *daga izquierda*, worked the bolts holding the grating free of the stone. He set it aside and gestured toward the opening. "After you, messieurs."

Perrin shot Teodoro a dark look before kneeling in the muck. "I don't want to know what this is, do I? The smell alone is enough to turn my stomach."

"Just go," Aristide ordered.

Perrin pulled himself clear of the culvert and drew his sword while he waited for the others to follow. When Aristide came through a moment later, Perrin grumbled, "You owe me a new pair of breeches. The smell will never come out of these."

"We'll worry about that when we're safely home," Aristide replied as Léandre and then Teodoro crawled through the hole. "Let's find Raúl and get out of here."

"The *comte* said he was in the dungeon beneath the kitchen?" Teodoro verified.

"Yes," Aristide said. "The middens are the lowest part of the castle, so we have only to work our way up until we find him."

"Judging from the chimney we passed, the kitchen should be to our right." Teodoro kept his hand on his sword hilt as they moved silently along the dark, narrow corridor. A short way ahead, a glow became visible, though they could not yet see its source.

Aristide, who had taken the lead, halted them with a raised hand. "Most likely there's a sconce or a lantern lit around this corner. Since they wouldn't bother lighting an empty storeroom, if we're fortunate we'll find our friend soon."

The quiet hiss of swords leaving their scabbards seemed to echo against the dank stone walls. Aristide sidled forward until he could ease his head around the corner where the corridor turned. "One guard," he whispered to the others.

"What are we waiting for?" Perrin took a step forward, but Aristide motioned him back.

"The *comte* all but told us how to find Raúl. I would not repay his assistance by killing his men," Aristide cautioned.

"Only if there is no other way," Léandre agreed.

Teodoro said nothing but nodded curtly.

As one, they stepped around the corner. The guard jumped to his feet, sword in hand, but he made no move to engage them. "He is ill," Teodoro murmured to Aristide, taking in the guard's pale complexion and the beads of sweat at his temples despite the coolness of the corridor.

"Drop your sword and give us the keys, and we will leave you unharmed," Aristide ordered.

"I can't do that," the guard said. "My lord gave me orders."

"We have no fight with the *comte* or with you," Aristide continued, stepping closer. He kept his sword pointed toward the floor, as unthreatening as possible without putting it away. "We simply wish to retrieve our friend and be on our way." The guard's arm shook as he kept the sword pointed toward them. "You're sick. You need to be in bed resting, not here in a cold hallway guarding a man who has done no wrong."

"It's for his protection," the guard said. "The *prévôt* will be here and—"

"We are not his enemy." Aristide took another step forward. Only a few more and he would be close enough to knock the guard's sword out of his hand, but Teodoro did not intend to leave aught to chance. "He saved my life along with many others, including your lord's son and heir and the queen herself."

While Aristide kept the guard talking, Teodoro slid against the inside wall, moving slowly enough not to draw attention. At his mention of the queen, the guard's eyes widened and Teodoro made his move. Drawing the *daga izquierda* from the back of his belt, he hit the guard at the base of his skull with the heavy hilt, knocking him to the ground. A second blow ensured he was unconscious.

Teodoro pulled the bandanna from around his head and tossed it to Aristide to tie the guard's hands while he knelt to search for the guard's keys. After snatching the ring from the unconscious man's belt, he bent his attention to finding the key that fit the lock of the thick wooden door at the end of the corridor.

"Raúl!" he called when one of the keys finally turned the bolt. The inside of the cell was dark and he could see no one within, but the *comte* would not have set a guard on an empty cell. He hoped that did not mean his friend was too injured to answer. "Raúl!"

RAÚL STIRRED at the sound of the heavy door of his cell grating on the stone floor. He lifted his head from where he had pillowed it on his knees, huddled in the corner of his cot, conserving his warmth against the chills that racked him. The sliver of light from the corridor hurt his eyes, and he squinted to make out the silhouette of the guard. He'd done what little he could for the man while his herbs lasted, but he had no more energy left.

The shape in the door called his name, and Raúl shook his head, sure he was hallucinating, but the vision did not change. "Teo?" He slid his legs to the floor and tried to stand, the dank walls tilting around him. Drawing a deep breath, he found his balance and took an unsteady step forward. "Is Gerrard with you?"

Teodoro crossed the room to steady him, catching him as his knees gave out. He slumped heavily against Teodoro's arm. "No, we have no word from him, but you can no longer wait for him. You need to leave France now."

Raúl shook his head in instinctive rejection. He had promised to meet Gerrard here. If he went back to Spain alone, it would be a betrayal of all the promises they had made to each other. "I can't leave without him."

"We can discuss that from the safety of the ambassador's drawing room," another voice interrupted. Raúl blinked to try to force his eyes to focus. Aristide… which meant Léandre and Perrin were not far behind. Had they all come to rescue him? "He wouldn't be looking for you in the *comte*'s dungeon anyway."

With Teodoro's support he made it into the corridor, where Léandre looked up from binding the unconscious guard's wrists. "I think we'd be wise to take no further advantage of the *comte*'s hospitality. As it is, we'll be lucky to get away before this one wakes to raise the alarm."

"Don't hurt him," Raúl interjected. "He was kind to me in his way."

Léandre pulled a kerchief from the guard's pocket and stuffed it into his mouth. "That should keep him from shouting should he come to his senses before we're outside the walls. Now let's go before Perrin loses his patience and does something rash."

"What do you want me to do?" Perrin grumbled. "You dragged me here with the promise of an adventure, and I've barely even drawn my sword, much less seen any adventure."

"So you did not draw your sword while Aristide and I supped and we waited for night to fall?" Teodoro retorted. "I would have sworn that was how you and Léandre passed your time."

The interplay, so very familiar, would have brought a smile to Raúl's face on any other day, but drained as he was and with no word yet from Gerrard, he could not summon the expression.

"Come, *amigo mío*," Teodoro urged, leading him down the corridor. "Once we have you safe, we will decide how to get word to Gerrard. He would not appreciate your leaving yourself in danger."

Raúl knew Teodoro was right, but his thoughts swam in a muddle in his pounding head. He reached for his sword, meaning to reply that he was not helpless to defend himself, only to remember it was somewhere in the attic quarters the *comte* had originally given him. Something nagged at him, but it was not until they'd crawled through a reeking culvert to the fresher outside air that his mind began to clear from the dark thoughts he'd nearly succumbed to. Staying close to the encircling walls, they'd reached a narrow door, Raúl still leaning on Teodoro's supporting arm, when the whicker of a horse stopped him in his tracks. "Martiya!"

"*Maldito sea*, Aristide, get him to safety," Teodoro cursed. "I'll find his brute of a horse and meet you under the cover of the forest."

"Not alone," Perrin said. "I know how well you fight, but if the *comte* tries to stop you, you'll need backup."

"They aren't likely to waste men guarding the stables," Teodoro objected. "And his horse won't let anyone else near him."

"Do you know where the stables are?" Aristide countered. "Because I saw them as I walked through the village earlier. Perrin and Léandre will stay with Raúl. I will show you where the stables are so you can rescue Raúl's horse, and if it comes to a fight, you won't be alone." He started back up the narrow road. "Come, we're wasting time. The faster we rescue Raúl's horse, the less likely we are to be caught should the guard get free and raise the alarm."

"Go," Raúl urged, pushing away from Teodoro's side. He wavered for a moment but found his balance. "I'll be fine once on Martiya's back. He won't let me come to harm."

Teodoro threw him a dark look but sped off after Aristide, leaving Raúl to follow Perrin and Léandre to where the other horses stood tethered among the trees outside the village walls. He leaned against a trunk, his breath coming heavily from even the minor exertion of their escape from the *comte*'s cellars.

"Here," Léandre said, holding out a wineskin. "It's not good wine, but it will fortify your blood. I don't know if we will face pursuit tonight, but we must be prepared to ride hard as soon as Teodoro and Aristide return with your horse."

"We should put him on one of our horses and send him to safety now," Perrin said. "He's in no state to fight if it comes to that."

"My sword is unfortunately in the *comte*'s keeping," Raúl replied after taking a draft of the wine. Léandre was right—it wasn't very good— but he could feel it warming his blood. He bent to pull the dagger from his boot, though it took a moment for his head to stop spinning when he straightened. "This is too small to be of much use except for throwing. If one of you has a larger dagger to spare, I would appreciate it, though I will forego the loan of a horse." He took another pull of the wine, a ghost of a smile twisting his lips. "None of you would get a leg over Martiya in any case. He might let Teo lead him, but I doubt even he could ride him for long."

Perrin muttered something about stupid nags that Raúl chose to ignore. Raúl had seen the company horses Perrin and Léandre rode. While they were decent animals, they had none of the loyalty that Raúl could count on from Martiya.

"Here," Léandre said, drawing a long dagger from his belt. "Benoît has taken it upon himself to make sure we are all armed as well as Aristide."

Raúl hefted the blade in his hand. It was well balanced and the edge keen. "Your friend is no mean swordsmith," he commented, tucking the knife into his belt. Circumstances would be dire were any to come close enough for the blade to be of use, but having it reassured him as nothing other than Gerrard's presence could.

The minutes passed slowly, but Raúl noted his pulse had slowed and his breathing came more easily by the time Teodoro and Aristide reappeared, the former leading his agitated stallion. He murmured softly as he approached, and Martiya nudged him sharply, as if upbraiding him for leaving him alone in unfamiliar quarters. Raúl dipped his head in apology, then ruffled Martiya's forelock before clutching his mane to swing into the saddle.

As if that were the signal they'd waited for, the others mounted as well. Raúl leaned forward in the saddle, the reins in one hand and Martiya's mane in the other, as they rode into the forest.

SEVENTEEN

GERRARD MADE his way through the streets of Arles toward the villa one of the night watchmen had indicated was rented by an Englishman. Gerrard wasn't sure such a high profile was a good thing for Christian and his retinue, but he wouldn't complain about it now since it made finding Christian—and more importantly Raúl—easier. He rode into the courtyard and tied Nubarrón to a post when no stableboy came running. He had started up the stairs when the door opened and Esteban stepped out. "Gerrard, I am glad to see you!"

"Not that I am sorry to see you either, but to what do I owe the enthusiasm?" Gerrard asked.

"You'd best come inside and speak with Christian," Esteban said, his expression shuttered.

Gerrard followed him inside, but Esteban's demeanor was so unlike his normal high spirits, it awoke a sense of foreboding. "Where is Raúl?" he asked sharply. "His caravan told me he was here with you."

"Come inside and talk to Christian," Esteban repeated, his words doing nothing to settle Gerrard's nerves.

Esteban led him inside to a simple parlor, so unlike the luxury Christian could have commanded had he so desired. Christian looked up from the desk where he sat working on correspondence. "Gerrard, thank goodness you've finally come!"

"Where is Raúl?" Gerrard said, too worried to bother with the niceties. "The caravan said he was here, but clearly he is not."

"Come and sit down." Christian rose from the desk and moved to a settee, beckoning for Gerrard to join him. "Esteban, perhaps some wine? You must be thirsty from the road."

Esteban left the room as Gerrard sat beside Christian. "Not that a glass of wine won't be welcome, but where is Raúl?" His voice rose at the repeated question, but he couldn't bring himself to care.

"There was a sickness in the nearby village," Christian began. Gerrard blanched, and Christian grasped his arm, continuing quickly.

"Raúl went to assist at the request of the *comte* du Saint-Rémy de Provence. You know he would never refuse a request to help others."

Gerrard nodded his agreement. "He spends too much of himself at times, but he will never hear me when I tell him so." Esteban returned with a tray of wine, and Gerrard took a glass, drinking deeply before he went on. "So he is still at this village?"

"If all has gone well, he is on his way back here now," Christian said. "Teo and the musketeers went to fetch him."

Christian had chosen his words too carefully. "I don't like the sound of that," Gerrard said. "What aren't you telling me?"

Christian sighed. "The villagers didn't react well to having a gypsy in their midst and blamed him for the sickness. You've traveled with Raúl. You've seen how it goes. The *comte* was keeping Raúl confined for his own protection. Teo disagreed and rode to Saint-Rémy to bring him back here. I expected them back last night, but they haven't arrived yet. I'm hoping they decided to spend the night in an inn rather than riding in the dark."

"Confined for his own protection? Jailed, you mean?" Gerrard rose to his feet, the wine turning to bile in his throat. "How far a ride is it to Saint-Rémy?" Gerrard asked.

"An hour, maybe two," Christian replied. "The musketeers rode with Teo in the event the *comte* needed… persuasion… to let Raúl leave with them."

"And you can just sit here and wait for them?" Gerrard snapped, pacing restlessly, visions of what might come to Raúl should the *comte* refuse to free him filling his mind.

"I couldn't go with them yesterday," Christian said. "I was summoned to attend the king. As much as I count Raúl my friend—and you of all people know how much I owe him—I could not refuse the invitation. I have done nothing but pace and worry since then, but I fear to only fuel the flames if I ride after them now. And what if I miss them on the road? If they are hiding from fear of being found, I would only draw attention to them."

Gerrard could see the sense in Christian's words, but the idea of waiting even a second longer when Raúl could be in danger chafed at his pride. "Perhaps, perhaps not, but I cannot sit here idly knowing Raúl could be in danger. You can stay here or come with me, as you please, but I will leave as soon as I give Nubarrón some water."

"If you left from Saintes-Maries-de-la-Mer this morning, he has already traveled far. You could borrow one of our horses and give him a chance to rest," Christian offered, rising and starting toward the door as he spoke. "It would take but a few minutes to ready one for you to ride. No longer than giving Nubarrón a drink, and you would travel faster with a fresh horse."

"Do you have one who could carry me at speed?" Gerrard followed Christian back toward the courtyard. Nubarrón was no longer where Gerrard had left him, but he could hear the gelding's distinctive whinny from the stable on the other side. Esteban must have moved him inside, out of the sun.

Before Christian could answer, a clatter of hooves on cobblestones made them both look up. Five horses entered the courtyard, but Gerrard had eyes for only one of them. Without even waiting for them to come to a halt, he ran toward the dark-coated stallion carrying a precious burden. "Raúl!"

Martiya pranced as Raúl pulled on the reins before coming to a halt inches from Gerrard. Raúl slid from the saddle into Gerrard's embrace, and all the long, weary months they'd spent apart vanished as Gerrard lowered his head to capture Raúl's lips in a fierce kiss.

Raúl felt far too thin in his arms, and while he returned the kiss with as much eagerness as Gerrard put into it, the fire he associated with his lover's mouth was absent. He lifted his head and peered into Raúl's wan face. "You've exhausted yourself. Come, you need a bath and to rest. You'll fall sick if you aren't careful."

"The *comte* does not believe Raúl guilty of any wrongdoing, but he is keenly aware of the demands of his villagers," Aristide said. "He has summoned a *prévôt* to oversee Raúl's trial. Someone will expect an explanation for his disappearance."

"And since we removed Raúl without his blessing, it would perhaps be a good idea to disappear before the *comte* comes to ask for him back," Teodoro added.

"They would take him over my dead body," Gerrard growled, pulling Raúl protectively against his side.

"You wouldn't be alone in defending him," Christian replied, "but I think the wisest route is to put some distance between you and the men likely to be looking for you. The farther away you are, the harder you will be to find. Esteban can gather Raúl's things while you eat a quick meal to see you on your way."

"Do we have time?" Gerrard asked Teodoro.

"If the *comte* doesn't discover that Raúl is missing until breakfast this morning, we have a few hours' lead on him. Enough for you both to eat."

"And while I do think the *comte* will come looking eventually, I felt he was reacting to pressure in sending for the *prévôt*, not to his own feelings on the matter," Aristide added. "He will make a show of it for appearances' sake, but I don't think he will do more than what will be required to save face. If you can reach Montpellier, you should be safe."

As far as Gerrard was concerned, they wouldn't be safe until they were back at Hawkins Hall, but Montpellier gave them a relay point along the way. They could be there in a little more than two days, depending on how hard Raúl could ride. From there they could go on to Bordeaux and be out of France—and the *comte*'s reach—as quickly as possible. Martiya looked rested, but Gerrard would take no risks with Raúl's health. They would halt at the first sign of weakness and only ride on when Raúl was ready.

"I would like to wash, even before dining, if I may," Raúl said. "A basin and cloth will be fine, but I should like to leave the memory of the *comte*'s cell behind us when we ride."

"Of course you need to wash," Christian agreed wholeheartedly, with a glance at Teodoro that, no surprise to Gerrard, simmered with heat. "Gerrard, take him to the room to the left of the stairs. We'll have water and food sent up to you."

"We had best return to court ourselves," Aristide said, making Gerrard wonder if he had seen the answering spark in Teodoro's hooded gaze. "Safe journeys, my friends, wherever your path may take you."

"My thanks to you all for your assistance," Raúl replied.

"'Twas the least we could do after you saved Aristide's life," Léandre said. "All for one and one for all, you know."

"I am no musketeer," Raúl demurred.

Perrin snorted. "Only because you don't wish to be. If you ever decided to don the tabard, we'd make you one of us in a heartbeat." He turned to Gerrard. "I'd tell you to take care of him, but I can see you already are. You have friends in France, if you ever have call to return." He offered a short bow and turned back to his horse. Aristide and Léandre followed suit, and all three of them clattered out of the courtyard.

Gerrard guided Raúl toward the stairs as soon as they disappeared from sight. Teodoro and Christian would understand. They knew what separation and fear felt like. Gerrard had guarded their privacy when they were reunited. They would guard his and Raúl's now.

"I hope you have no plans to take Perrin up on his offer," Gerrard growled as soon as the door closed behind them and he pulled Raúl back into his arms. "I would have you out of France and out of the reach of any *comte* or *prévôt* or any other who would threaten you." He meant to say more, but having Raúl beside him again was more potent than any of his memories. He could do nothing but claim his mouth in a kiss fueled by all the longing of their months apart. "Lord, but I missed you," he said when the need for breath finally drew them apart.

Raúl made no effort to move from his embrace, soothing the tension that had not left Gerrard since they separated. "I could not breathe for missing you," Raúl admitted. "And while I am sensible to the honor of Perrin's offer, I am no more fit to be a musketeer than I was to serve the king of Spain when he offered. My place is where it has always been— with my people and with you."

A knock at the door drew their attention. Gerrard was loath to let Raúl go even long enough to open the door, but he knew how Raúl felt about showing weakness to others. That he had leaned on Gerrard so much already with others around was a testament to how worn down he was. "Sit," Gerrard urged. "That will be water or food. I will take it and send the servant on his way."

"There should be clean clothes in that armoire," Raúl said as he bent to remove his boots. "After wearing these for the past sennight, I will be glad to be rid of them."

Gerrard set the plate of meat, bread, and cheeses the kitchen maid delivered on the dresser and turned back to Raúl before he could unfasten the collar of his doublet. "I'll do that," he murmured, kneeling before him to slip the ties free and gently lift the fabric over Raúl's head. He tossed it aside and kissed a path down the cords of Raúl's throat, then turned his head to rest it against Raúl's chest. Raúl's breath rose and fell unsteadily, which Gerrard would rejoice in if he were sure he was the cause of it. "You've exhausted yourself," he admonished, running a palm down Raúl's side. Raúl was always slender, but the ribs beneath the skin were too prominent for Gerrard's liking. "You give and give to others and forget to reserve anything for yourself."

"It is a failing of mine," Raúl said, "especially when you are not around to remind me." He coughed fitfully into his hand, only increasing Gerrard's worry.

"Tell me truly. Are you well enough to ride? I understand the reasons not to be here should the *comte* come looking, but I would not endanger you by pushing you when you are already so worn down." Gerrard tipped Raúl's head up so their gazes met as he waited for an answer. He didn't think Raúl would lie to him, but he needed to see the truth of his answer in his eyes.

Raúl traced a finger down Gerrard's cheek. "I will be well now that we are together again. It may take a few days to recover fully, but I can certainly ride back to Saintes-Maries-de-la-Mer to meet with the caravan. From there we can take our time returning to Spain."

Gerrard sighed. He had hoped to have this conversation in more agreeable circumstances. "I returned to Hawkins Hall to find my father, brother, and nephew all dead. If I return to Spain with you, the estate and all its dependents will be left with nothing because my son is too young to take up the title, and his mother is no noble to guide him in my stead. I had hoped to persuade you to return to England with me."

"To England?" Raúl hoped he kept his apprehension—to say truly, his dismay—at Gerrard's words from his response. Of course Gerrard would want to return to England. Not only was the barrier of his father's disapproval gone, but he had an estate, a title, and a son to return to—responsibilities Raúl knew Gerrard would feel keenly. But where would he fit in Gerrard's new responsibilities? Teodoro had accompanied Christian to the Ranleigh estates, it was true, but he had done so in a role as bodyguard that, while some might suspect was more, none would dare to question. An itinerant Rom healer had no such role to play in Gerrard's new life.

"Of course you must return to your son," he said softly. "It was good of you to come to tell me yourself rather than—" He broke off in another spate of coughing. When he had recovered, he continued, "Your place is with him and your estate now, of course, but I—I cannot go with you."

Gerrard pressed a cup of water to his lips. "Drink," he ordered. Raúl took a few sips obediently, though Gerrard's care would only prolong the inevitable separation. He wanted to pull away, but he couldn't make his body cooperate. He needed Gerrard too much, although he would have to learn to live without him again. When he had drunk enough, he pushed the cup away.

"Thank you."

"You never have to thank me for taking care of you," Gerrard said. He brushed Raúl's hair back behind his ear and stroked Raúl's cheekbone. "I love you, remember?"

How could he forget? And yet it would not be enough. He had let himself dream, but he should have known better. He summoned a smile. "Of course I remember."

"Good. If you cannot come to England, we will return to Spain and go on as we always have," Gerrard said. "My estate manager will have to make do without my supervision until Randall is old enough to take on more responsibilities. I will not spend my life apart from you."

"And I will not be the one to keep you from your title and your son," Raúl retorted. "Gerrard Hawkins, swordsman for hire, could spend his time with whomever he wished. Sir Gerrard Hawkins of Hawkins Hall does not have that luxury."

"Sir Gerrard Hawkins only exists if I allow him to exist, and if his existence means losing the only person who has ever loved me for me rather than for what I could bring him, then Sir Gerrard will simply cease to exist," Gerrard all but shouted. "Nothing is more important to me than you. Do you understand that? Nothing!"

"Do you think I don't feel the same?" Raúl pulled Gerrard back to him and poured all his love and longing into his kiss. "My soul went with you when you left and only returned to me when you did. But I cannot and will not be the cause of you giving up your inheritance and your family. It would poison any life we might have together."

Gerrard shook his head even as he pulled Raúl more tightly against him. "And going back to England without you would poison any life I would have there. The only thing that kept me from walking away from it months ago was the thought that you might come back with me, and that if you did, I wanted to have something worth offering you."

"I would follow you gladly if I had anything to offer you in return." Despite his resolve, Raúl leaned against Gerrard's chest, drawing from his strength. "Unless England is far different than Spain or France, for a noble to consort with a Rom will gain you nothing but the scorn of your peers." He did not add that to be seen consorting with a male could bring him far worse. Christian and Teodoro seemed to have escaped any consequences, but Christian's rank was far higher than Gerrard's, and he had the plausibility of Teodoro's employment to shield them. Raúl had seen the horrors the Inquisition visited on men of their sort. England might not have the Church's persecution to deal with, but he would not put Gerrard at risk, even if the cost was his own happiness.

"I care nothing for the opinion of my peers," Gerrard said. "I am not Christian, to seek a life in politics, nor do I need them to think well of me so I might find a wife. I have an heir. Even if you did not return with me, I would not marry, and by the time Randall is old enough to think of such things, any scandal associated with my bachelorhood will be long forgotten. As for what you can offer, I have only ever needed one thing from you, and that is your love. But if that is not enough, the village is without a healer now. They have an apothecary, but I do not know him, much less have any sense of his skill. The village lost many to the same plague that killed my family. Having you there would reassure them, and if others wish to join us, there would be a place for them as well. We will need all the hands we can find to bring in the harvest, and that need will not diminish for years as the village struggles to replace the population we lost. There is a life to be built at Hawkins Hall, if you will share it with me. I will not force you into it, but you must let me make my own choice for my future as well."

Gerrard's arguments made sense, though Raúl wished he was more sure he wasn't simply giving in to his own desires. "I want nothing more than to share my life with you," he admitted, turning to meet Gerrard's gaze and hold his head in place with a hand on his cheek and the other buried in his hair. "Since that life requires you to return to Hawkins Hall, then that is where we will go, and somehow we will find a way to be together that will not put you at risk or scandalize your neighbors."

"I don't give a damn about what my neighbors think," Gerrard muttered. "All I care about is having you at my side where you belong, whether in England, in Spain, or somewhere else entirely."

Raúl leaned forward to claim one more kiss before pushing Gerrard away gently. "Then you had best let me wash and change into clean clothes so we can eat the food Christian sent up and then set off. It's a long way from here to England."

EIGHTEEN

"TELL ME about your son," Raúl asked as they gathered the few belongings he'd left at Christian and Teodoro's residence in Arles. "I have not heard you mention him before." That surprised him, given how much Gerrard seemed to enjoy the children of their caravan.

"He was my one regret when I left England," Gerrard said. "I knew his mother was pregnant—it was the reason my father and I argued—but I never got to see him born. His name is Randall. He is seven years old and everything I could wish for. He wanted to come with me to bring you home. I wouldn't let him come, but I promised him we would find some other adventure when he was a little older."

"You must have missed being there with him during these years." Raúl knew he would never have a child of his own, though he had watched Esteban grow and mature under Teodoro's guidance, and he felt a connection with all the children born in his *familia*. He imagined a younger version of Gerrard, with the same impulsive energy and generous spirit, and could not regret that he would have a chance to meet him. "Does he live with his mother?"

"For now," Gerrard said. "I have named him my heir, so he will need to come to the Hall soon to begin his education and training. As for missing him, that's perhaps too strong a word, for how can you miss someone you do not even know? I missed the idea of him. I wondered what he looked like and how he was faring, but I knew nothing more than that he had been born healthy and that Rebecca had named him Randall. I sent money to her when I could, but my brother didn't dare defy our father to send more news of him than that, even when he knew where to find me."

"He must be a very loving child, to have accepted you into his life so quickly." Raúl wondered whether the boy would be able to accept his father's companion so easily, but he kept that thought to himself. "Very much like his father." He stuffed the last of his clothing into a pack and turned to Gerrard. "That is everything. Let me thank Christian and Teo for all they have done, and we can take our leave."

"His mother was kind enough not to poison him against me, whatever her personal feelings in my regard," Gerrard said. He caught Raúl's hand and pulled him close to study his face. "Tell me truly. Are you well enough to ride? You have barely regained any of your color, and you could hardly stand when you dismounted Martiya."

"Since I would as soon not have the *comte*'s men come after me, I agree we should put as much ground between us and the village as we can. Martiya will not let me come to harm." He freed his hand and stroked Gerrard's hair. "Being with you restores me. I will be well."

"Then we will ride a few hours at least," Gerrard agreed, leaning into the caress. "As soon as we are safely away, though, I intend to take care of you properly."

Normally Raúl would have made some quip about being well able to care for himself, but after the events of the past weeks, he wanted nothing more than to lean on Gerrard's strength. "That sounds like a fine plan. Let us make our farewells to our friends and then ride."

Gerrard gave him a swift kiss and gestured for Raúl to lead the way. They walked down to the antechamber near the door, but no one was there. "Do we look for them or do we leave them a note?" Gerrard asked Raúl. "I have no desire to disturb them if they have sought privacy."

"They know we plan to ride soon," Raúl answered. "They would likely delay their need for… privacy… until we have gone."

Before they got farther than the hallway, their hosts rejoined them, and if Christian's hair appeared a bit disheveled and Teodoro's lips curved in a slight, possessive smile, Raúl didn't feel the need to comment upon it. He suspected he and Gerrard looked no better.

"Thank you again for your hospitality. I am sorry to have proved such a troublesome guest," Raúl said, embracing Teodoro and then Christian.

"It was becoming too quiet here," Teodoro answered, grasping Gerrard's shoulder and nodding when Gerrard returned the clasp. "Ride safely, *amigos míos*."

"Come see us if your path brings you back to England," Gerrard said. "If not, perhaps we will come visit you again when the life of a landowner becomes too stifling."

Christian laughed. "You are always welcome wherever we make our home." He embraced Gerrard. "Take the northern road toward Nimes and across to Albi from here. The *comte*, if he decides to pursue Raúl, will come from the south. Be happy, my old friend."

Raúl suspected those last words were not intended for his ears, but he hoped fervently he could make them come true for Gerrard's sake. He didn't know what awaited them in England, but he would do everything in his power to make the best of it.

Esteban had their horses waiting in the courtyard. Raúl embraced him, trying to see some hint of the babe he'd delivered—could it really be so long ago?—in the face of the young man he'd become. "Good luck in your wooing," he said with a fond smile. "Though it would be a rare maiden who could resist your charms for long."

"If all I wanted was to woo her, it would have been done long ago," Esteban said. "I want to marry her, and that is something else entirely. But thank you. I am hopeful she will say yes eventually. You will come back for the wedding, won't you? If there is one, of course."

"If you win her hand, nothing will keep me away," Raúl promised. He took Martiya's reins and mounted, pleased to be able to do so without assistance this time. Being with Gerrard made all the difference in the world. Gerrard mounted as well and gave a final wave to their gathered friends. Raúl took a deep breath and rode out of the courtyard, hoping their new adventure would prove as successful as their previous ones.

GERRARD KEPT a sharp eye on Raúl as they rode toward Nimes. They would not make it there tonight, given the hour when they had set out from Arles, but they could camp along the road and be there by lunch tomorrow. Nimes was not quite as far away as Montpellier, but it was a large enough city to allow them some anonymity while they rested for a day and a night to allow Raúl to recover. Raúl could say what he liked, but Gerrard saw the bone-deep weariness in the line of Raúl's shoulders as they rode. Martiya was being careful of him, fortunately, rather than being fractious as he sometimes was, but even that was not enough to reassure Gerrard completely.

"Another hour and we can start looking for a place to rest tonight. A copse of trees or an overhang that will provide shelter and cover from any who might seek us," he said.

"I have never traveled to the western coast, so I am not familiar with this road," Raúl answered. "But I will keep an eye out for a likely spot."

It was slightly more than an hour later, the sun approaching the horizon behind them, before Raúl slowed his horse and pointed to a rocky outcrop just ahead. "We might find something there that would suit."

To Gerrard's eye, Raúl's coloring seemed gray in the gathering dusk. "Even if the best we can manage is some shelter to keep us hidden from the road and enough dry wood to build a fire, I will be content. I slept outside as often as I did in an inn on my way from England."

Raúl nodded his agreement, so Gerrard turned Nubarrón toward the cliff until he found a deep enough overhang to shelter them for the night. "I will gather some firewood," he offered. "Can you set up camp for us and take care of the horses?"

"Of course." Raúl dismounted and tethered Martiya to a tree before returning to take Nubarrón's reins. This close, Gerrard could see dark circles beneath his eyes. He started to speak, but Raúl put a hand to his lips. "Find wood. As warm as the day was, it will cool quickly once the sun sets. I will appreciate a fire." He clucked to Nubarrón, leading him to a tree close to Martiya, who snorted. Gerrard wondered whether the two horses had missed each other. Shaking his head at the fanciful thought, he turned his attention to finding tinder for their fire.

The area around their grotto was heavily forested, giving Gerrard plenty of wood to choose from without having to walk far. He filled his arms and headed back to their campsite. Raúl had untacked the horses and spread their blankets together a little distance from where the horses grazed. He set down the wood and dug in his pack for his flint. The dry wood caught the sparks quickly. Gerrard blew on it to fan the flames, and soon he had a merry fire going. "I think I spied some meat and cheese in the packs Esteban prepared for us. Are you hungry? I could set some snares if you don't want that, but that probably won't gain us anything before morning, and by tomorrow afternoon, we will be in Nimes and can take a room in an inn."

"That will depend on what Esteban gathered for us." Raúl reached for the packs he had removed from the horses and dug inside, coming up with several paper-wrapped parcels and a bottle of wine. He rummaged a little more before holding the bottle out to Gerrard. "Apparently Esteban forgot to include glasses, or he feared they would break during the ride."

Gerrard pried the cork loose and passed the bottle back to Raúl. He would drink some of the wine, but Raúl needed it more than he did. He had regained a little of his color, Gerrard thought, but that might have been the light from the flames playing tricks on his eyes. "I think we can drink from the same bottle, don't you? I'm more likely to catch any illness you might have from kissing you than I am from sharing a bottle of wine."

"Ah, but should you catch anything from me, I could treat you," Raúl said with a smile before taking a swallow of the wine. "Esteban has a passable palate," he commented, handing the bottle back to Gerrard. "Let us see what he has sent to accompany it." Unwrapping the parcels revealed a fat cured sausage, a wedge of golden cheese, and several small loaves of crusty bread.

Raúl used the knife he pulled from his belt to slice the cheese and sausage into chunks. "As good a meal as we could find in many an inn," he asserted before biting into a wedge of cheese.

Gerrard served himself as well, his gaze on the knife Raúl had used. "Is that a new dagger? I don't recognize it."

"Perrin gave it to me," Raúl answered. "The *comte* relieved me of my weapons before confining me to his cellar, and none of us thought to ask for their return on our departure." He speared a piece of sausage with the point before continuing. "It was kind of Perrin to leave this with me, but we shall have to see about replacing my sword at the next large town. I doubt the *comte* will send men so far to hunt for one troublesome Rom, but I would like to be able to defend myself in any eventuality."

"We should be able to find a weapon smith in Nimes," Gerrard said. He pushed down the rage that rose in him at the idea of Raúl being confined. "I've half a mind to find this *comte* and demand the return of your belongings on principle. He had no right to confine you when you had done nothing wrong."

"He did his best to keep me safe, by his measure." Raúl took another sip of wine. "He was not cruel, though perhaps he was not as courageous as he might be. He preferred, like Pilate, to wash his hands and leave my fate to the local *prévôt*. I had not as much faith in the outcome of such a plan as he did."

"I don't blame you," Gerrard said. "I would have had little faith either. None of that explains why you are so weary, though. I have known you to weather incredible hardships without such a drain to your strength. I had hoped your pilgrimage would restore you, not leave you drained."

"It did." Raúl's eyes shone briefly, and he stretched out a hand to clasp Gerrard's. "I wish you could have been there with me. There is always such power in the procession." He drew back his hand, and his eyes dimmed. "Afterward, though…." He sighed. "Esteban fetched me—you heard he is quite smitten with one of the queen's ladies-in-waiting? She confided in him that the queen was expecting again but was ill and in fear of losing the babe. He thought I might help, and perhaps I could have if the ghoul they call a court physician didn't think bleeding was the sure cure to any ailment." He shook his head, his expression sorrowful. "I did my best, but she lost the babe. Christian and Teo took me under their protection, until the *comte* asked me to attend to his son before he was claimed by what seemed to be the same sickness. I did what I could for the boy, who may well recover, though the illness has since spread among the *comte*'s servants and, I fear, the village as well."

"I'm sorry," Gerrard said. He knew how personally Raúl took every patient he treated, but when the case involved a child, it hit him even harder. To lose one tore at the very fabric of his being. "I should have been here. I wanted to come sooner, but there was always one more thing that had to be done first. I shouldn't have delayed."

"You are here now, and that is all that matters." Raúl took a final slice of cheese and sat back with a satisfied sigh. "I don't think I could eat another bite."

Gerrard gave him a critical once-over. "You should. You are far too thin. You are always slender, but I am twice your size right now. I'm afraid to touch you for fear I will hurt you."

Raúl took the bottle of wine from Gerrard's hand and set it aside before leaning forward, settling his palms on Gerrard's shoulders. "Have I not told you time and again not to underestimate an opponent simply because he is smaller than you?" He pushed Gerrard back until they were lying on the blankets. "Must I demonstrate it anew?"

"It would appear you must," Gerrard said as he stroked back the hair that had fallen over Raúl's forehead. He would keep his touch gentle and loving rather than let loose the wildness inside him despite Raúl's insistence he was well, but he had no strength to push Raúl away.

NINETEEN

ONCE HE had Gerrard recumbent, Raúl paused, savoring the joy of Gerrard's strong body beneath him. Desire kindled at his core, but for the moment he was content to let Gerrard's warmth ease the chill that had penetrated him since entering the *comte*'s cellar. He framed Gerrard's face in his palms and bent to kiss the creases that worried his brow. "Did I mention that I missed you?"

"Once or twice," Gerrard said with a smile. He draped his arms over Raúl's shoulders, holding him but not pulling him any closer. Raúl recognized the gambit for what it was, but he couldn't make himself complain. Gerrard was here with him again. Nothing else mattered in the face of that one ineluctable truth.

"It bears repeating." He let his lips wander a random path over Gerrard's face, dropping soft kisses over his shining eyes, his strong cheekbones, his stubbled chin. Following the line of his jaw to an ear, he tugged gently at the golden ring adorning its lobe. "You still wear it."

"Of course I do," Gerrard said. He turned his head to show it off. "It was all I had of you, save the memories that never leave me. I don't ever plan on removing it. Unless you decide you want it back."

Raúl traced the whorls with his tongue, his lips curling into a smile when Gerrard shivered beneath him. "Never," he whispered, bestowing a final kiss before turning to pay equal attention to its unpierced mate. "It pleased me to think you wore it, though I would not have blamed you if you removed it upon claiming your title. I often wondered what you were doing at any particular moment, and hoped you were thinking of me as I was of you."

"I fear you will be disappointed when we reach Hawkins Hall and you see the true import of my title," Gerrard said with a smile, although his voice was gratifyingly husky to Raúl's ears. "I am not Christian, nor does my family estate even begin to rival his in importance. I'm a minor landowner, so minor that were it not for a distant ancestor siding with King Edward IV, we would not even have a title. The only people who care about me are my tenants, and they are too dependent on my goodwill and management to question my choices overly loud." He pulled Raúl into a deep kiss, the most passionate he had given Raúl since their reunion in Christian's courtyard. "And I thought of nothing but you any time I had the slightest freedom from the demands of my people."

Raúl opened himself fully to Gerrard's kiss, the heat of its ardor driving away the last chills and sparking the desire that had never died, despite their separation. "You were always in my thoughts, day and night." This time it was his turn to kiss Gerrard, claiming his mouth and remapping its contours, from the full lips to the even teeth to the back of its palate. The taste intoxicated him more than the wine, and he indulged himself in its headiness until the need to draw breath forced them apart. "Especially at night."

"The nights were unbearable," Gerrard agreed. "I fell asleep to thoughts of you, dreamed of you while I slept, and awoke with your name on my lips and the memory of your hands on my body. I hid many a set of smallclothes to clean in my wash basin, lest my old nurse wonder what I was doing alone in my room."

"And what were you doing?" Raúl teased, though the hardness against his abdomen was proof enough that Gerrard's memories had been as vivid as his own. He shifted to reach the strong cords of Gerrard's neck and mouthed down them until he could nuzzle the pulse beating at the base of his throat. That the movement rubbed his own erection against Gerrard's was a most pleasing side effect.

"Yearning for you," Gerrard replied with a groan. He bucked his hips up against Raúl's. "Wishing you were there with me, just as you are now, except with fewer clothes between us."

"That can be soon remedied." Raúl tugged at the laces of Gerrard's doublet, nipping at each bit of firm chest this revealed. When it was not enough to allow him access to Gerrard's nipples, he eased back just enough to run his hands behind and tug at the hem. "Lean forward so I can take this off."

Gerrard curled up enough that Raúl could get the doublet and shirt over his head, leaving him bare to the waist. As soon as his arms were free of his garments, Gerrard reached for Raúl's shirt as well and pulled it up, stroking the sensitive skin over Raúl's ribs as he did. "Do not overdo," Gerrard said. "I am not underestimating you, I swear, but I saw how weakened you were by your ordeal. I do not want to make that worse."

Raúl took a moment to rub his cheek against the soft hair thatching Gerrard's chest before responding. "Can you not feel how much I have recovered?" He canted his hips to make it more obvious while he sought out a furled nipple to lip and then worry gently with his teeth. "I need this, *mi corazón*. I need you. Don't make us wait any longer."

Gerrard groaned and tangled his fingers in Raúl's hair. "You will be the death of me."

Raúl smiled against Gerrard's skin and moved up to kiss him. He understood Gerrard's concern. He would feel the same way if their positions were reversed, but he knew his own strength, and he knew how much the simple joy of being with Gerrard again restored him. Doubt and despair, more than any physical cause, were the source of his ailment, and Gerrard's presence chased those away like so many shadows in sunlight.

"But then I could not do this," Raúl protested, turning his head to repeat his ministrations to the other side of Gerrard's chest, the side over his heart. The strong, steady beat confirmed that Gerrard was indeed beneath him—not the frail wraith of memory but the vital, loving partner of his soul. The masculine scent of sweat and desire whetted his appetite for more, and he slid lower, following the planes of Gerrard's abdomen. "Or this," he added, dipping his fingers beneath the waist of Gerrard's breeches.

Gerrard lifted his hips, jostling Raúl in his precarious perch. He dug his fingers into Gerrard's sides, winning a surprised laugh and another jerk from his lover. "Careful," Gerrard said, "or I will unseat you entirely."

"You are far easier to manage than Martiya," Raúl retorted, rejoicing at the laughter bubbling up at their simple banter. He managed to unfasten enough of Gerrard's breeches to push them down his thighs. The scent of arousal was even stronger here, making his mouth water. He planted his knees on either side of Gerrard's long legs and shifted until he could close his lips around the tempting shaft.

Gerrard muffled his shout with the heel of his hand. Raúl knew they shouldn't draw attention to themselves, but after months of separation, he wanted to hear the noises Gerrard made. He reached up and pulled Gerrard's hand away, entwining his fingers with Gerrard's as he returned his attention to Gerrard's cock. The appetite that had deserted him as they ate dinner returned with a vengeance now that he had such a delectable treat to entice him.

He licked, lapped, and nibbled greedily, Gerrard's moans and writhing enough to tell him he could readily bring him to joy this way. But as much as he hungered for the sharp, salty taste of Gerrard's release, the emptiness he'd carried with him all the months of their parting clamored to be filled. He took the long, thick cock as far into his mouth as he could, relaxing his throat to swallow around the head, releasing it wet and slick with his saliva. Hastily he pushed his own breeches down his legs to his knees, then shifted forward again until Gerrard's shaft slotted behind his own.

Gerrard caught his hips in his big hands. "No. There is oil in my pack. You have to be able to ride tomorrow, and spit is not enough to ease the way. Not after so long apart. You can get it or I will, but I will not hurt you."

Raúl begrudged even a momentary separation, but his healer's practical voice told him Gerrard was right. He swung one leg over Gerrard's body, just enough to allow him to stretch an arm for the pack while keeping his other thigh pressed to Gerrard's. Once his searching fingers closed around the familiar bottle, he tossed the pack aside and knelt over Gerrard again, removed the cork, and drizzled the viscous fluid over the crown of his cock.

Gerrard caught some of the oil on his fingers and reached between Raúl's widespread thighs in search of his entrance. Raúl shifted to meet him. Gerrard's fingers wouldn't be enough and his patience for preparation wouldn't last long, but the fullness they provided would be better than nothing.

He endured the probing as long as he could, distracting himself with the nearly as powerful temptation of Gerrard's mouth, until the need to join fully in the most primal of ways would no longer be denied. "Enough," he gasped, reaching back to close his fist around Gerrard's shaft. He stroked up and down a time or two, spreading the oil, and then guided it to his entrance, where Gerrard's fingers still spread him. "Inside. Now."

Gerrard slipped his fingers from their berth and closed his hands around Raúl's hips again, but this time instead of stopping him, they urged him down. Raúl groaned as he sank onto the thick shaft. It stung, even with the preparation, his muscles no longer used to the feel of

Gerrard inside him, but he didn't care. They were together again, as fully and completely as possible. When his buttocks rested against Gerrard's thighs, he paused to catch his breath and let his body adjust.

He bent forward to rest his forehead against Gerrard's, his eyes closing to better focus on the connection binding them, a part of him had feared he would never feel again. Gerrard slid his hands from Raúl's hips and up his back, demanding nothing but the pleasure of skin against skin. Slowly Raúl began to rock against him, the gentle stirring enough to send tingles of bliss shivering through his limbs.

Raúl could feel the tension in Gerrard's body, the way he held himself back, even now. "Stop worrying and just be with me," Raúl urged. Gerrard pulled Raúl down into a deep, claiming kiss and bucked up into him once before stilling again to let Raúl set the pace.

"It will be over before it has ever begun if I do that," Gerrard said when they broke the kiss to breathe.

"Then we will simply rest a time and begin again." Raúl moved more purposefully, relishing the stretch as he rose up until just the head of Gerrard's cock filled his opening, then sank down to envelop him fully again. Despite his protest, Gerrard arched beneath him, their bodies working in tandem, the thrusts growing ever stronger until flesh slapped against flesh and Raúl could scarcely fill his lungs for the power of it.

Gerrard ran his hands over Raúl's chest, detailing each of his ribs and the lines of muscle along his stomach before sliding up to tweak Raúl's nipples. Each touch sent a fresh jolt of need through Raúl, a reminder of everything he had almost lost. He gasped and arched into the caress, losing the rhythm of their joining. In one smooth movement, Gerrard pulled Raúl down against him and rolled them over, tucking Raúl beneath his bulk. His next thrust drove all the air from Raúl's lungs.

Losing his breath was a small price in exchange for the weight of Gerrard's body holding him down, grounding him. Raúl wrapped his legs around Gerrard to bind him closer. He grasped the dark hair, dislodging it from its queue, and pulled Gerrard's head down, taking his mouth and thrusting with his tongue in pale imitation of Gerrard thrusting into him. Squeezing around the fullness, as if he could hold Gerrard inside him, he chased his fulfilment even as he wished this moment could never end.

Gerrard rocked into him once, twice, three times more before telltale shudders racked his body and Raúl felt the flood of heat inside him that signaled Gerrard's release. He moaned in delight as he arched into the sensation. Gerrard collapsed atop him, all sweaty skin and hard muscles, the hair on his stomach providing friction for Raúl's cock. It wouldn't be enough, but he could wait for a time while Gerrard caught his breath. A moment later, Gerrard pushed up on one elbow and wrapped his hand around Raúl's cock. "Come for me, *mi amor*."

Gerrard's voice, husky with satiation, might have been enough to push him over on its own, but the sure, firm clasp of his hand, the familiar calluses from sword and carving tools tantalizing the sensitive flesh, set him soaring. He shuddered and cried out Gerrard's name as his cock emptied between them. Gerrard continued to stroke him gently, the creamy fluid easing the way, until his trembling eased and he lay boneless and blissful.

Gerrard used the edge of his shirt to clean them up and then stretched out on the blanket next to Raúl. He nuzzled his neck and let out a replete sigh. "No dream will ever be even close to as good as being here with you. You should rest. We must ride on tomorrow."

Raúl bestirred himself enough to refasten his breeches but found himself too weary to even reach for his shirt—not that he would willingly give up the thrill of bare skin against his. Gerrard would simply have to keep them both warm. He turned to spoon against Gerrard's chest. "Waking beside you will be all I can ask from any dream. You are everything I need." His eyes drifted closed to the reassurance of Gerrard's heartbeat.

TWENTY

BORDEAUX WAS much as it had been when Gerrard debarked nearly a month ago, only this time he had Raúl by his side, and that made all manner of problems less annoying. They would find an inn to stay in while they waited for a ship that would sail in the direction of England. Gerrard would not complain about the rest, as eager as he was to be home. Raúl had grown stronger with each passing day, but Gerrard could still see hints of lingering effects, and he wanted them gone entirely. "The inn where I stayed the night I landed in Bordeaux is just down the street. We should be able to get a room there while we wait for a ship."

Raúl had inspected the ships at port with interest while Gerrard interviewed the captains to arrange their transport. "I have never journeyed by ship until now," he admitted as they made their way to the inn. "I look forward to the experience."

"Have I truly found something you have never done before?" Gerrard teased. "Esteban will be shocked. I shall have to tell him when next we meet."

"Teo and I marched to Flanders with the rest of the king's troops. My travels since then have been on horseback or with the caravan. I have been on small boats a time or two, but nothing of the size of these." He paused when they reached the entry of the inn. "I have never visited England either. Even Esteban has the better of me there."

"We shall remedy both those things shortly, and then Esteban can go back to believing there is nothing you cannot do," Gerrard said with a smile. "It will be three days at least before the next ship sails to England."

"It appears the *comte* was not so eager for my return as we feared," Raúl said. "We will have time to send word to Christian and Teo that we made the coast without incident and arranged our passage." He nudged Gerrard with his shoulder. "Let us see what the innkeeper can provide for our dinner. I find the sea air has sharpened my appetite."

"If it has sharpened all your appetites, you may wear me out," Gerrard said. "I can never keep up with you as it is."

"I have never had cause to complain," Raúl answered with a smile as he followed Gerrard into the common room. True to his word, he ate a hearty meal, so much more his normal, energetic self that Gerrard deemed him recovered from the malady that had stolen his strength.

They lingered over their wine, enjoying the boisterous atmosphere. It was a welcome change from riding late and leaving early. When they had finished the bottle and the tavern's patrons began to trickle out, Gerrard pushed back from the table and smiled at Raúl. "Shall we to bed?"

Mindful of proprieties, he didn't take Raúl's hand or caress the curve of his ass—though he was sorely tempted—while following him up the stairs to their room. Once the door closed behind them, though, he spun Raúl around and held him against the wood with the press of his body. "Do you know how many nights I dreamed of doing this while we were apart?" he growled, not waiting for an answer before claiming Raúl's mouth in a predatory kiss.

"As many as I dreamed of you doing it," Raúl replied when Gerrard lifted his head. "Hurried couplings in the woods are no longer enough, *mi amor*. I need to savor you."

Gerrard had never heard a better idea in his life. "I am yours to do with as you please."

"Then to begin, you wear far too many clothes."

Gerrard couldn't agree more. Nights in the open air could grow chill, but they had remained at least partly dressed as much in the event anyone came across them as to stay warm, and now he craved the feel of Raúl's body against his with nothing between them. He quickly assisted Raúl in undressing them both, leaving their garments scattered where they fell. They could tidy up later.

Raúl pushed him to sit at the edge of the mattress and knelt before him. "I could not taste near enough of you last night," he murmured, tantalizing Gerrard with kisses that never lingered long enough in any one place.

Gerrard spread his legs and leaned back on his elbows to give Raúl easy access to his body. He didn't ask what Raúl had planned. It didn't matter. Whatever it was, Gerrard would enjoy it. "Taste all you wish tonight. I meant what I said. I am yours."

As if driven to prove it, Raúl covered Gerrard's hands with his own to hold him in place and leaned forward. Beginning at Gerrard's throat, he mapped each inch of skin with kisses and laps and nips and once, on his abdomen, with a suckling kiss that left a bruise none but the two of them would see. Gerrard tensed in anticipation as Raúl bent his head to nuzzle at the crease of his thigh, but ignored his swollen cock to continue his ministrations down his outstretched leg.

The accumulated scruff from days of imprisonment followed by days of travel tickled the sensitive skin at the back of Gerrard's knee as Raúl nipped playfully at the tendon there. "Don't tease," he begged, even knowing it was pointless and Raúl would do as he pleased. He so rarely took Gerrard that when he did, it left Gerrard destroyed and begging for more. Gerrard hoped tonight would be one of those nights.

"Roll over," Raúl commanded once he'd made his way along both legs. Gerrard was quick to comply, the drag of the rough coverlet against his erection making him push away from it. Raúl slid his palms up the back of Gerrard's thighs to grasp the globes of his ass and squeeze, wringing a deep groan from Gerrard's throat. To his dismay Raúl did not linger, rising farther to run tender kisses along the planes of his back. He wasn't too proud to plead when Raúl seemed set to bypass them again in favor of kissing his way down the back of Gerrard's legs.

"Please," he rasped, his voice husky from desire. "It's been too long." His pleading rarely failed to move Raúl, but he had been known on occasion to draw things out for the pleasure of hearing Gerrard beg. If that was the case tonight, Gerrard would beg until he couldn't speak another word.

Perhaps Raúl felt as needy as Gerrard did, because he squeezed again, pulling the globes apart. The warmth of Raúl's breath made Gerrard's skin quiver. Then the flat of Raúl's tongue swept up the crease and back down again. Gerrard couldn't hold back the low moan of pleasure. "Again," he husked, sliding his knees apart to open himself even more fully to Raúl's mouth.

Raúl acceded to his pleading, teasing him with long, slow passes up and down his crack. Gerrard moaned louder with each one, hoping to encourage Raúl to continue. Raúl pushed one of his thighs up even higher, so Gerrard shifted until he could get his knee under him. "All yours," he repeated.

"Mine," Raúl agreed, sliding a hand upward until he could cup Gerrard's sac in his palm. He speared his tongue into the furled opening, and Gerrard had to bite his fist to keep from shouting at the decadent warmth. As deeply as Raúl plundered, though, it wasn't enough, leaving Gerrard aching for more. Before he could beg again, Raúl eased a long finger beside his tongue, the added length enough to brush Gerrard's most sensitive spot. He arched into the touch, forcing Raúl deeper. "Yes," he groaned, "yes, so good...."

His finger still teasing inside, Raúl pulled Gerrard around until he could close his mouth around Gerrard's cock. That was all it took for Gerrard to climax, his muscles tightening as he pulsed down Raúl's throat. When his shaking limbs finally stilled, he caught Raúl's shoulder and drew him up into a kiss, the saltiness of his release sharp on his tongue.

"Have you tasted your fill?" Gerrard asked.

"For now," Raúl replied, shifting on the bed so Gerrard could feel his still-hard shaft. Gerrard gave it a lingering stroke. A thrill ran through him at the way Raúl whispered his name. It would take him time to recover, but Raúl's husky voice would speed up the process if anything could.

"What shall I do for you?" he asked.

"I haven't said I'm through with you yet," Raúl said with a smile. He ran a palm down Gerrard's back, still damp with sweat, and stroked over the swell of his ass. "There is one more place I would reclaim, if you are willing."

Gerrard rolled quickly to his knees, offering himself to his lover. Raúl asked so rarely that Gerrard was not about to say no when he did. He shivered at the thought of the pleasure Raúl could bring him. "I have missed the feeling of you inside me."

Raúl gently nudged Gerrard onto his back. "As I have missed you. I spent too many nights dreaming of being able to love you again. I want to see your face when I do." He leaned in to kiss Gerrard again, deeply, before rising to rummage in his pack, returning with the bottle of oil in his hand. "We will need to find a market or an apothecary before we take ship. I need to replenish my herbs, and it would do well to ensure we have enough of this for the journey."

"Bordeaux surely has plenty of opportunity to find both," Gerrard said as he pulled his knees up to his chest. "Do not be stingy with it. It has been many months since I last loved you this way. I will need all the preparation your patience will allow." As desperate as he was to feel Raúl inside him, he had never learned the knack of opening to Raúl without the benefit of extended preparation. Then again, Raúl was too talented with his fingers for Gerrard to want to rush.

"It seems you were complaining about my patience just a few moments ago." Raúl took any sting from his words by coating his fingers generously with oil before rubbing them over Gerrard's crease. "But I can take my time. I have not yet tasted my fill of you." His oiled finger slid in more easily than when wetted with saliva alone. He knelt between Gerrard's splayed knees and lapped at his cock, which was already beginning to stiffen again.

Gerrard's entrance loosened more quickly than he expected as Raúl stretched him with expert fingers. He tantalized Gerrard's sweet spot, only brushing over it every fourth or fifth pass, until Gerrard was once again trembling with desire. "And once again, your patience outlasts mine," he gasped when Raúl pegged him with a particularly lingering thrust. "Take me. Please."

"It is not taking or giving. We are joining together." Raúl coated his cock with oil and slid in slowly, caressing Gerrard's face as he watched his eyes for any sign of discomfort. To his surprise, Gerrard felt none, opening to take Raúl in as readily as if they had been made to fit together this way. Perhaps they had. It had never felt this way with any other lover.

"I love you," Gerrard said, for no other words fit the gravity of the moment. He didn't have Christian's way with words, to spout poetry on demand, but surely those three little words would tell Raúl everything that was in Gerrard's heart.

"*Te quiero*, Gerrard." Raúl clung to Gerrard's shoulders, his abdomen brushing Gerrard's cock with each rocking thrust. "Te quiero para siempre, lo que viene." He bent to mate their mouths, and Gerrard opened to him there, too, meeting Raúl's tongue with his own as he spiraled toward a second climax.

Gerrard clenched around Raúl's cock, determined to bring Raúl to completion before finding his own release. Raúl groaned and jerked against Gerrard, emptying himself into Gerrard's passage. The rush of heat triggered Gerrard's orgasm as well.

Feeling quite satisfactorily ravished and replete, Gerrard rolled to his side and stretched out his legs, carrying Raúl with him. "We should clean up, but at the moment I've no mind to move," he murmured, pressing a gentle kiss to Raúl's cheek. Raúl wrapped a leg over Gerrard, holding him close. "I take it you agree?"

"We could never move again and I would be happy," Raúl said. Gerrard thought of all that waited for them in England. Raúl might well have the right of it.

TWENTY-ONE

THE MORNING of their departure dawned to a ruddy sky as they walked from the inn to the docks to take ship. Gerrard's face bore a slight frown, but Raúl felt surprisingly sanguine about their journey; certainly more so than when Gerrard first proposed it. Their reunion had proven, had he needed any convincing, that a life without Gerrard would be no life at all. Since they were still in public view, he forbore to take Gerrard's hand, but he smiled as he shifted his pack—now replenished with an adequate supply of herbs and essential oils—to his other shoulder so he could walk that much closer to Gerrard's side.

"How long will it take to sail from here to England?" he asked.

"If the winds are with us, we will be at sea for four days," Gerrard replied. "If they are against us, it may take longer. I am more worried for Martiya and the state of the captain's hold than I am for anything else. I don't see him being happy in confinement for that long. Fortunately we will have a good, long ride ahead of us when we land in Plymouth. Depending on what time of day we land and whether we leave immediately, it may take us twelve days to reach Hawkins Hall from the coast."

"That is good—he will have a chance to stretch his legs after days a-sea," Raúl said as they turned toward the stables near the port where Gerrard had suggested they leave their mounts, since it was much larger than the space at their inn. "He did not appear best pleased with me when we visited yesterday. With luck, being freed from his stall for even a short time will make it easier to coax him aboard the *Magpie*."

"Having Nubarrón with him may help as well," Gerrard said as they reached the stable and reclaimed their mounts and gear. "He's as much a calming influence on Martiya as you are on me."

Raúl inwardly cursed the need for decorum that prevented him pulling Gerrard into his arms and rewarding the sentiment with a kiss. He settled for a comradely clap on the shoulder before swinging into Martiya's saddle. The black horse danced for a few paces, making sure Raúl knew of his displeasure at the days of inactivity, then shook his head and started forward, Gerrard on Nubarrón following behind. "Is there nowhere we can let them run before we must take ship?" Raúl asked, eyeing the crowded streets around them dubiously.

"We have a short time before we must be aboard so as not to miss the tide. We could try to get outside the walls to give them a brief run before we come back to sail," Gerrard said, "but the captain made it clear he will not wait on us if we're not there when he's ready to leave. That is coin I would rather not lose."

"No, indeed," Raúl agreed. "Martiya will need to endure for a few more days." He patted the stallion's neck as he settled into a sedate pace, hooves clattering on the uneven cobblestones. The calm lasted until the port came into view. Martiya shied at the approach to the bobbing ship, until Raúl dismounted and took the horse's head between his hands, rubbed beneath his forelock, and quietly murmured a few words in in his native tongue. Martiya shook his head but relented enough to allow Raúl to lead him across the rickety plank and into the ship's hold.

Gerrard followed with Nubarrón, who didn't put up nearly the fuss. Raúl supposed this was the gelding's third crossing at least, enough to have grown used to the sounds and smells of a ship. Hopefully Gerrard's prediction would hold and Nubarrón would calm Martiya's nerves once they were settled in the hold. Either way, Raúl would be in for quite a ride when they first started off after landing in Plymouth.

They settled the horses and went back to the deck to meet the captain. Gerrard had brought only a limited amount of gold with him from England, and Raúl had urged him not to spend it all on convincing one of the officers to give up his private cabin for the passage. They would be fine in with the sailors for a few nights. If they had sought passage to the colonies, he would have requested better quarters, but he had served in the wars in Flanders. He could share bunk space again.

The captain passed them off to the quartermaster, who showed them to the crew's quarters, a large open area with several dozen hammocks strung between posts. "Any empty hammock is yours for the night," he said. "Just stay out of the way of my crew."

"We can spend most of our time on deck," Raúl suggested. While he'd regret being unable to sleep in Gerrard's arms, he reminded himself it was for only a few nights. He would simply have to endure, as much as Martiya would.

"I have found that makes the crossing much easier to endure," Gerrard agreed. "The sight of the horizon helps with adjusting to the waves. We will hope for a calm passage rather than the storms that often plague the Bay of Biscay and the channel."

Raúl eyed the leaden clouds to the west when they returned topside but said nothing. He was no sailor, though he'd spent enough wet nights during his days in the *tercio* and afterward to read the skies' tidings. The *Magpie* seemed a sound ship, and its captain a sober man—he would have to trust them both should the weather worsen.

As soon as all the cargo was on board, the captain ordered the lines cast off and the sails raised. The ship creaked into motion, lifted by the rising tide of the Gironde estuary and the currents of the Garonne and Dordogne rivers. Gerrard braced his hand on the railing of the ship. Raúl copied his posture, intending to take as many cues from Gerrard as he could so as not to advertise his inexperience with sailing.

He watched the wharves and buildings of Bordeaux shrink as the ship's sails filled with the rising breeze, until they were swallowed up in a gray haze. Staring at the vanishing shoreline left him with an unwelcome sense of discomfort, so he transferred his attention to the crew scrambling up and down the rigging, the masts as high as trees above his head. Something twisted dizzily inside him, and he bit back a frown. He had not expected to feel any pangs at leaving France. He turned his attention instead to Gerrard and edged a bit closer along the rail, until their shoulders touched.

The warmth that emanated from Gerrard's body soothed him even with the wind eddying around them. Gerrard moved his hand along the rail until their fingers brushed. It wasn't the comfort Raúl might have sought if they were alone, but it steadied him. This was just one more grand adventure to undertake at Gerrard's side. Gerrard had followed blindly everywhere Raúl had led him. Raúl could put his trust in Gerrard now.

"Shall we eat?" Gerrard asked. "It will be cold meat and hard bread for the journey, but we will find an inn with some good English food as soon as we land."

Even though they had left the inn before breakfast to catch the tide, Raúl found the suggestion of eating made his stomach curl. "Perhaps later, though you should eat if you're hungry." He raised a hand to tweak at Gerrard's raised eyebrow. "I assure you I am recovered," he said, since

Gerrard had insisted on feeding him at every plausible interval during their time on the road and at the inn, insisting he was still too thin. "Food simply does not appeal at the moment."

Gerrard didn't look convinced, but he dug in one of their packs for the provisions they had packed. The smell of the strong goat cheese assaulted Raúl's nostrils. For all that he normally loved all types of cheese, today it was more than he could take. He stumbled a few steps away from Gerrard and emptied his stomach over the railing. When the heaving passed, he turned to see Gerrard watching him with a worried frown. "Do you have herbs that would settle your stomach? We haven't even reached open water yet. The trip will get rougher before it gets better."

The thought of putting anything into his stomach threatened to make it roil again, but if Gerrard was right, he would need to prevent the nausea from getting any worse. He unearthed some savory from his pack and chewed a few leaves, washing it down with a sip of water from his canteen. It would serve better brewed into a tea, but he suspected the captain would not look favorably on his request to start a fire to boil some water. After a few minutes, the queasiness began to settle, and he could raise his gaze from the deck without his surroundings swimming around his head.

"If it would be easier to bear from below, you need not stay up here," Gerrard said. "I don't want you to be miserable the whole trip."

"Nay, I've spent enough time in close quarters of late," Raúl replied. The thought of returning to the stuffiness of the dark lower decks was almost enough to make him ill again. "Perhaps the breeze will refresh me." He set his teeth and leaned against the rail again, willing his uneasy stomach to settle.

THE BREEZE had stiffened into a strong wind by the time they reached open water. Gerrard watched helplessly as the green tinge to Raúl's skin grew worse with each rocking wave. The sky overhead was dark with clouds and the coming night, and Gerrard worried what the evening would bring. The only good thing he could say for the weather was that the captain said they were making good time and would arrive in Plymouth ahead of the predicted schedule.

"We should try to get some rest," Gerrard said. "If you can sleep, perhaps you will feel better, or at least not feel the waves while you slumber."

Raúl swallowed heavily as he straightened from the rail. "If you think it best," he agreed. "You are the experienced sailor."

Gerrard took his arm, heedless of whether anyone might be watching. He could justify the touch as assisting his ailing friend, should any remark upon it. He steered Raúl carefully across the deck, beginning to grow slippery from spray blowing across the sides as the ship bucked the waves, and down the narrow stairs to the crew's quarters. The room was empty, all hands on deck in the eventuality the weather grew worse, he supposed. Grateful for the privacy, he drew Raúl into his arms. Raúl's skin felt clammy, his throat warmer than Gerrard thought usual when he pressed a kiss there. "Come lie down and see if you can sleep."

The hammocks were hardly the most comfortable bed Gerrard had ever slept in, but they swayed with the movement of the ship, a rocking motion Gerrard had always found comforting. He hoped Raúl would find it the same. Raúl didn't look any more at ease in the hammock than he had at the rail of the ship, but sleep would take time to come. "Do you need anything? More of your herbs? A bite to eat?"

Raúl shook his head and bit his lip before answering. "No food, and it is too soon for another dose of herbs. It seemed to have little effect in any case." He lay back on the hammock and closed his eyes. "Is it always so?" he asked.

"No, there is a storm brewing, though we are ahead of it and may make it to Plymouth before it hits. It was not this rough when I sailed from England. My other two crossings have been across the Channel, which is more protected from the storms," Gerrard said. "Is there aught else I can do to help you?"

"Calm the seas to make our passage smoother?"

"Would that I could," Gerrard said, "but I don't command the elements. You should try to sleep. If nothing else, the time will pass more quickly if you do. Would any of your herbs help with that?"

"I know not how my stomach would tolerate it," Raúl said softly. "Forgive me for being such a troublesome companion. You will begin to wish you'd left me in France."

"Never," Gerrard swore. "A bit of seasickness is a small price to pay for having you safe and home with me. If I cannot help you, I will at least stay with you and hope you draw some comfort from my presence. I should have paid for a cabin so I could lie beside you and hold you close."

Raúl shifted in the hammock until he could stretch out a hand toward Gerrard, who took it in his own and squeezed gently. He would hear anyone coming down the stairs and could release his clasp should that happen. The cabin was quiet except for the creaks and groans of the ship around them, and he had hopes that Raúl might sleep, but as the hours wore on, the tossing increased until their hammocks were swinging with each slap of the waves against the hull.

An especially rough jolt tore Raúl's hand from his, and Raúl sat up suddenly, raising the hand to cover his mouth. "I need to go above," he declared, getting unsteadily to his feet.

Gerrard grabbed Raúl's arm to help guide him toward the steps. The deck pitched beneath their feet as they crossed the room. The moment their heads cleared the deck, rain lashed at them, soaking their heads quickly. "Get below!" the boatswain yelled before they could reach the top step.

Gerrard looked at Raúl. "Will the fresh air help?"

Without answering, Raúl raised his face to the sky, heedless of the cold, stinging rain beating against it. Or perhaps it helped, Gerrard thought, having no experience of seasickness himself to judge by. Raúl took a step toward the rail, but the crewman stepped in his way, pushing him back. "I said get below and stay out of our way!"

Raúl stumbled and Gerrard caught him in his arms, sparing a glare for the boatswain that boded ill for the man should Gerrard cross paths with him once they reached land. "Come back below," he murmured, leaving his arm around Raúl as he led him back to the crew quarters.

He helped Raúl back into the hammock, although perhaps the rocking would make things worse, except that the deck was no better. Once Raúl was settled, he cast around for a bucket. If Raúl was going to be sick again, emptying a bucket would be easier than swabbing the floor. Water dripped from the ceiling, seeping down from the deck above, but at least it wasn't as drenching as the storm had been. He would take that as a blessing.

Raúl settled for only a few minutes before he sat up suddenly and bent over the bucket, emptying the little he had in his stomach. Feeling helpless, Gerrard stood and stroked the wet hair from Raúl's face as the retching continued. When Raúl finally made to sit, Gerrard helped him to his feet and held him for a long moment. Raúl leaned into the embrace, and Gerrard could feel minute tremors shaking him. "Some water?" Raúl rasped, his voice raw.

Gerrard dug out the waterskin from their packs and held it to Raúl's lips. He hated not being able to do anything for Raúl. "Not too fast," he warned as Raúl tipped his head back. "You don't want to choke yourself." As soon as he said it, he felt foolish. Raúl was the healer, not him.

Raúl spat the first mouthful into the bucket and then sipped slowly before handing the skin back to Gerrard. "You'd make a good healer," he said, as if he knew Gerrard's thought.

"I have had the best of models," Gerrard replied, stroking Raúl's face. "I only wish there were more I could do for you now. The hammock is perhaps more comfortable than the wet floor, but if you come down here with me, I will offer what comfort my arms can provide."

"More than you know," Raúl murmured, resting his head against Gerrard's chest.

Gerrard dropped a kiss into his hair and moved to lean against one of the beams supporting the deck above them. He slid down until he could sit on the floor, heedless of the water soaking through his breeches. He settled Raúl on his lap, hoping to keep him somewhat drier, and wrapped his arms around him, still wishing he could do more to ease his suffering.

TWENTY-TWO

THE FOUR days it took their ship to travel from Bordeaux to Plymouth were the longest Raúl could remember having to endure. The storm struck in the predawn hours of their second day at sea, the waves tossing the craft from side to side with enough force to tip them from their hammocks, had he not been huddled on the cabin floor in Gerrard's arms. Indeed, at times it felt to Raúl as if the ship would pitch over onto its side and be swept under, and in those moments a small part of him could almost welcome it, would it mean an end to the roiling in his gut. Gerrard stroked his hair and held the bucket for him and murmured quiet encouragement in between Raúl's bouts of retching.

Raúl had no idea how long the storm actually lasted—it seemed an eternity to him—but at length the sea calmed, at least somewhat. When they dared attempt going on deck again, the captain greeted them cheerily. "A bit of a blow, but it's passed us now, and it looks like clear skies and calm seas the rest of the way."

Even "calm seas" were a torment to Raúl. He managed to keep the urge to vomit under control by eating as little as possible, though he knew to drink as much water as he could. Gerrard fretted, but Raúl assured him he could endure the few remaining days without wasting away. Still, by the time they left the ship at the dock in Plymouth, he was tempted to kiss the solid, unshifting ground beneath his feet.

"The inn where I stayed on my way to France is just off the docks," Gerrard said. "They will have a place for the horses and a room for us, and we will rest here a day or two until you are recovered." Raúl wanted to tell him not to fuss, but were their places reversed, he would be just as bad.

His first impression of England was that it differed little from France, though that could be simply because both Plymouth and Bordeaux were port towns. He could pick out few words in the babble of voices around him, though. "You will need to help me practice my English," he told Gerrard as they waited for their horses to be brought up from below deck. He hoped Martiya had weathered the passage better than he had.

"With pleasure," Gerrard said. "And when I am not around, I'm sure Randall will be delighted to help. It's not often he is the one who knows more than those around him. Although he may demand to learn Spanish in return."

One of the sailors led Nubarrón down the gangplank to the dock. Raúl could hear Martiya putting up a fuss, but he didn't offer to help. Even for his precious stallion, he wasn't sure he could bear to set foot on the ship again so soon.

The sailor who led the black down the gangplank seemed undamaged, though, and when Raúl took the bridle from his hand, Martiya butted his shoulder until he reached up to scratch under his forelock. "No more sea voyages for us, eh?" he murmured softly. The thought was a sobering one. For better or worse, he was committed to accompanying Gerrard and somehow finding a way to make a life in this new land.

"If we must take one again, we will go directly across the Channel," Gerrard said. "A half-day's sail instead of four days. Come, the inn is not far. We'll all feel better for a rest in a bed that doesn't move."

Raúl followed Gerrard and Nubarrón off the docks and into the yard of a bustling inn. The innkeeper recognized Gerrard, adding to Raúl's worries. Gerrard might say he was no one important, but he had made enough of an impression for the innkeeper to remember him. It didn't matter, though. He'd made his decision, and now he would find a way to live with it.

"Do you have space for two horses and a room for weary travelers?" Gerrard asked the innkeeper.

"Of course, sir," the innkeeper replied. One of the stableboys came running over to take the horses.

"Careful with Martiya," Gerrard warned the lad. "He has a bit of a temper, and he's spent four days confined on a ship to get here with us."

"I'll take good care of him," the boy said.

Despite understanding one word in four, Raúl was surprised at how much of the conversation he could follow from context and facial expressions. There was no mistaking the way the innkeeper bowed and fawned over Gerrard as he accompanied them into the taproom, pausing with a gesture to the tables in a clear offer of refreshment. Gerrard shook his head, his response urging their host to lead them up a flight of stairs to a bedchamber looking over the harbor.

"I told him you had been ill on the ship, and I wished to stay with you so I could make sure the illness passed now that we were back on land," Gerrard said after the innkeeper left them alone in the room. "He thought it most considerate of me to take such care of one in my employ. I didn't bother to correct him. I hope you don't mind."

"In Spain, you followed my lead without complaint." Raúl took advantage of the privacy to claim a short kiss, though in truth he was too weary to wish for more than to rest in Gerrard's arms for more than a few unsettled moments. "I can do no less for you, now that we are in your country."

"As long as you tell me if something is amiss," Gerrard said. "Come, you should lie down until your stomach settles, and then we will call for food. It will take us nearly two weeks to get to Hawkins Hall once we start out. You were only beginning to regain your strength when we sailed. I would prefer to linger here a few days until we are sure you're well enough for the journey. Better to wait a day or two and travel with no problems than to have you fall ill on the road and face even more delays without the benefit of a comfortable inn."

"Only if you lie down with me." Raúl pulled off his boots and settled onto the bed. The thin straw mattress felt as soft as the down coverlet he'd slept beneath the night following King Philip's rescue, compared to the rough twine of the hammock aboard ship. All that was missing was Gerrard beside him. He rolled onto his side and beckoned to Gerrard to join him.

Gerrard removed his own boots and outer garments and stretched out on the mattress next to Raúl. Despite the warmth of the room—not even the breeze through the window could make it anything other than a midsummer day—Raúl moved closer to Gerrard. His clothes had dried so his body suffered from no lingering cold, but the chill that had sunk into his soul during their separation still struck him at odd times, and only Gerrard's nearness could chase it away.

"This is what was missing the past few nights. I rest best when you are next to me," Gerrard said as he pulled Raúl into his arms.

Raúl rested his head against Gerrard's heart and let his eyes drift shut. *God willing, nothing else will take you from my side.*

FOR HAVING been gone two months, Gerrard expected to see more change upon his return to Hawkins Hall, but other than the fields having grown taller as the season passed, he could see little difference.

Except the most obvious one, of course: the presence of Raúl beside him. They spent two days at the inn in Plymouth before Raúl insisted he was well enough to begin the travel on to Gerrard's estate. Gerrard had set an easy pace the first few days, but Martiya wanted to run and Raúl seemed no worse for letting him, so he stopped insisting they halt early to rest. In truth, he was eager to be home and to start convincing Raúl that they could build a life together in England that would be worth the challenges.

He tried to view the Hall itself through an outsider's eyes, hoping it would meet Raúl's approval. It was not large as manor houses went, but it had space enough for both of them and Randall besides, as well as room for guests if ever Christian and Teodoro decided to come visiting. "Welcome home," he said, turning to Raúl. It still felt odd to speak English with Raúl after so many years of speaking only Spanish, but Raúl had insisted he would learn faster if he had no choice, so Gerrard had made every effort to speak only English since they landed. He had a facility with language that Gerrard had always envied, and it was no different this time.

Raúl smiled but didn't answer immediately, making Gerrard wonder if he'd been too presumptuous. He *wanted* Raúl to think of Hawkins Hall as home, but he could recognize it would take time for that to happen. "How much of the land we rode through is yours?" Raúl asked as they continued toward the stables. "It looks well tended."

"We have been on the estate for the past hour or so," Gerrard said. "The bulk of the estate lies north of the manor house. That's where the village is. Most of the farmers choose to live in the village and ride out to tend their fields. It's not as if the estate is large enough for that to be difficult. We could ride across the entire length before lunch, even if we lingered over breakfast."

"I would like to see it," Raúl answered. "After the depredations of illness you described, it would have been easy for the fields to have gone to weeds. You and your tenants must have worked hard to prevent that. I have little experience of farming, but your fields seem as verdant as any we rode through on the way here."

The unease in Raúl's posture tore at Gerrard's heart. He wanted this to be a happy moment for Raúl, and perhaps in time it would become a good memory, but right now, it wasn't. "Tomorrow we will ride out so you can see the estate," he said. "I know what will happen when we get to the Hall today. Agatha will insist on feeding us and settling us in our rooms and mothering us as if we were Randall's age instead of grown men. And when that is done, she will insist we send word to Randall. If I know my son at all, he will be at the Hall not ten minutes later, and that is only if news of our arrival doesn't reach him before Agatha's message. We will not have a moment's peace before we retire for the night, I fear."

"I look forward to meeting your son," Raúl said, smiling. "And the others you have spoken of. They will have missed you during your absence, though I doubt as much as I did."

"They have a different claim on me than you do," Gerrard said, relieved to see Raúl's smile. "I truly believe we can build a life here together, but if I am wrong, your claim will always be the most important." They approached the stables, and the new groom came out to greet them.

"Welcome home, Sir Gerrard. And I see you haven't come alone. What a beautiful horse that one is!"

Gerrard swung down from Nubarrón's back. "Hello, Hopson. That's Martiya. He's a bit headstrong, although nothing a good run now and then won't cure. I'm sure you can find space for him in the stable with Nubarrón."

"Of course," Hopson replied.

"Good, and this is my friend Raúl. He'll be staying with me at the Hall. If he needs anything, consider it as you would a request from me."

"As you wish, Sir Gerrard. Welcome to Hawkins Hall, Sir Raúl."

Gerrard nearly laughed at Raúl's expression when he realized the groom had ennobled him. "Merely Raúl," he answered with a quirk of his lips. "Thank you for caring for Martiya."

Hopson looked to Gerrard for confirmation, which Gerrard gave with a slight nod. He wouldn't have corrected the stableman, but that was for Raúl to decide. "We can take them for a run tonight after dinner. That way you can see him settled before you sleep."

Raúl gave a final pat to Martiya's neck before following Gerrard across the stable yard toward the entrance to the Hall. Their arrival must have been heard inside, for as they neared it the door flew open and Agatha came bustling out, while Herndon stood in the doorway with more restraint but no less curiosity, it seemed to Gerrard.

"Welcome home, Sir Gerrard," Agatha said. "You were gone too long. Everyone started to worry."

By which she meant that she had started to worry, Gerrard thought with a smile. "It is no short trip to France, even when one doesn't have to cross the country to reach one's destination. I traveled as quickly as possible. Fortunately Raúl was exactly where I expected him to be, and I didn't have to waste time searching for him." He had not expected to find Raúl prisoner in a *comte*'s dungeon, but Teodoro and the others had remedied that situation as he arrived. Agatha did not need all the details. "It would do us both good to bathe and change before dinner. Neither of us is dressed for polite company. Will you have my mother's rooms made up for Raúl? I doubt many of the other rooms are ready for guests."

"Of course, Sir Gerrard," Agatha replied.

He introduced Raúl to them both, not missing Herndon's raised eyebrow as he took in the scarf Raúl had tied over his hair and the sash and pouches at his waist. Agatha dropped a curtsey, and Herndon inclined his head. "Shall I bring all the bags to your room, Sir Gerrard?"

"No need—neither of us has more than would fit in our saddlebags. We'll carry them up ourselves." He didn't need Herndon following them when he had every intention of welcoming Raúl home with a kiss as soon as the bedroom door closed behind them.

Agatha tutted and fussed about guests arriving with so little baggage, but Gerrard ignored her. She had to have something to fuss about or she wasn't happy. He led Raúl up the stairs to the master suite. He didn't think anyone had followed them, but he made a show of going through the door to his mother's room with Raúl rather than going directly to his own room. Once the door closed behind, he pulled Raúl into his arms and kissed him thoroughly.

Raúl returned the kiss with equal hunger but drew back at last with a smile sparkling his eyes. "What, if anything, did you tell your people about me? I am plainly not what they expected."

"I told them I had taken work with a band of traveling merchants," Gerrard replied, "and that you relied on me and I couldn't abandon you without an explanation. As for the rest, I felt the less I said the better, for fear my… enthusiasm would betray more than I was willing for them to know. Especially if you decided not to return with me."

"There was no fear of that, though I confess during my time with the *comte*, there was a moment when I wondered if I would have the chance." Raúl ran a hand across Gerrard's chest. "I would like to wash before aught else. I have seldom felt truly clean since leaving the *comte*'s cellar. How long do we have before your Agatha comes to make up the room? I would not wish to shock her sensibilities."

"The estate was in much disarray when I arrived. Unless Herndon and Kellan, my man of business, were more efficient than I could dare to hope, the best we will be able to do for a bath right now is an ewer of water and a clean rag," Gerrard said. "Perhaps tonight, we might heat water in the kitchen and use the tub in the laundry to bathe properly. Given they didn't know to expect us, there is probably no hot water waiting. Agatha will be along in a few minutes with linens and water for us both." He pushed open the connecting door to reveal his bedroom. "You're welcome to join me once she leaves."

Raúl laughed, the sound doing much to ease Gerrard's concerns. "Such convenience! 'Twill be far easier thus for us to share a bed without remark." His expression sobered as he continued, "I presume that is your intent?"

"I have no intention of denying what you mean to me," Gerrard replied. "But neither do I see the benefit of forcing it on my staff. If having this room be yours in name allows them the illusion of you being a visiting friend, so be it. But these rooms are yours by right as well, for they were my mother's when my father was lord here and would have been my sister-in-law's had my brother outlived my father. England may not have the Inquisition to fear, but discretion here is as much a necessity as it was in Spain, at least among those who are not in our confidence. It is a sleight of hand, nothing more."

"So I am the wife, is that what you are saying?" Raúl's laughter was evident behind the words, and he pressed Gerrard back against the door with a predatory grin. "We shall have that discussion another time, I think." He kissed Gerrard with clear promise of what might come later, and Gerrard was about to damn Agatha or anyone else who might interrupt them when Raúl released him. "I understand the need for discretion. We have been spoiled by our time with Christian and Teo, but I will do nothing to put your reputation at risk, with your servants and tenants or with your peers."

"You are the other half of my heart," Gerrard said, switching to Spanish for a moment, "but those around us have not the words to understand that."

A tap at the door broke them apart. Gerrard stepped back so Raúl could open the door to Agatha, her arms full of linens and—as Gerrard had predicted—a pitcher of water.

"Here, let me take that," Gerrard said, grabbing the ewer before it could spill.

"Helping your friend get settled?" Agatha asked him with a smile. "You always were a considerate boy."

Gerrard could feel Raúl laughing at him.

"It seemed the least I could do when I have dragged him all the way here," Gerrard replied.

"You will have to tell me about his youth someday," Raúl said, his eyes twinkling. "I expect he was a handful—I still find him so at times."

Gerrard was sure his cheeks were scarlet, but he held his tongue. As much as an alliance between Raúl and Agatha was sure to lead to many such embarrassing moments, it would also give them their best chance at someday having the kind of freedom Christian and Teodoro enjoyed. If Agatha accepted them, the rest of the household would follow suit for fear of her wrath.

"Oh, the stories I could tell you." Agatha cackled.

"After we have bathed," Gerrard said. "You can regale Raúl with stories of my childhood exploits over dinner."

"Don't think I won't," Agatha said with a shake of her head. "Mr. Beecham should be back by dinnertime also. He's done a fine job while you've been away, making sure the villagers have all they need."

That assuaged the one concern Gerrard had left over his absence. Agatha finished with the bed and smiled indulgently at them. "Take your time. I'll make sure Mrs. Cullen has dinner ready when you come down."

She left, shutting the door behind them. She couldn't have meant her words the way Gerrard wanted her to mean them, but that didn't stop him from pulling Raúl in for another kiss. They would need to freshen up and go down before she came looking for them again, but for now, he had everything he needed right there in his arms.

TWENTY-THREE

RAÚL FOLLOWED Gerrard down the staircase before Agatha found it necessary to send for them. The long ride from Plymouth had given him ample time to recover from his humbling bout of seasickness as well as any lingering effects of his time at the *comte*'s, but after their long absence he still sought the strength to be found in Gerrard's arms. Their few minutes of privacy hadn't been nearly enough, but there would be tonight—and all the nights to come—to spend together.

He shouldn't have been surprised at how naturally Gerrard fit in his new role as lord of the manor, but Raúl still found the change slightly disconcerting. After they'd washed up, Gerrard had changed into fresh garments for dinner, their style a bit more formal than anything Raúl had seen him wear before. Raúl had pulled a clean shirt from his pack, aware of the contrast in their apparel as he had seldom been before. Christian had little use for formality outside that required by his state appearances, but Raúl well knew that Christian was not a typical nobleman. It was yet to be seen whether Gerrard would follow his model.

Gerrard led him into a parlor and gestured for him to take a seat. "Kellan, my man of business, will certainly join us for dinner. When I first came home, the estate manager's house was empty and we had families in need, so I moved one of the farmers into it. Since Kellan is unmarried, I saw no reason to evict them when he could use one of the guest rooms in the Hall. An unconventional arrangement, I know, but the one that seemed most expedient. I was most concerned with getting things in place so I could come meet you as I promised."

"It may draw less comment if both of us reside in the hall," Raúl said, settling into a plushly upholstered chair. Whoever had decorated Hawkins Hall had more grandiose taste in accommodation than Christian did. Telling himself to stop comparing everything he saw to his one experience with nobility, he watched Gerrard pour them each a glass of wine before sitting in the chair beside his. "Tell me about Kellan—is that his given or surname?"

"His given name," Gerrard said. "Kellan Beecham, cousin to my closest neighbor, Sir Thomas Beecham. Sir Thomas and my brother were good friends when we were children. Kellan is a younger son who had a falling-out with his brother over their opinions on the good running of an estate. Since his opinions were in line with mine, and since Sir Thomas vouched for him when I mentioned needing an estate manager, I hired him."

The door to the parlor opened and a young man walked in. "Sir Gerrard, welcome home."

Gerrard rose from his seat to shake the man's hand. "Thank you, Kellan. It's good to be back. And this is the friend I was telling you about. Raúl, this is Kellan Beecham, our man of business. Kellan, my friend Raúl."

Raúl glanced at Gerrard at his use of the word "our," but Gerrard only smiled at him. Deciding that discretion was the best course, at least for the moment, Raúl extended his hand. Kellan—since that was how Gerrard introduced him, though Raúl suspected most nobles didn't refer to their business agents by first name—took Raúl's hand in a firm clasp.

"I have heard much of you when Sir Gerrard spoke of his time away," Kellan said with no hint of anything but genuine interest in his voice. "I keep hoping for more details of what must have been a most unusual life, but all he has shared so far are tantalizing glimpses."

If Gerrard had said little, it wasn't Raúl's place to expand upon it. "He has spoken most appreciatively of your efforts on his behalf. He has been much concerned with the welfare of his tenants since the title fell to him."

Before Kellan could reply, the front door slammed open again and a child's voice rang through the foyer. "Papa! Papa, where are you? They said you were home."

"In here," Gerrard replied with a smile Raúl recognized as the one he reserved for the caravan's children. He stepped forward as a bundle of youthful energy came flying into the room. The boy—so clearly Gerrard's son even if he hadn't called Gerrard "Papa"—jumped into Gerrard's arms. Gerrard caught him and spun him around before setting him down. "Is that how we act in front of guests?" Gerrard asked, but Raúl could hear the teasing in his voice.

"No, Papa, but you were gone so long. I was afraid you weren't coming back."

"I promised I would," Gerrard said. "Come, say hello to Raúl."

"Hello, sir," the boy said politely. "I'm Randall Hawkins. It's nice to meet you."

Raúl bent a knee to the ground so he could address the boy at his level. "And I am Raúl. You are very like your papa."

"That's what my mother says," Randall said with a wry smile. "I don't think she means it the same way you do."

"No, when she says it, it's because we're stubborn and headstrong," Gerrard said with a laugh. "Does she know you're here? Because if she is looking for you for supper, it will be on my head."

"I told Grandfather, and he said he would tell her," Randall replied. "He said I could stay for supper if you agreed. Say you agree. Please?"

"You must be on your best behavior," Gerrard said with mock seriousness. He winked at Raúl over Randall's head. "You want to make a good impression on Raúl and Mr. Beecham, don't you?"

"I'll be the perfect gentleman," Randall promised. Raúl smiled at him and stood. The boy studied him for a moment and asked, "Are you the gypsy Papa stayed with?"

"I am a Rom," Raúl answered, "and yes, your father traveled with my caravan for a time."

"Papa said he would take me with him the next time he travels. And he said you have a horse almost as grand as Nubarrón, only I must not go near him if you aren't around. Could I see him? I promise not to do anything to startle him. Papa lets me ride on Nubarrón, though he always rides behind me." Randall chattered without leaving a pause for Raúl to answer.

"Randall, a gentleman lets people answer before he asks the next question," Gerrard chided gently. "If you don't allow Raúl to speak, how will you learn the answers you seek?"

"I'm sorry, Papa, but I have so many questions."

"Sir Gerrard, sirs, dinner is served," Herndon intoned from the doorway. "Ah, I did not see Master Randall come in. Will he be staying for dinner?"

"Yes, Herndon. Please set another place for him?" Gerrard requested.

"Of course, Sir Gerrard," Herndon said with a slight bow.

Gerrard turned to Raúl. "Shall we go see what marvel Mrs. Cullen has whipped up for us tonight?"

DINNER PROVED to be a feast of several courses, accompanied by wine, with fruit and cheese for dessert. The conversation flowed easily, between Kellan bringing Gerrard up to date on the progress made in the village and Randall asking Gerrard to tell him more about his adventures while he was away—stories Kellan seemed almost as eager to hear. By the time the last dishes were cleared away from the table, several hours had passed and the sky was darkening behind the dining room windows.

"We had best send you home with one of the grooms before your mother begins to worry," Gerrard said, ruffling Randall's hair.

"Can't I stay? I want to hear more stories," Randall pleaded.

"Not tonight since we haven't discussed it with your mother, but now that I am back, we'll prepare a room for you to come here to stay."

Randall pouted all the way out the door, but he hugged Gerrard tightly before leaving.

"I will bid you good night as well," Kellan said after they had seen Randall off. "Sir Gerrard, will you have time to sit down and go over the books with me tomorrow? Our discussion at dinner notwithstanding, I would like to show you the actual figures."

"I had planned to spend tomorrow riding the estate with Raúl. I want him to feel at home here as quickly as possible," Gerrard said. "Perhaps the day after?"

"Of course," Kellan agreed. "I trust you will find all in order. It is a pleasure to meet you, Raúl. I look forward to our better acquaintance."

"As do I," Raúl agreed. After Kellan left for his room, he turned to Gerrard with a smile. "He seems most capable, despite his youthful appearance. I see you have learned your lesson about judging by looks alone."

Gerrard smiled as Raúl had intended. "You taught me that lesson well, *mi corazón*. Shall we retire as well or would you care for a glass of port first?"

Raúl shook his head. "I am content." As they started toward the staircase, he rubbed his stomach. "Though if your cook means to feed us that well every day, I shall need to join your tenants in the fields to work it off."

"Mrs. Cullen thinks I am too thin," Gerrard said. "She will consider you emaciated and make it her mission to fatten you up. You'll meet her at breakfast tomorrow."

"It will not always be this easy," Raúl warned when they reached Gerrard's room and closed the door behind them. "Your son, like you, is predisposed to find everyone agreeable, and your Mr. Beecham may have said nothing during dinner, but I doubt he will remain ignorant of what I am to you for long." He drew Gerrard down for a kiss. "Nor will the pretext of separate rooms fool your housekeeper."

"Kellan suspects already, I think," Gerrard said. "I was not as subtle as perhaps I should have been when I was telling him about you before I came to find you." He ran a hand through his hair and sat down on the bed. "I don't pretend to know how this will work, but I know I don't want to do it without you. I can't do it without you. I am not important enough to need a bodyguard always at my side nor poor enough any longer to use money as an excuse to share lodgings as Perrin and Léandre do. The village has an apothecary, though he has not your gift for healing, but even if the village accepted you as their healer, it would not explain why you live in the manor with me. It will come down to people accepting us or not, and if they don't, we will return to Spain. I will name Kellan the executor of my estate until Randall reaches his majority, and we will hope for the best. But I have to try. I owe my family that much."

"I have spent my life knowing some people think ill of me, for being Rom if nothing else. Their opinions matter not to me, but it is not the same for you." He drew Gerrard to the bed to sit beside him. "In the day I have been here, it is clear how much your son and your people mean to you, and how much better their lives will be for your being here. It is your calling as much as healing is mine. We will make a life together somehow, because there is no life for me without you, and some will accept that and some will not. We can hope most are like your Kellan, who if he does suspect seems not to care. 'Our' man of business?" he asked with a pointed glance.

Gerrard shrugged as his cheeks turned pink. "What is mine is yours. You have shared your life with me for the past five… no, it is six years now. The day passed while we were apart. I will share mine with you now. I will share mine with you now. Besides, the more people we have on our side, the better off we'll be. But I will attempt to be more discreet in my words if it bothers you."

"Only so far as they may put you at risk." Raúl allowed himself a moment's regret that they were not still with his *familia* in Spain, where he and Gerrard had been accepted no differently than any other couple. "I would we could be honest about our love, but that is not the world we live in."

"I will be careful until we are more established here. A time will come when the villagers will think no more of us than they do of anyone else. I have to believe that."

"Let us hope you are right. If your villagers are anything like your household staff, they well appreciate your worth already." He clasped Gerrard's shoulders to draw him closer. "Now, I believe we have better things to do with our time, have we not?"

Gerrard moved into Raúl's embrace eagerly. "I can think of several very pleasant ways to spend the rest of our evening. Unless you had a suggestion, of course."

"Tell me what you would suggest," Raúl said.

Gerrard let his mind wander back to the nights spent alone and the favorite memories that had kept him warm. "I would have you take me, although I spent more than a few nights dreaming of all the things I would do to you before we reach that point."

"I am at your service, though I would suggest removing this very elegant doublet to begin with." Raúl pushed it back from Gerrard's shoulders and busied himself at the neckline of the fine linen shirt beneath, letting Gerrard struggle to free his arms before he could reach for Raúl in turn.

Gerrard shucked the doublet quickly, though he did lay it aside carefully rather than toss it to the floor. Once his arms were free, he tugged at the laces on Raúl's shirt, loosening it enough to trace the line of Raúl's collarbone with his thumb. "How shall I see to you first?" he asked, his voice the husky purr that always made Raúl shiver in anticipation. "Hands? Mouth?"

"Why not both?" Raúl challenged before making use of each himself, tugging Gerrard's shirt over his head and leaning forward to taste the broad, hair-dusted chest. "You were not alone in spending nights dreaming of this."

Gerrard arched into the caress, his back bowing as Raúl licked over one taut nipple. Gerrard clawed at Raúl's back but made no effort to take back control of their interactions despite his offer.

That suited Raúl, at least for the moment. He nudged Gerrard back to open more of his chest to his attentions, savoring the hint of soap from their ablutions before dinner and the muskier scent as he moved down Gerrard's abdomen. When the waist of Gerrard's breeches halted his progress, he reversed direction, nipping and licking a leisurely path until he could claim Gerrard's mouth.

Gerrard sucked Raúl's tongue into his mouth and ran his hands down to cup Raúl's ass. He rutted against Raúl, already fully hard. "I missed this," Gerrard groaned when they broke the kiss to breathe. "No one has ever made me feel the way you do when you touch me."

Raúl leaned forward, pressing Gerrard fully onto his back and resting his forearms on either side of Gerrard's shoulders, so their bodies rubbed together. His shirt muted the sensation he craved, and he pulled it off roughly so that skin met skin. "This is what I missed," he answered, "the warmth of your body against mine. I could not rid myself of the chill all the time we were apart."

"In this heat?" Gerrard asked. Despite his questioning words, he pulled Raúl back into his arms, enveloping his torso in strength and warmth. "You need not move farther than this until we go down to breakfast in the morning."

"A tempting prospect," Raúl said, flexing his hips against Gerrard's arousal. "But perhaps we should remove the rest of our garments first? I would feel all of you."

Gerrard stepped back enough to reach for the laces on Raúl's breeches. He pushed them down and off, then stripped away his own clothes. "Better?" he asked as he drew Raúl against him once again.

"Much," Raúl affirmed, nudging Gerrard back onto the bed and lying within the cradle of his legs, their hard shafts aligned. He flexed his hips, claiming Gerrard's mouth again as they rubbed together, the friction of skin against skin easing with the slickness of their growing arousal.

Gerrard met him halfway, lifting his hips against each downward motion of Raúl's body, his feet planted firmly on the bed to increase his range of motion. He could easily have lifted Raúl from the bed and rolled him if he'd wanted to. That he chose to remain mostly quiescent and give Raúl the control of their joining was a tribute to his trust and his love. Raúl prayed he would never give Gerrard cause to question either of those things.

He pushed up on his forearms and broke the kiss to gaze at Gerrard's face. Gerrard's pupils were wide with desire and warm with emotion. "*Kamaù tut*, Gerrard," Raúl murmured, brushing a strand of hair from Gerrard's brow. The muscles beneath him trembled, and Raúl gave silent thanks for the fate that had brought this powerful, loving man into his life.

"I love you too," Gerrard replied as he leaned into Raúl's caress. He angled his head for a kiss, which Raúl gave him gladly. Gerrard parted his lips, inviting Raúl inside, and Raúl took advantage of the offer, plundering Gerrard's mouth and wringing a groan from his lover's throat. He wanted to devour him, worship him, fuck him until he couldn't move, and hold him so tightly he wouldn't want to.

When Gerrard eased back to draw a gasping breath, Raúl turned that hunger to Gerrard's magnificent body. Years of loving had taught him all the places Gerrard was most sensitive, and he used that knowledge now to touch and tease and nip and suck, to bring Gerrard to the same level of need. His cock throbbed almost painfully, but he ignored its ache as he slid down Gerrard's sculpted torso, leaving a trail of nips and bites in his wake. Some primal part of his mind reveled in branding Gerrard as his, knowing no one but he would see the marks but that Gerrard would feel them tomorrow. Whatever claims of family and duty demanded Gerrard's time, he would remember Raúl's claim above all.

Gerrard buried his fingers in Raúl's hair, urging him on without guiding him, leaving all the control of their interactions firmly in Raúl's hands. "More," Gerrard gasped when Raúl sucked on the tendon where hip joined thigh. Raúl looked up to meet Gerrard's gaze, dark with lust and love and desperation. Without looking away, he put his mouth back to the sensitive spot and bit down, gently at first but with increasing intensity as Gerrard held his gaze. Only when his head fell back and a deep moan escaped him did Raúl release the bite. He licked over the already purpling spot with a sense of deep satisfaction.

The heaving rise and fall of Gerrard's chest was still too steady for Raúl's taste, so he moved lower, avoiding the heavy cock that all but begged for his attention. Instead he nipped down the firm muscle of Gerrard's thigh, hard enough to be felt but not to bruise, until he reached the bend of Gerrard's knee. He didn't need the shudder that shook Gerrard's frame to remind him that this was one of his most sensitive spots. Gerrard angled his leg to give Raúl more access, and Raúl licked over the crease at the back of Gerrard's knee, winning a deep moan. He closed his teeth over the tender flesh and suckled, savoring the saltiness of sweat and the unique taste of Gerrard's skin.

"*Maldito sea*, Raúl," Gerrard cursed. He thrashed on the bed, all but his leg in Raúl's hands. He made no move to pull away despite his cursing and writhing. "Fuck me."

"Patience, *mi corazón*," Raúl chided, though in truth his own control was wearing thin. But Gerrard could still speak, so he wasn't as frantic with need as Raúl would have him. He nipped his way up Gerrard's other leg until he reached the tangle of dark hair, redolent with musk. Gerrard arched up wildly when Raúl nuzzled into the thatch, catching a few hairs between his teeth and tugging before lapping at the heavy balls below. He drew them into his mouth, teasing at them with his tongue until Gerrard groaned loudly.

Sounds continued to fall from Gerrard's mouth, Raúl's name and some that might have been words, though they made no sense. That was the incoherency Raúl wanted. Gerrard dug his heels into Raúl's back as he lifted his hips to angle his body to give Raúl better access. Even that was more control than Raúl wanted him to have. He braced Gerrard's hips with his hands and licked over the smooth skin behind his sac and into the crease beyond. Every muscle in Gerrard's body went taut at the contact.

Raúl was nearly as tense, resisting the urge to simply push into the clenching iris beneath him and claim Gerrard in the most basic of ways. *Just a little more*, he promised himself, wetting the wrinkled skin until it was slick and then pressing inside with his tongue. Gerrard bucked as wildly as Martiya had ever done beneath him, and Raúl pushed back, holding him in place as he drove his tongue deep and slid it out, over and over in foretaste of the claiming to come.

Gerrard shouted hoarsely above him as he trembled with each press of Raúl's tongue. It wouldn't be enough to ease the way, but the longer he lingered now, the less time he would have to take with his fingers and oil.

Oil…. He hadn't seen Gerrard remove it from his saddlebags. "Where is the oil? If I take you with naught but spit to ease the way, you won't be fit to ride Nubarrón tomorrow."

The time it took for his words to register with Gerrard proved, as much as the tremors that racked him, how mindless Raúl had driven his lover. "Saddlebag," Gerrard said hoarsely, turning his head toward where they still lay on the floor beside the door.

Raúl rewarded him with a plundering kiss before drawing away. "Do not move," he warned as he stood to rummage through the leather satchel, strewing its contents heedlessly across the floor until his fingers closed around the vial he sought. When he returned to the bed, Gerrard lay as he had left him, hands gripping the bedding, legs spread wide, knees bent and open for him. "*Hermoso*. What a beautiful sight," he murmured, taking a moment to appreciate the bounty spread before him.

"You are the beautiful one," Gerrard countered, reaching for Raúl and pulling him back into place. Raúl settled on top of Gerrard and kissed him deeply, but that position didn't allow him the access he needed to prepare Gerrard for their joining. He urged Gerrard to straighten one leg so he could roll more easily to the side and slide his fingers to the spot he had so recently teased with his tongue.

Gerrard moved willingly to the new position, bending his upper leg to open himself more fully. Raúl rewarded him with a final swipe of his tongue down the damp crease before opening the vial and dipping his fingers into the viscous oil. He rubbed them together and then spread the slickness over the portal, tracing its ridges with his fingertips. Gerrard pushed into the touch, cursing when Raúl didn't push inward immediately. "Now," he demanded, turning a pleading glare over his shoulder but still making no move to wrest control from Raúl.

Raúl's cock was making the same demand, but he wanted to return Gerrard to a state of incoherent need before taking him. He slid his index finger into the tight heat, twisting to coat the sides of the passage, while he ran his other hand over Gerrard's hip to wrap it around his cock. "Open for me," he whispered. "Give yourself to me, *amado*."

Gerrard's body opened at his command, as if the words were all it took to send him back to the edge of mindlessness. Raúl added a second finger easily. Gerrard had never relaxed so quickly into the stretch. Apparently he needed this as much as Raúl did.

When his third finger pushed inside with little resistance, Raúl twisted them until he could brush over the seat of Gerrard's pleasure. Gerrard's cock jumped in his grasp, a driblet of fluid easing his stroke. Gerrard undulated between the slide of Raúl's clasp around his shaft and the thickness of the fingers spreading him, so beautiful in his need that

Raúl leaned forward to take his mouth, his tongue matching the rhythm of Gerrard's rocking, his own hips moving in synchrony.

Gerrard broke away to gasp, "Now! Please." His voice broke on the last word as Raúl twisted his fingers against his sweet spot, the sound more a sob than a word. Patience at an end, Raúl slipped his fingers from Gerrard's passage and replaced it with his cock, driving deep in one sure stroke to join their bodies as completely as possible.

A sound that could only be described as a howl issued from Gerrard's throat. Raúl silenced it with his mouth, sparing a thought to hope Gerrard's rooms were far enough from any others that it might go unnoticed. Then Gerrard clenched around him, squeezing his cock and chasing any thought from his mind but that of driving Gerrard wild with pleasure.

It only took a few thrusts before Gerrard began shaking beneath him, his body quaking with the need for release. Gerrard reached for his cock, but Raúl batted his hand away. "Like this," he growled in Gerrard's ear. "Just my cock in your ass. Come for me."

"Make me," Gerrard gasped back.

"You think to… challenge me?" Raúl's voice broke as a wave of sensation swept along his nerves. He would need to keep tight rein on his own arousal if he was to bring Gerrard to bliss first. Grasping Gerrard's hips, he rolled them both onto their stomachs and pressed Gerrard to the bedding so he could plow deep, then draw back and thrust again, gauging by the Gerrard's gasp that he was hitting just the right spot. He leaned back and gave in to the urge to take Gerrard with all the wildness flaring inside him. Gerrard met him thrust for thrust, the force of their coupling shaking the bed frame. *"Rendirse, amante.* Let go."

Gerrard cried out again, his muscles clenching around Raúl's erection as his cock disgorged its load onto his belly. Raúl pumped through the constriction, finding his own release in the tight depths. He collapsed on top of Gerrard, panting for breath. The smell of musk prolonged his pleasure as he buried his face against Gerrard's neck and let contentment sink into his bones.

Eventually, Gerrard shifted beneath him, rolling Raúl to the side so he could rise and bring back a damp cloth to clean them both. Then he pulled Raúl into his arms, settling them with Raúl's head pillowed against his chest. "I should challenge you more often if that is the result."

Raúl smiled and mouthed at the temptingly close nipple. "Let us hope your shouts haven't convinced your servants that I'm torturing you in here."

"If anything, they will be jealous that I am loved so well," Gerrard replied. He shifted a little so he was resting on the pillows and then kissed the top of Raúl's head. "They may not be so jealous of my inability to ride tomorrow, but it will be worth any lingering discomfort. Sleep well."

Surprisingly, Raúl did.

TWENTY-FOUR

RAÚL WOKE before Gerrard the next morning, the first light of dawn just brightening the eastern sky outside the master bedroom's windows. He took a moment to give silent thanks for the man sleeping beside him, and then another to assess their first day together at Hawkins Hall. The reception from Gerrard's retainers had been more positive than he had dared to hope and said much for the loyalty and love his *inglés* had won among them. Whether the farmers and villagers would prove as accepting—to say nothing of Gerrard's peers among the local gentry—remained to be seen.

Hearing the sounds of stirring below stairs, he'd moved to sit up when a strong arm wrapped itself around his waist, pinning him to the bed.

"Where do you think you're going?" Gerrard murmured in a husky voice.

"I thought to return to my—to the other bedchamber before your servants rouse."

Gerrard frowned in a way Raúl would have found irresistible on most occasions, but they could not afford to be discovered, least of all so quickly.

"It is only the first day and already I tire of this," Gerrard said with a sigh, "but you are right. It would not do for them to find us abed together. I will knock when it is time to descend for breakfast. Agatha will bring water for me to wash. Expect her to bring some for you as well."

"We will endure it because we must." Raúl claimed what he meant to be a brief kiss, though Gerrard held him in place when he would have pulled away. When he showed no sign of releasing him, Raúl nipped his lower lip. "Enough. I must give my bed at least the appearance of having been slept in before your Agatha arrives."

Gerrard's sigh turned into a yawn, and Raúl made his escape. After closing the connecting door behind him, he turned down the bedding and rumpled the linens and put enough of a dent in the pillow to convince at least a cursory examiner that he'd spent the night in the room. He had just reached for his pack to pull out clean garments when a tap sounded on the hallway door.

"I've brought water for you, sir," Agatha called through the door. "May I bring it inside?"

"One moment," Raúl called back. If he had to live in a house with servants, he might have to invest in a proper nightshirt rather than risk scandalizing Mistress Agatha by opening the door in nothing more than the long linen shirt he wore beneath his jerkin. For now he pulled on a pair of breeches as well before opening the door.

"Dressed already?" Agatha asked as she bustled inside with an ewer of water in her hands. "If I'd realized you were such an early riser, I'd have brought the water sooner."

"Do not go to more trouble on my account," Raúl said, taking the pitcher from her. He remembered she had been Gerrard's nursemaid and judged her to be at least twenty years older than he—no longer a young woman, though spry enough still for her age. "Whenever you are accustomed to seeing to Gerrard will suit for me."

Agatha's glance reminded him he should have said "Sir Gerrard," but he hoped the pretext of their friendship would excuse his informality. "Cook will have breakfast on the table shortly," she said, dropping a curtsey before leaving the room.

Raúl stripped again and used the water and a cloth by the basin to wash away the evidence of his and Gerrard's amorous activities. It wasn't a hot bath, but it would do for now. If they spent the day touring the estate as they had discussed, he would need a bath come evening. He would ask Gerrard how difficult it would be to arrange for one later.

Ablutions complete, he dressed again and waited for Gerrard's knock. He was tempted to let himself back in through the connecting door, but he had no idea if Gerrard kept a valet. He couldn't really imagine his lover with a body servant, but they were in England now, on Gerrard's estate, not wandering through Spain and France with his caravan.

The tap—again on the hall door—came a few minutes later. He opened it to find Gerrard dressed in riding breeches, boots, and a buff doublet with rows of many buttons down either side, his dark hair pulled back in a sedate queue. He glanced at his cotton shirt, breeches, and leather jerkin—one of the few sets of clean garments remaining in his pack. He understood Gerrard needed to dress to his station, especially as they would be visiting his estates in his role as landlord. The casual attire that would suit a sword for hire or a peripatetic tradesman was no longer appropriate for Sir Gerrard of Hawkins Hall. Raúl had never been troubled by Christian donning court attire, or even Teodoro on the occasions he needed to accompany the ambassador to a formal affair of state. Seeing Gerrard dressed as befit a baronet should be no different, and yet somehow it was.

He shook off the feeling and joined Gerrard in the hallway. "You look very fine this morning. Doubtless the evening's rest agreed with you."

"It did me good to sleep in my own bed again," Gerrard said, the way his gaze traveled Raúl's body making the unspoken *with you* understood. "I hope you rested well in your new room."

"I find the amenities here much to my liking." He let his gaze roam appreciatively over Gerrard as well, before he would need to guard himself to be circumspect in the presence of others. "Your housekeeper mentioned breakfast. You must tell her she need not curtsey to me," he added as Gerrard started down the stairs. "I am no lord to require such niceties."

"I will speak with her," Gerrard said, "but I make no promises. Agatha has been running my life and the lives of everyone around her for longer than I've been alive. She will listen or not, as she pleases."

He ushered Raúl into the dining room. "Breakfast is laid out on the buffet. Help yourself to whatever appeals."

Raúl hoped the variety and quantity of foodstuffs arrayed on the sideboard were in honor of Gerrard's return home and not a sample of what he could expect every day. His entire caravan could have feasted on the offerings with ample to spare. He selected a few sausages and a poached egg and took a seat at the large table. Gerrard was still filling his plate when his man of business entered.

"Good morning, Sir Gerrard, Raúl," he greeted them with a smile.

"Good morning, Kellan," Gerrard said. "How are you this fine morning?"

"Quite well, thank you," Kellan replied. "I have a few things I'd like to discuss with you if you have time today. You mentioned riding out to the village, and I wouldn't wish to delay you, but a few of them are urgent."

"I don't mind waiting while you speak with Kellan," Raúl said, not wanting to keep Gerrard from his responsibilities. He would have to find something to do to keep himself occupied while Gerrard saw to his tasks as lord of the manor, but that would come in time as he saw where his skills could best be put to use.

"If you're sure," Gerrard said. "We will go over things quickly so you don't have to wait too long."

"You have responsibilities I would not see you defer. Our tour can wait."

"It may be a bit warmer later in the day, but not as warm as Spain in the summer." Gerrard smiled as he took the seat beside Raúl.

"Your pardon, Raúl," Kellan said after filling his own plate and taking a seat across the table from them, "but I have not learned your surname."

"Among Rom, such names are not needed," Raúl explained. "Everyone knows everyone else within a *familia*, and among different *compagnia*, should there be two with the same name, referencing one's father is enough to avoid any confusion."

"What was your father's name?" Gerrard asked.

"Tomasis," Raúl replied. "Thomas, in your tongue."

"So you would be Raúl, Tomasis's son?" When Raúl nodded, he continued, "Raúl Tomason does not sound too amiss."

The name sounded strange to Raúl's ears, but if it would help him to fit more easily into Gerrard's world, he would grow to accept it.

"I still long to hear more of your adventures together," Kellan said. "The hints Sir Gerrard has dropped make it all sound quite fascinating."

"Perhaps the telling would be interesting," Raúl allowed. "The living was at times...." He turned to Gerrard as his English failed him.

"Tedious?" Gerrard suggested with a smile.

"Yes," Raúl agreed. "Like all battles, it was many hours of boredom followed by brief moments of danger."

Kellan raised an eyebrow. "I suspect even your idle time was far from boring. It must certainly have been more exciting than studying with my tutor or keeping my brother's books." He swallowed a morsel of ham. "Though perhaps danger is best appreciated in small doses."

"We seldom had the luxury of choice in such situations." While that was not strictly true—they might have elected not to join Teodoro and Christian in exposing the *conde* de la Rocha, or in rescuing Aristide from the Queen Mother's machinations—he could not imagine doing so. "Perhaps you will find it so yourself in time." Kellan seemed quite young, though perhaps that was just Raúl himself feeling his age.

"I would not begrudge Kellan his own adventure, though I fear the demands of the estate will keep him too occupied to seek one," Gerrard added.

"You say that like we sought the adventures we found ourselves involved in," Raúl replied with a smile. He turned his attention to his breakfast then, not wanting to say more than he should. Kellan's open interest would make it so easy to talk of Teodoro and Christian, of the musketeers, and of the time they had spent together, both in battle and in repose, but any one of those stories could damn them all if he said the wrong thing—or if Kellan drew the right conclusions.

Gerrard turned the conversation back to conditions on the estate after that, and once they had finished their meals, he and Kellan repaired upstairs to look over the account books. Not caring to return to his purported bedchamber, Raúl lingered in the dining room until the housekeeper appeared, seeming startled to find him still sitting there.

"I'm sorry, sir, it was so quiet in here I thought everyone had finished. Is there anything more I can get you?"

"Indeed not," Raúl replied with a smile, hoping to calm her agitation. "I could not do justice to all as it was. I hope your cook does not plan to feed us so every morning."

"You could stand a bit of fattening up, sir, if you don't mind my saying so," Agatha retorted, picking up a serving dish. "And Sir Gerrard has a hearty appetite, as I expect you know."

She turned to gather up another platter before Raúl could judge what she meant by the comment. "Let me help you with these," he offered, rising to stack the plates from the table and pick up several others from the sideboard. "You'll have to guide me to the kitchen."

She looked like she might protest his help, but he gave her his best healer stare and she finally nodded and led him down the hall toward the kitchen. From his vantage point a few steps behind her, he noticed how she braced herself to take the few short steps down into the kitchen. "Is it your knee that troubles you or your hip?" he asked as he deposited the dishes on the table.

"My hip," she said. "How did you know?"

"I can see it in the way you walk," Raúl said. "I am something of a healer among my own people. I could give you something that might help, if you are willing."

"The stairs don't get any easier," Agatha allowed. "I take some dandelion tea when the pains get too bad, but if you know of aught that works better, I'd be glad to hear it."

"Let us finish clearing up, and I will see what I have that might serve." After returning to the dining room, Raúl filled his arms with as many of the remaining dishes as he could and followed Agatha into the kitchen.

"Here now, Sir Gerrard's guest shouldn't be acting like a footman," Mrs. Cullen objected when Raúl deposited his load on the table.

"I volunteered," Raúl was quick to interject. "I wanted to thank you again for preparing such fine meals for us."

The cook flushed and stammered her thanks. Once the sideboard was cleared of the last of the serving pieces, Raúl returned to his rooms, Agatha fast on his heels. He placed his pack upon the bed—rumpled enough, he hoped, to convince her it had been slept in—and extracted his pouch of remedies.

"A tea of juniper berries may help ease the pain." He handed her a packet, then dug a bit farther and followed it with a small vial. "Oil of peppermint may also be of help. Massage a bit of it into the joint when it pains you."

"'Tis kind of you," Agatha said, taking what he offered. "I've known Sir Gerrard since he was a babe. He was always a good boy, but he never learned to temper his hotheadedness. He and his father were alike in that—too alike you might say, if you saw how things ended between them."

Raúl hummed noncommittally. He had seen examples of Gerrard's hotheadedness himself, most notably the first time they met.

"He's different since he came back, more... settled. From what he's said of his travels, I suspect we have you to thank for that."

"Any difference you perceive is solely to Gerrard—Sir Gerrard's credit," Raúl was quick to correct himself. "As you see, I have been used to accompanying him in less formal circumstances, but it is clear how deeply he feels his responsibilities here."

Agatha's eyes narrowed. "Take credit where credit is due. You're not at all what I expected when Sir Gerrard told me he'd been traveling with a band of merchants. I don't rightly know what to make of you, but Sir Gerrard is happy, and for now I'll be satisfied with that." She gave the bed a pointed look. "Make sure it stays that way."

Raúl wasn't sure whether she meant the bed or keeping Gerrard happy, but the latter at least he could promise his best to ensure. "As we both want the same thing, I am sure we shall deal well together," he said. "So long as you remember that Sir Gerrard is the only nobleman here, and make me no more curtseys."

Agatha's eyes twinkled as she dropped into an exaggerated curtsey far more suited to visiting royalty than to a simple gypsy. "I'm entitled to show respect where I will. Good day to you, Sir Raúl."

She straightened and left him alone in the room.

Raúl bit back a grin as he returned his pack to the floor and then headed back downstairs. He suspected that Agatha's regard, once won, could do much to ease his way with the remainder of Gerrard's dependents. Returning to the dining room, he found Gerrard and Kellan waiting.

"My apologies for the delay," he said. "Agatha and I were discussing herbal remedies."

"If you've an interest in herb lore, you must meet Turner, our apothecary, when we go into the village," Kellan said. "He's a dab hand from what I've seen."

"Kellan had some business to attend to as well, so I invited him to join us as far as the village. He may not ride the whole estate with us, but this way he can show me what repairs have been made in my absence," Gerrard added.

"I welcome the chance to further our acquaintance." While he might regret the constraint Kellan's presence would put upon their discourse, as Gerrard's agent, Kellan played an important role in Gerrard's life. Getting to know him better could only benefit them both.

When they entered the stables, Raúl could hear Martiya's protests even before the stalls came in view. "For your groom's sake, I hope he has not been so vocal all night."

Gerrard chuckled. "He never did like being penned in. We'll give him a good run today and see if that helps him settle. If not, we'll see if we can find another option for him. For the sake of my groom and my stable."

One of the grooms came running up. "Sir Gerrard, that demon horse—"

"We'll see to him," Gerrard interrupted.

Raúl was already at the stall door, scolding Martiya quietly in Spanish while rubbing behind his ears. "I am not the only one who needs to learn a new language," he told Gerrard when he had calmed the stallion enough to leave him for a moment to gather his tack. "He's never at his best among strangers, but here he cannot even understand what your grooms say."

"It might be easier to teach them a few words in Spanish, enough to calm him down, rather than expect him to learn English," Gerrard replied. "I will see if any of them are interested when we return from our ride. I know you prefer to care for him yourself, and I will never discourage you from doing so, but it would be useful if he could come to know and trust at least one of them as well."

It amused Raúl to see Gerrard standing by while grooms busied themselves saddling Nubarrón and Kellan's mount. He tacked up Martiya himself, not wanting to risk one of the grooms being kicked or worse, but Gerrard was right. "We're both going to have to get used to living in a different world," he murmured in Martiya's ear as he mounted to follow Gerrard out of the stable yard.

Twenty-Five

GERRARD TRIED to see the village through Raúl's eyes as they rode past the tavern toward the apothecary. Perhaps not the usual first stop, but Gerrard could see the tension investing Raúl's frame, and a visit to the tavern so soon after breakfast, or to the tailor for new clothes or any of the more "logical" first stops, would do nothing to ease it. A chance to sit and talk herb lore with the only person Gerrard knew who could even come close to Raúl's knowledge, though, would relax Raúl in a way nothing else Gerrard could do in public would.

"If you wish to go ahead and tend to your business, there's no reason to wait for us," he told Kellan. "We can meet at the tavern to talk later. I suspect Raúl and I will be here awhile."

Kellan nodded and veered off in the direction of the tailor's. Gerrard would offer Raúl a visit to the shop later. He would never force his lover to change his way of dress, but if Raúl wished for new clothes in the style of his new home, Gerrard would be happy to oblige. He guided Nubarrón to the blacksmith's shop where he could leave both horses in the field behind the forge. "They'll be safe here while we walk through the village, and we won't have to worry about them bothering anyone either."

"That is for the best. I will let Martiya have a good long gallop before we return home, but the ride here was not long enough to settle him. He would not appreciate being penned in a stall so soon after tasting freedom."

"Sir Gerrard," Warren called as they let the horses loose in the field. "I'd heard you returned. Does that great beast of yours need new shoes again already?"

"Hello, Warren," Gerrard replied. "No, we thought merely to use your field for a few hours. Nubarrón would be fine in the stable at the tavern, but Martiya is less even-tempered. He'll be happier chasing around your field than he would be closed up again. I didn't think you'd mind."

Warren came to the edge of the fence and looked at the two horses. "That's a mighty fine one. He belong to your friend?"

"He does indeed. Warren, this is my friend Raúl Tomason. Raúl, John Warren, our blacksmith."

Raúl raised an eyebrow but offered Warren his hand. "Martiya has not been shod in some time. When he is better accustomed to his new home, I may have need of your services."

"'Twill be my pleasure to work on such a fine beast, Mr. Tomason."

After they took their leave of the blacksmith and headed toward the apothecary shop, Raúl shook his head. "I wonder if I will ever grow used to hearing myself addressed as 'Mr. Tomason.'"

"As they get to know you better, you can ask them to call you Raúl, or Mr. Raúl at least. Some will, some won't, but it will not always be as strange as it is now, I promise." Adjusting to life in the gypsy caravan had not been easy, but with time and familiarity, Gerrard had come to be at his ease there. The same would hold true of Raúl here in the village. "But for now, we should meet Turner. I expect he will be your first conquest in town."

They found the apothecary consulting with a young mother about her infant's colic. Raúl watched the interaction, nodding silently when Turner recommended feeding the babe a weak chamomile tea and asked the woman to return the next day if the child's pains had gotten no better.

"Mr. Turner, here is the friend I spoke with you about," Gerrard said when the woman had left the small shop with Turner's packet in hand. "Raúl, our village apothecary, Arthur Turner."

"Pleased to meet you, Mr. Turner," Raúl said with a bow of his head. "Sir Gerrard has spoken highly of you. I hope you won't mind if I come to visit from time to time. Not many share my passion for healing."

"I would sincerely welcome it," Turner said with a smile. "I have found there is always more to learn, and remedies that provide ease for one may have no effect on another. And it is even more challenging when the patient cannot speak to describe their symptoms, as in the case you just saw. I can only judge from the mother's description and suggest something else if this does not serve."

"I have found an infusion of basil in water to be helpful in such case," Raúl offered, "and a warm poultice if the pains are especially strong."

"I have tried mint tea as well, but have never thought of suggesting basil," Turner replied eagerly. "What proportion to the water do you find works best?"

"Gentlemen," Gerrard interrupted. "If you will excuse me, I will leave you to your discussions and see to my own business. Raúl, join me at the tavern when you and Mr. Turner have finished."

"Or come to fetch me when you are ready to ride on if we are still talking," Raúl said with a knowing smile. "It may be years before Mr. Turner and I finish."

"You do not need to exchange all your knowledge today," Gerrard reminded them both with an indulgent smile of his own. Raúl might hide it better, but he was just as eager to confer with a congenial spirit as Turner was. "'Tis a discussion you can resume at any time."

Since Turner had already gestured for Raúl to join him behind the counter to examine his store of medicines, Gerrard took his leave unnoticed and headed down the road to the tailor, where Kellan was just finishing his transaction.

"Have you lost him already?" Kellan asked with a grin.

"Alas, I am no match for the lure of Mr. Turner's company," Gerrard admitted. "I may need to pull him away bodily to bring him back to the Hall before dark."

"He is… a most interesting man," Kellan said. "How did you come to meet him?"

Gerrard chuckled. "I underestimated him. He could have killed me for it. Instead he taught me a lesson that has saved my life any number of times since then."

"He must indeed have hidden depths," Kellan observed, "for looking at the two of you, most would assume you could best him easily."

"You make the same mistake I did," Gerrard said, "but he has taught me that speed and cunning are more than a match for brute strength."

"You have a unique friendship," Kellan observed.

Gerrard looked at him sharply, hoping Kellan meant those words at face value or, if not, that they indicated his approval. "I would imagine any friendship that began with one nearly killing the other, followed quickly by trying to stop the assassination of a king, would be unique."

"I meant no offense," Kellan said quickly. "I am in your employ, but I hope you know you can always count me your friend as well.

Perhaps a more conventional friendship, but no less deeply felt, at least on my part."

Gerrard bowed his head in acknowledgment. He might never have the same openness that Christian and Teodoro enjoyed with their entourage—of two, though that was the way they wanted it—but he would take what he could get and be grateful for it. "I suggested he should meet me at the tavern when he and Mr. Turner have finished their conversation. Would you care to join me, or have you other business to attend to in town?"

"Nay, I had but to order some new shirts, and Johnson has my measure now. I would be pleased to join you."

"I shall need to bring Raúl on a similar errand soon, I suspect." Gerrard thought for a moment of placing an order on Raúl's behalf—he could give a near enough estimate of his measurements—but thought better of it. Raúl might not have quite Teodoro's prickly sense of pride, but he would no doubt prefer to pick out his own clothing. "Let us refresh ourselves at the tavern, then."

"Sir Gerrard, welcome back! And Mr. Beecham, always a pleasure," Cowden said as they walked in. "What can I bring you this fine summer morn?"

"A pint wouldn't go amiss," Gerrard replied. "For all that the sun hasn't hit its peak yet, it's already quite warm."

"I'll have the same, please," Kellan added.

They found a table near the door and settled in to wait for Raúl. Gerrard suspected it wouldn't be a short wait.

OVER AN hour—and two pints of ale—later, Gerrard gave up on the idea that Raúl would join them. "I think I shall have to roust Raúl from Mr. Turner's apothecary if I have any hope of finishing our visit to the estate."

"I wish you luck," Kellan said. "I will ride back to the manor house and let Mrs. Cullen know not to expect you for luncheon. I have some work to see to, so I will bid you a good afternoon."

"The same to you," Gerrard said. "You may tell her we will be back in time for dinner, although not an early one. We will take advantage of all the daylight we can."

"I will give her the message," Kellan promised.

GERRARD WALKED back to the apothecary, not at all surprised to find Raúl and Turner with their heads together as they studied an old text. Whether it was in English, Spanish, or Latin, he didn't know. "Gentleman, I have come to drag Mr. Tomason away. We have other stops to make this afternoon."

"Take it with you," Turner urged. "It will give you another excuse to visit when you return it."

"I need not the excuse, but I thank you for the loan of your book. It has been my great pleasure to make your acquaintance, Mr. Turner."

"And mine to make yours, sir. I look forward to your next visit."

"I assure you it will be soon, but for today, I promised to show Raúl the rest of the estate," Gerrard added. "A good day to you, Mr. Turner."

"And to you, Sir Gerrard, Raúl."

"Are you well pleased with your visit?" Gerrard asked Raúl as they walked back toward Warren's field and their horses. Raúl appeared more at ease than he had been since they landed in England, but Gerrard wanted to make sure.

"Most pleased," Raúl said. "Here is somewhere I can be truly useful to you and your village. Mr. Turner is better than many in his profession I have met. I have no fear in that regard, but we have been to different places and learned from different sources. I have things I can teach him just as I have things to learn from him."

"Good," Gerrard said. "I want you to be happy here."

"I am with you—how could I be otherwise? But I mean to do as well to fit into your life here as you have done to fit into mine."

Regardless of who might be watching, Gerrard took Raúl's hand and squeezed it. He wished he could do more, but helping Raúl fit into life in England unfortunately meant being circumspect in public. Raúl met his gaze with a warm smile but drew back his hand before they reached the smithy.

Warren was busy with a customer, so they whistled for their horses, mounted, and waved their thanks as they took to the road.

"Where to next?" Raúl asked.

"I thought to show you some of the farms before we pass by to visit Randall and to discuss his move to the Hall with his mother," Gerrard said. "And we need to give Martiya a good run at some point before we go to visit. I don't want her refusing to let him come because she fears what Martiya will do."

"Is it safe to go for a gallop along these lanes?" Raúl asked. "You know the area, and I do not."

"The farmers would prefer us to use the lanes rather than their fields," Gerrard said. "This lane leads through the estate and eventually on to the village that depends on Kellan's cousin. Give Martiya his head. Nubarrón and I will keep up as we can. If you get to the next village, wait for us there."

Raúl nodded his agreement, then leaned forward over Martiya's neck to murmur in his ear and loosened the reins. Martiya broke immediately into a gallop, and Gerrard paused for a moment to admire the sight of Raúl and his steed racing almost as one before tapping Nubarrón with his heels to urge the larger horse to follow. Memories of the first mad race to the *conde* de la Rocha's country estate filled his mind as they sped against the wind. How much both their lives had changed since that day! Not that he would change a moment of it.

He caught up with Raúl—Raúl and Martiya stopped to wait for him—near the border of his estate and Beecham's. "See that tree line?" he asked when he was close enough not to have to yell. Raúl nodded. "That's where the Hawkins estate ends and the Beecham estate begins. At some point Sir Thomas will come calling, I'm sure. He recommended Kellan to me in the first place and seems to have taken quite an interest in having a Hawkins living in the Hall. Good for the neighborhood, he said."

"Should I be worried?" Raúl asked.

"He's happily married, if that's what you mean," Gerrard said. "If you're worried about what he might think of you when he visits, I will say what I have said from the beginning. I care nothing for the opinion of local society because I don't need their goodwill beyond perhaps working together to bring in all the crops this fall, with the deaths we've all had in the villages. I had intended to ask if some of your caravan would come to England with us, but we left France too quickly. I am a Hawkins, living in the Hall, and I have a son to follow after me. He can hardly complain that I have left things unstable."

"If he is as amiable as his cousin, I shall be pleased to meet him." Raúl glanced around him. "Your fields seem well tended, despite the tenants lost to the plague. It says much for the effort those remaining have exerted to keep them so."

"No one wants to face starvation this winter," Gerrard said. "I would do my best to meet their needs, but I did not collect rents in the spring because of the plague, and I spent much of our reserve seeing to improvements so we would not lose even more people. Without a rich harvest, there would be only so much I could do, and I think they realize that."

"I meant to praise, not criticize," Raúl said. "Remember how Javier spoke of the tenants on the *conde*'s estate. There was no loyalty or respect there. Your tenants obviously care for the land almost as if it were their own."

"As it might well be." Gerrard turned Nubarrón at a more sedate pace toward the nearest holdings. "Some of our tenants have held their land for generations. And whatever my father's faults, he did not believe in wringing every bit of yield from the land. He might have been slow to expend coin to repair their cotes, but he did not begrudge the farmers their fair share of the harvest."

"And we shall follow in his footsteps," Raúl replied. "Martiya has had his run. He will be more polite now, if you're ready to visit Randall."

Gerrard feared how that visit would go. Rebecca had none of the instinctive respect for his position that many of the other villagers gave him. She wouldn't hesitate to make any concerns she might have quite clear, and she wouldn't bother with putting things nicely either. Still, better to get it over with and have it behind them. "Randall will be thrilled to see you again, and even more so if you take him for a ride on Martiya."

"I can trust him to behave now," Raúl agreed with a pat to the stallion's neck.

Gerrard didn't ever trust Martiya to do anything, but he trusted Raúl, and that was all that mattered. If Raúl said Martiya would behave, Martiya would behave. He turned Nubarrón toward Rebecca's father's farm and braced himself for the upcoming confrontation. He didn't want to fight with Rebecca, but he would not let her push him to choose between his son and his lover.

"Raúl!"

Randall's voice, bright with excitement, carried down the lane to them as they neared the farm.

"So you will yell for Raúl and not for your own father?" Gerrard teased when they reached the boy.

"I have already ridden on Nubarrón, but Raúl said I might ride Martiya," Randall exclaimed.

"Randall!" Rebecca's voice sounded loudly as she appeared at the doorway of the cottage. "What have I told you about running out—" She stopped short when she saw Gerrard, the expression on her face far from welcoming. "I expect you've come to take my son from me."

"I have come to speak with you," Gerrard said, "but perhaps it would be better if Raúl took Randall for a ride while we do so. He will enjoy that far more than listening to our discussion."

Rebecca frowned, but she didn't protest when Raúl bent low to pull Randall up on the saddle in front of him. Gerrard waved as Raúl let Randall help him hold the reins while they rode back along the lane.

"Before I left for the Continent, you were demanding to know when I would be back so he could move up to the Hall," Gerrard said when they were alone. "Have you changed your mind?"

Her gaze followed Martiya and his riders until they disappeared around a curve in the lane. "I did not think it would be so hard to let him go," she said softly. "I know he will have a better life than I can give him as your heir, but I shall miss him."

"I am not taking him across the sea, Rebecca," Gerrard replied gently. "The Beeches is not so far from here that you cannot come to visit him. You are welcome to spend time with him at the Hall as often as you like, as he will be free to come and visit you."

"And when you marry and have a legitimate child to replace him," Rebecca said. "What then?"

"I told you before that I have no intention of marrying," Gerrard said, "and that holds true. The papers have been filed naming Randall my heir. He won't be replaced."

She didn't look convinced, but Gerrard wasn't ready to tell her that in his heart, he had pledged his troth to Raúl. She would understand that even less than she would understand his decision to stay a bachelor. "And I suppose next you'll be telling me I have nothing to fear from the heathen gypsy who just rode away with him?"

"Do you truly believe I would have brought him here and introduced him to Randall if I believed for an instant that he posed any threat to our son?" Gerrard asked. She was only spouting the prejudice born of ignorance that so many people shared, but it irked him nonetheless.

"Who knows what godless ideas he will expose Randall to?" Rebecca continued undeterred.

He debated telling her that far from being godless, Raúl was a good Catholic in his way, but to Rebecca's mind that would be even more damning than his being a gypsy. "I will ensure that Randall continues to practice his faith," he said instead. It would mean accompanying him to church every Sunday, a practice he had long fallen from himself, but it would do no harm. In fact, he expected talk would begin if the lord of Hawkins Hall failed to present himself at church once he was established to be in residence once more.

"That will be something, at least," she grumbled. "I don't suppose I can stop you anyway."

Legally she was right. As Randall's father all the rights were his, but he had never wanted this kind of rancor between them. "Rebecca," he said gently, "tell me what is wrong. Or better yet, tell me how I can reassure you that this will not be as terrible as you seem to fear. I have never wanted there to be anger between us, and yet I can't seem to satisfy you."

"It is so easy for men to simply ride away when faced with a situation they dislike." Rebecca walked to the fence separating the cottage grounds from the lane and leaned against it, watching for Randall's return. "Leaving women to keep the house and tend the sick and raise the children. I have a chance for a life with Ben Hull, but I will still worry about my father and my son, even if I am no longer in the same village with them. You say you are here to stay, and for the tenants' sake I hope it is true, but what is to keep you from deciding one day that you are tired of domesticity and disappearing again?"

"My word," Gerrard said. "Which means as little to you as a passing fancy, I know, but I don't know how else to convince you. I left because I felt I had no other choice, but my father is gone now. Those reasons no longer exist. And while I have friends in France and in Spain, Viscount Aldwych will undoubtedly visit England again at some point, and the others may well accompany him." He took a moment to savor the thought of the rowdy musketeers shaking up life in his sleepy village, but more likely they would stay in Paris and he and Raúl—and possibly Randall—would go to the capital to visit there.

"I suppose I will have to be satisfied with that." Rebecca straightened when Martiya reappeared at the end of the lane, Randall laughing happily as he urged the steed on. "It will take a few minutes to pack up his clothes. You might take him to say good-bye to his grandsire before you return to the Hall. Father is working in the east field today."

"I will bring him to visit often," Gerrard promised. "I have no intention to keep him from his family."

Rebecca's expression betrayed her skepticism, but she headed inside the cottage without further words.

Gerrard leaned heavily against the fence. The conversation had left him drained, no matter that he had gotten what he wanted—Rebecca's agreement for Randall to move to the Hall. He smiled at Randall when he bounced off Martiya into Gerrard's arms.

"I rode Martiya, Papa! Raúl let me hold the reins and everything!"

"And was he a good horse?" Gerrard asked.

"Of course he was. Raúl wouldn't let him be anything but good."

Gerrard laughed. Trust his son to have Raúl pegged already. "Shall we walk out to say good-bye to your grandfather before we go back to the Hall? Your mother is packing your things so you can stay there tonight."

"I can really stay?" Randall's eyes were as big as saucers. "I didn't think she'd say yes."

Gerrard wondered how much of her upcoming marriage Rebecca had explained to Randall, but it was not a task he intended to undertake for her. "Yes, she has, though you will continue to see her and your grandfather as often as you all wish."

Randall flung his arms around Gerrard's neck and hugged him. Gerrard met Raúl's gaze over Randall's tumbled curls and smiled. "We'll see how happy he remains once Agatha begins instructing him in the deportment proper to a nobleman's son," he said. "She was quick enough to tweak my ear when my behavior fell short of her standards."

"She could not be more proud of you now," Raúl answered. "Mayhap that goodwill shall carry over to your son."

Gerrard hoped so. With no lady mother to teach him, Randall would learn most of the social graces from Agatha, at least until Gerrard could arrange a tutor for him. He would have to see to that eventually, but first he wanted Randall settled and comfortable in his new home. He might have to call on Sir Thomas Beecham after all to see if he could recommend someone.

Someone else who might not approve of his situation.

He pushed the thought away. He was home with Raúl and Randall. He couldn't ask for more.

TWENTY-SIX

"TELL ME again, Raúl, how you and Papa saved the life of the musketeer!" Randall tugged on the sleeve of the doublet Gerrard had convinced Raúl to have the village tailor make him, along with an armoire full of shirts, breeches, and neckcloths—not so many, after much discussion, as Gerrard had assured him were necessary, but still more garments than Raúl had ever owned.

"'Twas chance, or some would say providence, that we found Aristide's tabard on the road," Raúl said, picking Randall up and then sitting the boy on his lap. "Since we were traveling to visit your father's friend, Viscount Aldwych, who is ambassador to the French court and well acquainted with several of the king's musketeers, we brought it to his attention and were able to lead Aristide's companions to where he was being held prisoner."

"And then?" Randall said. "What happened then?"

Raúl smiled. Randall could probably have told the story as well as Raúl did, as often as he and Gerrard had recounted it—careful to edit it for young ears—but Randall never let either of them stop the tale until they reached the end.

"Then we rescued the horses and set the barn on fire to draw out the evil queen's guards," Raúl said. In France he would never have spoken against the Queen Mother, but in England, where the French were already the devil simply for existing, he could cast Marie de Medici in a different light. "When they all came running to put out the fire, we snuck inside to find Aristide. He was wounded badly enough that we hid in a nearby inn until he was well enough to ride. Viscount Aldwych and the other two musketeers—"

"Léandre and Perrin!"

"Yes, Léandre and Perrin rode back to Paris with Viscount Aldwych and Señor Ciéza de Vivar to warn the king of the threat to his throne," Raúl said.

"And the king chopped the evil queen's head off," Randall added. When Raúl shook his head, Randall set his jaw in a manner that strongly resembled his father's expression when Gerrard became stubborn. "Well, he should have! She was wicked!"

As much as he might have agreed, Raúl wasn't about to tarnish Randall's innocence with an explanation of why it wasn't politically expedient for the king of France to execute his own mother, even when she plotted against him.

"He has you there," Gerrard said with a chuckle, entering the sitting room adjacent to Randall's quarters.

Raúl shrugged. He could hardly argue with Gerrard. "The king loves his mother, even when she is wicked," he said instead. "You wouldn't want anything to happen to your mother, would you?"

"No," Randall said. "I wouldn't want anything to happen to her."

"And King Louis feels the same way," Raúl said. Maybe it wasn't the full truth, but it appeased the boy for now.

"Randall, Agatha is waiting for you," Gerrard said. "We will see you at dinner, though. Listen to her."

"Yes, Papa," Randall said as he scampered out of the room.

"You haven't yet managed to teach him to walk like a young nobleman," Raúl said with a smile.

"No more did I at his age." Gerrard settled into the window seat beside Raúl and wrapped an arm around his shoulder. Raúl relaxed into the embrace, relishing the moment of privacy. "Though he is old enough to need more than Agatha's guidance. I think the tutor Sir Thomas recommended will serve."

"Another of his many cousins?" Raúl asked. Their neighbor Sir Thomas Beecham was the only titled member of a large and close-knit family and did his best to promote the interests of his relatives when he could. Raúl approved; the members of his *compagnia* in Spain cared for each other's interests in much the same way. The momentary pang of homesickness faded when Gerrard spoke.

"Yes, and young enough to have the energy to keep up with Randall that Agatha lacks," Gerrard confirmed. "Though she would tweak my ear if she heard me impugn her thus."

Raúl laughed. He had seen Agatha tweak Gerrard's ear more than once since his arrival in England. Fortunately his herbs had worked on her aching joints so she absolved Raúl from such discipline. "Good. We shall hope he is as easy an addition to the household as Kellan was. How soon can we expect him to start?"

"He is finishing up his last term at university." Gerrard brushed a strand of hair behind Raúl's ear and nuzzled at the ring in his lobe. "He will be available as soon as the term ends. And he is so eager for this chance to prove himself, especially after speaking with Kellan, that I suspect he will fit in well."

Raúl shifted to allow Gerrard better access and raised a hand to the matching ring Gerrard still wore. To his surprise, few had commented on it, apparently accepting it as a harmless eccentricity their lord had acquired during his time abroad. So far Raúl seemed to have been accepted in much the same manner.

He slid his hand down Gerrard's neck to draw him into a kiss. Gerrard responded eagerly, and Raúl was reaching his other hand toward the ties at Gerrard's throat when a sound made him raise his head and draw back.

"Sir Gerrard?" Agatha sounded distressed.

"Go see what she needs," Raúl said. "I'll be here when you come back."

Gerrard gave him one more quick kiss before opening the sitting room door. "Yes, Agatha?"

"Oh, thank goodness I've found you. I have word from the village. Rebecca has fallen ill. Some of the villagers say it's the plague come back to finish the rest of us off. I told them to stop being fanciful and to send for Mr. Turner, but I thought you should know as well."

Raúl's intention to wait for Gerrard to return couldn't withstand the prickle of alarm at hearing that one of the villagers—Randall's mother, of all people—had fallen ill. He rose and walked to Gerrard's side. If Agatha was surprised to see him, she hid it well or counted it unimportant in the face of her obvious concern.

"We'll come at once," Gerrard assured her, then turned to Raúl. "I'll get the horses saddled. Gather what you need and meet me there."

Raúl nodded his agreement but reached out to clasp Gerrard's hand. "Rebecca seemed in fine health when last we saw her. Don't fear the worst before we can determine the truth of what ails her."

Raúl gathered his bag of herbs. If they needed something he didn't have, they could send Mr. Turner for it. Between the two of them, they had made sure the apothecary was well stocked. And if all else failed, he had the gift of Sainte Sara in his hands.

By the time he joined Gerrard at the stables, Gerrard had Martiya saddled and one of the grooms was leading Nubarrón out to join them. Raúl took Martiya's reins and mounted, waiting only for Gerrard to do the same before spurring Martiya toward the farm where Rebecca lived. Gerrard would keep up or catch up. Raúl might have told him not to panic, but he pushed forward nonetheless.

Rebecca's father stood at the door with a frown on his face when Raúl arrived and dismounted. "Where can I put Martiya that he won't do harm to anyone?" he asked.

Rebecca's father looked like he might protest, but Turner came to the door. "Raúl, good, you're here. Put that beast somewhere. I need your opinion on what might best suit."

Gerrard rode up and dismounted, then took Martiya's reins from Raúl's hands. "I'll see to the horses. Check on Rebecca, please."

Turner was already speaking as Raúl turned to follow him inside the farmhouse. "She collapsed while preparing luncheon, it seems. Her father found her and helped her into bed, then came for me. She says she has felt unwell for the past several days and had little appetite, which may account for her swooning."

Rebecca lay in bed, the coverlet pulled to her chin despite the day's warmth. Raúl knelt beside her and touched her hand where it lay outside the quilt. Her skin felt warm and clammy, and it took a moment for her eyes to flutter open. When she recognized him, she drew her hand away.

"What are you doing here?" she asked. Her voice was weak but not hoarse.

"I am something of a healer," Raúl said. "Will you let me help you?"

"How do I know you won't use some heathen medicine on me and make me worse?" she demanded.

"Mr. Tomason and I have spent hours discussing herbs and tinctures," Turner replied. "I have found him most knowledgeable. Anything he gives you will be as good or better than anything I could prepare."

Rebecca didn't look convinced, but Raúl doubted words would do it. "I will tell you everything I have planned, and you may decide for yourself if you wish to let me proceed."

"I've tried giving her yarrow tea to reduce the fever, but she could not keep it down," Turner told him softly. "Perhaps elderflower would be more gentle?"

"Fever is a symptom, not a disease in itself," Raúl reminded the apothecary. "Let us see if we can determine what ails her first, as that may tell us how best to treat her." He turned back to the bed. "Mistress Rebecca, may I take your hand again?"

Rebecca looked skeptical but slid her hand across the coverlet. It trembled as he lifted it, and Raúl closed his fingers around her wrist to measure her pulse. "How long have you been feeling out of sorts?"

"Since my son left," she said bitterly.

Raúl frowned. That had been three weeks. "The same symptoms the whole time?"

"No, they have grown worse. I thought it was nothing, nerves over Randall leaving, but the past few days I haven't been able to keep anything down but the barest broth."

"When did the fever start?"

"Yesterday, perhaps," Rebecca replied. "I'm not sure. It was one more misery on top of a miserable week."

Randall had visited twice during the weeks Rebecca was ailing and had not mentioned anything unusual, though it was hard to judge how much the boy would have noticed. "May I have your other hand?" Raúl asked, clasping both when Rebecca shifted enough for him to reach them without leaning across her. He would like to listen to her breathing to know if her lungs were clear, but he deemed a request to lay his head against her back or, worse, her chest would be sharply rebuffed. He would need to use other means to gain the information he needed.

Keeping his grip light, Raúl closed his eyes and reached out with his senses. Rebecca's pulse was a bit fast, though that could be uneasiness at his presence or anxiousness at the situation in general. What he could hear of her breathing was regular and clear, without hitch or cough. He could wish for privacy for what he would need to do next, but there was no pretext he could use that would convince Turner and Rebecca's father to leave him alone with her.

A hand settled over his shoulder, and Raúl felt the strength and assurance of Gerrard's presence settle into his core. He reached out again, murmuring a prayer to Sainte Sara under his breath and opening himself to whatever Rebecca's spirit could tell him. He sensed weariness and weakness for lack of nutrition, but none of the bone-deep ache and debility the plague brought in its wake. He was about to withdraw when he felt an unexpected spark of presence that explained much. He squeezed Rebecca's hands gently, offering his gift to its fullest. He had failed Queen Anne in this; he would not fail Rebecca.

"I don't think it is anything too serious," Raúl said. "Exhaustion, a bit of weakness from not being able to eat. I suggest some ginger tea to settle your stomach, plenty of broth, and perhaps some toast soaked in milk to keep your strength up, and rest. If you begin to feel worse, you should send for us, of course, but I see no reason for alarm." He pulled some dried ginger root from his satchel of herbs. "Mr. Turner, could you show Mistress Rebecca's father how to prepare a tea for her? The stronger the better."

"Of course," Turner said.

Raúl caught Gerrard's eye and tipped his head toward the door. Gerrard frowned but withdrew, leaving Raúl alone with Rebecca.

"Do not worry too much, if you can help it. I would, however, think of setting a date for your wedding. Perhaps sooner rather than later."

He waited for comprehension to dawn on Rebecca's face. "Are you sure?"

He was, but he could hardly explain how. "Sure enough, but a few more weeks will show if I'm wrong. Right or wrong, my remedies will not hurt you or the babe. But I meant it when I said to send for us if you begin to feel worse. I would not have you lose the child to stubborn pride."

Rebecca settled a hand over her stomach, a far gentler expression warming her face. "Oh, Ben will be so happy. He's always said he wants a family to carry on the craft. I hadn't wanted him to set the banns until Randall was settled, but now...."

"Randall will always be your son," Raúl assured her. "Neither his living with Gerrard nor your starting a new family will change that."

"No, of course not, but it will be easier to start a new life if I am not asking Ben to accept another man's son into his house," Rebecca said. "You must understand. I love Randall with all my heart, but being the mother of a bastard son is not easy, and when the father is the son of the lord of the manor...."

Raúl could imagine it all too easily. Teodoro had married Margarita to protect Esteban from just such a fate. Unlike Esteban, had Teodoro not claimed him, Randall had a father who loved him. "There are many things I do not know in this world," he said slowly, "but as a healer, I have seen many families from many situations. I know what it looks like when a father loves his son. Gerrard may not have been here for the first years of Randall's life, but he is utterly devoted to Randall now."

"I believe you are right, or I would never have let Randall to go live with him, baronet or no." For a moment Raúl saw the spirit and determination that must have attracted Gerrard. She caressed her belly with her fingertips, as though searching for confirmation of the new life within, and her eyelashes fluttered closed.

"Rest," Raúl murmured quietly. He closed the door behind him and rejoined the others in the kitchen. "She will be well," he assured her father. "Give her as much of the ginger tea as she wishes to help the nausea, and be sure she eats even if she says she is not hungry. Perhaps one of the women from the village can help see to your meals and cleaning until she is better?"

"I've been meaning to look into it," her father said. "She'll be off to marry young Hull soon, and it's not fair to keep her tied to me." Raúl doubted it would be difficult for him to find a helpmeet. He was still a hearty man, and the plague had left the village with several likely widows.

They took their leave then and returned to where Gerrard had tethered their horses. When they were mounted and on the road toward home, Gerrard guided Nubarrón close to Martiya's side. "Tell me the truth now. What is wrong with Rebecca?"

"I would not lie to any of you," Raúl said. "Not her father, not her, and especially not to you. She will be well. You left home too soon to see whatever toll carrying Randall took on her, but you spent enough time watching young ones in the caravan because their mothers were ill. You know what pregnancy can do to a woman, especially one worn down by the challenges of raising other children."

Gerrard was quiet for so long that Raúl began to worry. "Gerrard, what is it?"

"I loved her once, you know. I wanted to marry her, but my father refused. For some years after I left, I dreamed of making my fortune and returning for her despite my father's decree."

"Do you still love her?" Raúl asked.

"Not the way I love you, but she is the mother of my child. Except now she's the mother of another man's child instead."

Raúl shook his head. "Not instead. What was it Esteban said about Teo? A heart that big? A mother's heart always has room for more without it taking anything away from the ones already there. You know that."

"Yes, I do." Gerrard grinned the mischievous smile that never failed to warm Raúl, whether he saw it on Randall's face or his father's. "Let's head home. I've a mind to resume where we were before Agatha interrupted us, and I intend to prove you have no reason to feel jealous of Rebecca." He clapped his heels to Nubarrón's side and took off.

Raúl let him ride a bit ahead, admiring the fine view of man and beast, before leaning over Martiya's neck and whispering in his ear. The black nickered and lengthened his stride, and Raúl gave him his head. Martiya had the advantage of Raúl's smaller weight on his back. He could win if he wanted to, but victory could put Gerrard in an even… better mood. Raúl wasn't jealous of Rebecca, but he was by no means averse to letting Gerrard prove he didn't need to be. He smiled all the way back to the manor.

EPILOGUE

"HOW MUCH farther, Papa?" Randall bounced to the carriage window and pressed his nose against the glass, gazing raptly at the French countryside.

Gerrard rolled his eyes at Raúl but answered patiently, "If we meet no delays, we should reach Paris before suppertime." At the beginning of their journey to Paris for Esteban's wedding, he'd instructed Randall that he could ask once per day how much longer the trip would last, and after a few reminders, Randall had not abused the privilege.

"And I can meet the musketeers, and Christian and Teo!"

"Viscount Aldwych and Señor Ciéza de Vivar, yes, since we will be the Viscount's guests at his *hôtel particulier*," Gerrard said. "You must remember to address them properly, Randall."

"Yes, Papa." Randall crossed to the other side of the carriage and peered out the window beside Raúl, though it offered no different view. "And I must address Aristide, Léandre, and Perrin as *M. le Mousquetaire* or monsieur."

"At least until they grant you permission to address them more familiarly." Raúl settled Randall onto the seat beside him. "They have their duties to the king, so you may not meet them before the wedding, but I am sure they will attend the ceremony. Esteban wrote that Queen Anne, at least, will attend since Marie-Agnès is one of her ladies-in-waiting."

Gerrard gave silent thanks once again for Raúl's gift with children. The three-week trip to Paris had been long and tedious for a nine-year-old boy used to running free across their estate for hours each day. Mr. Beecham the tutor—not to be confused with Mr. Beecham the estate manager, and didn't that make for interesting dinner conversations—believed in teaching Randall everything he could outside the schoolroom, leaving only reading and ciphering for the time they spent indoors at a desk. The hours spent on the ship as they crossed the channel provided some outlet for Randall—and, fortunately, minimal discomfort for Raúl, since the channel was calm during the half-day crossing from Dover to

Calais—but they would all be glad when they reached Paris and Randall could escape the confines of the carriage again.

"If you behave like the young gentleman you are, we will see if we can visit musketeer headquarters before we leave Paris," Gerrard offered, "but only if you remember your manners."

"I'll remember, Papa. I promise," Randall said.

Gerrard believed Randall would try, with a reward like that hanging in the balance. He also knew less than a year of living as a nobleman's son had only begun to curb the boy's natural tendencies for boisterousness. Then again, being in the musketeers hadn't managed that for Léandre and Perrin, so Randall would fit right in.

The farmlands outside the carriage could only hold Randall's interest for so long, and soon he rested his head against Raúl's shoulder and dozed. Raúl smiled across the seat at Gerrard. "Quite a different journey than riding at all speed with the prospect of a sword fight at the end, is it not?"

"Let us hope there are no sword fights on this excursion," Gerrard answered. "Randall may see this as a grand adventure, but attending Esteban's nuptials and returning home safely will be excitement enough for me. I suppose I am growing old and stolid."

"You are growing into being a father."

And what a wonderful feeling that had turned out to be. He had sent money whenever he had it during the years he had spent on the Continent, but beyond that, he had not envisioned a life with his son. Now he could not envision a life without him. Before he could say anything else, shouts from outside the carriage drew his attention. He frowned and reached for his sword. He had hoped the trip would pass with no problems, but it seemed they would not be so lucky.

"Bonjour, *le carosse*! Gerrard, Raúl, is that you?"

Gerrard slumped back against his seat in relief while Raúl lowered the window and leaned out to greet their friends. The movement jostled Randall awake, and he squirmed around Raúl to poke his head out the window also.

"Léandre, Perrin, well met! What brings you out to the countryside?"

"Teodoro told us you were expected to arrive today, along with Gerrard's son, so we decided to give you a proper welcome to France." Perrin reined in his horse as the carriage slowed to a stop. "This must be young Master Hawkins himself."

"Bonjour, Messieurs les Mousquetaires," Randall said formally, adding a small bow as best he could with his head and shoulders out the carriage window.

"Why, 'tis Gerrard in miniature!" Léandre added, removing his hat with a flourish and bowing over his horse's neck in return.

"He is my son," Gerrard muttered inside the carriage. With Raúl and Randall both leaning out the window, he would never fit.

"You are monsieur Léandre, and you are monsieur Perrin, right?" Randall asked, pointing to the two men in turn. "Papa and Raúl have told me all about your adventures."

"You are right, Master Hawkins," Léandre said. "You have a good eye. We are only an hour from Paris on horseback. Do you suppose your father would agree to let you ride with us so we can show you the sights?"

"Oh, Papa, please?" Randall said, pulling back inside.

Gerrard shared an indulgent smile with Raúl. "You did use your best manners." He opened the carriage door and stepped down. Randall darted out after him, stopping far enough away from the musketeers' horses to avoid a chance nip or kick.

"Our nags aren't as fractious as Raúl's beast," Perrin said with a smile and extended a hand. Randall ran to him and was quickly pulled into the saddle in front of him.

"Though you'd do well to be cautious of Aristide's Orphée, should you meet him," Léandre added. "He would have joined us, but he has duty at court today. He is looking forward to seeing you both and meeting young Master Hawkins as well."

"We will meet you at Christian's residence for dinner," Perrin said. "Enjoy your carriage ride."

Before Gerrard could say so much as be careful, they spurred their horses and galloped back down the road toward Paris, Randall's peals of laughter sounding around them.

"They will see him safe," Raúl said at Gerrard's side.

"I know that, but a part of me wanted to see his face when he first entered Paris and when he arrived at the musketeers' headquarters," Gerrard said. "He will tell me more about it than I could possibly want to know over dinner, but it's not the same."

"No, but they have given him a memory he will treasure his entire life," Raúl said. "Even in England, where the French are the devil, the musketeers are dashing heroes out of every child's imagination. He will be the envy of Sir Thomas's children when he tells them of his adventures."

"And it gives me the chance to have you to myself for the next hour," Gerrard added, pulling Raúl back into the carriage and closing the curtains before knocking to signal the coachman to drive on.

"THERE, YOU look the perfectly respectable *inglés* once again." Raúl straightened Gerrard's doublet as the carriage clattered over the cobblestoned streets of Paris. They still maintained discretion in public, though Raúl suspected that Agatha as well as Herndon and both the Beechams had come to understand the nature of their relationship. How well they accepted it he could not say, though he supposed their continued presence at Hawkins Hall was its own answer. Randall was, as could be expected, far more open in his acceptance. He'd startled them both when, after breakfast one morning before they left, he'd told Gerrard, "You don't have to wait until I go to kiss Raúl if you want. I won't tell anyone else." Gerrard had spoken with Randall about not sharing everything he knew with those around him, but Raúl hoped to have a moment with Esteban. If anyone would understand the position Randall was in, it was Teodoro's son.

The carriage had not even drawn to a halt yet when the door to Christian's *hôtel particulier* opened and Christian came hurrying out, Teodoro following close behind. "You're here! We weren't sure you'd make it today."

Raúl laughed and jumped down from the carriage as soon as it stopped. The year he had spent in England with Gerrard was the longest he had gone without seeing Teodoro since they'd met, and as much as he loved Gerrard, he'd missed his best friend. "We came as quickly as we could, although traveling for a wedding is very different than traveling at speed, especially with a child along."

"How long are you staying?" Teodoro asked.

"A few weeks at least, before we go on to Spain. Gerrard wishes to invite some of my *compagnia* to settle on his estate. We can but hope Randall will find the second half of our journey as grand an adventure as it has been for him so far."

"Where is Randall?" Christian asked when Gerrard exited the carriage alone. "I've looked forward to meeting him."

"Perrin and Léandre met us outside the city and took him for a ride." Gerrard pulled Christian into a hug and then offered Teodoro a handclasp. "I expect it won't be much longer before he will have worn out their patience, and they'll be glad to hand him back to us."

"How is Esteban?" Raúl asked Teodoro as the carriage driver began unloading their luggage.

"It is hard to say, since he spends so much of his time with his betrothed that we seldom see him," Teodoro answered. "We will send word you have arrived. If anything can coax him from Marie-Agnès's side, it will be that."

"We shall hope that is sufficient enticement," Gerrard said with a smile. "I have a small favor to ask him, if he can make time for the son of an old friend."

"He will make time," Christian said. "Teo is right that we rarely see him, but when we do, he speaks of your arrival with much excitement. There is still a bit of the boy who idolized Raúl in him, for all that he is a man grown these days. As the wedding approaches, Marie-Agnès's time will be taken up with the last-minute plans, and Esteban will be back to haunting these halls, I'm sure."

Raúl laughed. "Is he that nervous?"

Teodoro's lips twitched. "Only that she will change her mind."

"There is proof that he loves her," Raúl said. "He must respect her enough not to have bedded her yet, or he would have no fears in that regard."

"If he has any fears, it is of the queen's reaction should she learn one of her ladies-in-waiting had been despoiled before marriage," Christian added.

"How fares the queen?" Raúl asked. His failure to save the babe she'd lost would always haunt him, though seeing Rebecca wed and safely delivered of a healthy son had brought its own balm to his spirit.

"We see her rarely, but she always has a smile and a nod for us when we do," Christian said. "As ever, the cardinal is a thorn in her side. Esteban could give you more news."

The clatter of hooves drew their attention. Léandre and Perrin rode into the courtyard with Randall perched in front of Perrin, a delighted smile on his face.

"Papa!"

He threw himself from the saddle into Gerrard's arms. Raúl might have worried if he hadn't seen Randall dismount that way numerous times over the past year. Randall had complete faith that his father's arms would always be there to catch him.

"I saw the musketeers' headquarters, and I met M. Aristide, and we rode past the Louvre where the king and queen live, though not the evil queen, right, Papa?"

Christian raised an eyebrow, and Gerrard shook his head. "No, though perhaps we should not speak about that during our visit. Randall, these are my friends, Christian Blackwood, the Viscount Aldwych, and Teodoro Ciéza de Vivar. Gentlemen, my son, Randall Hawkins."

"It is a pleasure to meet you, Master Hawkins," Christian said, shaking Randall's hand. "You really are very like your father."

"Papa says you are the best swordsman he has ever met," Randall said to Teodoro, though his voice hinted at his doubt that anyone could be better than his father. "He will not let me use a sword yet, but I will be a swordsman too when I am older."

"He sounds very like Esteban to me," Teodoro said with a wink for Raúl. He turned his attention back to Randall. "And with your father and Raúl as your teachers, I have every faith you will be a good one. But if there is one lesson I can give you, it would be this. Only draw your sword if you intend to use it. Knowing when not to use it is as much a battle as any fight you will ever be in."

"That sounds like a lesson Christian taught you," Raúl said.

Teodoro shrugged. "Who better to learn it from?"

Raúl couldn't argue with that, not when Christian's ability with words had saved Teodoro's life when all the swords in the world would have been useless.

"Shall we go inside and get you settled?" Christian interrupted. "I imagine a chance to refresh yourselves would be welcome. I know how long a trip it is from London when you must travel with a carriage and retinue, no matter how small."

"Nothing could keep us from Esteban's wedding," Raúl said as they entered the hotel.

"Not even the prospect of another channel crossing," Gerrard added.

RANDALL YAWNED as they finished dessert. Gerrard started to rise to take him upstairs to bed, but Javier stopped him. "You stay and enjoy your port with the others. I can see the young master to bed."

"Thank you," Gerrard said. He would have done it, but they had so little time in Paris that he hated to miss even a few minutes of the one evening they were guaranteed to have everyone together. Tomorrow would see Esteban wed. He had asked to spend the evening before with his father and their closest friends.

Javier gathered Randall into his arms despite the boy's token protests.

"Go with Javier," Gerrard said. "You need a good night's sleep before the wedding tomorrow."

That assured Randall's cooperation, fortunately.

"We can take our port here or we can retire to the salon," Christian said when Javier and Randall had left.

"Let's be comfortable," Perrin suggested. "After all, we have a long night ahead to celebrate with the bridegroom." He toasted Esteban with his glass before draining it.

"Just remember that Esteban must be sober enough to play his part in the wedding tomorrow," Teodoro cautioned as they followed Christian from the dining room into the larger salon.

"I don't plan to overindulge," Esteban said with a laugh. "A few tipsy evenings when I was young—and suffering through Teo's 'remedies' the mornings after—taught me my lesson."

"Says the graybeard," Léandre interjected. "You have years yet to learn to carry your drink."

"Or not, if his lady keeps a tight rein on him," Aristide said with a smile. "'Twill be important to keep your lady wife happy. Even if you must make a sacrifice or two to do so."

"I've seen his bride," Perrin said with an exaggerated leer. "I'm sure it will be no sacrifice to keep her happy."

"And what would you know about pleasing a lady?" Léandre teased.

Perrin looked around the room, pretending to count on his fingers. "As much, I would imagine, as most any of us here. Gerrard has a son, so perhaps he has a bit of experience he could share with Esteban. Eh, Gerrard?"

"Don't rush her," Gerrard said. "She has spent her whole life being taught the value of chastity. Give her time to adjust to the thought of being your lover as well as your wife."

"Assure her that you love her as well as desire her," Benoît said softly from where he sat at Aristide's side. Gerrard remembered that he had lost a wife and child before the musketeers found him near death on the roadside. "That means taking the time to see to her pleasure before seeking your own."

"Or to see to hers even if you lose control of your own," Perrin added.

"You'd know about that," Léandre said with a bawdy grin.

"I've never left you unsatisfied," Perrin retorted. "Though there can always be a first time."

"That will be no hardship," Esteban assured them while Léandre did his best to coax Perrin out of his dudgeon.

"Oh, he thinks he knows how to please a woman," Aristide said. "Have you had much experience?"

Esteban flushed but didn't back down. "More than some in this room, I'd wager."

Aristide tipped his head in acknowledgment of the retort. "I'd not wager against you, but don't think for a moment that everything you learned with light-skirts applies to your lady."

"Though I've known some light-skirts to be more honest than some ladies," Léandre commented, having won a smile and a kiss from Perrin.

"Not that you have aught to do with either any longer," Perrin said smugly.

"And that is the greatest gift you can give to her," Raúl said. "Keep your promise to cleave only to her. The rest—what she likes, what you like, how you live together—will work itself out as long as she trusts that your eyes—and the rest of you—are not wandering."

Gerrard met Raúl's gaze in silent apology for his own lack of trust, but this was not the time for memories of times and problems long past. "Although you may have found an area at which your own expertise surpasses Raúl's own."

"Do not disillusion me by telling me there is a second thing Raúl is not expert at!" Esteban protested.

Teodoro raised an eyebrow at Gerrard. "If you believe that, perhaps you do not know Raúl so well as you think you do, even now."

Gerrard glanced at Raúl, who met his gaze with an inscrutable expression that made Esteban laugh. "I know that look well! It means he's not going to give you an answer, no matter how much you beg."

"Perhaps Gerrard has methods of persuasion you did not," Christian suggested, making Esteban flush again.

"Or perhaps I've learned from past mistakes and don't need to know every detail of Raúl's past to know that his present and his future are mine," Gerrard said firmly. "In that, at least, you have an advantage over all of us. You need not fear some specter from her past coming back to haunt the present. She, however, does not have that assurance unless you give it to her."

"And saying it once or twice will not be enough," Christian said. "Jealousy is an ugly thing, best beaten by unfailing devotion. Tell her you love her as often as you can."

"And take her to bed even more often," Perrin added. "What?" he said when Léandre swatted him. "If he's sleeping with her, he isn't running around town lifting someone else's skirts."

"Let her take the lead when she wishes as well," Benoît said. "She won't know how to ask at first. You must let her know you welcome her interest too."

"Most importantly of all," Teodoro said gravely, "remember that whatever comes, you will face it together, and that whatever you face, you have a family—however unconventional—who will be here if you need us."

Gerrard looked around the room at the gathered men: Léandre and Perrin lounging across the furniture; Aristide like a regal caged lion with Benoît ever at his side; Teodoro and Christian, who had proven more than once that they would die for each other if that was what it took; and finally at Raúl, who had given up everything to come home with Gerrard. Unconventional certainly applied, but Teodoro was right. This was his family. Teodoro had raised Esteban, with Christian's aid, to a young man any parent would be proud of. With Raúl's help, he would bring Randall up to be the same.

Gerrard raised his glass in a toast. "To Esteban and his lady. May they share a love that's deep and true."

Glasses were raised and drained around the room. Gerrard recognized the looks on his friends' faces. More than one vow would be reaffirmed tonight in anticipation of Esteban's vows tomorrow. Weddings were good for the soul, it seemed, a validation of all the risks they'd taken for love.

Growing up in Chicago, NICKI BENNETT spent every Saturday at the central library, losing herself in the world of books. A voracious reader, she eventually found it difficult to find enough of the kind of stories she liked to read and decided to start writing them herself.

When ARIEL TACHNA was twelve years old, she discovered two things: the French language and romance novels. Those two loves have defined her ever since. By the time she finished high school, she'd written four novels, none of which anyone would want to read now, featuring a young woman who was—you guessed it—bilingual. That girl was everything Ariel wanted to be at age twelve and wasn't.

She now lives on the outskirts of Houston with her husband (who also speaks French), her kids (who understand French even when they're too lazy to speak it back), and their two dogs (who steadfastly refuse to answer any French commands).

Visit Ariel:

Website: www.arieltachna.com
Facebook: www.facebook.com/ArielTachna
E-mail: arieltachna@gmail.com

CHECKMATE

Nicki Bennett
and
Ariel Tachna

All for Love: Book One

When sword-for-hire Teodoro Ciéza de Vivar accepts a commission to "rescue" Lord Christian Blackwood from unsuitable influences, he has no idea he's landed himself in the middle of a plot to assassinate King Philip IV of Spain and blame the English ambassador for the deed. Nor does he expect the spoiled child he's sent to retrieve to be a handsome, engaging young man.

As Teodoro and Christian face down enemies at every turn, they fall more and more in love, an emotion they can't safely indulge with the threat of the Inquisition looming over them. It will take all their combined guile and influence to outmaneuver the powerful men who would see them separated… or even killed.

www.dreamspinnerpress.com

ALL FOR ONE

Nicki Bennett
and
Ariel Tachna

All for Love: Book Two

Aristide, Léandre, and Perrin pledge only three loyalties in life: their king, their captain, and their passion for each other. So when the musketeers discover a plan to accuse M. de Tréville of treason, the initial impulse to kill the messenger, Benoît, is tempered by their need to unmask the plotter. But their first two suspects, the English ambassador and Cardinal Richelieu, prove to be innocent, forcing the musketeers to delve deeper into the inner machinations of the French court.

Meanwhile, Aristide finds himself falling in love with the ill-fated messenger, a blacksmith without a home who rouses all of his protective, possessive instincts. Benoît, however, has no interest in any man. Torn between desire and duty, Aristide must find a way to protect the king and clear his captain's name—all while heeding the demands of his heart.

www.dreamspinnerpress.com

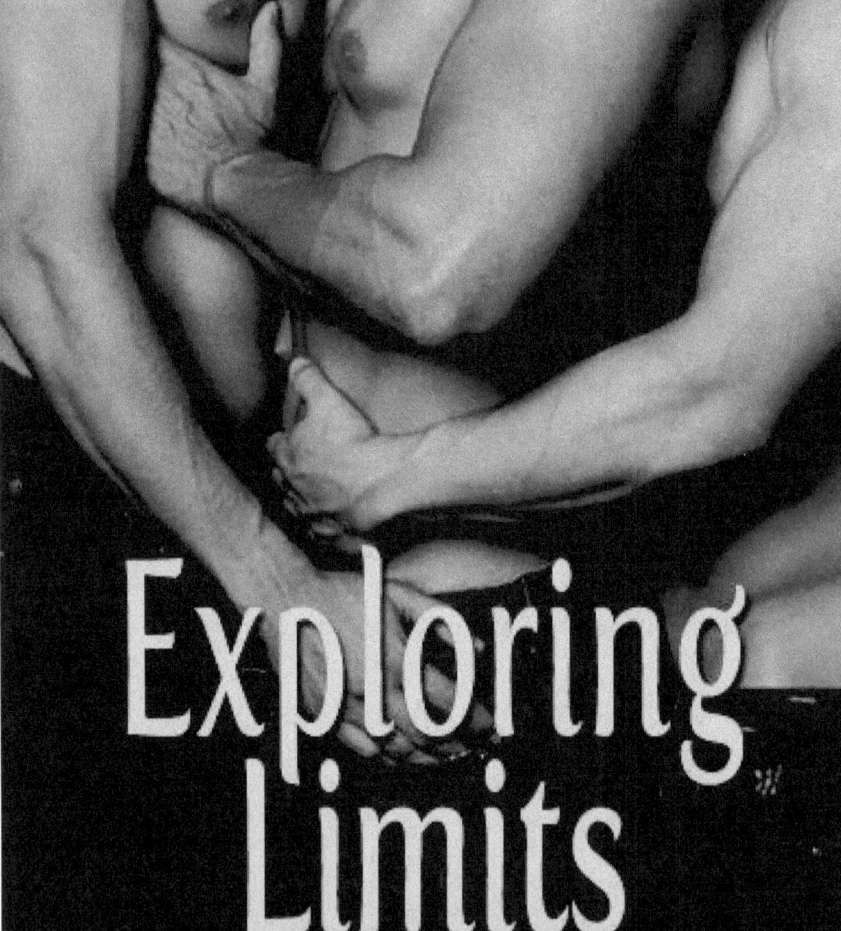

Exploring
Limits

NICKI BENNETT AND ARIEL TACHNA

Exploring Limits: Book One

Jonathan Braedon's successful acting career and consideration for his young son have always kept him from acting on his attraction to men. Newly cast as King Arthur in a BBC miniseries, he manages to conceal his interest in co-stars Devon Aldridge and Kit Webster—but Kit and Devon are just as interested in him. Rather than fighting over Jonathan, the two decide to seduce him together. Jonathan might have been able to hide his attraction to Devon and Kit individually… but together, they're too much to resist.

The three find themselves deciding what they want out of their lovemaking and their relationship, exploring options they'd never before considered or thought they'd left behind. Add a touch of kink to the mix, and Jonathan, Devon, and Kit discover that the perceived limits of the past are really just the beginning.

www.dreamspinnerpress.com

Nicki Bennett &
Ariel Tachna

HOT
CARGO

Captured and accused of piracy, privateer Blaise Risner, captain of the Golden Stallion, finds himself in a clinch - literally - with Confederation Admiral Peter Keller, who promises to see justice done by way of hard labor. But when the chemistry between them rivals the heat of the twin Talixin suns, the dominant admiral decides he wants to handle the rehabilitation of the provocative pirate himself. After their first close encounter, Blaise figures that serving Keller in such a personal capacity won't be such a terrible sentence.

Keller dispenses his own forms of painful justice and sensual discipline, which usually involve a not-so-resistant Blaise on his knees bound and determined to give as good as he gets. The privateer can't deny that suffering the handsome admiral's punishments makes him burn like the fires of the Horsehead Nebula. Serving in the roles of prisoner and captor defines their 'relationship', but no power can stop a shooting star … the star of startling passion that flares every time they touch.

Just when Blaise thinks he can navigate the treacherous asteroid field of emotion to find common ground with Keller, an interstellar war tears them apart. Through it all, Blaise's desire for his captor stands as tall and strong as the monoliths of Maraven, and he'll go to the very edge of the galaxy and back if that's what it takes to crack the ice around the admiral's heart.

www.dreamspinnerpress.com

UNDER
THE
SKIN

NICKI BENNETT
AND ARIEL TACHNA

Police detective Patrick Flaherty has no illusions about Russian mobster Alexei Boczar, but that doesn't stop his fascination with the bodyguard to one of the most ruthless families in Chicago's growing Eastern European crime community. From the moment Patrick meets Alexei's eyes over the body of another Russian mobster, Alexei is a thorn in Patrick's side, refusing to cooperate with the police and turning all of Patrick's questions back on him. Alexei's hard-as-nails persona whets Patrick's professional determination to get the information he's sure the gangster is hiding, while personally Patrick just wants to get his hands on Alexei's hard body.

The tattoos marking Alexei's skin tell the story of his criminal past, but the more Patrick learns about Alexei, the more he wants to know, until he finds himself over his head in a relationship that might cost him his job and could well cost Alexei his life. Alexei is equally fascinated by Patrick's willingness to overlook his past and even his present associations, but he has secrets of his own that could drive a wedge between them forever.

www.dreamspinnerpress.com